FINDING SOPHIE

FINDING SOPHIE

A NOVEL

IMRAN MAHMOOD

BANTAM BOOKS

New York

Published in the United States by Bantam Books, an imprint of Random House, a division of Penguin Random House LLC, New York.

BANTAM & B colophon is a registered trademark of Penguin Random House LLC.

Hardback ISBN 978-0-593-72358-6
Ebook ISBN 978-0-593-72359-3

Printed in the United States of America on acid-free paper

randomhousebooks.com

2 4 6 8 9 7 5 3 1

First Edition

Book design by Alexis Capitini

For Mama, my light

To Shahida, who gave me life
To Sadia, who changed my life
To Zoha, who made my life
To Shifa, who completed my life

I have beheld the whole of all, wherein
My Heart had any interest in this Life
To be disrent and torn from off my Hopes
That nothing now is left. Why then live on?

—SAMUEL TAYLOR COLERIDGE, "DESPAIR"

Have we not expanded your chest
And relieved you of the burden
Which weighed so heavily on your back
And exalted you in renown?
So truly with hardship comes ease.
Surely with hardship comes ease.
So, whenever you are free, stand in worship
And to your Lord alone turn in hope.

—SURA 94, "AL INSHIRAH—THE EXPANSION"

FINDING SOPHIE

ONE

NOW

OLD BAILEY
COURTROOM THREE

I'VE BEEN WAITING A YEAR FOR MY TRIAL BUT NOW THAT I'M HERE I CAN'T contain the panic blooming in my gut. I am in the glass-walled dock of Court Three of the Old Bailey. The courtroom, paneled in satin-wood, is cavernous. The desks in front of me cascade gently down four rows, narrow and impractical-looking. In the distance the judge's bench is attended by a pair of empty red leather chairs. The room brims with decades-old scents.

I am drowning.

My barrister, Stan Stevens, is middle-aged with streaks of silver in his otherwise black hair. He is small but he bristles with energy as if permanently plugged into a power source. His voice is shrill and sometimes he shouts, even at me, his client. But I like him. There's always a gleam in his eye as if he knows things nobody else does. He barrels toward me and slaps his hand on the glass wall.

"Jailer. Can I speak to my client? Just in here is fine." The security guard opens the door to let him in and then locks it again.

Stevens sits next to me, eyes flashing. "Okay. I don't want you to react to the prosecution speech. I know this prosecutor. He's a tit but he's not stupid. I mean, he's not as clever as me but he is cleverer than you. Don't give him an excuse to stitch you up. And when the jury comes in: don't look at them."

"Why?"

"Because if you're looking at them, they'll think you're trying to get their sympathy. Juries don't like being played."

I nod but can't help noticing the slimness of the black file in his hand as I do. It seems almost empty.

"Have we got any more from Braintree?" I ask him.

"Braintree, the OIC? I thought he was called Brown or something."

I've had to learn this new language. OIC—officer in the case. "No, the cell-site expert," I say slowly.

He riffles through the few pages in his file. "Don't worry about the cell-site stuff yet. That's days away. We'll get a witness batting order soon and I'll see when he's on. We can talk about cell-site the day before he's due to give evidence against you. No point doing it sooner."

"She," I say pointedly. "Braintree is a woman."

"That's what I said. She. The judge will be in soon, so I better get back," he says, and exits the dock. The door behind me opens, but before I can turn to see what's going on, Stevens returns. "And don't object to any of the jury when they are being sworn in. They'll ask if you want to object but you're not allowed to. It's just a convention. It's stupid, I know."

I agree quickly so that I can finally turn and see the commotion behind me.

My heart stops.

This is only the second time in my life that this has happened.

A loud bang from deep inside the courtroom starts my heart again. There is a collective scrape as everyone shuffles to their feet. The judge, a small woman with the face of an owl, takes up the central red chair.

The usher shouts, "Would all persons having business in the Central Criminal Court this day draw near and give your attention. God save the king."

I can't believe it's come to this.

TWO

HARRY

TODAY IS LIKE YESTERDAY AND YESTERDAY IS LIKE THE DAY BEFORE. BUT there are days, before all those yesterdays, that are different. They're the days of S—.

And yet nothing has changed. My heart still beats blood through my veins. My eyes still open when I wake, and still see. My legs still want to walk me into the kitchen every morning and sit me down at the table. I fill my body with food so that my heart keeps beating and chases the blood all around my body, all over again. Endlessly.

Nothing has changed.

Everything has changed.

I can see Zara from S—'s window. She is in the garden pruning the mock orange. She tends it as if it is a person—strokes its leaves. Whispers to it. When she planted it, it was the size of a houseplant but now it's reached over the fence into next-door's garden, and scatters blossoms over the yellow flags when the wind blows.

As I leave S—'s room I let all the objects in it pummel me. Scraps of makeup, blunted eyebrow pencils, jewelry that lies where she left it. All of it a reprimand. In the corner of her mirror is a calling card—cheap and purple. I have seen it so often that it has blended into the background. On it there is a black cat in silhouette stepping over a fat white moon. In an arch along the top, the letters T A R O T, and beneath in smaller white font: UNLOCK YOUR BLOCK AND MANIFEST SUCCESS.

Then, in a smile underneath, the letters K A T Y A.

I turn away when something clicks into place. There were a few cash withdrawals of fifty pounds from S——'s bank account. I'd assumed it was pocket money, but who needed cash these days? Maybe it was for K A T Y A. I put the card in my wallet.

In the kitchen I call Zara in for breakfast. She looks back at me from under the wide brim of her sun hat. She smiles and tells me she is coming. If you didn't know her, you'd mistake that smile for joy.

The smell of grass and wet earth chases her in. She rolls off her gloves and deposits them on the counter.

"Peanut butter?" I ask, and then spread it onto her toast as she takes a seat. "What's your day doing?"

She takes a tiny bite and puts the toast down. The bones across her chest are becoming more pronounced. I see her every day and still I have noticed it. "Just birthday stuff. Need to choose a cake design for the party. She likes butterflies, so I was thinking of something like a cake with wings. Made to look like a butterfly."

I eat my breakfast hungrily. My appetite has taken me over these days. I look down. My plate is more dinner than breakfast. Leftover roast chicken, and fresh eggs and tomatoes. "Sounds nice," I say, as I steadily demolish my plate, watching hers all the while. "You need to eat."

"How can I?" She sighs.

How can she?

Last night was the same. Different routes, but the destination as barren as ever.

After eating, I go into the loft study. A large map of South London decorates one wall. On it I have drawn lines in red marker, dotted once but now joined. There are only nine roads that she could have taken from ours. After that she'd be on the main road with traffic cameras and CCTV. They'd have seen her.

I have now spoken to at least one person from every household on each of those nine roads. It has taken just over five weeks but I can join the last of the red dotted lines on the map.

Every single household.

Except one.

I left questionnaires. When they didn't fill them in, I knocked on their doors. I dodged their excuses, came back when there was a better time—there's never a great time to intrude, in London. They open the door as if they have twenty saucepans on the go and a crying child to rescue from chewing on a nest of cables. But the point is that I have spoken to them all. And I am as sure as I can be that none of them saw S——.

Nobody saw anything suspicious. None of the few who had been spoken to by police had anything different to say to me, they said. They told the police everything.

But that one house catches in the back of my throat like a hair.

Number 210—on our very own street.

We have to pass it on our way to the shops at the bottom of the road or if we need to go into town. That means every day we pass it at least twice—once on the way out and once as we come back. Whenever I walk past, I knock. Hard. But he's never answered. And I can't help wondering why.

I sit at my desk and open my laptop. The early August sun gives the walnut a whisky glow. I find the HM Land Registry website, register quickly, and then type in the address, making sure I am careful with the number: 2-1-0. I know his name already from the police—John Douglas—but I want it here in black-and-white in case there's something in it. A minute later I am looking at the Office Copy Entry that I have printed off. Under the words Proprietorship Register, it says *Title absolute* followed by a date, presumably of purchase, and then a name in capital letters: JONATHAN DOUGLAS HERMAN. I turn the name around in my mouth. There's something in it that razors through my skin. Herman. I have to go.

When I started the driving, two days after S—— vanished, I told Zara that I had to go and clear my head. And now, almost six weeks on, that's what I still say. I think we both know that I'm not clearing my head.

We both know that I am hunting.

THREE

ZARA

It is morning, but Harry's asleep.

I don't know how he finds sleep among all the noise. There's so much of it. I never knew it was there before. Or maybe it wasn't and it's come from the empty space Sophie left. Nature abhors a vacuum, so all this noise gathers from everywhere and fills it. It buzzes in me as I move through this glue that the world has left me in.

I peel away the bedcovers and roll onto my feet. Harry is a stone. I look at him before leaving the room. He is in two places at once but I know that neither of them is a place from which he can break the surface and take a breath. There are no breathing holes. So I leave the warmth of this bed early every morning to find a pocket of what seems like air but isn't. And every morning he lies as still as meat.

I stand at Sophie's door—the clasp now gone and the only evidence of it ever having been there six tiny screw holes. Whenever I see them my stomach knots.

I steal into Sophie's room and curl onto the edge of her bed. I'm too terrified of moving all the way into the middle. If I do that, I think it will swallow me whole, the emotional power of her.

It doesn't smell of her here anymore. But I have a secret thing that

I know. I know that she has left fragments of herself. There are cells and hairs, yes. But also things that only I'm aware of. The best way to explain it is to ask you to imagine an empty church—it can be anywhere. When you walk in you can feel all the prayers whispering in the eaves and around the pews.

I don't feel it at the mosque. The peace is more buttery there, warmer, and life is more prominent than the loss of it. But I like the church better for peace. The coolness seems to quiver so that when you stand for a few minutes under its cloak, it becomes part of you.

The twentieth of August is Sophie's birthday. She needs clothes more than anything else. I've been through her wardrobe and most of her things are faded and past their best. Perhaps a sparkly dress and some shoes to go with it. She's not going to get much wear out of them at university, but everyone needs something special. Later I'll trawl through the John Lewis website for party dresses. She won't forgive me for buying something without running it by her. In fact, I hope she won't forgive me. I pray for that.

I struggle back onto my feet and rub my arms in long sweeps from my shoulders to my fingertips. I can't indulge the darkness anymore. The first time, it seduces you. It beckons you with a soft hand and shows you its delights. In there you can close your eyes and fall into its long sleep. Its caress soothes you beyond words and that softness is hard to get up from—harder the longer you stay in it. But when you do finally claw free from its arms, you emerge, exhausted. And then you're out here, in the world, uncovered and raw.

I shake it free and leave the room.

In the sunny kitchen I mix the cake ingredients and sprinkle in a prayer with the flour so that the entire thing becomes imbued with its power. You don't have to believe in it. It's the same to me whether you do or don't. I don't believe in living and yet, here I am.

When the cake is baked I'll decorate it to be like a butterfly with wings. Harry knows I want a party for Sophie. Not a party but a memorial. No! Before you even think it, not that kind of memorial. I want it for people to remember her—not as she was but as she *is*. If enough of us remember her again, then I think we can force her back into our lives.

I make a practice cake with wings but it isn't a butterfly. This one is an angel, for the angels that I dispatch every night with Harry when he goes out to look for Sophie. An entire column of them rising like the Angels of Mons.

While it bakes, I sit in the garden because the sunshine splashes on the grass and the leaves keep me afloat. I can't enjoy the sun like I once did, but still, it paints hope into the colors.

After lunch, I dust the rooms. It's a quiet job that I can do without too much exertion. I start at the bottom and work my way up. The spray sends the scent of wax into the air. It reminds me of my mother, always cleaning and scrubbing and vacuuming. And now here I am echoing her memory despite everything that I did to escape a life of it.

By the time I get to the loft my hands are throbbing. I shouldn't be getting arthritis at forty. But my body has sensed what is happening to my mind and is doing everything to catch up. My hair has silver strands that run like streamers through the deep brown. There are patches of discoloration on my cheeks and under my eyes.

The chart on the wall is now complete. The red dashes are all joined. He's been to every house. Whatever slender hope there was is now deep in the acid whorls of my stomach, being eaten away. As I leave the room I glance at the desk. One of the papers is a formal-looking document. It's a title deed or something for number 210. Why has he printed that off? I know we suspect that house. Whenever we walk past it we knock on the door and wait for a minute before slowly, lingeringly, moving off again. There's never anyone in. But what can this document help, except to tell us a name that we already know—Douglas? Then I read it and see he's called Herman, but it doesn't mean anything to me. I've not heard this name before.

The police never formally suspected Douglas—*Herman*—because there was nothing to go on. He didn't have anything to tell them so they didn't have any reason to follow up. But maybe they could look at him again. We've ruled everyone else out for them—that must mean something, right?

I get out my phone and hit the Amazon app. I scroll through the last few things I ordered and look for the thing that came in the biggest box. A plastic bin for the recycling. Now that I have this new name, maybe a delivery will make him open up. If I follow the progress of the delivery, I can be waiting there when he opens the door. And when he does and I see his face, I'll know. A mother can know things that don't follow ordinary laws. There are threads of light connecting me to Sophie, like piano strings. I can feel her when they vibrate. That's how I know she's alive. And when I see him, this *Herman,* I'll know whether he's been close enough to trip those wires.

FOUR

HARRY

IT'S LATE WHEN ZARA WAKES ME WITH A CUP OF TEA. SHE STAYS WITH ME until I drink it. Sometimes I get the feeling that she wants to reach across to me and take my hand or burrow into my body, but she doesn't have the strength. She's being held together by something more powerful than mere skin and tissue but it's stretched so thin that it's translucent. "Did you eat dinner?"

"Yes," she says so quickly that it makes my heart sink. "Lasagna. I've left you a dish in the fridge for later."

I sip at the tea. "How did the cake turn out?" We are reduced to this, Zara making cake for our missing daughter without any question of whether she will be there to taste it—whether she is even *anywhere* anymore—and me asking how it turned out.

She sees the absurdity of it but wants to, has to keep playing. "Nicely," she says. "It's just the practice one—but it was okay."

I want to tell her I've been everywhere I know that S— has connections. The swimming pool where she took her lessons when she was just six years old, until she was twelve. I've scoured the local park and the little den at the edge by the orchard where she used to drag me, in case some primal memory has taken her back there. I've stopped at every bubble tea shop, arts café, and fast-food place she has ever been. I know the chances of finding her are nearly zero. That, in a strange way, isn't really the point. I just need to touch a memory so that it sparks the next one.

There is that one house left: number 210.

Zara opens her mouth to say something but whatever was being formed loses its shape and drops out of her. I lay a hand on top of hers.

"Tell me," she says, sliding her hand away. "Can you still feel her?"

I used to think this was a rhetorical question but I know that she wants me to say that I can feel her through the ether.

"If she's still alive, I'll find her," I say.

She stands and walks to the door. "Then you'll find her," she says, and leaves.

I DRESS AND take the car keys off the hook and call out as I slam the door. "I'm just going to clear my head." I have nothing but time. I left work on July 5, the day S— went missing, and neither of us has been to the school since. I called and simply told them that we wouldn't be coming back. The head teacher, Mrs. Cooper, assured me that we could take as much time as we needed and the school has continued paying our salaries.

So I'm making the time count.

I drive. The way out takes me past number 210 and I pull over opposite. The streetlamps burn white. Our street is a row of terraced houses, almost identical but for the odd architectural flourish here and there. I'd wanted to live closer to the school, on the leafier side of the borough, but this was as close as we could afford. If you asked her, Zara would tell you she prefers it here. Architects, musicians, and council tenants living cheek by jowl. At night you can hear shrieks and not know whether they are from drunken art students making their precarious ways home, or from foxes.

A few of the houses are double-fronted; some have narrow flats squeezed into the spaces that might have been planned as passageways to the rear yards. But on the whole, they are the same. Identical columned porticos with twists chased into the plasterwork. Double-arched windows in the upper floors. And small front gardens. An ordinary modern mix of renters and owners—of flats and whole houses.

Except 210. Number 210 is different. Where other houses have dwarf walls or privet hedges, this one has a high-walled front garden— well over six feet tall. Across the top perches a wooden trellis wound through with ivy. Instead of meeting a front door, there's a pair of tall wooden gates in the wall—padlocked, with a letter box for mail. The gates are covered in small circular dents. I stand back and gaze up at the windows—two double windows, both veiled in yellowed net curtains and heavy blue ones beyond those.

There is no bell on the painted wooden gates, and no knocker. I take the small hammer I keep in the boot for this purpose and rap repeatedly on the gate. One of the curtains in the windows parts and shows a splinter of light. I can't see his face. But he must see mine. I look up and wave.

"Mr. Herman. Just a minute of your time, please?" I shout, using the name I now know. The night is becoming blanketed in the evening traffic, so I need my voice to loft over the noise. He drops the curtain, snuffing out the light from the window. He won't come out. He's never come out. I return to my car and drive.

I LOOK DOWN at the small glossy card in my hand. The purple ink is cheap and has bled into the white font. It is soft at the edges as if it's been handled again and again.

I have checked her bank statements. I know how much she spends when she says she goes to Chicken Hut at lunchtime instead of the school canteen. I know when she's bought two lunches so that her friend Emily can have one because her mum doesn't allow her junk food. I know that on Mother's Day last March she ordered delivery coffee and some pastries for Zara from us both because she knew I'd forget.

Because I *do* forget things.

I even forget things about S—. If I lose my grip on too many of those things—as they vanish, so will she. I lived my whole life around her, and the things I have let sink are legion—criminal. I've dredged up a handful of things from the millions I've lost. Things like how she was obsessed with *Star Wars* for two years, between ages eight and ten. And how she could recite every word from *Return of the Jedi*. And how later, in her teens, she'd find it impossible to memorize even a short poem.

But I'm not allowed to forget anything more—in case I forget something important.

There's no bank payment that relates to this tarot thing. Just the cash withdrawals. Eight separate weekly withdrawals of fifty pounds last year.

I look again at the card. I'm furious at the idea that this person took money from my daughter and strung her along with lies so many times. I call.

"Hi, is that Katya?"

A pause.

"Are you free to do a reading?"

An accented voice replies. "Is thirty pounds telephone. Forty pounds Zoom. Fifty pounds face-to-face. When you would like?"

"Actually, I'm free now. I'm standing outside your place."

I sense the hesitation.

"How do you get my details?"

"Recommendation. I have your card."

After a beat, she lightens up. "Sure. I have cancellation. Give me five minutes."

There are three flats in this building, judging by the buzzers. Two have name labels, one doesn't. I press that one. A tinny voice answers and tells me to come to the ground-floor side entrance. I do and wait at the peeling green door. It's late. She doesn't know what's coming.

FIVE

ZARA

I CAN'T SLEEP. WHAT I KNOW NOW ABOUT SLEEP THAT I DIDN'T BEFORE and that only came to me when I was on the computer is that both you and the computer only sleep when nobody's tapping. You have to stop. It only comes when you stop. I can't stop. How can I stop? She's somewhere.

Here are the things that I think when I lie awake, staring into the dark. When I tell you them, maybe you won't sleep either.

1. Sophie gets dry skin on her elbows. She likes Body Shop satsuma butter. When she runs out she gets annoyed and won't put anything else on until she gets more.
2. When she watches TV, she likes to sit with a bowl on her lap filled with crisps that she tells everyone have Mum's secret ingredient in them. It's not secret. I just squeeze lime juice and sprinkle chili and lemon powder over them.
3. She needs socks when she sleeps, otherwise her feet get cold and she can't stay asleep.
4. I have to have my shower before she does because when she leaves, the mats are sodden.

5. She's left her rose quartz at home—her protection. She'll
   be distraught without it.

She was just ten when she first became interested in the occult.
Back then, it was in a predictably childish way. When her friends
came for sleepovers, the Ouija board would come out so they could
scare one another. Her friends grew out of it, but Sophie clung on.
She started collecting ephemera. There were tarot card packs, books
on witches and on the healing power of crystals. A book called *1001
Spells for the Modern Witch*. Once when we were on a family trip to
Brighton, she insisted on spending the best part of an hour in a shop
that specialized in selling mystical trinkets and other fluff. I didn't
mind. Harry minded. And he minded most when she asked for
twenty pounds for a personalized horoscope. After taking down
some basic details—date and time of birth—the middle-aged woman
behind the counter handed her a four-page report hot off the printer.
There were streaks across the page where the toner had run dry.

"It's all nonsense, Soph," Harry said, tutting. "It's come off a
copier, for Chrissake."

"It's still real," she said. "You don't know what happens to people
when they die. They have to go somewhere."

"Do they?" he said. "Maybe they don't."

She looked at me then because she knew I believed in life after
death. "Nobody knows for sure," I said, shepherding her out of the
shop. "But if you think of the world as a teacher, then one thing it
might be teaching us, in plants, for example, is that things die, but
that they come back. Or that when fruit falls, the flesh rots, but the
seeds live and create again. Transform. Everything is connected to
everything else."

And Sophie smiled at that. It was as if a load had lifted from her
tiny shoulders. But now, I don't know if it's true anymore. If it were
true, and Sophie were gone, I *would* be able to feel it. I *would*. I know
it. But I don't feel anything. I see her there, gazing at me like a ghost
from the ceiling, but it isn't a real person. It's a projection.

Later I log in to Sophie's Facebook account. Getting her actual account details was impossible. The privacy laws apparently prevent
me from unlocking the account. Even if she were dead and the pic-

tures in there were the only ones we had, they still wouldn't do it. They offered to memorialize her account, but she isn't dead. Even DS Holly can't access it. I thought she might be able to in case there was evidence on it, but apparently it's not as simple as that.

So I have made my own Facebook account for Sophie. She really used other social media more, like Insta and Snap, but I can't get on with those. I don't understand them enough to do anything useful. All I want to do is post some pictures of her and reach out to some of her friends. The police have spoken to most of them, but I know what girls of that age are like. They don't just come out with important information the first time you sit them down. Especially not to the police. No. Getting anything from teenage girls is a much more involved process—like trying to tame a wild pony.

I post the most recent picture I have. It shows her with her head bent over her desk, the lamplight burnishing her hair. I was in the doorway watching her. I took it without her knowing. I post it now because I want them to think of her as alive and to really believe it.

Emily, her best friend, is on the cusp of telling me something important. I know because every time I message her, she switches the conversation immediately to Sophie. She wants to talk about her but I can't be too thirsty, otherwise she'll spook. I left our chat last night telling her how I was beginning to lose hope. How the police have taken what little evidence they have as far as they can. How unless we can get them something more . . . and then I left it there, too upset to continue.

Sure enough, there is a new message from Emily on WhatsApp.
R U Awake?

I don't like to phone her because the difference in the pitches of our voices reminds her that she's talking to me, not Sophie. So text is best. I have Sophie's picture on my profile so every time Emily opens up the chat, she sees her. She knows it's not Sophie she's speaking to, but maybe she likes to fool herself into thinking it. I'm doing the same thing with her. I chat to her and it feels like Sophie's there somewhere, waiting to come in and tell me off for speaking to her friends behind her back.

Yes. U can't sleep either?

I been thinking about Soph

> Me too. I'm going to have a party for her birthday. Will u help me organize it?

 K

Then there is a pause, and it is like I can hear her breath being held. I hold my own.

 ...

 ...

> I don't knw if she told u but . . .

This is the moment. I know it could be nothing because what feels important to a teenage girl can be anything from a misplucked eyebrow to a fatal disease. I wait. The dreaded dots appear on the screen and I hold on to my breath.

 ...

It's okay. Go on, I say to encourage her.

> About her bf

Best friend? As soon as I type that, I remember all the BFFs from a decade ago and just as quickly I know it's not best friend.

> She told me not to tell anyone

> Emily. Please. It could be important

And just like that, she is gone. I've spooked her. I look at the time and it's 1:11. I want to call her immediately. If she doesn't pick up the phone, I want to drive round to her house and shake it out of her. It's been weeks . . . How can Emily not have told us?

SIX

HARRY

SHE IS VERY STRIKING. A MASS OF BROWN CURLS AROUND FINE FEATURES. Deep brown eyes. A spray of pale freckles across her nose. She has on overalls that give her the look of a children's presenter.

She studies me for a second before pulling back the chain. "Come in."

I follow her into a small living space with an adjoining kitchen. It is tired-looking. There are damp patches on the ceiling. The smell of mold makes me wonder whether I am breathing in spores with every lungful.

"What you prefer?" she asks, sitting at a small beaten-up kitchen table. It's covered in clutter: a small fruit bowl with a solitary, sad-looking apple, a folded utility bill, paper clips, some stray tubes of dried pasta. All of it as if designed to break any kind of spell.

"Sorry?" I drag my eyes away from the window frames, blooming with dark spots.

"Cards? Runes? Numbers?" She gives me just the hint of a smile.

"Whatever is better."

She takes some ordinary playing cards out of a cutlery drawer and returns to the table and sits. "It's all the same," she says. I can't tell when she says this if she is being frank about her fraud or not.

"Is it?"

She pulls her hair free of the scrunchie that was taming it and covers it with a diaphanous shawl. I roll my eyes because now it seems like we have fallen fully into farce.

"Donations first, please," she says. I resist the temptation to roll my eyes again as I hand over fifty pounds. She puts it into a small tea tin.

"Ask the cards your question."

"I want to know where my daughter is."

She glances up at me as she lays out the cards. "What is her name?"

I can't bring myself to say it. Plus, S— might not have used her real name. "I have a picture," I say, and pull out the flyer I made, where her eyes are still catching the sun.

"I know her!" she says. "Sophie." She reads the name off the flyer, but her eyes are wide with recognition.

"She kept your card in her room."

She looks crestfallen. "How is she?"

"I don't know. She's missing. I just said."

"Shit. I'm sorry. I didn't know you meant *missing* missing."

"Almost six weeks," I say, and feel the edge of my voice about to fray into tears.

She puts a hand over her face. "Oh no." She wipes a tear from each eye with the pads of her ring fingers. "I'm so sorry." She reaches into her tin and hands me back my money. "I can't take this."

This takes the ground away. I had intended to tear strips off her. My anger at the way she manipulated my daughter with this stuff is so raw. But this has unseated me.

"Keep it, please. I just want to ask you some questions about her."

"Of course."

"Did you know her? Or get to know her?"

She dabs again at her eyes. "She came few times. Always polite, and she was knowledgeable, you know, about the art."

I take it in. "What did she come here for? Was she unhappy—was there something upsetting her?"

She pulls the veil off her hair and folds it into a wad. "Nothing especially. She was asking about love." She sees me react and jumps in again quickly. "But this is normal thing for young girls. Trust me."

"She wasn't upset or worried or frightened to you?"

"No. She was always—*happy*."

"When did you see her last?" I ask.

"Oh," she says, gazing up into a corner of her memory. "Maybe April?"

That fits in with the last fifty-pound withdrawal. "If there's anything you remember—"

"Of course," she says, looking at the flyer. "I'll call the number. But please take the money."

"No. You keep it. Please."

She puts the money reluctantly back into the tin and then gathers up the cards. Next to her on the table her phone buzzes incessantly until she turns it off. She shuffles the deck and closes her eyes before laying the cards out once again. "Let me read for you."

"No. Honestly. It's okay. Take that call if you like."

"It's just landlord. He wants me to go." She puts away her phone and starts to arrange the cards.

"There's no need for a reading. I don't believe in it."

She ignores me, and draws a pack of cigarettes from a pocket of her cardigan. "Even if you don't believe in the moon, it is still the moon."

She turns over the first few cards and stops.

I lean in. There is a ten of spades, a king of clubs turned over.

When I look up, the color has drained from her. "I don't think it's the right moment. Sorry," she says.

"No. Go on. What is it?"

Katya picks away at a sliver of skin on her bottom lip. "Let me lay cards again," she says, and gathers them up. A moment later they are shuffled and relaid. Her face drops.

"What? You have to say. I want to hear it." And I do want to. I don't know why, but it suddenly in this moment is the most important thing.

She hesitates. Her eyes flutter like wings until she catches my look. "I cannot see her."

My heart stops. "What does that mean?"

Her eyes water, and whatever it is doesn't seem manufactured. She is scared. "There is a block."

I wait for her to say more.

"Like a wall," she says at last.

"I know what a block is," I say, irritated. "What *is* the block?" I feel myself swept up in this and it's setting my skin aflame.

"No, no," she says. "A wall. There is a wall." She stares into space and for a moment whatever she is seeing is not in the room.

"She's hiding in the walls."

The hairs on the back of my neck prick up. "What do you mean, she's hiding in the walls? Physically?"

"No. Not *she* is hiding. But she hides *something,* I think. In the walls. But I can't be certain."

WHEN I DRIVE home, I take the corners hard, accelerating all the way. The house is cloaked in darkness. I open the door softly and tiptoe to the bathroom.

I step straight into the shower. The evening has left me shaken. But even as I soap it all away, the thought is waiting for me, scratching away for the slightest air in which to emerge. I force the idea away but I am now kneeling with my head on the floor of the shower. And it's all I can do to stop myself from turning it all off. Everything off.

Zara is asleep. I don't want to wake her even though more than anything else I want to lie down next to her and be near the warmth of her body. I wrap a towel around my waist and go into the loft.

I've exhausted my options. I don't know what else is left to follow up. I open the sash windows for some fresh air. The backs of houses and flats bask in swaths of darkening light. I lean to the side of the frame so that I can crane a view of the skyline to the far left. In the distance I make out, in a cluster, the Gherkin, the Scalpel, and the Shard, spots of gold shining off the glass. I open the window and immediately I can smell burning plastic. I lean out to see what's causing it and just make out wisps of black smoke drifting in ribbons from high walls. It has to be number 210, I think, counting the gardens. I can't see any part of the garden, garrisoned as it is by the wall. The smoke continues to snake up, polluting the innocent sky.

What is he doing behind those walls?

SEVEN

ZARA

BREAKFAST IS BEING COOKED. SUNDAY IS WAFFLE DAY—*WAS.* HARRY tries to make it feel as though some things can remain the same.

I think about Emily and the news about Sophie's boyfriend, and just those words together are enough to put stones in my stomach. Sophie never mentioned a boyfriend. She's never had one—not openly. I knew about the crushes and fancies and the red-faced boys I'd say hello to when I collected her. This boyfriend, though, I had no idea about. I'm angry at Emily for this. The time to have told me this was in the first days, not now, weeks later. We could have lost important things in evidence. And now I don't know if I should suspect a boyfriend whose name I don't even know.

Churning at the bottom of all of this is that last argument we had with Sophie. It shouldn't have been an argument at all. But we as parents were just unprepared, I think, for her transition from child to adult. I know on a rational level, *knew then,* that the stubborn streak, the shouting, the pushing—the constant pushing—was just Sophie subconsciously readying herself, *training* herself, for a dangerous world. She had to fight us so that when she was out there, she would know how to fight back. Rebellion is just growth.

That conversation wasn't the last one we had but it's the one that won't go away. Sophie wanted to waitress over the summer at the Pig, the local gastropub. We'd been there only a few times but as teachers living in the area local to the school, we avoided it for fear of bumping into other parents.

It's a nice pub, though it's never quite shaken off its old reputation as a villain's pub. But these days it's more hipster than gangster. Exactly the right sort of crowd if your daughter is going to work there. But I didn't, *we* didn't like the manager. It was nothing you could put your finger on. He was creepy, that's all. When we spoke to him about Sophie waitressing there over the summer he held her gaze for longer than he needed to. When we tried to draw him back into the conversation it was as if his eyes were magnets pulling at her.

"No. Absolutely not," Harry said when we got home. "I'll find you a job somewhere else."

"Dad!" she said, arms tightly crossed. "You're a control freak."

"I'm a protecting-my-daughter freak," he said, and turned to me for support.

"Honey. You don't know enough about men yet. Dad's right."

She blazed off to her room. Later I went in to see if she was okay and found her on her bed clutching her frog, Robbit. Sometimes she did a good impression of being an adult. Most of the time, in fact. She liked black coffee. She did her own laundry and occasionally made breakfast for us all. But looking at her then, her dark mahogany hair skimming her brows, her knees up high by her chin, she was twelve years old again. Time expanding and contracting so quickly that both these moments, and every second in between, must have been happening at the same time.

"You don't trust me," she said, flaring again.

"We trust *you,*" I said. "We don't trust *him.*"

"Then let me decide how to deal with him. You can't protect me from everyone. I'm going to uni this year. Are you going to be there vetting all my part-time jobs?"

She was right. "No, honey. But I would if I could." I smiled and reached over to pat her leg. She pulled it back from me and slid off the bed.

"Where are you going?" I asked.

"For a walk," she said, and stalked off, calling out as she descended the steps. "If I'm allowed to go for a walk on my own without you."

And though that wasn't when she vanished, it was the start of it. She began to go out for walks every evening. She'd come home some days with dark paint staining her fingers. I was so mystified that I even suspected she might have been spraying graffiti but I checked her bags and there were never any spray cans.

Still.

We shouldn't have done what we did.

In the kitchen Harry lays a plate with a single waffle in front of me. The look on his face is one of resignation more than anything else. I feel sorry for the painful attempt at eating that he will have to sit through. And I am sorry for me that I have to be watched by him, infantilized, making sure that I eat enough to survive.

I take a big forkful and chew through the taste of cardboard and sugar. If I take a big enough first bite, he'll ease off me for twenty minutes.

"Did you clear your head?" I ask him.

He nods. He looks as though he is about to say something but has decided against it. "What's your day doing?" he asks.

I brighten my face with a smile I don't know how to use anymore. I'm going to turn up at Emily's house. I haven't seen her since Sophie went missing.

"Maybe I'll go to a yoga class," I say. I want to speak to Emily alone because she'll clam up if Harry's there. "What about you?"

"I'll be in the loft just going through some stuff," he says.

Once he's cleared up the breakfast things and headed upstairs, I check on my Amazon order for number 210. Delivery is estimated to take place within the hour. I track it and see that it is only one stop away. Quickly I pull on a pair of sneakers and head out the door, shutting it softly behind me.

EIGHT

HARRY

ZARA IS OUT. SOMETIMES SHE PRETENDS TO DO THINGS, YOGA OR INTER-val training, or have coffee with friends but I don't think she goes. Mainly she goes for long walks. She slips out without ceremony and comes back, drained to gray. She spends a bit of each day in S—'s room. If I had to guess, I'd say that she rations her time there. I caught her once under the duvet. I watched her from a crack in the door, and then some minutes later she hauled herself out and every second of that withdrawal was like watching hooks being pulled from her skin. She hated leaving that bed. I hated it *for* her.

She's on another walk. I wash my face and hide out in the loft. The charts on the wall have to come down soon. There is anger in the red lines. *Why haven't you been able to do more?* It's my mind, I think. It's not that well designed for this job. I can do some things well. I can do logical thought and I can follow a plan from point A to B. But I can't find that spark of brilliance that I need to solve this.

Next to the chart are some more flyers of S— that I had made. It's not a real photo—it's a composite. One of the teachers from school, Alex Musset, photoshopped it so that she is wearing in the picture what she was wearing when she went missing. She has the same butterfly clips, the gold hoop earrings she'd been wearing this last year, and the enamel butterfly pendant. She loves that pendant. On that day she had it on over a black mohair sweater, the sleeves pulled down. The image of her face on the leaflet is unreal because of the editing. She looks like what I imagine a robot will look like once the technology is good enough. Not quite human. But the eyes are definitely hers. She follows me round the room telling me that I have everything I need here. I just need to see it.

At the window I peer sideways again but can't see anything of the Herman house. But behind it there is a lower fence where it borders a small block of flats. It's perhaps six feet—about my height—and is rimmed with foliage from bushes sprouting from the flats' communal garden. Behind that there is a big London plane tree. He has privacy from anyone looking from the flats, but if you stood at the fence you'd be able to see into his garden, just. You'd have to fight your way through the greenery, though.

I rummage around in the shed for my hedge trimmer and an extension cord. Instead of walking past number 210 to get to the street behind, I take the long way around so there's no chance he might see me.

The block of flats behind his house is nicely put together. Not too large—around eight flats—and well-kept. There is an off-street parking area and behind it a gate that leads to communal gardens at the back. The gate is open.

I stride through confidently. There are a few shrubs that need pruning but other than that it's neat and tidy. I aim for the plane tree and nose around as if I am sizing up a job. The hedge behind the tree is in need of a trim, which gives me an excuse to delve in and pull at the growth. I push all the way in and reach the fence that borders number 210. I stand on my toes and peer over the top but it's difficult to get a decent view. I step back. The fence panels have vertical boards rather than horizontal ones and the clean face has been offered up to the side I'm on. With a claw hammer I could prize away some of those boards and squeeze through. They'd come off without much noise.

Behind me I sense the twitch of a blind from the flats and I make a pretense of checking my phone. I gaze at the screen and shake my head for show, before leaving and making my way home. Maybe if I can get close enough to the house at night, I'll see something or hear a voice. Something that isn't quite right. A small risk for a potentially large return. I'll have to come back once it gets dark—like a criminal.

The thought hangs like fog.

At school, among the staff, I'm the safe one. My lesson plans are tight and well structured. I run chess club. I'm the teacher who has the least pushback from the kids and I like to think that's because I give them certainty. I'm not spontaneous but I am reliable. And now I'm not. Now I'm a pinball.

NINE

ZARA

THE SUN STAINS THE PAVEMENT IN SQUARES OF HOT COLOR. IN THE OLD days, I always gravitated toward the sunnier side of the street, yearning for the sun's hand on my skin. Now I have no preference—light or shade. The absence of my daughter makes me ambivalent about everything, has stolen everything I could care about.

In case I have to wait, I take the car. I nose my little Fiat off the curb and drive it down the road to number 210. I park opposite to give me a good view of the front and switch off the engine. Sophie always liked it. It's a car designed for teenage girls. The interior is off-white with navy piping. The steering wheel is small but chunky, giving it the air of a toy. It is the kind of car Audrey Hepburn would have been filmed in. There are candy wrappers in the passenger well and the gearstick is a totem pole of hair bands and scrunchies. A pair of her glasses, lenses smudged with lipstick, are still perched against the windshield. I can't bear to move them. And suddenly, I'm back ten years, just like that.

The first time I took her to the optician's, she was eight. When the optician told me that she needed to wear glasses, I was devastated. Sophie, though, was surprisingly pleased about it. She picked out a pair of pale blue Disney specs and bounced on her heels with excitement as they were being made up. Her glee lasted all the way home, and continued into the weekend. She wore them at every opportunity, wiping the glass with her special cloth. On Monday she went into school wearing them. She'd studied her new face in the hallway mirror and smiled in a dozen different poses before she left the house. She peered out at me from behind the small frames and grinned, swishing her dark hair.

When she came out of school at three-thirty, the glasses were nowhere to be seen.

"They broke," she said when I asked her. "But maybe we can get contact lenses? Emily says they're safer for sports."

LATER I FOUND the glasses at the bottom of her book bag, intact in their case. She couldn't get on with contact lenses and ended up with a pair of glasses that didn't upset her as much as the Disney ones evidently had. They were silver and grown-up and they gave her a serious expression that she never quite lost after that. I can't move the pair that are now in the car. If I hold them, I will become deconstructed and cascade to the floor like a thousand glass marbles.

The noise of a van slamming its doors jolts me from the reverie. From the rear of a chocolate-brown van, a man emerges with a large box. He takes it to the high gates of number 210 and bangs on them with the side of his clenched hand. I step out of the car and cross the road. The delivery man pays no attention to me waiting in his long shadow. He bangs again and the sound of the front door opening somewhere behind the wall trips something in my chest. I haven't thought about what I want to say to him. I just want to see his face. As if sensing my presence, the rattle of the door stops and instead a voice sails over.

"Yeah?"

"Delivery, Mr. Herman."

"From?" the voice continues.

"Amazon," says the driver, irritated.

"No, thank you," he says firmly after a beat.

"What, mate?"

"I don't order anything from 'em. Amazon."

The man swears under his breath. "Maybe it's a present."

"Don't think so."

He looks around and swears quietly again. "Fucking people," he says. "Are you Mr. Herman?" Louder.

"Yeah."

"Then it's for you."

"No, thanks. Don't want it."

The delivery man sees me now, lurking, and turns his attention to me. "Do you know him?" he asks, throwing a thumb in his direction.

I pat my chest in surprise. "No. I just saw your van and wondered if you had a delivery for 51?"

He checks his device. "Nah, sorry, love," he says, and climbs back into his van and drives away.

As I get into my car I look up at the windows of the house on the upper floor. A curtain twitches and then is pulled away, and I see him there peering out onto the pavement in front of his gate. He's about to go when he catches me looking. Even from this distance we are able to lock eyes. His face is veiled by the dirt on his panes, but there is something ghoulish about him. He is still as a block of ice. I take a picture quickly on my phone. Then he shakes his head slowly and deliberately, as if warning me, before pulling the curtains across again.

TEN

HARRY

W HEN I GET HOME, I SPLASH WATER ON MY FACE AND CATCH MY REFLEC-
tion. I have the face of a stranger. My skin is dull and saggy and has
lost whatever youth it once concealed. I vacillate between going to
bed and going to the loft. In the end I do neither and go into S—'s
room.

I hardly ever come in here. The fading scent of perfume and hair
spray mingled with the emptiness is usually too much. But today,
with the light falling as it does, in loud shouts across her bed, it is less
overwhelming. I kneel on the floor and put my face into the duvet.
Where is she? She should be here. I slide my hands under her pillow
and touch something plastic. It's Zara's hair clip. She's been in here
again.

I phone Zara to ask about dinner but she doesn't answer. I check
her location on the app but it's switched off. We are supposed to leave
the app on. We are meant to quietly let the other know where we are
at all times, for comfort.

I know she's okay—that she's safe, I mean. It's a feature of the universe that it disrupts what is good and even and steady. What is already spoiled seems to avoid the worst of it. The devil looks at us and
says, "Nothing more needed here."

I still worry.

I was never frightened for S— when she started slipping out in the evenings. It was just after we'd told her she couldn't work at the pub. When she came back after an hour or two, she'd avoid us both and barrel straight into her room. It wasn't the being out that worried me, it was the deep, treacly silence. She treated us as though we had crossed some kind of line in the sand. Maybe we had. Maybe she had grown out of the sacred skin we had reared her in. Now that I think about it, I do ask myself whether she was trying to tell us something important. And that if we wouldn't listen then she would stop trying to talk.

In the mornings she'd seem different—she was still quiet but the quality of her silence was different, less resentful, more disappointed, I suppose. She seemed unassailable in a way. She didn't seem vulnerable. I was wrong. I used to think that vulnerability was a kind of magnetic force around a person that drew in darkness. Now I think it is the opposite. It's the light that makes you vulnerable.

I think back, as I always do, to what we did. Zara blames me. I'm not sure whether I take all the responsibility or not. I'm not even sure that I wouldn't do the same thing again. She said she was *leaving*. Leaving? Where would she have gone? To a friend's? Maybe. But we had no way of knowing that's what she would do.

We had to ground her. We hated it—the nannying—even more than she did—but what choice did we have?

ELEVEN

NOW

OLD BAILEY
COURTROOM THREE

THE PROSECUTION HAS INSTRUCTED A SILK, A KING'S COUNSEL, MR. ALfred, to prosecute this case. He's no older than Stevens, my barrister, but he does have a polish that mine doesn't. When he stands at his lectern he is as still as a lake. But his eyes blink rapidly, like a hawk's.

The jury is sworn in laboriously. Since I'm not to look at them I have to make deductions from their voices alone. Seven women and five men. One of the men speaks with an Irish accent and one of the women swore on the Quran. Exactly half of them swore on a religious book and the other half "affirmed" as they agreed to give "true verdicts according to the evidence."

Mrs. Justice Foulkes watches me over heavy, black-rimmed glasses. The clerk turns to the judge once all the jury are done. "All sworn, my lady." The judge leans toward the goggling jury and tells them the rules of her court. She draws the words out like golden thread, slowly and carefully, so that there is no doubt about what she is saying.

"Don't use the internet to conduct your own research and do not search social media for details of this case," she says.

"You are not to reveal details of this case to anybody outside your number. If you were to do that, and I were to discover it, I would be left with an unenviable decision about whether to send you to prison." One or two of the jurors laugh until they see that she is serious. They cough away their smiles and the judge continues the remainder of her address in a vale of silence.

Once she has terrified them sufficiently, she smiles at Alfred. "The Crown will now open the case."

I go over everything again and again in my head. It is a routine. At night on my prison bunk, I ask myself the questions that I think Alfred will ask me. I answer them in different ways, using different phrasing or emphasis but the answers are always the same in substance.

When Stevens came to see me at the prison for a conference, I asked him what the prosecutor was like. "Don't worry about what he's like," he snapped. "Worry about what you're like."

Now Alfred arranges himself at his lectern and smiles affably. "Ladies and gentlemen. And nonbinary folk," he says, to muted smiles. "Mr. and Mrs. King are conscientious schoolteachers in schools where they are underpaid and overworked but valued. But extraordinary circumstances intervened in their lives and changed them forever. They were overwhelmed by a tragedy that no parent should have to suffer. They lost their teenage daughter. One day just over a year ago, their daughter, Sophie King, walked out the door and never came back. Her body has not been found. But contrary to what you may have heard, you don't need a body to prove a murder. The circumstances alone, in some cases, are enough to put beyond doubt that a murder has taken place. Mr. and Mrs. King suspect their daughter has been murdered. They know it deep in their bones. Even without a body."

TWELVE

ZARA

I STAND OUTSIDE THE DOOR AND, DRESSED AS I AM, FEEL SELF-CONSCIOUS. I look smart but unfamiliar and I wish I had thought of that when I decided I was coming here. Emily opens the door, and seeing her framed in the doorway breaks my heart a little. She seems so small. It takes her a moment to register me but when she does, she turns pale.

"Mrs. King," she says, recovering.

"Emily," I say, and seeing her, it's all I can do to keep the tears from coming. I draw her into a hug. "How are you?"

She nods.

"And Mum?"

"She's fine." She looks behind her to check. "Can we maybe go for a walk?"

Her road is smarter than ours. The houses are grander, cleaner, and the gardens are bigger. There is the faint flush of wealth all around. Emily and Sophie have spent hours and hours in each other's houses over the years. They always preferred Emily's, though.

We amble down the road until we reach a patch of green that is a cross between a large verge and a small grove or park. It is fenced off on one side with low railings and a bench. On the opposite side are houses. We sit. She brings her legs up, tucking pink suede pumps beneath her. I have to remind myself that she's lost her best friend too. Not lost—but is without her.

"How are you, Em?"

"I'm good," she says sadly.

"I didn't know she had a boyfriend," I say.

She crinkles her eyes against the sun. "I know. She didn't want anyone to know."

"Who is he?"

"I never met him. But Sophie was really into him." She stops herself.

I take a breath. So many questions argue for space. "Emily. You have to tell me everything you know. What's his name, where did she meet him? How long has she known him? *Everything*."

She stares down at her hands, small and bitten at the nails. "She only told me a week before she . . . went. She didn't tell me his name—she just called him 'D.' He's older, I know that. He used to pick her up in his car and they went for drives in the evenings."

The thought of it drips fear through my body. "How much older?"

"I'm not sure. I saw a picture of someone on her phone. He was nice-looking, I guess."

I'm infuriated by how her mind goes straight to whether he is good-looking or not.

"Come on, Em. You're her best friend. She must have wanted you to meet him."

"No," she says, shaking her head. "She was really secretive about him. Like, paranoid almost. I kept asking to meet him and she was always like, soon. Not yet."

I take this in. "Do you know what he does or where he lives?" My hands are trembling.

"I *think* he works in a restaurant or a café or something."

"Do you mean after school?"

"No, he's not at school. He's like more than twenty. He's a man."

The last weeks before she vanished, Sophie had been very changeable. Some days she'd be low and irascible. Other times she'd go to school glowing and I remember wondering—*worrying*—whether there was a boy at school she had a crush on. But this boy Emily was telling me about—this *man*—worked in a restaurant. He wasn't a schoolboy. I cycle the words through my head trying to find a fit for them. "Wait. Did she ever mention the Pig? It's a gastropub near where we live."

She mulls it over carefully. "I want to say yes, but I don't know for sure."

I hesitate over the next question but it's the most important one. I keep it in my heart for a second longer. Once it's out. It's out forever.

"Was she sleeping with him?"

Her pale blue eyes widen at the question before she reddens and shakes her head. "I don't think so."

I sit in silence as she fidgets next to me. The minutes stretch. I want to melt away from here. "Emily, I can't believe you waited so long to tell me."

She has tears in her eyes. "I'm sorry. But—"

"But what?"

She shifts again. "At first I didn't think she was really missing. I thought she was maybe just staying with D."

"But why would you think that?" I say, incensed.

The words are cracked when they come. "Because. She told me what you did to her."

ON THE WAY home, all this information fizzes in my head. She had a boyfriend. I'm so angry at the things that teenage girls *think* are important against the things that so obviously are.

But as I walk I allow myself to let go of my anger. She's still a child. I concentrate on Sophie. I'm not upset at her having a boyfriend. I'm upset that this was kept secret from me, because things that hide under that blanket are never good.

And he's a man. Who is out in the world. With my *child*.

THIRTEEN

HARRY

MY PHONE LIGHTS UP WHEN I TOUCH IT—IT'S NINE-THIRTY P.M.

Zara is out again. I'm not a controlling sort of person. I don't care how often she goes out or what the reason is. But ever since S—, I worry about her because she doesn't worry about herself enough.

I check her location expecting it to be off again but it's not. She's at the Pig. Why has she gone there? Before S— she avoided going there in case she bumped into any of the parents at the school. So why now, and who was she meeting there—a friend, Sadia, maybe? These days Zara struggles to speak to me, let alone meet a friend, at night, in a pub. And it's *that* pub. The one that S— wanted to work in, the one whose manager I spoke to about S— being underage.

Within minutes I am striding toward it, the smell of hot tarmac rising off the road. Something energetic but unpredictable is powering me forward. I have to get hold of this feeling before I walk in or I'll say and do things that I will regret. This measured and calculated part of me that I have learned to make peace with has begun to fray into disorder ever since she vanished. I don't feel comfortable in my own skin now. The longer she has been away, the more brazen I have begun to feel in the world. Something animalistic, pantherlike, has started to inflect my moods and movements. I know it's overcorrection but it is hard to stop my own yearning for balance.

I tumble through the door at speed and scan the pub for Zara. The noise and the lights drive up an anger that I have no particular reason to feel. I find her at a bleached wooden table in the corner alone. She has a drink and her handbag on the table. She is muttering to herself, and then she puts both hands on the surface and stands up. That face—I've seen it before. Determined.

I reach her before she has squeezed out of the space.

She looks up when she sees my shadow. "Harry? What's happened?"

I sit us down. "Nothing. Why are you here?"

She takes up her glass and I see her hand is trembling. "No reason. Just needed a drink."

I sniff her glass. "Of water?"

She pulls it back from me and picks her handbag off the table and stands up. "Well, you've ruined it now."

I follow her out into the hot night. "What's going on, Zara?"

"Nothing."

"It's not nothing," I say, trying to make her face me. "Why are you here?"

She shrugs me off until we reach the point in the road where we can go left past number 210 or right and avoid it altogether. She takes the left. We haven't really spoken in weeks and now that we are finally on the brim of saying something, she is about to spike it.

We walk in silence until we get to the bottom of our road and she stops. "We can't keep doing this. Something has to change."

"What do you mean?"

"I don't know. I feel as though we are coming apart."

I move round to face her, conscious that we are stopped right outside number 210. "What do you mean?"

"I don't know," she says, throwing her hands in the air.

"What's that supposed to mean?"

"It means, take me with you."

I stare at her waiting for a clue to tell me what she's talking about.

"What am *I* supposed to do? Did you ever even think about that?

While you're off distracting yourself from every painful second of this . . . hell. What am I supposed to do? I'm drowning."

"We're both drowning."

"I know that. But we're drowning separately."

What she is saying now has had weeks to ferment. I can't catch it up in time to say anything sensible. "What?"

"Take. Me. With. You," she shouts, and the next thing I know she is hammering her fists at the gates to 210. "Open the fucking door. For one fucking second. Just open it!"

The curtains from above move aside and I see the shape of a man. He has something to his ear.

"Come on," I say, pulling her along by the elbow. "Before he calls the police."

At home I lead her into the lounge. We don't sit here much. The open-plan kitchen is where we spend our time so when we come in here it smells unfamiliar. I switch on the lamps.

"I wasn't sure that you wanted to be involved," I say softly. "I know how hard you find the days as it is."

She stares at me for some seconds, her eyes electric. I don't recognize this face anymore. There was always a smooth grace to Zara. Everything was effortless. People were drawn to her. But now that warmth has intensified so much that to be near her is to be burned. Why shouldn't she be angry? I'm angry.

"Maybe I do want to be involved now. I can't sit here and go from room to room every day being flattened by all the things in here that are Sophie. I have to *do* something."

"I don't know what else is left. I've gone over and over her last movements. I've looked at all the papers that Holly left with us. I've run out of rope myself. I don't know where else to look for her."

Her head snaps back. "Her?"

"Yes. What?"

She gathers herself together and stands up. "Forget it. I'm going to bed."

I lean back into the sofa, confused and exasperated by this. "What?" I shout after her.

"We have to do *this* together or . . . I don't think I can carry on with all this weight on me. I need you to help me, Harry."

"I'm trying to help!"

"Are you?"

"Yes. But you're walking away."

She stops and looks at the ceiling before turning to me. "How can you help me if you can't even say our daughter's name?"

The tears come and I look at the carpet until the patterns are in a blur. Zara is still there waiting when I look up.

"I can't."

"You can," she says. "You have to. How can you keep her alive if you can't say her name? Sophie. Sophie. Sophie. Say it. You have to say her name, Harry."

LATER WHEN I am lying in bed I think about this, why I can't say her name. And I think then about Katya and the reading she gave about walls.

I don't believe in any of this. I know the way it works. She picks up on things and reframes them. She knows that S— is missing and that if she's alive she's likely to be trapped somewhere. If there are no walls then it was just a metaphor.

But now Katya comes up around me like a ghost. I can't convince myself about her. She seemed genuine. And now I'm asking myself whether she believes what she is saying because she has convinced herself of her own powers, or whether it's because she can do something I can't: articulate my fears.

"Come back again," she'd said—*pleaded*.

"Thanks," I'd said in the doorway as I was leaving. "But I don't believe in magic. Anymore."

But maybe I have to believe in something.

FOURTEEN

ZARA

HERE IS THE THOUGHT TAPPING ON THE INSIDE OF MY SKULL. TAP, TAP, tap. Usually I bury it. Drown it out with noise. With anything. But it's back.

Was she suffering? Did she feel that she had to do something to herself? Now that I face it hard in the light, I'm sure the answer is no. Sophie wasn't in misery. She was a teenager who, like all teenagers, painted her experiences in more lurid colors than they warranted. I know teenagers, I teach them. And I know psychology—I have an A level in it. And I know that for all her angst, her quite plain and everyday anxiety, she's not a candidate for suicide. And I know this most of all for the simple fact that I think *I* could be one.

I take my laptop and update the Facebook page for Sophie. Her last post ended with a quote from a Radiohead song, so each day I like to put some lyrics from a band that I think she might like. The Roaring Muds was the last thing she listened to.

We're all in this life with differing
Amounts of skin in any particular
Game that we are playing

A few of her friends have posted messages of support. There is a surprising lack of anything negative. I scroll through the friends of hers who have friended me to see if there are any boys I don't recognize, but there aren't. If the boyfriend is on here, it's either Jack, Rolf, Sheeny, or Bobby—kids she's known since she was five years old. Kids *I* have known since Sophie was five. But then—this boy was apparently a man. So it's none of those.

I post a message to ask the group if anyone knows about Sophie having a boyfriend. Once the post is live, my insides crawl a little with the shame I know Sophie would feel if she read it. I have to be the one to feel that for her while she isn't here to do it for herself. The embarrassment snakes up the veins in my arms and down my spine. I close my eyes and let it take me over for a moment.

I need to go back to the Pig but the thought of it is like dredging up something filthy.

The phone rings.

"Hi, it's DS Holly. Have you got a second?"

My heart flips at the sound of her voice. It always does this even though I know that if there was news, she would come to me in person. She'd have that decency. "Of course."

"We've had Sophie's medical records through."

"Okay," I say slowly, my heart rippling.

"Um, how to put this. Were you aware of any issues?"

I'm conscious of blinking away the creeping anxiety. "What kind of issues?"

FIFTEEN

HARRY

THE NIGHT IS HEAVY AND I AM AWAKE SO THAT I CAN TRY TO RECONNECT with S——. Every day that passes is another day that my memories of S—— yellow and curl. If I don't remember her she will vanish again—become nothing. That is what I worry about. I worry that I am killing her all over again.

I can tell you things about her. She liked wearing ripped jeans. She loved eating Nutella from the jar with a spoon and when a spoon wasn't available, her finger. She slept till midday at the weekends if she wasn't shaken out of her bed. She liked filling her ears with silver ware. She sang in a soft voice when she thought nobody was listening. She left the bath mats wet. If you told her to do something, she would wait five minutes before doing anything so she wasn't "following orders." She liked the smell of coffee and grass. She hated coriander. And now hearing myself like this, I stop and realize with a jolt that I've killed her again. I've put her in the past.

The phone silently rings and I answer it to a number I don't recognize. It's late. Zara is asleep and I don't want my voice to wake her. I hurry up the stairs to the loft with the handset. "Hello?"

"Harry?" A woman's voice.

"Yes," I say, and I'm conscious that my heart is beating hard.

"Katya," she says. "I'm sorry to call but I think you should come back again."

I sigh. "Why, Katya? What purpose does it serve?"

"We have to look in order to find. Yes?"

"Yes, but—"

"And my instinct tell me we have to look for this wall. I feel she's there waiting."

"And you always follow your instincts, do you?"

"Harry. I made mistake once before of not following the messages that are left for us. I'll never make that mistake again. Come back. Bring something of Sophia's."

Whenever anyone mis-says her name it is immediately discordant and it takes me a second to reset. "I'm sorry," I say eventually. "I don't think so."

When I end the call, I stare at the wall. Could this be the wall that Katya is talking about? Is the clue here in these red lines? The picture of S——. The light on her cheek still beaming at light speed from that distant sun. All that time and motion ongoing, in some eternal vibration. She was so young. Too young to be gone.

I catch myself again. I have to stop this. She lives. Even Katya seems to have faith in her as a living, breathing person. Not a corpse.

And now I think that I can't stand in the way. How can I? I don't believe her but it doesn't matter. She wants to look, so I can't stop her from looking. If we could persuade everyone to look, we could find her alive. And I wouldn't have to wind back time or believe in magic to save her.

Zara prays. I don't stop her, even though that is the same thing. She finds peace in it.

The loft has become at once a sanctuary and a prison to me. When I'm here I want to escape. When I'm not here, I want to come back and to work at something.

I stay until I am deep into the velvet part of the night. Then I pad silently downstairs and crawl into bed with Zara. She is lost to the dark places she is dragged to every night. If I could pull her free from there, I would.

But I am determined to find a way of doing it.

SIXTEEN

ZARA

I WAKE TO SEE HARRY NEXT TO ME. IN THE BRIGHT FILTERED LIGHT, HE looks tired, old even. His skin is gray.

I run through the first of the morning's hurdles in my head—breakfast and how to avoid it. I am turning over whether just to say out loud that I don't want to eat so that I don't have to appease him any longer with this daily dance when the door knocker bangs. It's so loud that it makes me jump and shakes Harry out of his sleep.

I head down in a green cotton dressing gown, my brow holding a crease through every step. It's seven A.M. on a Monday. Who could it be?

Behind the door is a face I know. "Oh," I say. "I thought you were coming later."

"Sorry. Busy today. Can I come in?"

Harry appears at the top of the stairs in boxers and a T-shirt. "DS Holly?" he says, his voice strained with panic. He follows us to the kitchen and remains standing in the doorway as Holly and I sit.

"Can I get you some coffee?" I ask.

"No, thank you. So, as I mentioned yesterday, Sophie's medical records came through. We didn't have any real reason to check them but it can sometimes be useful."

Harry rubs his hair. "Sorry, you mentioned *yesterday*?"

"What did you find?" I say, ignoring him.

Holly reaches into her bag, removes an iPad, and opens up a page. "Here," she says, pointing.

I look over at the page and my heart begins to throb in my chest. I look up at Harry and want him to leave, to not have to see this. We don't both need to know. I can carry it alone.

"What am I looking at?" he says, coming in.

Holly looks at us, but me particularly. "It's the pill."

I shake my head, but Harry is pacing the floor and muttering about whether it was even possible. "She wasn't even seeing anyone," he says.

I hold up a hand so we can let Holly finish but she's looking at me now, questioningly.

"Was she seeing anyone?" Holly asks me.

I hesitate. "I went to see Emily yesterday. She told me that there was a boy. Older."

Harry's face struggles to keep its shape. It quivers at the edges. "You never mentioned that."

"Harry. Can we not do this now?"

Holly hovers as if she has to leave but I need to keep her here. "She doesn't know how long it was going on for—maybe only a few weeks."

"Do you have a name for him?"

"No," I say. "Emily said she thinks he might be called 'D.' That's all I know. And he drives. She thought he worked in a restaurant or a pub maybe."

Harry spreads his hands on the table and takes a seat. "The Pig? Is that why you were there last night? Who is he? Can't be that many people there it could be."

"I don't know. He might not be working there. She only said he might work in a restaurant."

"Then why are we still sitting here?" Harry says, standing up and casting around for his keys.

Holly stands too. "Don't. Please," she says to Harry. "Leave it to me. I'll make some inquiries. I know the Pig. I'll swing by there and speak to Andrew Pugh, the landlord, this evening." She gathers her belongings. "Look, I have to be off. But I'll keep you updated." She sees herself out.

Harry is still staring at me in disbelief. "After everything you've been saying."

"What?" I say, but I know what.

"I can't believe you'd keep this from me."

"But this is exactly what I mean, Harry," I say, moving deeper into the kitchen. "We're becoming these people we don't know. I'm desperate."

He moves so that he is standing next to me. "No. Don't do that. I haven't kept anything from you."

I laugh but can't keep the bitterness out. "Seriously? All those late drives. All that—that *stuff* in the loft. All of it, you've kept the whole lot from me. I don't know anything about what you're doing. I don't want you to misunderstand me, Harry. I appreciate it. I am so grateful that you are out there doing everything you can to find our daughter. I am. But I need to be a part of it. To be told at the very least. I feel so—"

"So—what?"

"Alone, Harry. I'm alone. You've left me all alone."

He raises his hands at me in frustration and I brace myself for more anger and recrimination, but instead he slides down the side of the cabinet till he is sitting on the floor, sobbing. He looks up at me, wet. "I haven't found a thing, Zara. Nothing!"

For a second, I stall, and then I touch the top of his head. "I'm sorry," I say. I don't know what to do with his tears. I can't hold both his grief and mine. After a minute he stops and climbs slowly to his feet. His joints crack, the suppleness they once knew gone. He wipes his eyes with the heels of his hands and coughs away some of the grief.

"If there's ever anything concrete to share, I will."

"Something concrete?" I say in disbelief. "Have you not been listening to a word? Talk to me. Tell me what you're doing. Include me."

He stands with his hands on his hips as if making a decision.

"Okay. Fine," he says, throwing his hands up. "I saw a clairvoyant the other night."

I'm so surprised that for a second, I think I haven't heard him properly. "What? Have you lost your mind, Harry?"

"Not any clairvoyant. That card on her mirror. The tarot one. I called the number and went to see her. I didn't know whether she had ever even been. I was just trying something new."

"And?"

"And, well, nothing. She said some crap about a wall or her being behind a wall. I didn't understand it. But there you are. Not concrete. That's the kind of shit I'm trawling through."

BY THE TIME the evening has come around, the sadness has lifted a layer. They never tell you that the grief comes in hard, thick blocks made up of a thousand whisper-thin skins. On the best days, a few will peel away and a gram or less of the weight will lift from your shoulders. But most days you're lucky to peel away just one leaf. And at night whatever you have managed to shed in the day before returns to its place and bonds just as tightly as it did before.

At dinner, Harry fills our plates. Pizza on one side, salad on the other. Moisture drips off our wineglasses.

"Thank you. For telling me about the clairvoyant."

He nods but says nothing.

"I sent a bin to number 210 the other day." He is staring at my food and I can't bear it.

"A bin? Why?"

"I thought I might get him to open the gate and I could see what he looked like."

He seems to turn the information around in his head. "And did you see him?"

"No but I took a picture of him in the window," I say, and show him the blurry image. "He wouldn't come to the door. I waited outside as the delivery guy tried to persuade him to open it, but he wouldn't."

He stares at the image before pushing his food around his plate. "There's something about that guy that doesn't quite add up."

"Herman?" I say, and when he narrows his eyes at me, I add, "I found his name on your desk."

He puts a piece of food in his mouth. "There's something not right about a man who builds such high walls around his house and never comes out of it. It's the only house on the road that looks like that. The only house I've ever seen like it. Who has walls that high around their front garden?"

"You really think he's involved?" I ask. We have been knocking on that door for six weeks, twice a day. At first it was just to get him to answer the questionnaire. And I thought he was simply hard to get hold of. Now it feels like more than that. The energy around that house feels more malevolent now that I know the owner's name, now that I've seen his outline behind its windows.

"I'm not sure," he says, getting up. "But I plan to find out. To-night."

SEVENTEEN

HARRY

I'M DRESSED IN BLACK. IN MY HAND IS A SMALL CLOTH BACKPACK WITH pruning shears, a hammer, some pliers, and a screwdriver. Zara is sitting at the bottom of the stairs.

"I don't want you to go."

A deep sigh escapes my lungs. It sounds accusatory and I don't want that. "This is why I don't tell you everything."

"I don't mean you shouldn't do something—just do something that you've thought through. What are you going to do when you get there?"

"I'll look around."

"Inside the house?"

"Maybe. I won't know till I get there," I say, and sidle past her. "I just want to make sure there's nothing obvious. The police have never been inside. There might be her clothes in the garden or her shoes in the hallway. We have no idea. I just want to see if there's anything to justify my, *our* suspicion."

"Then I should come too."

"No, you shouldn't," I say, and hold her gaze. She stares at me for a second longer than is comfortable before dropping her arms.

"Fine. But be careful."

— — —

I MAKE MY way quickly to the rear of number 210, taking the same route as before. This time the gate to access the rear of the flats is shut. But it's okay. I am sure I can climb over without too much trouble. I look up at the façade. The lights are all out. It's after midnight so it's not a surprise. But I have to be deathly quiet because in this valley of silence every sound is multiplied.

I move toward the gate but keep close to the walls just in case. Once I am at the gate I see that there's not much to grip. I'll have to take a run at it to get my arms over the top and then haul myself over.

But as I pelt forward, a blaze of white light floods the area from security lights I hadn't noticed. I have no choice but to vault the gate because I am already in full flight. Speed and adrenaline take me over and I land surprisingly softly at the bottom. I sit completely still, my back flat against the door, gasping until the light ticks off again. We had one of these. It set off every time someone passed by on the street, so we removed it. I just have to hope that this one is the same and the residents are used to it going off.

Once my eyes have adjusted, I move so that I can see the windows of the flats. No shards of light as blinds and curtains are pulled away. I look to see if there are any security lights here but there don't seem to be. There is only one door at the back and it is protected by an alarm and a heavy wrought iron gate.

I wait another minute and then creep forward, staying low the whole time, until I touch Herman's fence. The greenery that covers it comes away quickly with the pruning shears. I take out my hammer and lever off nails until an entire plank is free. I do the same with the next two, as quietly as I can, until there's a gap large enough for me to get through. But as I squeeze through, suddenly there's a crack—loud as a target pistol—as the fence panel splits from the force. I drop to the earth and hide in the shadows of the tree. I wait, as my heart bangs out the seconds. I'm used to holding my breath when I have to. I used to shoot years ago, and the breath was the most important thing to control. I listen. Nothing. I relax. I lay the fence panels gently on the ground and slide in.

The scent of burned plastic hits me as soon as I am on the other side of the fence.

Where was that smell coming from? There is no moon to give me any light and my phone torch would be a flare in this thick darkness. I wait, and then to my right I see the dark outline of a bin. I move carefully toward it, keeping low and as close to the fence as I can. There is heavy undergrowth along sections that conspires to trip me every meter or so. The scent here is the kind of sweet decay that comes at night in any garden, but mixed with burned plastic. When I reach the bin, I see that, as I had thought, it is an incinerator. I lift the lid, taking care to muffle the sound by using both hands. I peer in but the darkness makes it impossible to see much inside. There is certainly ash.

I reach in and grab a fistful of debris, most of which passes like sand through my fingers. Some large pieces remain, though, and I deposit them carefully into my backpack. I have no idea what it all is in this light, but it doesn't feel like garden waste. It is smooth and plasticky with hard edges where the plastic has melted and then solidified.

I take another look up at the house. My vision has adjusted now to the dark and I can see the outline of the rear aspect clearly. There are two windows at the ground level and a glazed door. Above that there are two windows on each floor for the next two floors, and at the top a loft conversion with a Juliet balcony. Juliet. I get a rush of memory from when I was set to teach Shakespeare to S—'s class in year seven. She sulked as soon as she found out that I was teaching her class. She begged me not to, but it was only when Zara found her gouging blue lines into the dining table with a ballpoint pen that I finally relented. It was the right decision. The deputy head, Robert Delancey, took the class and S— got an A. She'd never have done as well with me— it was Rob's specialist subject. But still I wonder whether giving in to her like that was a mistake.

When I consider all the mistakes I made with her, I am submerged by the weight of them. They come like straws in the wind, weightless. But then you turn and find that you can't move under the weight of all of those tiny, insignificant mistakes. I can't make another. Not now. I shake myself back here.

None of the windows betrays any light at all, not even a splinter. In the ground-floor window I notice a small hinged pane at the top that looks as if it hasn't been shut properly. It's not large enough to get through but there might be a way of reaching in and pulling open a handle for the larger pane beneath. I move quick and low toward the façade. To the right, the building recedes two meters before continuing along. And in that recess must be the kitchen door. The darkness is so thick that even with the time my eyes have had to adjust, I can't see anything until I'm very close.

It's why I don't see the half-height shed hunched in the far corner. Or the dog until it lunges at me, barking for all its life.

EIGHTEEN

ZARA

WHILE HARRY IS OUT *DOING* AGAIN I AM HERE WAITING AGAIN WITH ALL these memory shades.

It's been three-quarters of an hour. I don't know what that means—whether he's been caught or whether he's deep in Herman's house, prowling. If you knew him as I know him, you would never be able to reconcile the man I'd married and spent twenty years with, with this man who goes off into the night.

I could weep for what it has made him but I don't have tears for him as well. Besides, I need him on the other side of the wall I'm hiding behind to do whatever unspeakable thing he hopes will get Sophie back. He doesn't trust the police to get the job done.

I don't think I do either.

Holly going to the pub to look for the boyfriend, for example. How is that going to help? If Sophie was seeing someone there, why would he suddenly admit that to the police now? And if it's an older man seeing a seventeen-year-old girl—he'd run for the hills.

I remember again the night that we grounded her. I know she was seventeen and I know that she needed to spread her wings to try out the world. But she had been out twice the week before and her sleep was suffering. In the mornings she emerged with circles inked under her eyes. And I didn't believe the last-minute study session at the house of a friend we hadn't ever heard about.

"I told you, she's Emily's cousin! From Sweden."

"But what, she's living here now?" I'd said.

She bristled. "I don't know, do I?"

"Where does she live?"

"I don't know. I'm going to meet Emily at hers and then we'll walk down there."

"Do you mind if I call Emily?" I asked softly.

"Yes, I mind. Because that means you don't trust me."

"Okay, fine," I said, backing out of her room. "I'll speak to Dad but I don't think we can let you go this time."

She laughed bitterly. "You can't stop me. I'm an adult."

"No, you're not. You're still my responsibility for another year. When you're eighteen we can talk about giving you more independence."

Harry and I were drinking tea in the living room when we heard the elephant thumps from above. We exchanged glances but continued watching TV. A second later, the sound of her hurtling down the stairs. She passed the living room and headed straight for the front door.

"No, you don't," Harry said, and leaped up into the hall just in time to slam the front door shut before she managed to slip out.

And then she attacked Harry, clawing at his face. I ran to pull her away but she rounded on me.

"This is so toxic. I can't believe you're just enabling him. You can't keep me here. I'll just leave when you're asleep." She stormed off to her room.

Later, once the chaos had ebbed away, I asked Harry, "What are we going to do?" I meant about the situation—all this resistance that had come from nowhere.

"Tonight? I'm going to put a padlock on her door."

"I mean, we have to sit down with her. Get to the bottom of all this *behavior*."

"Tonight padlock. Tomorrow talk."

— — —

I SIT ON the stair and search my phone's location app for him. He has been a blip at the rear garden of 210 for fifteen or twenty minutes. But now he is moving. I can't tell where he is. For a second it looks as if he is inside the house, but the blue dot is hovering so that it's sometimes within the boundary and sometimes outside it. I can't call him—it could be disastrous.

And then, just like that, the light goes out altogether. He is offline.

NINETEEN

NOW

OLD BAILEY
COURTROOM THREE

SOPHIE ARRIVED IN THE WORLD SMALL AND ANGRY AND SUCKING AT AN invisible nipple. In a way, she took us completely by surprise even though we had yearned for her. But we didn't have the imagination to understand how life-destroying a baby would be. I don't mean that the way it sounds. I mean that she tore the fabric of everything we knew apart. We used to lie in bed watching TV, a tray of croissants and coffee between us. In the afternoons we'd sit through long lunches or visit art galleries. We used to be undefined by anything but ourselves. Then Sophie came and all that changed. She became a supermassive center of gravity. Our tiny individual worlds revolved around her the minute she erupted into being.

But what we lost, we gained elsewhere. Our limits became labile and elastic. We could love, for example, to heights we'd never known.

Now as I watch the prosecutor continue his address to the jury, all I can do is think about the space, fathoms deep, that her absence has carved out of me.

"Undoubtedly, this was murder. A knife was buried deep into the victim's jugular vein. A life was snuffed out." He turns back to his lectern and takes a breath.

"I pause a moment to try to consider what it must have felt like for Mr. and Mrs. King. I can't, however much I try, imagine their pain. Their daughter, still only a teenager, gone."

The jury turns to look, their eyes flicking between us. I can see the sympathy like syrup dripping off their collective gaze. They pity us, but we are nothing but exhibits in a Victorian museum. They are moved by our pain but they can't stand to look at it long enough to feel it.

TWENTY

HARRY

I HAVE TO GET AWAY AS FAST AS I CAN. THAT BLOOD-FILLED BARK COMES again. And now the heavy rustle of linked chain feeding itself through at a rip. At this time of night, its owner won't get to me in time to save me.

The hammering in my chest fills every space. I run. I fall. And as I fall I pick myself up and run again, every muscle and sinew cooperating to drive my legs as fast as they can.

More barking sends spikes of fear through me. My skin is tingling in terror.

I am still blind in this low light and I run for the gap in the fence that I know is there but cannot see. The barking is now at full volume, wet and angry and right behind me, as heavy as meat. I fall but scramble up again. I am back on my feet but now a searing, tearing pain takes my ankle as the dog grips my foot.

In panic I try to scramble away but it clamps down again. It has just the spongy heel of my running shoe and it is shaking it so hard that if it was my ankle it would be in shreds. I clamber away, sacrificing my shoe to the dog. It lunges at me again but is brought up short with a yelp. Mercifully, the chain must have stretched taut.

I don't look back. The ground is now lit by a shaft of light that must be coming from a window from the house. I see the gap I made in the fence and hurl myself at the loose planks.

Once on the other side, I hurdle the double gate, triggering the floodlighting. But I don't care, I'm free. I don't stop running until I reach my door. Zara opens it before my key is out. Her face is washed in concern.

"What happened?" she says, letting me through. She catches sight of my socked foot, bloody at the ankle.

I drop onto the stair, the backpack at my feet. "Dog," I offer by way of explanation, panting.

"My God," she says, and spins away to the kitchen, returning moments later with some antiseptic and paper towels. She peels away the sock and dabs the wound clean. I steal a look. Now that it's clean, it's hardly there at all. Four puncture wounds and a long scratch.

"What happened?"

"Dog," I say again. "The bastard's got a guard dog. Alsatian." My breathing is still heavy.

Zara is wringing her hands. "So, you didn't see anything? None of Sophie's things, her clothes, nothing?"

I shake my head.

She hesitates. "So, it was wasted?" she says. Now that the words are out, there's a shadow of regret over her features.

I consider this. "No," I say at last, "not wasted." It's never completely wasted. There's always some sand to add to the scales. You can't see it a grain at a time, but when you stand back after some time, you begin to see the heap and the scales will move. "I found things out."

She turns now and looks up at me. "What things?"

"That place, for example," I say. "It's dark. I mean it's *kept* dark. The windows are double-curtained. There are those high walls. And now a massive fucking guard dog. The guy's hiding something. I know it."

Her voice is papery. "It's the middle of the night. Why would there be any lights on?"

"It's more than that. Most of the houses I passed on the way even at this time had a hint of activity. A light in the hallway. An overflowing bin. Something to tell you that there's life there."

"There was a dog. That's life."

"Never mind," I say, the irritation building. "There's something off there, that's all."

I think of the bag and the scraps of rubbish that lie in there awaiting me. I can't show her. I can't expect to keep her hope stoked on a
handful of ashes. But it does mean something to me. What was he
burning? Why was he destroying something that he could have
thrown in a bin? It had to be important.

ZARA IS ASLEEP. Her breath is like a whisper. Since S——, she sleeps as
if on the rim of a pool. She can't let herself fall in.

I slip out of bed and steal down the stairs and get my backpack.
Silently I pad back up the stairs and continue on to the loft. The
easiest way is to clear my desk and tip it all onto the surface. A lot of
gray and black ash flutters out first and then out clatter some lumps
of charred black-and-white material. There is something hard and
stringy that resolves at the other end into a flat glossy strip. Then bits
of hard plastic. One piece is round—white in the center like a cog,
encased in black plastic. I know what this is. It's a VHS videocassette.
He's burning videos.

The piece that I have in my hands looks as though it still has some
tape in it that's been protected by the case. I unspool it carefully. In
minutes I have a couple of meters of tape. Most of it is shriveled at
the edges but some has survived.

One piece twice the length of my arm looks intact. I hold a section
of it under the lamp but of course it's not cine film. You can't see
anything on the surface at all. I roll up the good film loosely and drop
it into an A4 envelope. I know how to make this play. When we were
kids, my brother Caspar and I used to fix VHS tapes for Mum and
Dad when they got mangled. And then when word got out, for the
rest of the village.

I open the window to get a lungful of air. At this hour the world
outside feels metallic and bloody. Things happen under cover of
darkness. The insects roam around freely on the earth like fingers on
skin. Wolves and wild dogs roam in packs. Men cut through the night
like ships through the sea.

S—— is out there somewhere and all I want is to tear open the tissue
that separates us and pull her back through into safety.

TWENTY-ONE

ZARA

"I'M AFRAID I JUST CAN'T," SADIA SAYS, AND SMILES IN THAT WAY SHE does when she thinks she's being empathetic.

"Except you can," I say, imploring her. "This is Sophie we're talking about! She's missing. I can't think why you wouldn't want to help me."

She shifts in her chair. "Because of ethics. I still need her consent, Zara. You knew that when I agreed to take her as a patient."

Anger that I have kept with me, simmering in my body all these weeks, begins to leak through. "Just how do I get Sophie's consent when nobody can find her? The police have been combing the bloody city for weeks and there isn't a trace of her. Maybe you can tell me where she is so I can get her fucking consent?"

She reaches a small hand out to touch mine. "The police have her medical records; could you ask them?"

"The police only have her last six months of records. I want them all. And why are you prescribing her the pill? I honestly thought having a friend as her GP would mean that you'd take more care with her!"

"I'm sorry," she says. "I can't talk to you about this, Zara."

I stand and find myself huffing. There must be a law here somewhere that allows me to access her records. Harry's brother, Caspar, is a solicitor.

"Isn't your first duty to preserve her life? What if there's something in there that could help the police find her?"

"Then the police can get an order—like they did to get the records they already have." She stops. "Here," she says then, handing me a piece of paper. "Tom's renewed your diazepam prescription. But he wants you to make an appointment before he repeats again."

I stalk away from the surgery, my face hot. Outside, a wind has kicked up from nowhere that smothers me as I stride into it.

When I get home my head is pulsing with hot anger. I need to get this feeling under control. If I let it colonize me, it will finish me. I want to claw these intrusive thoughts from my brain.

I head up to Sophie's room. In here there are still traces of her to find. I have to root all my feelings for her in something physical.

But today I can't be in her room. Not without her. Not today.

My girl. My sweet little girl, where are you?

TWENTY-TWO

HARRY

THE BITE ON MY ANKLE STILL FEELS RAW, BUT I WON'T STOP BEING GRATE-ful that I managed to get away from the dog before it could do worse. I plug the video player into the TV, slot in the newly repaired cassette, and press play. It takes a few minutes of static before an image flickers onscreen.

The side of a man's face hovers into view. This is a home video—there is no doubt about that. The colors are stonewashed on the screen, the edges of the images lazy and indistinct. My heart quickens because at first it seems like it might be him, Herman, but then I don't know what he looks like, beyond Zara's hazy picture of him in the window. White, middle-aged maybe, and tall, judging as best as I can. This face is younger. But then the tape is older.

I sit on the floor and continue to watch. The man is in a room of a house. The curtains are drawn and a single bulb burns white overhead. When he moves out of shot I see a chair, an ordinary kitchen chair, in the middle of the room. After a minute he goes to the door and leads someone in. I can't see who because his body is obscuring the person. I turn up the volume but there is no sound, just this macabre mime.

He sits the girl in the chair and gives her a glass of what looks like Coke. She takes a sip and smiles at the camera. She can be no more than fourteen. Her lips are the pink of candy floss.

And then the tape goes blank.

I rush to the bathroom and throw up. I feel suddenly exhausted by it all. Whatever is on this tape must be thirty or more years old. She, whoever she is, must be in her forties now. My age. I blinked and traveled back and forth in time, like a miracle.

Once I have washed my face I stare into the mirror. I'm aging before my very eyes. Not just in the traditional cinematic way, with smile lines and gray at the temples. It's frailty that is creeping up on me. My shoulders, once rounded with muscle, are now nubs of bone. My lips are dry and beginning to hang low, as though some bit of elastic has been cut from higher up my face. When I look at myself, I see my father.

I climb up to the loft. From the window the odor of burning plastic is again wafting through. I peer out and see plumes of inky smoke billowing up from the corner of Herman's garden. I get the binoculars and focus them on the boundary line. I can just see the top of a faded red baseball cap bobbing around a smoking bin. Then I see that Herman is on his knees, screwing strips of timber to the rear fence, repairing the gap I made.

After a few minutes he is back at the bin and poking around inside with a stick, giving the fire a surge of flame. I pan around and see a pile of videocassettes on the ground waiting to go in. But as I shut the window tightly, I can't escape the question that is now taking hold more and more firmly. Who burns old videotapes unless they have something to hide?

I watch him and suddenly it is as clear as day, from the slope in his shoulder and the angle of his neck, that the man in the video is Herman. For a few minutes I am lost to myself. The thoughts won't arrange themselves into an order that I can process. I know what I have to do but against that is what I *want* to do, and what I want to do is so much more visceral.

I call Holly. She doesn't answer it and the call goes to voicemail. "DS Holly, it's Harry. Sorry. Look. I have some important evidence in the case that you need to come and look at. It can't wait. You need to come as soon as you get this message." And then as I am about to end the call, I add, "Or at least *call* me."

I eject the tape carefully, place it into an envelope, and take it to the kitchen. For the next hour, I stare at it, the possibilities cycling through my head. Herman is out there right now, burning everything incriminating that he has. He knows someone was snooping around last night. He's spooked.

Later when Zara comes home, her face flushed from the outside, I am still fizzing. There must be a crazed expression on my face because she is immediately on edge.

"What's happened?"

"I think I've found something, Zara. Something important."

"What is it?" she asks, holding her breath.

"That," I say, pointing to the envelope on the kitchen table. "Holly is on her way."

TWENTY-THREE

ZARA

HOLLY IS HUNCHED OVER THE TABLE, IMPATIENT FOR HARRY TO FINISH. "I understand all of that," she says. "And as I said, I will get this looked at. But you have to listen to what I'm saying. Even if this might have once contained something—"

"Abduction," Harry says firmly. "On film. Of what looks like a child."

"Even if it does show that, there's a limited amount we can do with it."

"What do you mean?" he asks.

"Well," she says, looking around the room. Her untamed black hair is hanging in wisps around her face, making her seem frivolous. "So far, you've committed an offense of attempted burglary, or being on enclosed premises, and you broke his fence, so that's criminal damage on top. If that," she says, pointing to the envelope, "was evidence, you've contaminated the exhibit by tearing it apart and taping it to another tape. And that's without the shit we'd get into over continuity."

"Continuity?" I say.

"Someone needs to say that exhibit was found by X police officer at the scene. And that officer placed it in an evidence bag to preserve the forensics. And then it was handed to another copper, Y, who signed it into property—where another person, Z, booked it in, and so on until it got to a lab where *professionals* reconstructed it."

"Okay, but—" Harry says.

"What we have here is a mutilated bit of tape that, as far as we can say, came from you. Who could have got it from anywhere."

Harry rolls his sleeves up and combs both hands through his hair. "What about the man's house? Once your guys have looked at it and confirmed that it looks like him, surely that can give you grounds to go around there and search the house?"

She sighs. "Not really, Harry. We'd never get a warrant on the basis of a bit of forty-year-old tape that you stole from his bin."

For a moment we sit under a seam of silence. Harry and Holly are avoiding each other's eyes and I'm looking from one to the other waiting for the heat to evaporate. Finally, I break the stalemate.

"But if . . . if it is *something,* maybe you can at least speak to him? See what he says about it. There's a young girl on that tape."

She picks up the envelope and seals it carefully in a clear plastic evidence bag. "She *was* a young girl. She's not now. And for all I know, she might be his niece or daughter, *if* that is even him on the tape." She catches herself as her voice sails into the roof. "I'll go around there. See what he says," she says. "But if he won't open the door, I doubt there's anything we can do."

"But you will have tried at least," Harry says, as she heads to the front door.

I race after her and touch her back. "Before you go, DS Holly, I need your help with something. Is there a way you can get Sophie's medical records going back a year or two? The surgery won't give them to me."

"Why?" she asks, turning at the door.

"No particular reason. I just thought maybe if something was going on with her then we might need to go a bit further back."

She pauses. "I'll make a request when I have a chance. It'll take time, though, so don't hold your breath. But most of all, please just trust us to do our job."

TWENTY-FOUR

HARRY

IN THE EVENING, WHEN THE SKY IS FIRE TOUCHED, I GRAB MY KEYS FROM my chest of drawers. As I pass it, I feel a pull from S—'s room. The door is shut tight but I can smell something sulfurous that gets stronger as I approach it.

But inside it is as it always is, and the scent evaporates. The small, soft frog that S— used to love is on the floor, under the bed. I pull him free.

At night, once the lights were out, I would hear her singing made-up songs to him. For a year or two she couldn't sleep without him, but after she started school he was relegated first to the foot of the bed and later the floor. In the last few years he spent most of his time being trodden on. I tried to kidnap him once for myself, for the memories it had created in the folds of that time. But she found him and restored him to his rightful place on the floor.

I pick him up. There is a ball of fluff on his head, and that and the fact that he had a name once trick me into a sudden and deep sadness. Where are you?

I sit lightly on the bed, taking care not to disturb it. The wallpaper is peeling just a sliver and I get up to run my fingers over it. For a moment I am possessed irrationally by the thought that S— is behind this wall, as Katya said. I pull at the peeled pink curl and it comes away in a sharp triangular tear. Behind is just the buff backing paper. I soak a sponge from the bathroom and rub it on the paper. And peel away a few more stripes. Nothing.

I drag the bed out a little and start tearing off more, looking for evidence of a cavity in the wall. Then I start tapping the wall with the heel of my hand, all the way along.

But of course, there's nothing.

It's only eight P.M., but I have to get out of here. My throat is closing from the pressure of all this.

Before I know it, I have gotten into my car and driven into the depthless night. The car, Caspar's old one before he traded up, gives me comfort. I feel his energy in here—competent and capable. I should call him. It's been so long, but these days I find it hard to speak to people, even him.

I park outside Katya's flat. She answers the door in jeans and a white shirt. She smiles.

"You came back."

She pulls her glossy bronze hair back into a fistful of curls and wraps it in a scrunchie. "Come," she says, and takes me by the elbow. The touch sends a buzz of electricity through me.

In the kitchen, there are boxes filled with pots and pans. A dozen wooden and steel spoons poke out of one. The scent of patchouli argues with the smell of damp cardboard.

"What's going on here?"

She waves away my question. "Is nothing. Landlord."

I think about Caspar. He's a family lawyer but I'm sure he knows someone who does housing law.

"Anyway, sit, sit," she says, and offers me coffee from a pot in the center of the table. The clutter has been swept away but it still feels chaotic somehow. I lay her money on the table for her.

"No," she says. "I want to do this for Sophia."

The mistake she makes with her name sends me into a misstep again. She sees it.

"In my language, is Sophia," she says. "More beautiful. Suits her more." I return the money to my pocket, and whatever feelings I had that she might be a con artist dissipate.

"Shall we do cards? Did you bring something of hers?"

"He's called Robbit." I hand her the soft frog toy. She runs her hands lasciviously over it. She puts its body to her nose and breathes in the scent. "Good. It's good," she says. "I can feel her."

She meets my creased brow with a soft smile. "Cards," she says, and takes the pile and asks me to cut them.

"You do it," I say.

"Is better if you do it," she says seriously.

I cut the deck and hand her the two halves. She takes them and deals them out in an intricate pattern.

"Do I ask a question?" I hear the words from my lips, and I can almost see myself stepping out from my body and sitting next to myself. I don't know this man I've become.

"If you like. The cards are a map. A guide. You look at a map and can say where you want to go if you like. But is not necessary. The map remains the same."

The light is murky in here. The fluorescent strip bulb flickers. It's covered with cobwebs and candle soot, but Katya herself glows as she turns the cards dexterously. She puzzles over some longer than others.

"See," she says. "Spades and clubs. Maybe an older man. Here, four of clubs, betrayal." She stops then and looks at me, puzzled. "And this wall is still coming up."

I am swept up in this energy she has created around herself and the cards and me. "Like a high wall?" I say, thinking of 210. "Is this a physical wall or something else?"

"Is not like this. Not definitely one thing or another thing."

I stop for a moment. I don't know if I can ask this question. It is the only question there is. I close my eyes. "Is she alive?"

When I open my eyes, her face is like lit amber. "This I cannot answer. Time is not like a line."

"What do you mean?"

"In spirit, time is happening all at once. Past, present, and future are all now." Her hands are fanned. The nail beds are almonds, the varnish chipped at the ends.

"I don't understand," I say.

"When you look at cards everyone is dead and alive at the same time."

I watch her for evidence of guile but see none. I shake my head at her, lost.

"In the cards, this is happening or has happened or will happen." She stops and looks at me frankly. "Romeo and Juliet. Are they alive or dead?"

"Dead."

"Well, actually, depends on where you're in the play. Same here. This is *Romeo and Juliet*." She waves a hand over the cards. "The book. They are alive and dead at the same time."

"That doesn't help me much."

"I'm sorry," she says, and gathers the cards.

"I thought you might be able to tell me where to find her— *now*."

"With cards, no," she says.

"But there are other methods?"

She nods.

"Costs more?" As soon as I ask, I half regret it.

She reacts as though she has touched a live wire. "Okay, okay. You can go, Mr. King. This was mistake." She stands and folds her arms tight.

"What? Why?"

"I know what you people think. It's okay. *You* came here, you know? To me. I didn't follow you and beg you."

"I'm sorry," I say.

"Me too," she replies. She makes for the door but freezes when suddenly there is a loud knock. She puts a warm palm over my mouth and strains to listen. My skin tingles. She's physically so warm, as if her body can't contain her life without it spilling free.

A voice sails from behind the door. "Hi, Katie. It's Ahmed here. Can we have a chat?"

Katya signals for my silence with a flash of her eyes. "Landlord," she whispers. I nod in understanding. She holds her breath.

"Okay," he says after a moment. "I'll come again. But next time it'll be with bailiffs."

He waits a second as if for a change of heart and then his steps recede.

I look around. The boxes. The packed-away life.

She drops her hand from my mouth a beat too slowly. "Thank you," Katya says. "He has court order for me to leave but—"

I want to help her but don't know how. "I can ask Caspar, my brother. He's a lawyer. It's not his area but he might know someone who could do something."

She turns her back on me to take the coffee things to the sink. "I have no papers. No papers. No rights. Is okay."

"What will you do?"

She shrugs. "Look for more shitty places like this. Go back home—I don't know."

WHEN I GET home, I creep my way up to the loft and lie under the large roof light on the landing. The clouds move slowly across the glass, lit by a slice of moon. The evening with Katya has left me shaken. I don't believe in the things that she believes in and yet, there was something so certain in her manner. She looked at the cards as though there were words there to be read. No drama. Matter-of-fact. Just saying what she saw.

I stare at the wall and try to make sense of the red lines.

What am I missing?

TWENTY-FIVE

ZARA

When I wake, I'm alone. Harry must have slept in the spare or in the loft. It feels as though we are icebergs that have broken away from each other.

Instead of showering and getting dressed, I go straight into Sophie's room. When I open the door, I stall. The scene that greets me is chaos. The bed has been pulled into the middle of the room. It's been stripped of its covers and all the soft toys have been piled into a corner. There are curls of wallpaper on the floor where the headboard was. The wall has been left wounded.

I stare at it trying to process it. Why did he do this?

He's destroyed Sophie's room. I collapse onto the bed and sob until my skin tingles with endorphins. And then I unfold myself from the bed.

He's right. Sophie isn't how she left us any longer. She's not a baby anymore. When we get her back, she will be changed forever.

I find a corner and pick at the wallpaper. Some of it comes away in large sheets. Other parts cling to the wall. When I pull those shreds, I begin to cry, and I think it's because I feel as though I am peeling away my self from her. I spend the next hour spraying the wall and peeling whatever paper I can.

When I return with more water, I see the mounds of damp wallpaper I have made on the floor. The entire wall is stalagmites and stalactites of paper and plaster.

Then I notice something.

At the bottom, there is a space where the wall meets the skirting board. The plaster has come away to create a gap of about half an inch. Some stray wallpaper has tucked itself in there and I stoop to pull it clear. But there are other things there.

Hidden things.

I reach for whatever it is with my fingertips and pull until it scrapes free. It's a wad of folded paper. There's another wedge of paper. I pick that free too and open them both out on the bed. The thinner package is made up of a sheet of spiral-notebook paper. I unfold it to reveal a pen-and-ink drawing of a butterfly. It reminds me a little of her pendant. It is beautifully done in purple and indigo, but however beautiful, it can't distract me from what it was hiding. Dozens of small off-white pills. I quickly pick up the other packet. It's an envelope. Inside are cash and a slip of paper containing numbers and initials.

It's a lot of money. Much more money than she should have.

The world judders around me. What the hell was Sophie involved in?

I spread the money out, and then using only the tips of my fingers, I smooth out the paper with the numbers and initials. Next to it I empty the pills from the butterfly page and count them. Twenty-one pills. I take several pictures on my phone. This is what Holly meant when she was talking about the chain of evidence, I think. I want to make sure I have *continuity* before I call her.

Her phone rings three times before I end it. I can't tell her about this. It would make Sophie just another young person who went off the rails rather than the person I know she is. An innocent girl who has been taken by someone somewhere and who is relying on us to find her. *Expects* us to find her.

It really changes nothing. Sophie is still who she is. They're probably not hers. They're just things she's guarding for someone else. That was just her nature. Once, we were doing a spring-clean; Sophie would have been eleven. Harry tipped up her mattress to flip it and there, as bold as an Egyptian artifact, was a small gold box of cigarettes.

When we looked at her for an answer she didn't miss a beat. "They're not mine. They're Ophelia's. You know what her parents are like."

We did. They were like us. Harry and I exchanged a quick look. When she lied she usually gave herself away. I remember cycling through the possibilities. She never smelled of smoke. I did her laundry and always smelled her clothes to check them to see what had been worn. There was never cigarette smoke.

"But why you?" I'd asked her, worried that she was being bullied into it.

She'd shrugged. "Because she trusts me."

I SCOOP EVERYTHING into my hand and then into my pocket—the paper, the money, and the pills. I'll deal with it later. I just want some time to process.

In the kitchen I go through the breakfast ritual. Harry comes in as I'm walking my coffee to the garden. The rain last night has given everything an electric glow. The blossoms shimmer, invigorated. The grass shoots out, alive. And everywhere is the scent of a garden after a monsoon. I sip my coffee slowly. What was Sophie up to?

Harry waves at me through the door glass, halfheartedly, as he assembles his breakfast. When he joins me, I see from his eyes that if he slept, it wasn't well. He crouches next to me and tugs up a handful of bergamot leaves from a pot, releasing their scent.

"So, there's still Herman at number 210 to be followed up. And the boyfriend." He pauses as if weighing them up. "I still like Herman for it. There's something weird about him. It's not normal living like that. In hiding."

The secret from Sophie's room begins to burn inside my pocket. I want him to slow down so I can tell him about it. But he's too wired for it right now. Later.

"I've never seen him out. Or if I have, I didn't know it was him," I say.

He stands and wipes his hands on his jeans. "I think I saw him at his door once. Or the back of him. He was sneaking into his own house. Seemed paranoid about anyone getting even a glimpse."

Then, like an omen, my phone rings and the name DS Holly flashes up.

"Put it on speaker," he says, and leans across and does it for me. Holly's voice comes through clearly.

"Zara, Holly."

"Hi, DS Holly," I say, with the phone flat on my palm. I wait.

"Just Holly is fine. You called me," she says. Harry stares at me.

"Oh, just for any news," I lie. "Did you speak to anyone at the Pig?"

There is a hiss on the line and then her voice again loud and clear. "I've already told you that I'd keep you updated as and when there was any news." She sighs. "Every time you call, it takes me away from the investigation."

Harry takes the phone. "Hi, Holly. It's Harry. Did you speak to the pub guy—Andy?"

"I did. There's only one candidate who was working there at the relevant time. And he was part-time."

"And?"

"And it can't be him."

"Why not?" he asks.

"Because he has year-old twins. He hasn't got time to wash his face, let alone kidnap someone. He had to quit his job because he couldn't cope with the hours."

Harry takes my phone with him and walks around in circles with it, his brow creased. "And what about Herman? Did you look at the tape? It's him, isn't it? Has the lab been able to find more footage on the tape?"

She starts to speak, and I have to follow Harry as he paces to catch what she's saying.

"No. Look, the lab can't work that fast, and honestly, I've told them to put it on ice for now."

"What? Why?"

"I've told you why. We wouldn't be able to do anything even if it came back. It's contaminated. And we haven't got unlimited resources here."

"Can we pay for our own? I mean, our own expert."

A breeze blows a spray of last night's rain from the apple tree down my neck. I shiver.

"No. No. Don't do that. There's no point. And listen, I shouldn't be telling you this, but he's reported a break-in to his property. Fences broken. He said whoever it was attacked his dog. CID have been round to take a statement from him."

"Shit," Harry says.

"He has no idea who it was, but a running shoe was left behind by the suspect."

"Shit," Harry says again.

"Exactly. And if you start pushing this the wrong way, it's going to bite us all in the arse."

Harry throws his head to the sky in frustration. "So then, where are we? Have you got any more leads at all? Or are you closing the book?"

"Of course we aren't closing the investigation. But I'd be lying if I told you that there was a line of investigation that we haven't followed up. We've done everything we can. And now—"

"What?"

"We wait. Hope something turns up. Hope there's a sighting."

Harry holds out the phone to me, killing the call as he does. I go to take it but he doesn't let go.

"What?"

"What did you call her about? She was returning your call."

I can't tell him yet. His memory of her is all he has to propel him onward. And I need him to keep going. "I was calling for an update. As I said to Holly."

He lets go of the phone. "I know you're lying to me, Zara."

TWENTY-SIX

HARRY

WHEN THE DOORBELL RINGS AFTER 9 P.M., I BECOME IMMEDIATELY APPRE-hensive. But it's just an Amazon delivery. It's a camera drone. I smuggle it upstairs before Zara can see it. I skim the instructions and assemble the parts and then put it on to charge. By morning it will be fully charged.

Flipping through the manual, I see there are a million things to learn before I can safely use this machine. Setting pathways, correcting navigational drift, and not least of all, how to fly the damn thing without crashing it.

I need to do a few practice flights. Tomorrow morning.

I pull on a light sweater and head out. The air is still cool from the showers last night. As I step onto the pavement my feet seem to realize where I'm heading before my head does. I stop at number 210 and after hammering on the high gate with my fists, I head toward the Pig. The way Holly is dealing with this case makes my muscles burn with frustration. She's already drawn blinds over it, despite what she is telling us.

In this light the slick road takes on hues of purple and blue. I walk into the pub and into a tide of warm air and stale alcohol. There is music playing but there's so much chatter and life for it to fight through that it gets lost in places.

I order an IPA at the bar and scan the room for Andy as I wait for it to be pulled. The young woman serving pushes it over to me, carelessly, and takes my card. She can't be much more than eighteen, S—'s age. Her hair is pink. Her body is a sapling.

"You're the guy whose daughter went missing?" she says when she swipes the card. She is trying to keep her voice casual but it is strung taut.

I nod. I had left flyers here. In the early days of her going missing, I think I spoke to a girl serving and showed her the picture. But I can't be sure now looking at her whether it's the same one. If she'd had pink hair I think I'd remember.

She hands my card back but she lingers. She leans forward as if to say something but stops when one of the other bar staff calls out her name.

"Lola—can you go and change the barrel?"

She sighs and releases my card.

I walk away wondering whether she was about to say something. It was too gossamer to ask her about directly.

The first third of the pint pours down like silk on glass. And then the alcohol awakens my senses like a memory. My body recognizes this feeling and I have to treat it with care or I could sink.

Out of one eye I see Andy, the manager, on a small stepladder hanging or straightening some pictures. I take my pint and wade over to him. At the foot of the ladder I stare up at him and wait. When he comes down he almost walks into me.

"Sorry, didn't see you there."

"Can we talk?" I say. "Maybe outside."

He narrows his eyes in question. "Do I know you?"

"You do, as it happens. Won't take long."

His eyes do a sweep. He's been a barman long enough to know that in my sweater and clearly on my first pint, I'm no more of a threat than your average schoolteacher.

"Lola, just watch the till a second. I'll be outside."

Lola looks up from behind the bar and waves a hand at him.

I lead the way, and when I leave the warmth and clamor of the pub for the street, the sudden change discomposes me. A second ago, everything was dreamlike and now in this wet air, the mundanity is sobering.

"So?"

"My daughter came for a job here, six months ago," I say, balancing my glass on a window ledge.

"Okay," he says, and though his face betrays nothing, he stands, hands on hips, ready.

"We met you. All of us, I mean. Me, my daughter, my wife. Sat in that corner over there. And we met you." He takes a step back and takes another look at me.

"It's your daughter that went missing."

"I know," I say.

He drags a hand down his face. "I was sorry to hear about it. Just spoke to the police. Did what I could."

"Did you?" A car slides slowly past.

"Yes. They were asking about some lad we had working for us a while back. I gave his details."

There is a smear of sweat prickling his forehead.

"We know she was seeing someone that worked in a pub. Police thought it might have been him."

"Okay."

"Only I don't think it was a lad that she was seeing. I think it was a man. You know, an older man."

He bristles, he can see the turn this is taking and doesn't like it. "All right."

"I wondered if it was you." My heart patters as I say this. The words feel like an escaping djinn; there's no telling what they will summon.

"Me?" he says. He hasn't decided how to take this yet, I see. Whether to be affronted or surprised.

"You. I saw the way you looked at her. I warned you off her. I reminded you she was underage," I say as a gust of wind blows away the volume of my words.

"Okay. I think we're done," he says, and turns to go, but now it's not just the words that I can't control. I reach across and pull him back by the elbow. "I'm not done yet."

"Let go of my arm."

"Were you seeing my daughter?"

"I won't tell you again. Let go of my arm."

"You seem to have an eye for the young 'uns. That one in there, Lola. How old is she?"

The punch catches me hard in the chest and sends me and my drink scattering onto the curb. I land heavily. There is glass all over me, swimming in beer. Blood blooms from my right hand. A shooting pain runs down my hip as I scrabble clumsily to my feet. He stares at me, waiting. I'm not sure what I thought he'd do. Admit seeing my daughter? Admit having something to do with her vanishing off the face of the bloody earth? What was I expecting?

He shakes his head and then he's back inside the pub before I can say anything more.

I head back home with my face burning. I've never been hard or strong or athletic, but I've always imagined myself as courageous, ready if the need ever called. Having her, S——, solidified that belief. When I first held her, I was overcome with the visceral need not just to protect her but to assert my right to protect her. To invite circumstances in which I could prove that I could protect her. I wanted someone to test me. And I am ashamed that he beat me so easily—without a fight.

She was seeing someone who worked in a pub. This was the only pub she knew. I saw the look he'd given her. But if it is him, what good am I?

Outside number 210, I stop automatically. Now I'm overcome by the certainty that Herman, whether he has taken S—— or not, is responsible for the twist in the fabric of the world I'm in. Somehow, he's pulling the weave and making everything on it tumble.

Opposite, the low wall has a run of loose bricks on top jutting like teeth in a seven-year-old's mouth. I wiggle one free, the mortar still attached to the bottom, and hurl it at the first-floor window. When it smashes, the glass makes a sound like dropped bottles. I stand there, arms wide, waiting for the lights to come on. Seconds later, the fire of a light burns. Do I hear a scream? Is that voice a girl's? I wait, straining my ears. A shape emerges in the window behind the dirty net.

I wait for the net curtain to part but it doesn't. He sees me though I can't see him. I beckon him down, but he remains impassive behind that broken glass.

I head home, slowly. As I near, I look at my own windows and see the warmth of the light that blazes behind the glass in our bedroom. And I want to be there, in the seclusion of my bed and under the awning of my—complete—family, but none of that is real any longer. It was ripped away when they ripped S— away and along with her, all of time and space.

The walls that Katya spoke about—are they those high walls of Herman's? She comes now unbidden into my mind. Just being with her made me feel as though S— was out there somewhere just waiting to be reached by her. Katya makes me believe that I can find her. When I was there with her, I felt a spike of hope. She didn't deserve to incite that hope in me. It's all hocus-pocus. I have to keep reminding myself of that. There's no magic that can find my daughter. None.

TWENTY-SEVEN

ZARA

I TAKE THE PILLS OUT AND LOOK AT THEM. THEY ARE OFF-WHITE AND HAVE a star stamped in the middle. Apart from that there's no way of telling what they are from the pill itself. But I remember that at the school, the deputy head arranged for a drug expert from the Metropolitan Police to come in to teach the parents about drug use and what to look out for. Most of what was said back then has misted away. But a few wisps from the talk still linger. Illicit pills are often homemade and discolored. They sometimes have logos, just like these.

"Look out for 'tick lists,'" the drug expert had said. "Lists showing customers and amounts they owe."

I remember thinking that that felt outdated. "Isn't it all on phones and computers now?" someone asked.

No, we were told, paper was the usual choice now. Dealers knew they couldn't get rid of digital information as easily as paper.

I google "pills with star logo." Google thinks it's MDMA. Ecstasy. A class A drug. From what I can find online, if Sophie is caught with it, she's looking at prison—three years or more. I drop them into the toilet and flush them. They cling stubbornly to the bottom of the pan so I pour toilet cleaner over them and make the water so cloudy you can't see what's under the surface.

I keep the butterfly drawn in her own hand. It will not be the last thing she ever draws, I know that. But it has the character of a relic in the same way that her room has become a reliquary. I smooth it out and take it to her room, where I place it carefully between the leaves of a book.

Then I sit on her bed and count the money. There's £820. Way too much for Sophie to have in cash. Way too much for any teenager. The slip of paper looks like a tick list with initials down one side and figures on the other. She has totaled the sums and at the bottom in red pen has written:

£1960 short!!

Although it is a lot, it doesn't feel like enough to steal someone for. Hurt them, perhaps, but not vanish them. Even if you added the £820, the total is still under three thousand pounds. But I don't know enough about this world. Maybe that is enough to cause you serious trouble.

I look up and down the list. RN seems to owe the most at four hundred. And then EB owes £240. EB—could it be Emily? Emily Blake? CR owes the least, £210.

I don't know what Sophie's mixed up in but I'm certain that Emily does. I send her a message: Meet me in those gardens near your house. It's urgent. 5 pm.

WHEN IT'S TIME, I hurry out of the house, checking my phone as I lock up. Still no reply, so I assume that Emily and I are on. The postman arrives and hands me an official-looking letter, addressed to both Harry and me. The school wants us to come in for a keep-in-touch day. I suppose now the summer holidays are ending, they want some certainty. They're not alone in that. I'll show it to Harry later. He can go in. I have no interest.

My phone buzzes through a message from Emily.

Can't make it. Mum 😔 Sorry.

My hand shakes a little as I type the message in reply. The words keep coming out wildly misspelled and every time I have to correct it I feel myself edging closer and closer to some chasm.

> Emily. Make it. Or explain to mum why you owe Sophie £240 for Ecstasy.

A second later I see the dots.

> K. The Bakery.

The Bakery is a café with blanched wooden tables and ironwork chairs. The smell of coffee, chocolate, and croissants is warm on the air. I take a table at the back and order an espresso. I have no idea what kind of whipped caramel thing Emily will want.

I finish my coffee before I see Emily's small head bobbing in and searching for me. Her hands are wrapped tightly across her body. When she sees my raised hand, she doesn't smile but shuffles up to me and sits with her arms still folded.

"Drink?"

She shakes her head. "I can't be long."

I look around. The purl of middle-class chatter, pastel bright, is cover enough for this talk. "I found Sophie's pills." I stare at her dead in the eye when I say it so that I can know from her reactions.

"They weren't hers."

I have considered this, of course. But the more I think about it, the less likely that seems. That was her handwriting on the paper. Her butterfly drawing the pills were wrapped in. I want to believe that she'd never be mixed up in drugs. But I want truth more.

"I don't know how to make you see how serious this is, Emily. I know they're hers. How long has she been selling pills?"

She is tugging her sleeve over her hand and then shifts to bring her feet up onto the seat. "Not long. The guy she was seeing. It was him, I think."

"What was she doing, exactly?"

She chews her lip till it bleeds a little. "She didn't say."

"Well, what did she say?"

"She said she got told where to drop off and collect, and that was it."

Her face is streaked with regret but I don't care.

"But you ended up buying them?" I say, and I don't lose any of the edge in my voice because I don't want to give her any room to slip through.

She mumbles an answer that I don't catch and I slap the table with a hand. "Emily."

"Just for a party that I went to. They asked me to get some. Everyone was supposed to chip in but nobody did. But it's okay," she says, looking up. "I can pay it."

I take the list out of my bag and show her the names, or rather the initials of the ones that seem to owe money. "Do you know who these are?"

About halfway down she points with a bitten nail. "That could be Chloe Williams. And that, I think maybe, is a girl called Casey in the year above. Don't know anyone else."

I take the list back. "And do you know where Sophie was buying the pills? Who she owed this money to?"

"No. Just that it was to do with the guy she was seeing."

"But you don't know his name?"

"D. She called him D. That is all I know, I swear."

I pay for the coffee and walk her back out onto the pavement. "Don't buy or take any more drugs, Emily. If I find out that you've been messing around with that shit again . . ."

Her face is white and washed through in fear. "I don't. It was just that one time for a stupid party, and I thought that Sophie—"

I cut her off. "This guy, D. If I hear that you've been holding back any detail—*any* detail—I'm going straight to your mum with it all. And maybe the police as well."

She nods. "I'm sorry."

"It's too late for sorry. Do you have any idea how important this could have been for finding her? Weeks have gone by. More than a month!"

"I just—"

"Just what? Wanted to protect yourself from getting in trouble? This is too serious for you to have been this selfish."

"I thought she was hiding out with him. I didn't know—"

I leave her stranded on the pavement and return home the way I came.

I SIT ON the bed in Sophie's room. The walls still need peeling and then papering. There is mess everywhere, and I wish now I hadn't made it worse. I wipe my face, which is wet now with tears. Everything is a mess. My head spins and increases this feeling now building that I am losing my grip on the world. It's all moving too fast in competing directions. How am I supposed to keep any of the threads in my hands? How?

TWENTY-EIGHT

HARRY

I AM BACK TO SEE KATYA. I HADN'T INTENDED TO, BUT THE MORE I THINK about S— being lost out there, the more entangled she becomes with Katya, and the more clearly I feel I have to see her again. Even if it's all rubbish. She's the only connection I have to S— as she is now as opposed to how she was. There's a force connecting them, S— and Katya.

"You are back?" she says, opening her door in a sleeveless orange dress, her hair up in a loose knot. "I'm surprised, considering everything."

"I thought you'd be expecting me—clairvoyant and all that," I say.

She doesn't smile. "What do you want, Harry?" She folds her arms and I see the muscles in her shoulders turn from supple to ropelike.

I look away. I realize I don't know how to say this. "I just want to be close to her."

She turns in to her hallway but then stops, waiting for me to follow. "I'm making tea, if you want?"

A few minutes later I'm drinking strong, sweet mint tea from a small Moroccan glass. The damp box and patchouli smell of the room has already begun to feel comforting—exciting almost.

"You forgot to take your frog with you," she says solemnly. She leaves and returns with it a minute later. "Don't worry. I kept him in bedroom with me." When I don't take it from her, she hugs it absently like a child.

We sip silently. More boxes have sprouted, crammed with belongings.

"Things no better with the housing situation?"

She doesn't reply. After another minute of silence, she forces a smile. "Are you here for reading?"

I drink the rest of the tea in a single gulp. "No," I say, and then, "I just want to find her. That's all." I search my pockets for the money I brought and it comes out in loose glossy slips. Some of it falls to the floor, and when I reach for it, the tears start.

Katya gets up, puts my head in her arms, and holds me until they stop. Her bare arms are smooth against my face. Her warmth contains so much power that for a moment I just want to be lost to it. Then she returns to her seat, her face a stranger to what has just happened. She smiles in concern.

"We can try something, like I said before. But what I did not say was that it is not always safe."

I rub some blood back into my face. "I'm sorry, Katya. Honestly, I don't know why I came. I don't even believe in any of this."

"And I told you, it does not matter if you believe. You cannot affect power by your denial."

I consider this. Hocus-pocus always has this advantage, like religion, of being essentially untestable. I want to give her the fulfillment of having tried to search for her. I know how important it is.

"You want to try it?" she asks.

"What is it?"

"The ringed cup of Jamshaid."

I am disappointed by the hokeyness of it. "What's that?"

She reaches over and takes my empty tea glass and refills it. "It is a kind of scrying. You look into the cup when it is filled with water. The legend says you can see the goings-on in the seven heavens. But the reality is less"—she gropes for the right word—"fantastical."

She is on the edge of excitement. Her eyes implore me. "Okay, then let's do it. But I want to pay for it."

"You have paid," she says, indicating the cash.

"Whatever the full price is."

She rolls her eyes flamboyantly. "Even when you think it is all rubbish?"

I do think it is rubbish but at the same time it is magnetic. "Your time is still your time and you're using it to help me."

"I'm not taking more money," she says firmly.

"You could use the help," I say then.

"Help me another way, another day."

I concede and wait for whatever happens next. She catches my look. "No. Not now. I need to prepare. First, I have to be in a correct state. Give me a day or two, please."

As I leave she holds out Robbit.

"No. You keep him for now." So I have to come back, I think.

She takes him back into her chest and looks at me seriously. "If you want to do this, I have to make you a warning. If you don't follow guidance when it comes, sometimes bad thing can happen. So, think about this and let me know."

Even tiny, vanishingly slim chances are better than none. "I don't need to think about it."

"Okay," she says. "Then I will make preparations, for next time."

I get up.

"So, did you find the wall?"

"I think so," I say. "There is a man behind high walls near where we live. I think maybe that's what you're seeing."

"I don't know," she says. "But you will know, when we reach that time."

AT HOME I climb the stairs to hear the sound of Zara scraping. In S——'s bedroom, I see that she has continued where I left off and has removed almost all of the wallpaper. The walls are pink and smooth behind.

When I come in, she is holding up a roll of expensive-looking paper. It is black but shot through with gold and purple. It's handmade, I see now that she has unrolled it.

"New start," she says. "She will be changed when she comes back."

She puts the roll down and sits on the bed. Her pushed-up sleeves show how thin her arms have become. She doesn't look at me when she says the next thing. "I found drugs."

I'm shocked. "What? Where?"

"Behind the wall," she says, and I feel the tingle of hairs rising on my neck.

"The wall?" I sit down in shock.

"Actually, the skirting. Pills. Ecstasy, I think."

It takes a second to catch up with what I've been told. Then my mind begins to separate and scatter the information like light through a prism. Drugs? "She was taking drugs?"

"No. Not taking. At least I don't think she was taking them."

"What then?"

"Selling."

"What?"

"She was selling them. She's a—a dealer."

I can't process what I am hearing so I keep saying it. *What? What? What?* Until finally she snaps.

"Look," Zara says, producing a sheet of paper. "Remember when the drug expert came that time to the school, they said to look out for tick lists. This looks like a tick list. These," she says, running her finger down the list, "are the people who owe Sophie money still."

I read the initials and the sums and when I turn back to face her, Zara is already answering the questions I am still formulating. "School friends. This one is Emily. That one is someone called Casey in the year above. Don't know much about the others."

"And the drugs?"

"Down the loo. I flushed them. I didn't want them in the house."

"And Holly?" I say but I know the answer already. We can't have her recast as a drug dealer. They'd stop looking for her altogether.

"No."

"Who is she?"

"She's still Sophie," she says sadly.

This version of S——, this one that has drugs in her room and lists of people that she has been supplying to, is hard to hold. It's like a trapped animal. Every time I try to grasp it—to examine it—it struggles violently away. I don't know this S——. I can't believe it's her and now faced with it all, I'm wondering whether I was walking around with my eyes closed. These thoughts linger. If I'm not careful they'll begin to ferment.

"Can I have a look at that list?" She shows it to me again. "I'm going to try and speak to all the people on here," I say.

"I think *I* should do it," she says. "You can't be talking to teenage girls."

I rub my head and churn through the possibilities. She's right. "We do it together," I throw out as a last-ditch effort.

"No. I'll do it."

TWENTY-NINE

ZARA

In the morning after Harry has laid breakfast at my place and I have taken a bite, I spread out the tick list and log in to the school's intranet. There are four sets of initials that I need names and addresses for.

AG	
CR	
CW	
RN	

    I start with Sophie's class. If Emily is right about CW being Chloe Williams and CR being Casey someone, then AG *must* be Alex Godinet. I make a note of their telephone numbers and addresses and then find the others. RN is Ryan Nessa. Casey is harder to find because she's not in Sophie's class. A run through the R's gives me seven candidates in the year above Sophie's, but none of them have first names beginning with C. I check middle names and find Poppy Cassandra Richards. She must be Casey. I note her details too.

    Harry watches me from his breakfast as I write out the names. He is hunched over his plate, eating slowly. There is something wolfish about him today. I can tell that he wants to snatch the names up and set dogs off to chase them all down, but I can't let him. But I can't let him feel irrelevant either.

"How are you going to speak to them? Arrange a visit with the parents?"

I've been thinking the same thing, how to make contact with them. I can't just turn up at their homes. And the telephone numbers are all their parents' numbers. If I call them, I'll get them and not their children.

"I don't think that's going to go down well. And you know how kids clam up when their parents are there," I say. "It might be better to just do it at the party."

"Party?"

"The party. For Sophie. For God's sake, Harry. I've spoken to you about this!"

He flicks his eyes around the room. He's forgotten about it. Or had been nodding along all this time hoping I'd change my mind. "Okay. Good idea. We can do it next weekend."

Now that I have said it, I'm apprehensive about having people in the house to celebrate Sophie when the only person that I want here at home is Sophie.

"We can do it in the church hall," he says.

"They won't have any space at this short notice," I say.

"Well, let me find out at least," he snaps, and leaves the room.

We spend the rest of the day avoiding each other. He hides out in the loft and I in Sophie's bedroom, finishing off the statement wall. It doesn't take long, and when it's done I stand back and see that it's transformed not just the room and the way it looks but the air in here. The darkness is like the space behind the eye. It speaks of a deep and wrenching, serious change. It has the sick feeling I get in dreams when I realize I have torn off a limb or the skin off my face.

Harry comes in to look as I am tidying up the mess. "Looks good," he says. I can see that he is still bloated by secrets he's keeping inside him. He needs me to take them from him, but I can't.

Once darkness has fallen, I join him in the kitchen and pick at the dinner that he's made. We don't talk. And then I take myself off to bed while he spirits himself away to the loft again. I lie waiting for him but he doesn't come. In the beginning I was certain that we wouldn't be able to survive this catastrophe, but in that certainty, the way we sundered was more visceral. Now I see that the way we are coming apart, slowly and undramatically, is worse. It's like decay.

I hear him leave the house. The front door clicks softly and then in the distance the muddled thump of a closing car door and the sound of its engine coming to life and taking him away. Then I rise, phantomlike, and soundlessly I dress and leave too. My Fiat is neat in the road. Once inside I see the glasses and reach out to touch them but with the lightest of touches. I can't be making shrines right now.

In twenty minutes, I am parked outside the Turkish mosque. I've always liked it because it's a Sufi mosque. There's no shouting from the minbar. The women and the men appear to mingle freely. There's none of the oppressiveness that I grew up with. I expect it to be open, but I have never been here this late. I look up at the building, which is a converted church. There are long lancet windows along the flank, the glass stained in Moroccan blue. I approach the Gothic stone arch and push the door. It opens and as I enter, I feel the world behind me drop away at the threshold.

I sit in the semidarkness on the carpet and wrap my arms around my legs. The silence begins to hum and whine. I haven't practiced properly since I was a teenager. I don't pray the daily prayers—not even the Friday ones. But an urge descends over me to touch my forehead to the ground in *sajada*. The carpet is soft against my head and nose and under my palms. The blood rushes into the open pockets in my head until every thought is filled with it. The peace doesn't descend as much as it pushes through my veins. But when it comes, it floods my senses. I stay with my head pressed down and I pray until the carpet there is wet with tears.

Bring me back my girl.

When I sit back up, I feel lighter, as if a cloak has fallen from my shoulders. The painted lemon walls, that particular hue of yellow, sends me tumbling into a memory of me as a child, and then overlaid on it, one of Sophie. I'd had a doll as a child. It was a Barbie, and I'd wanted it so much that the yearning was physical. I'd see her on TV and moon over her. There was always something on a credit card that needed paying off. But then, unexpectedly, one day shortly after my mother died, Dad gave me a wrapped box. I was ten, so probably too old for it, but when I saw the Barbie I gasped. The thing I remember most vividly is that it wore a yellow Barbie Dream Glow dress that glowed in the dark.

I looked after her obsessively. Even as a child, I harbored a dream that I'd hand it down to my own daughter—long before I knew whether I'd have one or even wanted children. I kept her, Lanah, in a shoebox that I'd made up as a bed, and over the years, on my birthday, I made a point of looking in on her. I would ritually wipe away the dust with a damp flannel and then pack her away again in her yellow dress. And then the years came on in slabs. Harry first. Then the flat we bought and renovated. Then the wedding and the honeymoon and the holidays. Then Sophie. And the year of colic. And the teething. And the potty training and the nursery years, all grindingly slow and yet all passing at the speed of riffled pages in a book.

Sophie was four when she found her at the bottom of my wardrobe. "Oh, Mama, a doll!"

I knelt beside her and lifted her out of the box. "This is Lanah. This was Mama's favorite doll."

"Can I play with her? Please?"

"Of course you can. I saved her for you."

A week later, her dress was torn and her green-eyed face covered in red pen. *She wanted to wear makeup.* I looked at the doll and then Sophie in horror. All those years of care, gone. I confiscated her until she found her again and begged her back from me.

"I *will* look after her. I promise."

The next time I saw Lanah the dress was gone and her hair was a tangled cloud. And I shouted at Sophie for that. And she was just four. And I can see Sophie now, her dropped cheeks and liquid-filled eyes. I hate that I did that. I hate that I shouted at her for the sake of a cheap doll in cheap clothes. I don't know whether that one thing ruined half a lifetime of caring for Sophie. It feels as though I made a stain that I can't wash away.

I know it didn't. But I regret it more than my aching body will let me express. I want to reach deep into my belly through my mouth and grasp the stringed clot of it and pull it out and fling it. But in the absence of that there's nothing to do but to nourish it with my own body and wait till it takes me over.

THIRTY

HARRY

Zara is gone. I run around the house checking all the rooms, ending with the loft. Each empty room sends me into a deeper, galloping panic. Once I have done a sweep of the whole house and shouted for her, I check the ink-dark garden in case she's fallen or something. I stop and catch up with my breath. Her location is switched off and her phone is ringing out.

I slip out into the street and scan the road for her car. It's gone. It's okay. It's fine. She's gone for a drive. I go to the garden to try to calm myself down.

The night air is cool and has a dewy quality.

Number 210 is just there to the left. A few houses away. I go up and get the drone.

I take the controller and press the power button and immediately the motors whine like a horde of giant mosquitoes. The camera image is so sharp that I can pick out shapes I recognize from the neighboring gardens. The wooden garden table next door. The bike shed in the next one and a paddling pool left out in the one after. I count the gardens as I pass them, and when I reach the tenth one I make the drone hover steadily and turn the camera toward the house.

At first all I can see is some blurred brickwork, but a second later the focus becomes sharper. I back the drone away and then lift it up higher so that it's flying just below the soffits on the roofline. This gives me a decent view of the rear elevation. The two top-floor windows are lit up but not from the rooms. The light is from deeper inside the house—the hallway perhaps?—it's low but it reaches through the cracks the drawn curtains have left behind.

I hover around for a minute or so but there's nothing of interest. Then I fly around the right side of the house, and immediately I see the dog leaping from the kennel. I know she's barking because I can hear the sound as it echoes over the fences.

Quickly I pull the drone up and circle back around to head for home, but then the curtains fly apart. He must be looking out. I bank left for a better view and that's when I see his face. He's searching the night sky for the sound, and then he must see the green power light. In the monitor I see his eyes flicker. They appear to be looking right at me. I shiver though I know that he can't see me. He is seeing only the LED light of the camera, not me. But just as I talk myself down, he smiles right into the lens. And I drop the controller and send the drone hurtling downward.

I quickly recover the controller and pull the drone out of free fall. I fly back up to see if Herman is still there. The curtains are drawn again, but a second later they part and he is there, eyes like glowing charcoal. The sash window goes up. He pulls his arm back and, in that moment, I know he's going to throw something at me. I make the drone climb until I am certain it has just missed me, whatever he has thrown.

My palms are slippery and controlling the drone is becoming a challenge again. I wipe my hands on my shirt. I lower the drone until I see him staring at the camera again before disappearing into his room.

But he's left the window open.

I don't know whether the signal can survive inside his room, but the camera is recording and whatever I get might be good enough.

The window is open, I say to myself. Open.

I hold my breath and hover at the threshold. I wait, heart pounding. And then with a prayer, I send the drone in.

I see him. He freezes and then begins to flap his arms in alarm. I try to avoid him and the objects in the room but it's almost impossible. The camera shudders as the drone hits a wall lamp. But it straightens itself and I quickly find the collision-avoidance button and turn it on. The image settles. The room is dominated by an old bed with an ironwork bedstead. The covers have been thrown back. They're gray, as if they haven't been washed for months. Between the iron uprights on the headboard I can see what look like belts, tied round in a loop. A sick feeling spreads through my insides like spilled oil.

Herman ducks and then crawls out of the room. I spin the drone around to capture more footage. On one wall to the right is what looks like a giant black-and-purple stain. I pan round to get my bearings and to keep the window in view. I want to be able to make a quick exit when he returns. My heart is hammering.

I try to lower the drone but the anti-collision function won't let me drop below two feet off the ground. I do a quick scan of the room and then get ready to return. I remember with a pang that the SD card is in the drone. If he catches it and sees the footage he'll know where to send the police.

I climb carefully and hold the drone steady at the window just as the world goes sideways. He must have returned already. I don't have any audio so I couldn't hear him open the door. The image flickers and then corrects and I see him now to my right. He is still in his dirty vest, his eyes like burnt holes. He's holding a cushion. He swipes at the drone and my heart stumbles.

Quickly, I back out of range and aim for the window. With the camera facing the window I am blind behind me. As soon as the aperture is in front of me I maneuver out of the window. The footage rocks as though I have clipped the frame but I know I can't have with the anti-collision on. And then as the drone levels again I see a bright padded square spin in front of me. He's thrown the cushion and it's only just missed.

I bank the drone and race away, keeping his window in view for more projectiles. He leans out and watches me. If he keeps the drone in sight he'll see it land and find where I live. So I send it up high into the sky and wait for him to put his head inside again. But he waits too, as if he knows that when the battery runs low it will return

home. A bar on the controller tells me I have only a few minutes' flying time left. It's a risk to fly so high in case I go out of range but I
don't have any choice. I push the drone up and over his roof. It is
responding still to the controls so I follow the rooflines all the way
home and quickly bring it in.

In the bedroom, I put the camera into my sock drawer and then
push the SD card into the controller and have a closer look at the
footage. I'm amazed at the quality of the little drone camera. I can
see the gardens in outline, clear in the pale moonlit night. Then as the
drone turns I make out his house and then the window as it opens. I
follow the drone as it slides in, and then there is that huge purple
stain on the wall. I can't make it out—it seems deliberate, like a
mural, but before I can get a better look, the drone drops down and
the mural is out of sight.

I wind the footage on, stopping here and there to examine parts of
the room that I hadn't seen properly first time around. Then once I
finish I watch the entire thing all the way through again. There is no
sign of anything to do with S— but this is just one room. There's at
least another ten in that house, and he wouldn't keep her somewhere
with windows, where she could be seen.

I get to the part where the mural is again and I pause the image to
try and work out what I am looking at. A switch flicks in my subconscious. The picture resolves in part. That portion I am looking at
looks a little like the top wing of a butterfly.

The front door clatters. In the silence of this late hour, the sound
ricochets like saucepans down a well. I hide the controller just in
time to see Zara open the bedroom door.

Her eyes are swollen.

"Where've you been?" I try to keep my tone neutral.

"Just a drive," she says, and begins to dress for bed. "What about
you?"

"Same," I say, and then at the same time we both say, "I've been
thinking—"

"You first," she says, getting into bed.

"We should think about returning to work. The school's generos-
ity isn't endless. When do they want us to come in again?"

She flicks through her phone diary. "Week after next, Monday,
Wednesday, or Thursday between two and four P.M."

I reach for my phone to put the dates in. "What do you think?"

"I agree. For you, I mean. I can't," she says.

I climb into bed next to her, and sit staring at the light from my phone. "Why not?"

Zara faces me. "Could you stop looking for Sophie?"

"What?"

"I'm asking. Could you? Stop searching for her? If I asked you to?"

"No."

"Then it's the same. I can't stop her filling every space of my life."

We sit in a pool of quiet for some minutes. Finally, I have to ask. "Do you still blame me?" I take the heat out of the words so they lie, cooling. "For locking her in, two nights before she went missing?"

She scratches the cuticle of her thumb with the nail of her index finger. "No," she says, and then immediately changes her mind. "Yes. I do blame you. But I blame me too."

"We couldn't just let her wander out into the night, Zara!"

"No. But we could have spoken to her. *Talked* to her."

"She wasn't talking to us. That was the whole problem, don't you remember?"

She nods and then says, more to herself than me, "But we shouldn't have given up."

I think of that night. We only held on to the door until I could hastily screw on a latch. We only had the padlock there to keep her safe.

I let my thoughts become arrayed—ordered so I can make sense of them. It was all perfectly logical as a response. It was the right thing to do. It was. I would do it all again.

Wouldn't I?

THIRTY-ONE

NOW

OLD BAILEY
COURTROOM THREE

THE PROSECUTOR WAITS UNTIL THE EYES OF EVERYONE IN THE COURT-room return to him.

"There was a mural of a butterfly on the wall of Mr. Herman's bedroom. The one thing we know about Sophie King is how much she liked butterflies. She'd loved them from an early age, as a child visiting the Horniman Butterfly House in South London. As a teenager, she wore them in earrings, on necklaces or pendants. And she drew them whenever she could.

"Mr. Herman complained to police about a drone being used to spy on him at night. A drone, he told police, was flown in through his bedroom window in the middle of the night, three weeks before the murder. We can't prove who did that using direct evidence." He spears the jurors with a look before continuing.

"But there is some evidence, from which you can draw an inference, of who it was. You see, a drone was recovered by police in the basement of the Kings' home. It was acquired by Mr. King just days before Mr. Herman complained of a drone in his house. We say the conclusion is inescapable. Mr. King flew that drone into Mr. Herman's house in the dead of night. His drone must have captured an image of the butterfly. He had always been suspicious of the reclusive Mr. Herman but this must have been the missing jigsaw piece he had been looking for. Once he saw that butterfly, he completed the puzzle and made the connection between his missing daughter, Sophie, and Mr. Herman. It was a wrong connection.

"But one that led, inexorably, to a brutal, cold-blooded murder."

I look over at Harry. He is tensing under the weight of these words but I am not. On me, the words are a soft fog. Harry smiles to reassure me but I don't feel the need for his reassurance. I am certain. It all makes sense now, as if the world has suddenly become transparent and I can see its workings.

The prosecutor, Alfred, finishes his speech and then calls his first witness. After all the delays and the months spent trudging through mud, the speed we are traveling at now is dizzying. One day I was at home waiting for Sophie to walk in through the doors and then I blinked. And now a witness is giving evidence in a murder trial.

Harry leans forward so he can catch every word.

"Officer, tell us then, please, whether on discovering a drone in Mr. King's basement you had the opportunity to examine it?"

"I did."

"And what can you tell us about it?"

"It's a very powerful drone for a domestic unit. It has sufficient range to be flown from number 190, where Mr. King lived, to 210."

"Anything else?"

"Well. It's a camera drone."

"Is it?" Alfred asks dramatically, turning to the jury.

"Well—kind of. The camera has been removed."

"I see. So, we don't know whether any footage was recorded?"

"No, sir."

"Or what it might have shown us?"

"No, sir."

"And from Amazon purchase history you can confirm that it was purchased three weeks before the murder?"

"Just over three weeks."

"Thank you. Wait there," Alfred says to him as he takes his seat.

Harry's barrister, Stevens, stands up. He is immediately animated. "Mr. Chris."

"Cross."

"Cross, sorry. Whatever. That must be a military drone or something like that?" he says, leaning so far over his lectern that he is draped across it.

The officer scratches his head. "I don't think so. It's commercially available."

"Then it must be a very advanced drone."

The officer looks at him puzzled. Everyone seems a little puzzled.

"Because it talks," Stevens offers.

"Sorry?" he says.

Stevens stares across at the jury. "It talks, doesn't it? It must do because it told you that it went to number 210."

"I'm sorry, I don't—"

"I mean, how else do you know it went there?" There are titters from some in the courtroom. "If it didn't tell you? Did it record its movements somewhere? Like on a map?"

"No."

"Then at the risk of repeating myself, can you tell me how you know it went to number 210?"

He colors under the glare of the question. "I didn't say that it did."

"Oh. I thought you were here to tell us that it was flown into number 210 by Mr. King?"

"I can't say that. Just that it has the range to do that."

"But it's got the range to go that far in any direction, hasn't it?"

"Yes."

"Do you have a car, Mr. Chris?"

"Cross. Yes, I do."

"How far does it go on one tank? Five hundred miles?"

"About that, yes."

"So, you must have gone to Manchester and back this morning?"

There are smiles developing among the solicitors sitting in the row behind Stevens. They are enjoying this charade. But I can't see the humor in it.

"No."

"Well, of course you did. Because it's got the range, Mr. Chris—Cross."

The judge leans forward a little but even she appears to be holding on to her smile. "Mr. Stevens."

"That's all, thank you, my lady." He sits down, satisfied.

I look over at Harry and I see he is looking less tense. He gives me a half smile but I don't know what to do with it. I feel as though his smiles don't reach me anymore. I worry that nothing can reach me anymore.

THIRTY-TWO

ZARA

I DON'T WANT TO DO IT IN A CHURCH HALL. I WANT THE MOSQUE. I WANT people to stop and examine where they are and who they are and who Sophie is. She's more than they imagine for her. She's the child of traditions and rituals and prayers and prophets that go back hundreds of years. It took countless couplings, thousands of lifetimes, to bring her life into being. Every one of Sophie's ancestors had to survive plagues and hardships and starvations and persecutions to get her here. Before they arrive at the mosque her friends should already be thinking about who Sophie is.

"I want it at the Turkish mosque," I say as I load the washing machine the next morning. "They don't mind as long as it's outside prayer times. We only need a couple of hours."

"What Turkish mosque?"

"The one in Peckham."

He scratches his head as he dredges it up and even before he says it, I know he's going to say it and I know it's going to irritate me. "You mean St. Anne's? The converted church?"

The converted church, as if there's a defilement in the transition. A superior thing has diluted into this lower form. I know deep in my heart that it's not what he means, but there's no getting away from how different we are.

He looks at me to go on but I haven't thought it all through yet. There's an argument for inviting everyone she knows from the school and another one for just those specific people on the list. Part of me wants them to recognize, each of them, what binds them together to Sophie and to me. And to see the realization glitter in their eyes.

"I've downloaded the class details and I think that we invite the ones we know Sophie knows. And the ones on the list."

Harry leans against the counter, lost in thought. His face is pointed at his phone. "Set up a WhatsApp group, maybe?" he says eventually. "I'm sure Emily will want to help."

The name clangs. He wouldn't be so casual if he knew that she'd held information back that could have helped Sophie.

By lunchtime, I've made the booking, compiled the group, and sent a message inviting everyone. I don't want to bring the mood to the ground, so it's a "birthday party." I'll make the butterfly cake and order pizza.

No gifts please—if you really want to, a donation to MISSING— a missing persons charity—would be gratefully received by them, I add.

Sophie's room is finished, and with everything clean and polished it looks very striking. When I walk in there is initially this feeling of displacement, as if I've stepped into another dimension, into a room I don't know. When it adjusts itself to my eye, it's as though Sophie has grown up. From the shelf I pick up the book where I hid the butterfly drawing and tease it out. The dark, brooding inks on the page stir something deep within me. The beauty and delicacy of the creature in the violence of those colors. What was she feeling when she drew it? How much she must have been hurting.

Later, at around four, the doorbell sings and I answer it to a police officer in uniform. He looks to be about nineteen. My heart kicks and immediately my mouth dries. When I speak, the words come as if dragged across blades.

"What's happened?"

Harry emerges from somewhere and stands behind me, a hand on my shoulder. "What is it?"

The officer has splashes of red on his cheeks like two fat autumn leaves. He smiles. "Hi. Nothing to be alarmed about. We're conducting some routine inquiries. Can I come in?"

He sits at the kitchen table and lays down his radio on the polished oak. The remnants of lunch are still there, embarrassing me. Plates with food that Harry has eaten and I haven't. He seems not to mind the mess.

"We've had a complaint about a drone flying in this area. Obviously, it goes without saying that the flying of a drone in a residential area is illegal and you could be liable, if you're found guilty, to imprisonment or a substantial fine." He says it raised at the end like a question.

I sneak a look at Harry, who is nodding seriously at the officer.

"Okay, well, I haven't seen any. Have you, Zara?"

I shake my head though I've seen it charging in the loft. He'd told me he'd got it to look around the house. I told him not to.

"Well, as I say, just a routine inquiry. The complainant wasn't able to identify where the drone came from but we wanted to make sure you were aware of the potential dangers to life and limb. Not to mention privacy."

The way he garbles his sentences makes me want to force him to write down what he is saying and explain to him all the places in which he is going wrong.

"Yes. Well, we don't have a drone and have no intention of getting one, do we?"

Harry shakes his head.

"If you have children, I know many parents think it's a cool gift, but the rules are still there for them as well."

Once we have ushered him out I turn to Harry. "I told you it wasn't a good idea. What did you do?"

"Nothing. I flew it to his house. Had a look around."

"And?"

"And nothing."

"Nothing?" I say, so that I can ask him next whether that is now an end to it.

"Nothing. But that's just one room. What's in the others? That's the question."

I recoil at what he's just said. "Wait—room? You flew it *inside his house*?"

"What?" He looks at me as though confused.

"You can't do that, Harry. Are you crazy?"

"The window was open. You telling me that you wouldn't have gone in?"

The question hangs in the air and I don't know how to bring it down, how to burst it. Because I don't think I would have gone in if it had been me, and then I am ashamed that I wouldn't have. He looks at me and sees it too.

"So nothing stood out?" I ask at last.

"I mean, apart from serial-killer bedroom, no."

I stare at him, shocked at the blasé way he can say that. "What do you mean?"

"Nothing. One wall's been painted in weird colors."

"Weird how?"

"I'll show you."

He swipes quickly through his photos but a message flashes over the screen in a notification. I see it only for a moment before he swipes it away. He tenses next to me. The skin on his fingers glistens, leaving traces on the glass.

"What was that message?"

"Nothing," he says, too quickly.

"Show me."

"No, I'm showing you the drone pictures."

I stand up from the table and look down at him. "Show me the message."

He closes his eyes. "I will but I need to explain it." He puts the phone down and looks up at me.

"Go on then," I say. My heart is beating because I saw that it was a message from a woman.

Come to me whenever you can. I am ready for you.

THIRTY-THREE

HARRY

"You gave her Sophie's frog?"

"Yes. Wait," I say. "You believe me, right?"

She looks at me with eyes that are rimmed red and quivering. "Believe you? You mean that you're telling the truth? Of course I do. When have I ever disbelieved you? But *can* I believe what you did? No, Harry. I can't believe it."

"I needed to try something new."

"Don't even," she says, shaking her head.

"Well, how the hell else do you think we do this? Shutting our eyes and hoping? Leaving it to Holly? *Praying?*"

"You're having a go at me for *praying?* When you're doing fucking fortune-telling?"

She clutches her phone so tightly that her fingers, brittle after these weeks, seem about to snap.

I take a second because I am not completely sure about what I am thinking.

"She was right about the wall."

She stares at me, disbelieving. "You're not serious."

"So far it's the only hint of a clue that we've ever had. And," I add, "does it really even matter if it helps me find her?"

"Yes, it matters, Harry. This isn't happening to you. It's happening to us. I exist, Harry. Sophie is our daughter but she came from inside me. You can't keep doing this to me."

"In what way am I doing anything to *you*?"

"You're destroying me. Everything you do is scorched earth. You go and then you burn everything that you leave behind. But it's me, Harry. *I'm* behind you. I'm finding it hard enough just to keep—" And then she drops into a crouch against the wall, clutching her face.

I kneel so that I can reach her.

Finally, she drops her hands to reveal a tear-broken face. "How could you give her Sophie's frog? She *loves* that frog. And you've handed it over to some crackpot, like it's nothing? Like Sophie is nothing."

"I didn't *give* it to her. She—Katya—needed it to, I don't know, reach her. And I know. Don't think I don't know how you feel about this stuff. I do. But right now, she wants to look for her and I don't want to stop her."

Zara's eyes blaze. "That is Sophie's frog—it wasn't yours to give away."

"It's not been given away. I'll get it back!"

"But it won't be the same, will it? It will have *her* on it. It had Sophie on it and now, that's ruined."

"Okay, I think you're overreacting," I say, but regret it immediately. I let the echo of the words die away. "Can we talk about something else? We have the party to think about. We need to focus. She owed money to someone and then she disappeared. We need to know who that was."

Zara wipes her face with the backs of her hands and stands up. "I can't talk to you right now," she says. "And I'd prefer it if you slept in the spare."

I want to say that it makes no difference. That we are hardly in the same room together at night as it is and that when we are, we don't even touch. There's so much to say, but to say any of it I'd first have to crawl out from all this pain, and I'm just too tired. So instead I say, "Okay," and when the sun sets, I drag the winter duvet out from the wardrobe and head upstairs. I prefer the loft. It feels as though it's apart, somehow, from the rest of the grimy world below.

Dusk throws a tangerine glow onto the rooftops. The beauty of the sky hurts. I can't understand why, but it triggers something physical. S—'s picture on the flyer finds me again, and there she is, smiling. But this evening, the way she looks, the way the camera has caught her, is as if she is in the room, blinking away the low sun—her tiny butterfly pendant nestled in a dip in her breastbone—I think she is calling me.

I sit at the desk and make a note.

1. *The barman.* Andy. I haven't finished with him yet.
2. *Herman.* If I could just get a look inside his house.
3. *ALL the people on the tick list.* Zara doesn't want me near them but she's not going to stop me from speaking to them. Someone knows, has to know, who was supplying the drugs to her.

I lie on the duvet and stare at the ceiling until the glow becomes gloom and then only shadow. My phone buzzes with a message. It's from Katya.

> Come soon if you want to do this

I'm ashamed that when I read the message it sends a frill of excitement through me.

THIRTY-FOUR

ZARA

EVERYONE HAS RSVP'D TO SAY THAT THEY WILL COME. IN MY IMAGINA-tion I hear them calling one another on their phones and talking about how *weird* it is to be invited to a birthday party for a girl who they must think is dead. Even as I play the words in my head, the anger blooms. The insensitivity of young girls has never stopped slicing away at me. Some aren't just oblivious—some are decidedly venomous.

I've decorated the prayer hall with lots of paper butterflies and the cake is in the shape of a butterfly too. In one corner I have laid out fizzy drinks and plates for pizza that will arrive at one. A small speaker plays music that I know Sophie likes but which she'd hate that I know about. I have to make sure that they all keep Sophie in their minds as a person—flesh and blood. They have to picture her as if she is here but has popped to the shops and will be back in a minute.

Harry is emptying crisps into bowls. I've barely spoken to him all week.

—   —   —

BY THE TIME the pizza arrives, everyone who was expected is here. The chatter is like the noise from a flock of starlings. They are excited to see one another after so long on holiday. Some come in shyly, twisting their sleeves, holding gift bags. Others are loud and glittery in heels and makeup.

"I know you said no gifts but this is something she really wants," one girl, Phoebe, says. I've known Phoebe for a decade. She was once Sophie's best friend—in years seven and eight—but then found a different friend group.

I thank her, take the bag, and put it under the cake table. When I turn around, I get a surprise. It is Mrs. Cooper.

"Sheila-Anne?" We deliberately hadn't invited any of the teachers. We didn't want anything to make the kids feel inhibited. Having the two of us here, both teachers, is bad enough. But when I look at her and see her eyes, I am glad she's here. I haven't seen anyone from the school for nearly two months.

"Nina's mum mentioned it. Her little sister is at the summer club. I didn't mean to intrude. I just wanted to see how you are holding up," she says, reaching to kiss my cheek.

"Not good," I say, surprising myself. She looks at me with real sorrow and I suddenly feel myself crumble. She puts an arm gently around my shoulder and waits patiently until I stop crying. "I'm sorry," I say, and ease myself back.

"I won't stay," she says. "I just wanted to pay my respects. To you both." I look around for Harry but he's not immediately visible.

"Thank you," I say. "I'll let Harry know you came by."

"This is from all the teachers," she says, and hands me a card. I thank her and she heads awkwardly to the exit.

THE PIZZAS ARE devoured or untouched depending on who is holding the plate. I stand and watch their expressions. They are all about to tip into adulthood but can't see what a deep drop it is.

Harry calls everyone to the cake and starts to speak.

"Thank you for coming to celebrate our daughter's eighteenth birthday. Obviously, she isn't here and there's nothing we'd have wanted more than to see her celebrating with her friends—" He

stops, overcome by tears. He stands like that in a pool of light sur-
rounded by teenage girls, who watch him open-mouthed, fidgeting,
brazen. I wait for him to pick the thread up again but he can't seem
to find the end no matter how many times he tries. The girls look
to me.

I light the candles and because I don't know what else to do, I sing.
"Happy birthday to you. Happy birthday to you. Happy——" Nobody joins in and when I reach Sophie's name, I trail off and cough
the rest of the song away.

They all refuse cake. Some feign being full while others hold slices
of pizza in their hands and say they'll have some later. A few pretend
the cake is too pretty to eat. After a time their feet dance, and in their
whispers, I hear how some are preparing to leave. I begin to panic.
We haven't spoken to any of them yet. Harry is sitting near a wall on
a plastic chair and I rush over.

"They're getting ready to go. You take Chloe Williams and Alex
Godinet. I'll take Ryan Nessa and Casey Richards."

He springs to his feet and heads toward Chloe, whom he knows
better than I do because he had her in a class last year. I race after him.
"Don't frighten them."

"Seriously?"

"It's not what I mean. You start talking about drugs and they will
shut down. Be subtle."

He turns his palms down as if telling me to calm down and then
steps smartly away. I go to Ryan, who as one of the few boys is easy
to spot. He smiles nervously and a patch of dark red creeps up his
neck when I touch his arm.

"Ryan, thank you for coming."

"It's okay, miss," he says, reminding me that I am a teacher to these
young people well before I'm a human.

"Can I have a word?" I lead him in the direction of a chair. The
girl he was speaking to drifts off to a group of sparky kids laughing
loudly at something.

"Ryan. Look. You're not in trouble. But if you don't tell me the
truth you could be."

He blanches. "Is this about the E's?"

"How did you know?" I say, trying to bury my surprise.

"Some of the kids are talking about it."

"Emily?" I ask.

Ryan nods. "I don't know where she was getting them or any-thing. But I had Sophie's money ready for her, I swear. Then she didn't come to school the next day and so—"

I take a little time going over the details with him but there's noth-ing useful there. She'd been doing it for a few weeks as far as Ryan could tell.

"No more drugs, Ryan. I'd have to tell the school and you'd get expelled."

He sits up straight, alert. "You coming back to school, miss?"

"Maybe," I say. "Do you know Casey?"

He points to a tall girl with lank dark hair and heavy cheeks. She's nursing a Coke and is alone.

I thank him and go over to the girl. "Casey?"

She creases her brows.

"I don't think we've met, have we?"

Casey shakes her head. "No. I don't even know why you invited me. I wasn't Sophia's friend." Blunt but at least honest, which is wel-come.

"Sophie," I say, but she doesn't see the point I'm making. "You weren't her friend. But were you something else?"

She steps closer to me and I get the sense of how much bigger she is than me. A wave of something acidic comes off her skin. "I wasn't shagging her."

I lean back a little to get some air between us. She's awkward, that's all. "No, not that," I say, and then whisper at her. "Customer. You were her customer."

She scratches her head, releasing another cloud of vinegar scent. "For what?"

"Drugs," I hiss. "E's."

"No," she says, horrified. "I'm teetotal. My stepbrother died of an overdose."

WHEN THEY HAVE all left I gather up what look like the leavings after a storm. A tide of paper cups and plates washed up in odd places. One cup is impaled on a coat hook, dripping electric-orange syrup into a small pond on the carpet. As I rub the patch dry, Harry kneels next to me, balancing the dozen objects he has in his hands.

"Did you get anything?"

I shake my head. "She was definitely selling. For a few weeks."

He stands. "Shit. To who?"

"Ryan Nessa. I think I've scared him silly about it, though. What about you?"

"Nothing," he says, and shrugs when I wait for more.

"Is that it? Just nothing?"

"Yes," he says, and heads out to his car and loads the boot with some bags and returns for more without looking up.

The cake is still there on the table, untouched, like an insult. I re-light the candles, shut my eyes, and cup my hands.

I am here, Sophie. Waiting.

I finish my prayer and open my eyes to see Harry. It's time to blow the candles out. The wax has dripped all over the cake, leaving it looking like a Pollock.

He stares at the flickering candles as if unsure of me.

"What are you doing? They're all gone."

"For her birthday."

His legs twitch as if there are ants running down them. He fidgets as if to shake them off. "I know that. But she is not here."

I lean forward and blow. "Happy birthday, my little girl."

Then I cut a slice and break a piece off and eat it. And then when it's finished I break off another piece. There is a feverish quality to the way I am moving. When I finish that slice, I cut another and this time put the wedge straight into my mouth. Harry continues to stare. Without taking my eyes off him I put my hand straight into the cake and shove a fistful of it into my mouth.

"It has to be eaten," I say, spraying crumbs.

"All of it?"

"Yes! It's been prayed on."

"But all of it—right now?" he says.

I continue eating until the sickness wells up inside.

"Zara. Just stop. Please just stop for a second."

I shrug him off and make my way out of the mosque. He tails me, calling after me.

"Wait. Talk to me."

"You think she's dead!" I shout after him, and get in the car and drive home.

I just have time to unlock the door and deactivate the alarm when he arrives. He barges through the door. "I didn't mean that she was dead. I meant she's not *here*." He moves farther into the hallway so that I have to back either in or out to avoid touching him. I step out onto the path and walk.

"Where are you going?" he says, coming out after me. "We have to talk about this."

"No, we don't," I say, and stalk off down the street, him following me. He draws alongside me and continues in a stage whisper. "Zara!"

The sun has dropped below the horizon, causing the darkened light to shiver in the sky. He takes my elbow to stop me.

"Zara. Just stop. Please just stop for a second."

I shrug him off and continue toward the main road that runs like a river across the bottom of our street.

"Is it the frog? You can't be doing this over a toy. One that she didn't play with anymore."

And then I do stop. "Didn't?"

"What?"

"You said *didn't*. Not doesn't."

When I turn to face him, he has frozen, staring past me.

"Not now," he says, quietly. "Look."

THIRTY-FIVE

HARRY

THE AIR IS THICK LIKE WADDING ON MY SKIN.

"Look." I pull her gently behind a tree whose roots have blown the slabs off the pavement.

"Harry," Zara says, dragging her arms away from me.

"Shh. Look!" I say, insisting now. I point to the house—Herman's house—and Herman himself is there. His back is to the road and he is struggling with his key in the gate. I put a hand out to signal to Zara to stay put, and then quietly I hurry toward him. If he manages to open the door it will be too late. I'm no more than ten feet away when he looks up and sees me. I hear a voice and turn to see Zara rushing toward me from behind. Herman smiles uncertainly at me and returns to his key. The lock turns just as I pull up alongside him. A stale, pungent smell radiates off him.

"Harry," I hear Zara say next to me. "What—"

"It's okay," I say to her, without taking my eyes off him. "Mr. Herman and I are just going to have a chat."

Herman's eyes flash and he stiffens in alarm. The key in the lock has turned and he pushes the door open quickly. Before he can get in, I pull him back by his arms and slam the door shut again.

"Let me go!" he calls out loudly, his voice cracking at the edges. He shoves me off and puts his hand back on the key still in the lock. I push him out of the way and snatch up the keys.

In the yellow of the lamplight I see his eyes quiver. "Give me my keys back," he says.

I hold them aloft. "After we've had our chat."

"You can't do that." His voice has none of the German I expected it to have. Northern.

"I can." As he comes forward to snatch them I push him forcefully back, my forearm against his chest, pinning him to his door. His long gray hair sticks in places to his skin.

Zara begins to pull at me from behind—but her heart isn't in it. "Let him go, Harry."

"Tell me you don't want to know what he's hiding in there."

Sensing a chance, he pushes me back. "I'm calling the police."

I take a risk. "What with?" He is in slides and stained jogging bottoms. If he has a phone, it's not obvious where he's got it. He was just putting out his bins, probably.

He stops. I can't quite read the look on his face. There's fear there, sure, but something else too. Arrogance. "What do you want?"

"My daughter's missing. Has been for seven weeks."

"Don't know anything about 'em." He says it without pausing for thought.

"I think you do. Here," I say, getting my phone out and showing him my home screen. "That's her. You'd have seen her face on a flyer I've put through your door a dozen times."

He looks at the darkening sky and grimaces. "Told you. Don't know jack."

"So, can you tell us why you've never answered your door to us in the last nearly two months of knocking?"

He shifts on his slippered feet. "Don't have to answer the door if I don't want to."

I feel the blood rising into my head and cannot contain the flood that I know is coming. "Why? What do you think we might see?"

"Leave me alone," he says, and starts off down the road to escape.

I follow him and pull at his arms to hold him back. "My daughter is missing. Do you understand that? And I've been to every house in a half-mile radius. I've talked to everyone except you."

He stops. "I don't have nothing to do with it."

"Then talk to me. Why haven't you answered me when I've come calling?"

He shrugs me away and heads toward the main road. "I'm going to the police."

Zara is holding my hand to pull me back from something she thinks I am going to do. I unpick her grip.

"Fine," I say. "Let's go to the police. For a start, you can tell them why you're burning videos in your garden."

He freezes when he hears that and turns to face me. That mixture of fear and arrogance is back, etched again into his features. "That was you with the flying thing. The drone."

"What are you hiding?"

"I'm not talking to you. It was you broke into my garden. It was you flew that contraption in my house. I'm going to the police."

Before he can turn back again I leap onto him. My weight brings him crashing onto the pavement. He groans, but he's stronger than he seems. Close up, I can see he's not sixty but nearer fifty. His fingers now around my neck are a vise.

I roll onto my side to dislodge him, putting all my body weight onto him. He lets go. And then in the blur of this and the blood pounding behind my eyes, I hear Zara screaming hysterically. She's standing over me, pulling me back. Two young men join her and drag me off him.

"Stop! Stop!" she cries.

"It's okay. It's okay," I say, getting slowly to my feet. My hands are up by my ears, and when they see me talking to Zara, trying to calm her, the two men, students perhaps, recede to the edges of the pavement.

"Zara. It's okay. Come on. Let's go home." I throw the keys at Herman's feet. He quickly swipes them and runs back to his gate.

"No!" she screams, pushing me in his direction. "You have to stop him!"

I freeze. There is something dangling from her fingers.

THIRTY-SIX

ZARA

HERMAN BOLTS FOR HIS GATE. HARRY, STILL RED FROM EXERTION AND anger, is apologizing, maddeningly, for the scene he made.

"No!" I scream. "You have to stop him!"

He stoops to look at what I am holding out in my hand, myopic in this light. I see the moment his face changes from one creased in confusion to one swollen in anger.

"Is that . . . ?"

I nod. Harry runs at Herman, who is still fighting with his gate. As it opens, Harry leaps onto him again and brings him down in the open doorway. The urge to help, to do something physical, takes me over and before I'm aware of it, I'm pressing my hand into Herman's face. He claws it away, but now Harry has his hands against the man's neck.

"Get off," he says, choking.

Suddenly I am hauled to my feet by the two students from the street. They calmly lead me away, one on either side. Their arms are like rock when I stumble against them. My heart guns in my chest. They return to tear Harry away with more force.

"Leave him. You don't know what he's done!" I shout. But by the time they notice me shouting, Herman has slid inside his gate and slammed it. The two young men melt away leaving Harry and me staring at each other, panting.

"Show me," he says, and I drop the pendant into his hand.

A tiny purple butterfly. Enamel. Her pendant.

"Are you sure it's hers?"

I take it back from him and shine my phone torch on it. "It's the same one," I say, and I feel the blood thudding in my ears. "It was on the road exactly where he fell. He must have been *wearing* it."

"I'll call the police," he says, and dials. As he's waiting he quickly remembers. "Don't touch the pendant. Just hold it by the chain."

THE POLICE DO not dispatch a car with flashing lights and sirens. In the end, we're left having to call Holly. She's not on shift but agrees to drop by the house. Harry and I wait now, perched tightly on the edge of the sofa. From time to time, one of us paces before sitting back down again. Whatever is in my head is waiting for the chance to unfurl. Finally, Harry can't hold back any longer.

"I fucking knew it. I told you there was something about him. Has to be him. I've been everywhere else. Every house. I saw the insides of most of them. They invited me in. Talked to me. But this guy wouldn't even open the door. And what I saw. I haven't shown you the bedroom, it has—"

The doorbell startles us both. Harry opens it and ushers in a redeyed Holly. He's talking to her back, following her as she comes in. She stands at the threshold to the living room.

"Here," Harry says, handing her an envelope before she can sit down. "It's in there."

"You're certain it's Sophie's?"

I nod.

"I am. Zara is too. It's hers. I've even checked it against the photographs. Here," he says, and pulls a folded sheet from his pocket and opens it. It's one of Harry's flyers, the pendant just visible on the neckline of Sophie's black sweater.

She takes the flyer and looks at it briefly. "Did you touch it?"

"Only by the chain," I say.

Holly sits and scratches into a notebook she's produced from somewhere. "How did you come into possession of it exactly?"

They both look at me. I swallow. "As he told you over the phone, Harry was fighting with him—Herman from 210—and they were on the ground. I didn't see how they ended up there. And then I saw it on the pavement. I almost missed it."

She looks up from her pad. "Did you see him in possession of it?"

"Well, not, you know, in his hand or anything."

Holly wipes her face with a hand. "Did you see it fall from his person?"

"No. I saw it for the first time on the pavement. But it had to have come from him. There was nobody else there."

She faces Harry. "Earlier, Harry, you said there were two other people."

Harry moves closer to her and I can tell from the way he is standing that he is about to snap. "What's your point? I don't understand why you're being so dismissive."

"I'm not being dismissive. I'm trying to get the facts. Look," she says, producing an evidence bag and allowing Harry to drop it inside, "I'll get it sent to the lab. If Sophie's DNA's on it, then we might be able to get a search warrant. But . . ."

"But what?"

Holly looks up. "Don't get your hopes up."

Harry looms over her. He is so close to her that Holly is straining at the neck to meet his gaze. She stands, clearly uncomfortable.

"Do you understand it from our point of view? Her necklace. That," he adds, slapping the flyer with the back of his hand, "that she was wearing around her neck when she vanished. Do you get that? She vanished without a trace. You've been looking for seven weeks and you've got nothing. This is something."

Holly puts the bag into her pocket. "As I say. We will do what we can."

"Like what you did with the video?"

She turns to leave but then faces him. "For your information, we sent uniform round there to speak to him."

"And?"

"And nothing. He was clearing out his basement. Had no idea what was on the videos."

"And you believed that?"

"No. Not necessarily. But we can't prosecute him on that. We can't prove that he's in possession of anything illegal. The videos don't exist anymore. We can't even prove that he was in possession of the bit you stole from his garden. Burgled, in fact."

The silence that drops once she finishes speaking trails her as she leaves.

THE AIR IS still charged twenty minutes later. Harry is so electrified that when I touch him I think he's going to give me a shock.

"We just have to wait."

"I'm tired of waiting, Zara. It's been long enough now, hasn't it? They don't have any interest in this case anymore. They've stopped looking because—" he says, and then hauls himself up short.

"Go on."

"Nothing."

"Harry."

"They don't want to find bad news. That's it. They think it's over but I'm still going because it's not. It's not. We have to find whoever is responsible." His eyes are rimmed in fury.

I draw the curtains and wish hard that by the time I turn around he won't be there anymore. "Whoever that is?"

"You mean me?" He looks at me, shocked. "You've got to stop blaming me. And *yourself.*"

For seconds we simply stare at each other. "We locked her in her room," I say quietly.

"For one night, Zara. One night. And then we removed the lock."

"But don't you see, Harry? It was too late by then."

"Why?"

"You saw what she did."

"It was nothing. It didn't mean anything."

"She had a knife."

"On her bed. A tiny one."

"She was about to hurt herself."

"Or just mark herself."

I think back to that morning. How we'd unlocked the door expecting to find her room in chaos. But instead how we'd found her calmly drawing butterflies in pen all over her bare legs. There was an art scalpel on her bed on a single tissue paper.

"Marking herself is bad enough, Harry. It was a cry for help. A cry to us!"

THIRTY-SEVEN

HARRY

IT SWIRLS SO MUCH NOW THAT ALL THE COLORS ARE BLENDING. THE room. That horrible room that I flew the drone into. It's not *evidence* evidence but it is something. It means something when where you live is toxic and dark. That place is a mirror to what is happening inside his head. And then there's the stuff from the garden. I absolutely do not buy what he says about throwing out old videos. Who burns VHS or any plastic? The smoke is poisonous.

That wall with the strange colors—the huge butterfly that looked like something out of a horror movie. It wasn't right. And the pendant. *Her* pendant. Identical to the one she has. Identical to the one around her neck when she went missing. I can see it now, slipping from his neck and landing soundlessly on the pavement. Maybe he lured her into the house with the promise of a look at his butterfly mural. Perhaps he'd noticed her one day and caught a look at the butterflies in her hair or on her T-shirt and struck up a conversation with her. She'd have been taken in by that. She liked helping people. What had there been in her world to cause her any fear or caution?

I see her innocence, I realize now, in a stylized, naïve way. I can only see what I know. My daughter, just seventeen—a schoolgirl still—being taken in by a picture of a butterfly. But she wasn't this girl—selling cookies to neighbors like a kid in an American film. She was selling drugs. Like a kid in an American film.

This loft room has been my world for more than seven weeks but now it has to go. I peel away the map of the houses I've visited. All the red marks joined except the one at 210. After an hour or so of organizing and tidying, I have a pile of investigation materials amassed in one corner.

I had an idea overnight. I look for listings for rental properties at a reasonable price. Something not too close. Not too far. And then I call and make an appointment to view one in Whitechapel.

I find Zara in the kitchen staring out the window into the garden. She has grown so small I sometimes wonder whether her arms are going to wither into wings so that she can take off.

"You off to see Mrs. Cooper? At the school?" she says without turning.

I hold my laptop in front of me. "Yes, in a minute. Look, you can say no, but if you want to see Herman's room, I can show you," I say, and open it. She is right. I have been leaving her behind. It's not fair. Especially when I'm about to leave her even further.

The screen is still open at the footage of the drone. She sees it.

"Is that his house?"

"It is. But it's—grim."

She stands next to me. The scent of her fills me with sadness. It's not just the realization that she is so weak, but that I am. I'm about to lose the only thing I have left in the world. I feel like a man in space watching the only other human for a million miles drifting off into a cold, horizonless universe.

"Play it," she says. The drone footage flickers into life. The sight of him at the window. Then when he disappears, the inside of his bedroom. That old wrought iron headboard and then that huge purple butterfly on the wall, more grotesque than ever on reviewing.

Zara stiffens next to me at the horror of it.

"I'll turn it off. It is upsetting first time round."

"No," she says turning to me. Her face is rinsed through with alarm. "Don't."

"What is it?"

"That butterfly. I've seen it before."

"What do you mean?" I say.

Without answering she races out of the room. I resist the urge to tail her.

She returns holding a small piece of paper and unfolds it. The image is striking in its similarity. I stare at it and then at the screen. They aren't identical but one definitely came from the other.

"Where did you find this? Did she do it?"

She nods vigorously. "It was with the list. This one," she says, putting another slip of paper in my hand. That list is her handwriting. But the butterfly—is that definitely hers?

"Is there anything in her room? Something with more of her drawing on it?" I say, and then run to her room. I'm still not used to the new wallpaper, and when I walk in that feeling of stepping into a new dimension hits me. I go straight to her bookshelf and look through her spiral-bound notebooks. There are three in bright colors, backed in fabric. I flip through one and hand one to Zara. As I leaf through, I study the writing on the list. The handwriting is definitely a match, if there was any doubt.

"What are these books?"

"Homework jotters. Sophie uses them to make notes and write down any research."

"Anything with pictures?"

She flips through quickly and finds one and turns it on its side. "Not identical. But the same purple pen. And look at these curly ends with the three dots. It's the same. It can't be a coincidence."

I place it side by side with the butterfly picture. There's no question in my mind at all. "So, she drew this butterfly. And this butterfly was copied from his bedroom."

Zara sits on the bed next to me. Her face is shot through with pain. "I'll call Holly."

"No. Don't. You've seen how she is. All she's going to do is tell us that it's not enough to arrest him for. That it's not evidence. That it's more paranoia."

Zara takes the paper and studies the picture and then reaches across me for the list. "We never found CR." Her finger hovers under the letters. "There is something strange about it, though, isn't there?"

"What do you mean?" I look down and really see it for the first time as she says it.

"Look. It says RN 400 and under that EB 240. And then—"

"210 CR. In reverse. Maybe CR paid already?"

"Then why is it even on the list? The others have been scratched out once they've paid."

"Maybe CR was *owed* the money," I say, squinting across at it, trying to make sense of it.

"It's also right at the bottom—as if it's not on the list itself. Just, I don't know . . . an afterthought."

I return the books to the shelf. "I have to find a way of getting into that house."

"He has to leave at some point, surely. Maybe it's just a question of waiting. And when he's out, then—" She stops, caught up by the momentum of what she is saying.

"He was out Saturday night. Maybe he'll be out again."

"If it's not too late. If it hasn't been too late for weeks." Her face is riven with sadness. I don't know what to say to her anymore. There's no comfort I can give her that is capable of stanching a single one of her fears.

"You better go," she says at last. "Mrs. Cooper will be waiting."

I leave her there, on the bed, certain as I shut the door that I hear her crying. In the car, I match her, tear for tear.

THIRTY-EIGHT

ZARA

As soon as the front door closes I listen for the sound of the car engine and only when I am certain he is gone do I scream. I scream out all the anguish that is creeping its way into my heart. A song for Sophie. I scream hard into her pillow for my lost baby. All this fog around me muffles my voice and binds my arms. I need to reach her but I can't. I need to breathe but I can't. I need to live to be able to do it, but I can't.

I take two sedatives and swallow them. I know the effect will be more fog and less strength to climb my way out but it also will mean less pain.

The house sings in the silence. The silence sings in my ears.

I call out her name. "Sophie!"

And then again. "Sophie!"

And I fancy, just at the fringes of my senses, that I can hear her. She's running down the street toward the house. She stops at the door. Her keys are jangling and then here she is, pounding up the stairs. And then the noise—palpable now—of her breathing. Panting.

I close my eyes and lie on the bed, trying with every cell and sinew to hold on to the connection. And for once it is easy. I can hear the breathing, heavy and labored. I squeeze my eyes and listen harder. The rustle of fabric. Skin slapping on the banisters. She's here. My baby.

The door flies open. I sit up, rigid, eyes wide.

"Harry?"

"Look," he says. Harry is standing there with a deranged look in his eye. He is holding the list in his outstretched hand.

I rub my eyes, not understanding why he's here, and I think that if I rub them some more, I will wake and he will vanish. But he is still here, kneeling by my side and showing me the list.

"What's different about this one?" He is pointing at the "210 CR" entry.

"It's written the other way around from the others. We know that."

"Yes, we do," he says, and smacks the paper with the back of his hand. "But why?"

"I don't know! Why are you back?"

"Because it's not money owed. It's not even money. I realized when I passed it," he says, eyes wild.

And then a cold wash of realization runs down my face. "210 is Herman's door number. And CR is Clandon Road."

I am on my feet now and staring at the list, trying to process what is happening. Harry is talking still, wild. I find my phone and do a quick search before putting it to my ear.

"What are you doing?"

"Calling Holly."

Harry snatches the phone from me. "How many times? She isn't interested."

"Then what?"

"I don't know," he says, and looks away into the ceiling. After a minute he blinks and folds the paper into his pocket. "I'm going."

"Where?"

"To the house."

"He's not going to open up, Harry."

I follow him down the stairs and then as he leaves the kitchen for the garden. I tail him to the shed, until it swallows him up. When he emerges, he has a small but heavy object stretching a plastic bag in his hand. He edges past me and strides fast through the house.

"Wait. I'm coming," I say, and wriggle into my sneakers and chase him into the road, hopping. "Harry." The drugs in my blood are making my movements spongy. I fumble for my keys and shut the door before hurrying after him once again. He is ten paces ahead of me. I jog until I catch him.

"Wait!"

"You're not stopping me."

"No. I'm not. But slow down, Harry."

He doesn't stop till he is at the door to 210. The light in the sky, though ebbing away, is livid. The colors give the evening an unreal edge. I try to blink us away from this spot to another, however near. Because the primal part of me knows that this place is where the rest of it all will begin. The next phase of horror.

Harry glances at me once before banging hard on the gate with his fist. He pounds away for a minute until the dirty curtains in the window above shiver.

"Come down, Herman." He is shouting, and now net curtains and blinds from all around the street begin to split and crack behind their glass. "I'm not going away till you open the door."

"You know he won't come."

"I know."

"Come on. Let's call Holly. She has to do something about it. It's new evidence."

He pulls me by the elbow and whispers hot in my ear. "She was dealing drugs, Zara. I don't think that's going to make her care more about our daughter, do you?"

"Then what?"

"I'm going to talk to him," he says, stabbing a finger at the door. "Whether he wants to talk or not."

Harry lifts the carrier bag in his hand. It is taut as a water balloon. He wraps the plastic around the handle of what is obviously a small sledgehammer.

"You can't, Harry!"

He touches the lock with his left hand as if positioning it and then swings the hammer hard against metal. The lock pops in a single blow and the door is left to swing on its hinges. He waits for me to stop him. And I do want to stop him. I also want him to charge through and into the man's house. I want both things to play out simultaneously so that I can finally have some certainty about even a small decision like this. Because wherever I look, all I can see are these chasms in the road waiting to swallow me.

"I'm coming too," I say.

Harry nods and strides through the garden to the front door. The dirty white paint is thick but has flaked in places. There is a glazed panel—but not one that you can see through. It is leaded and the colored glass opacifies whatever might be behind it. Even when the lights blaze on, there are shadows.

"Are you sure?" I say.

"I have to," he says, and knocks on the door. Then, louder, he says, "Open it or I break it."

THIRTY-NINE

NOW

OLD BAILEY
COURTROOM THREE

EACH MORNING WHEN I LEAVE, I HAVE TO PACK ALL MY BELONGINGS—everything—into a transparent plastic sack to be taken with me in the van. If I don't and they end up taking me back to a different prison, then my things will be looted. The more experienced inmates have advised me in clear terms, "Take all your shit with you."

We're now into the second week of the prosecution's case and it's getting very close to the time I have to choose whether I give evidence. I already know what I'm going to do, so there's no stress there at least. Zara's here, but has barely looked at me since we began. She has the appearance of a woman who is drowning but doesn't want to struggle for breath anymore.

The witness now in the box is a large-set man with bloated cheeks. "Yes," he says in answer to a question that Alfred has asked. "In total there were fifteen full finger marks that can be attributed to Mr. King. By that, we mean there are sufficient quality and quantity of ridge flow and ridge characteristics in agreement with the reference sample with no unexplainable differences. There were a number of partial marks, some of which were inconclusive and others of which were insufficient to make reliable comparisons."

— — —

ALFRED SITS DOWN and offers the witness up to my barrister, Stevens. The jury sits forward whenever he gets up to speak. It's not, I think, because they like him or are siding with him. It's because when he starts asking questions, there's a smell of fireworks in the air.

"I've had a look at the finger marks, Mr. Weaver, but I'm afraid I couldn't find the information I wanted in the report." He looks at him with an impish grin.

"What exactly do you want to know? Perhaps I can help."

"The date."

"Sure, Mr. Stevens. The date the marks were developed is—"

"No. No. Not that date," he says, flapping his gown. "The date they were left on the walls and the door and everything else."

"Sorry?"

"Can you tell us when the marks were left? Mr. King admits—in fact, both Kings admit—being at the house a week or so before the murder of Mr. Herman. Do we know that Mr. King's prints weren't left then?"

"Well, prints tend to degrade over time. The likelihood of the lab being able to develop a good quality print decreases exponentially over time."

"I see," Stevens says. "So how many hours or days were these prints degraded when you lifted them?"

He smiles. "Well, we can't say."

"Exactly what I'm saying to you, Mr. Weaver. You can't say. You simply can't say."

Stevens looks down for a file and as he does, knocks over a glass of water on his desk. He swears audibly but the judge appears not to have noticed. "Mr. Weaver, the marks lifted were, according to this report, entirely on the ground floor of the house."

"That's correct."

"The body of Mr. Herman was discovered in his bedroom on the second floor. A flight and a half up."

"Yes."

"There were no prints up there?"

"None that we were able to develop that weren't accounted for by the deceased."

"Mr. Herman was found dead in a kitchen chair, correct?"

"Yes, I believe so."

"The chair was part of a matching set of four—the other three were in the kitchen, weren't they?"

"I can't say. I didn't examine the scene."

"Okay. Well, take it from me, if you would, for now, and if I'm wrong, Mr. Alfred will no doubt correct me. If the chair was carried up by the murderer, is there a good chance that a print would be left on the hard surfaces of the chair?"

"Possibly. Depending on how it was held. Palm marks aren't generally that reliable and an object like that might not always have contact with the fingertips."

"Was the chair examined?"

"Yes."

"Were any marks on it identified as belonging to Mr. King?"

"No."

"Is wood a good surface for prints?"

"Yes. It's usually an excellent surface for marks."

"The crime scene, as we see from the pictures, had a good deal of blood and blood spatter on the body, the chair, the carpet, the bed, the bedframe, and the walls of the bedroom."

"Yes."

"Were any of the prints lifted from the scene identified as belonging to Mr. King contaminated by any blood?"

"No."

"So, there were no bloody finger marks at all?"

He pauses as if searching for an alternative answer. "No," he says finally.

Stevens sits down but Alfred is on his feet again immediately. He fixes his wig so that it sits farther forward on his head. "If a person wears gloves when they handle objects, such as a chair, obviously there would be no prints?"

"Correct. And in fact, there were partial prints that had been wiped in such a way as to suggest a glove or something fabric might have overlaid the print."

"And it would be possible for the murderer to have put on gloves before venturing upstairs?"

"Certainly."

"Thank you. My lady, save for some questions for the OIC, the officer in the case, we are nearing the conclusion of the Crown's case." Alfred sits, satisfied, stealing a glance at Stevens who is sighing, annoyed, into his crossed arms.

The judge nods at Alfred and turns her attention to Stevens. "Thank you. Mr. Stevens, I suppose you'll want till tomorrow before you make a decision about calling any evidence?"

Stevens gets slowly to his feet. "Yes, please. I think I know the answer but best to be certain."

"Very well. We'll rise for today, then. You may close your case tomorrow, Mr. Alfred."

FORTY

HARRY

FROM DEEP INSIDE THE HOUSE, SOFT LIKE A MUFFLED DRUM, COMES HIS voice. "I'm calling the police."

"Call them. By the time they come, your door will be off its hinges."

His dark outline appears in the glass. "What do you want?"

"To talk to you," I say, and exchange a look with Zara.

"Then talk."

"Not through the door. Last chance or it's coming off."

He hesitates. "I've called 'em already."

"Fine." I raise the hammer and strike it hard against the lock. The metal pings and the door splinters at the frame. But it holds. I take a step back and once I've moved Zara out of the arc of my swing, I hit it again. Harder. Behind the wood, he yelps and then I hear footsteps in retreat. I hit it again. The frame splits under the force of the blow and opens a gap of a few centimeters. All I have to do is kick it.

Inside a cobweb-covered shade dangling from the ceiling throws dirty light onto a dirty carpet. A minute later the stench of a decade of sweat and dirt and piss fills my nose. The smell is so strong that I have to cover my nose with my forearm.

I signal to Zara to wait outside but she ignores me and is right here at my shoulder now, coughing away the ammonia. In places the hallway is a foot deep with leaflets and junk mail, but Herman is nowhere to be seen. A metal bowl with rotting food sits at the far end near the door to the garden. Herman appears at the door with a metal crowbar in his hand.

"You need to go," he says over barking that has now started up from somewhere in the house.

"No."

He stands as if in cement. "What do you want?"

"Why was she here? We know she was, so don't even try to lie."

"I don't know what you're on about."

"Our daughter, Sophie!" Zara says behind me.

And then he smiles. "Oh. The missing one. So they never found 'em, eh?"

I feel the weight of Zara behind me as she tries to squeeze past me. But I keep her back with an arm. "Why has she got your name on a list?"

"No idea," he says without thinking. It doesn't have his name on it but the fact that he hasn't denied it fills me with dread. He swallows as if the air is too dry in here.

The dog has stopped barking. "Why was my daughter here?"

Herman smiles out of the corner of his mouth, revealing a scattered line of sea-gray teeth. "I told you. I don't know anything about 'em."

"She was selling you drugs," I say, and keep my eyes glued to his. If there is a reaction, I need to see it. There should be surprise there, stretching his skin, but there's none. S— was here.

"Was she?" he says instead.

From above I hear something that sounds like something with weight, falling. He starts at the sound and I feel Zara move behind me, twisting round.

"I'm going upstairs," I say, taking a step toward the staircase.

"I don't think so," he says, stepping forward, his hands round the crowbar like a baseball bat.

I feel the pulse of blood in my ears. My mouth is a desert. Zara is bristling by my side, eager to get past. "Let's wait for the police," Zara says. I see the phone in her hand. She dials 999.

He smiles. "Yeah, let's do that. Let's just wait for 'em."

"I don't give a monkey's about the police. I'm going up." I don't trust the police not to arrest me and cart me off. I have to look upstairs now while I have the chance. I take a step and Herman doesn't move. I take another, and then I am on the first step. The way is lit through another dirty lampshade. The walls are filthy and there is nothing covering the stairs, not even varnish, just bands of old white paint on the edges leaving a stripe of mud-colored wood in the middle.

I take another step, keeping my eyes on him, and then I see the glint in his eyes as he lunges toward me. There's no way I can outrun his metal bar. He rounds the stairs and swings at me, sending me toppling backward. My leg screams in pain.

Even through the sharpness of the pain I am conscious that I need to get upstairs.

Zara has retreated to the threshold. Herman jumps on me with a fist round each end of the bar. I push back, furiously kicking, but he is determined to press it against my neck. He's trying to kill me. All I see is white then red as I fight for my life. I try to launch myself off the step but that searing pain in my leg has me hobbled.

Zara screams at Herman to get off me but he elbows her back with one arm, keeping the bar pressed against my neck with the other hand. He reaches round to swing a fist at Zara but she dodges it. He moves just enough to create space for me to push him and the bar away. "Don't come any nearer!" I shout to Zara.

"Leave him alone," Zara cries, but Herman is now trying to force me back under the bar.

A moment later, blue lights strobe into the hall with a piercing blip of siren. The crackle of the police radio scatters the tension immediately.

"In here," Zara calls, disappearing from view. She races back in, a second later. "Get off him! The police are here."

Herman eases off but stands blocking the doorway. Five minutes ago, he wanted us out and now he wants to trap us inside.

The static gets louder and with it, the voices of police officers—calm. Just another disturbance for them, no doubt, in a life full of chaos.

"Just approaching now. Advise send a unit," a male voice calls out.

"Body cam on?" another voice says, coming closer.

I lever myself off the stairs, ankle throbbing, and move toward the doorway. Herman doesn't back away even though the police are now easing their way through. An officer gets a head through the door to announce himself when Herman leans in to me.

"You'll never find 'em in a hundred years," he says, and then steps away to let the police in.

FORTY-ONE

ZARA

Harry and I are outside. We have been separated, and more police officers have arrived. The response seems heavy and immutable, like a crashed car. I'm talking to a female officer but she's not like Holly, bright and capable of being reasoned with. This one, slight and bird-like in stature, is unyielding. She continues to ask me her questions.

"So, you stood there while your husband smashed the door in?"

"You don't understand. We already have a detective dealing with the case. DS Holly from—"

"I'm not interested in that right now, madam. Basically, you're telling me that you trespassed into this gentleman's home, knowing that he didn't want you there. And to do that you broke two sets of locks with a hammer?"

"It wasn't me," I say slowly. "My husband."

"But you encouraged him by your presence."

She keeps talking to me about what I've done and how very much against the law it is. I feel the heat crawling on my neck, burning with frustration. "There's someone in the house, upstairs. I heard them. You have to look. He tried to kill my husband."

"Can you calm down, ma'am."

"Look upstairs!" I say, screaming now. "My daughter could be up there in that house. You have to go and look."

I crane my neck past her thick uniform and stab vest and see that Harry is being sat in the back of a squad car. "No," I say, reaching a hand out. "Don't take him away. This man," I say, pointing to Herman's house, "is the one you want. He has kidnapped my daughter. There's evidence—"

"Okay, madam."

"Don't let them take my husband away. Please!"

She finishes what she is writing and puts her pocketbook away. "Wait here. Don't move. I'll go and find out what's happening with him."

I follow her with my eyes to another officer where they have a muted discussion. A minute later she returns.

"Your husband's been arrested on suspicion of criminal damage. There may be other charges depending on what the householder says about what happened inside. We're just waiting for a paramedic to look at his leg before we take him to the station. But you're free to go for now."

"Has *anyone* looked upstairs? Has any one of these dozen officers," I say, looking around, "searched the house?"

"They're in there now. If they have grounds, they'll search."

My heart drops and I hear the murmur of Harry's voice.

"Can I speak to my husband?"

"Briefly, if it is absolutely necessary," she says.

I look quizzically at her.

"Like, if he has your keys and you need to get them back?" She nods seriously at me. "Go on."

When I get to the car, the officer standing there moves aside as I open the door. But he stays close enough to hear.

"They're waiting for an ambulance," Harry says.

"I know," I say, and look down at his leg. The jeans have been rolled up to display a ripening ugly bruise.

"It's not as bad as it looks," he says.

"What can I do?" I ask him.

He wipes a hand over his face. "Can you get hold of Holly and let her know?"

I nod. He beckons me closer with his head and then whispers when

I am near enough. "I just need her to pull some strings. Don't tell her what Herman said about never finding her."

I'm shocked by this. "Why not?" I ask, the sharpness in my voice surprising me. "He's practically admitted to kidnapping her!"

"Has he?"

"Yes."

"No, he hasn't. Even if he admits to saying it—which he won't— what is he saying that isn't, in fact, true? At least so far. Maybe he's right. We'll never find her."

"Harry!" I say, and before I know what I am doing, the flat of my palm strikes his face.

"All I mean," he says, putting up a hand where mine left his face, "is that they're not arresting him for that one comment."

The officer stands between us now as if preventing it from escalating. "Sorry, madam. Paramedics are here now. Got to get him checked."

Harry walks gingerly to the ambulance, flanked by the officer. As the officer moves, he mutters into his shoulder radio. Once Harry has been handed over, I try to get closer but a cheerful female paramedic brushes me back. "Won't be a minute, love. Just giving him the once-over."

When they have iced and sprayed his leg, the same officer walks him lazily back to the car and helps him in.

"I want to come too," I say to the officer. He is about to answer when Harry leans out of the open window.

"No. There's no point. Call Holly. She might get word to them before I get to the station. That's the only thing that might help." He thinks for a moment before adding, "And call Caspar. He'll know what to do."

"Okay," I say. A second later the car has gone and I am alone. I was alone before they even arrested him and took him away.

I find the officer who was dealing with me and ask her for the police station details, which I key into my phone. "How long will they hold him?"

"No idea."

I look at her until she catches on. "Don't wait up, that's all I can tell you."

"I'm going to drive there," I say.

"Love," she says, touching my arm. "Honestly. Don't. You won't see him. You won't be able to talk to him. It will be hours and hours. He'll be sleeping and you'll be awake on a cold steel bench. Go home. Get some sleep."

I walk through the copse of officers waiting, chatting merrily. There was nobody upstairs. They searched. A few of my neighbors stand in their doorways, watching the commotion as another police car slices through. Others simply turn and disappear into their homes. We've been here for ten years and only know the names of the people living to the immediate left of us. It's only now, seeing the faces of all these people who live just yards away, separated only by a skein of brick, that I realize how odd that is. I don't really know anyone here. Most of them have spoken to Harry—when he handed round the flyers. But nobody has ever called round to see us.

I shut my door on the world, still in a trance. Instead of going into our bedroom I go to Sophie's room. I crawl into her bed and feel a crevasse open up behind my head, deep and cold. I know I need to confront the possibility that Sophie might be dead but I can't. I conjure the question in my mind and then all there is, is a wall. No answer—just this block of granite.

I look at the newly finished wall. Handmade papers with a dark, brooding black-and-gold design that she will love. I stare into and behind the wall. Here, with this black depth behind me, I can slide between possibilities and find her.

And now here she is. I venture in and take Sophie's hand. She pulls me softly through, and in that dark velvet world I can see everything and nothing.

At first all I see are her hands as she leads me in. But then I see her face as she half turns, white and dusted with tiny diamonds. Her lips blue. She opens her mouth and although no sounds leave her I know what she means to tell me. She lives there now. And that I must let her live. I think about Katya and what she said to Harry about Sophie and a wall. This is what she meant. I can see it now.

Caspar has not returned my call so I shut my eyes and wait for the morning to wash in its pale light.

I turn in the bed and the day is here, sunlight shooting all over Sophie's room. I roll over and check my phone but there are no messages. I call him again and he answers.

"Sorry, Zara, I know. I got your message. I'm at the station now trying to speak to custody. I'll call you when there's news."

There is a space on the line as if he is struggling with whether to say something else. Then finally he blurts it out. "What were you thinking, Zara? You of all people. Harry, I get. But you? You're lucky they didn't arrest you on a joint enterprise."

"Do you know about the list?"

"Yes. But that is not a reason to go smashing a person's front door in."

"The man is not right, Caspar. Sophie was there. I know it. And—" Harry doesn't want me to mention what Herman said at the end to anyone, but I don't know why. If the police knew, I am sure it would change everything. And while I hold that information like a pill on my tongue, I realize that saying as well as not saying will change everything.

"What?" he asks after a minute.

"Nothing. Just can you let me know once he's out?"

"Of course," he says, and hangs up.

In the kitchen, I pour cereal into a bowl and drench it with milk. Once I have swirled it into a froth, I tip it into the waste bin.

I sit still in this empty house. Not a house anymore—a prison. I don't know if I will ever get the words out of my head. "You'll never find her in a hundred years."

There can be only one reason he said that.

FORTY-TWO

HARRY

CASPAR TOLD ME TO GO "NO COMMENT" TO EVERY QUESTION THEY ASKED. He couldn't act for me in the interview but said he'd call me a solicitor if I didn't want the duty solicitor. I didn't want either. I just wanted to get it over with, and to wait hours for a solicitor only to still say "no comment" seemed idiotic.

"You go back to your family," I said to Caspar. "I promise. I'll 'no comment' it all."

When it finally gets going, the interview is swift—twenty minutes from beginning to end.

Afterward I step out into the street and am surprised by how much light there is. From the plastic bag I was given at the station, I retrieve my keys and wallet and check my phone. It's 9:30 A.M. I've been up all night. I gaze at the pavement, its glitter shining improbably like cut gems. Lost for a moment until the shadow of a body over mine brings me back into the bright morning light.

"Harry. I'm glad I caught you. What on earth were you both doing?"

"DS Holly," I say, feeling a strange kinship with her. "Zara called you, then. Is she okay?"

"She's fine. You broke a man's door down over some initials on a list?"

"I wasn't thinking," I say, exhausted.

"I'm not sure I can make it go away. Victim's Charter and all that. And. You broke your way into his house with a sledgehammer." Her hair, normally pinned tight to her scalp, is loose from its grips. It must have been a long night for her too.

"If he'd just let us in or agreed to speak to me—for two minutes—"

"You can't force people to talk to you, unfortunately. Not even we can and we're the police."

I half smile because I've just proved that with my no-comment interview.

"What's going on, Harry? Is there something I need to know?"

"What has Zara said?"

"Nothing. But she seemed on the verge of telling me something. I don't think it would take much to tip her over into saying whatever it is that's bothering her."

I search her face for clues. "Look, she's going through a lot at the minute. Could you maybe give her some space?"

Holly bites her bottom lip. "Okay. And I'll see if I can have a word with Mr. Herman. No promises, though. He'd be well within his rights to insist on a prosecution. And speaking to the OIC—the officer in charge—he's thinking of aggravated burglary. Which, so you know, is serious. Double-figures serious."

"I wasn't burgling it."

"So you say. But what's a jury going to say? I'll get the charges looked at. I can tell them about our history, which might help, but a criminal damage will stick if I can't persuade the victim to drop it."

"Victim?" I say.

"Yes. Victim."

"What about that pendant? Is that not proof enough for you guys? The actual jewelry she was wearing."

She sighs. "Harry. They are checking it for DNA. But honest opinion—it's going to be hard to get a profile from something that small and on a surface like that. And then there's contamination. You've handled it. Your DNA might be on it. And if it does have his

DNA on it, and Sophie's, he could say it was transferred onto it from you when you touched him. And the object itself isn't unusual or unique. It's from a high street brand. They will have sold tens of thousands of these. It doesn't prove what you want it to."

I start to complain but sense finds me. "Okay. Look, I'm sorry. I'll write him an apology if it will help. Offer to pay for his repairs."

"I can't tell you what to do. Just . . . think before you do anything rash like this again. It could have ended very badly from what I've been told." She is staring at my leg. A coin of blood has dried on the cuff of my jeans. I pull it up to show her the bruise.

"Wasn't that bad," I say.

"Sounds like you got lucky."

"I can honestly say, DS Holly, that lucky is the last thing I feel."

IN THE TAXI home I allow my head to fall back into the headrest and think about what I have to do and the order in which I have to do it.

I've known for some time now, at least since the police refused to do anything about the videotape, that there's only one option.

S— is dead.

There was never really any doubt about that for some time. I think within days of her going missing, we all knew it. Holly knew it. I knew it. Zara pretends still not to know it—but she's always known it too. That's why she is so steeped in grief.

And now—seven weeks and more on—we are all still dancing around this burning effigy. We know that if we get too close, we burn. But we watch and dance and act out these rituals because that day when we have to confront the grief is a day we can't bear to live through. And so we say that she's still there. That she's hiding some-where and all these weeks she's just been waiting to come home. But that's madness. We are only a hair away from wrapping up her bones and sitting them in a rocking chair, facing her toward the window.

But I'm ready now, I think, to face the day I have been dreading. It's been too long.

FORTY-THREE

ZARA

Harry comes in just as I am going upstairs. I hear the rattle in the door and run down. His face is gray, like old meat. We both stop in our tracks as soon as we see each other. Shocked but not. Eventually he breaks the spell and nods at me as if I am an acquaintance he's passing in the park. "I need to talk to you."

It takes him a long time to tell me what he has to say. At first, I sit and say nothing. I don't know whether at some level I have been thinking the same thing he is now saying out loud.

The difference is that I don't want him to leave.

"I'll just get a few things together," he says, and looks down at the carpet.

"I don't understand why you have to leave."

"For you. I don't know how to help you, but I know my being here isn't doing it."

He is right about that. Whenever he's near, it feels as though his gravity is just ripping chunks out of my body. He doesn't mean to, but it's happening anyway.

I thought we were decaying. But we didn't fall apart gradually. It happened in a single calamitous moment—when Sophie vanished. It didn't just destroy us individually, but exploded us apart from each other. Since that moment we've been walking around with our eyes shut, ignoring the cratered earth we are in.

Still, I don't want him to go. He is all I have now. He avoids my eyes so he doesn't have to see the hurt in them.

"Just for a couple of weeks. Just to give you some space."

"What if I don't want space?"

"I don't want you being crushed," he says. "By me."

Whatever spider strands are tethering us together are only binding loosely a thoroughly broken thing. We stand in silence for a few moments, waiting for the gap in time that will let him pull away. Finally, he breaks the silence by just saying it. "I better go."

I watch from the doorway as he gets into his car. He glances sadly at me and then pulls away quickly. I don't want him to leave. Why would I want that? He's been a rock. Not a rock—a bed. He is the only thing in my life that can give me any comfort. I used to think of this as shared pain but it's not as easy as that. We are not simply two people experiencing the same tragedy. We are conjoined in it. When one of us breathes or dies, the other does too. Or is it a sacrifice? One of us has to die to give the other a chance of life.

I look at the paper that he's left me with his address on it. How quickly he transplanted himself into a different life. Separation.

I *was* upset that he gave away Sophie's frog, Robbit. Keeping her relics near me is the only way that I can hold on to her. The things Sophie has touched are like fingers stained deep red with henna. They carry scent and essence as well as color. I used to think that if I could add them all together, I could re-form her, a particle at a time. But they are never going to be more than carriers for memories. Each one a tiny film. But I don't need the thing itself for that. I can close my eyes and find the trail of light Sophie left just by thinking of her.

You'll never find 'em in a hundred years.

His eyes when he said the words were like dancing flames as he leaned in to Harry. I don't know what he meant by it. That she was dead and he knew it—because he was responsible? Or was it just vindictiveness? Whichever it was, he wanted to see the pain tear through our faces.

But the butterfly on his wall and on that paper—the one a tributary of the other. What else could it mean? Sophie was inside that room. And that is enough for me to want to talk to him. He spoke to her. He knows something about her that I don't.

I remember the first time that happened. She was at nursery and I had gone to collect her. She was three years old. When we walked home through the park, she told me about Sky.

"Sky showed how to put Sophie's thumb in the hole," she'd said, pulling her mitten through her sleeve.

"Who's Sky?" I asked, bending down to zip her coat.

"Sky," she said. *"Sky."*

And just like that, at three, Sophie knew people, adult people, that I didn't know anything about. She was her own person. And when that reel started to spin, it never, ever stopped. Every day she was more her own and less mine.

I find the tranquilizers in the bathroom cabinet and take two with a cupped handful of water from the tap. The day hasn't begun to grind yet but I know that with Harry gone it will imprison me in minutes.

The tablets work their way around my system fast, and soon I feel it as a breath of warm air over my whole body.

The day recedes quickly.

That thought cycles back again and again. Herman spoke to Sophie. I can't lose that thought. I can't lose it or reconcile it or make peace with it or do anything with it at all but let it wrap its chain around my neck like an anchor. It will always be there.

I don't know if I can do this horrible thing that I'm thinking now. A fantasy, really, induced by the chemicals streaming through my system.

But I can get the information. I don't have to decide anything beyond that. Just information. I always tell my students this. Get as much information as you can before deciding anything.

It doesn't take me long to discover that it's easy to search on the internet without leaving a bread crumb—a *cookie*—trail. All I need is to download a VPN app and switch it on.

I don't know who I am worried about seeing it. Harry maybe. I'd hate him to see what I was searching and how low I'd been brought. I think it would destroy him. But I realize that I don't know what he thinks of me now, in this broken state. Maybe by leaving he is just hacking me away like diseased wood. Maybe it wouldn't destroy him—just me.

I learn about tranquilizers and how many it will take to kill a living and breathing thing. There are complex calculations involving weight and medication strength. My head begins to hurt from the math. It's never been my strong point.

When I finally look up from my screen, I'm in a darkened kitchen with nothing but the blue of my screen for light. The night is heavy around my shoulders. The glass in the bifold doors throws back my reflection into the room. When I look, I see myself but as a ghoul. Or is it Sophie I see? I will the ghost to walk in and to devour me if she can. But she can't. I see her face now at the glass. She glows like the moon. Her skin sparkles as if with glitter. She smiles her blue smile at me and taps the glass. But she can't move away. Like me, she is powerless where she is.

I look down at the screen before shutting it down. Tomorrow I will walk a step further. That's all I need.

FORTY-FOUR

NOW

OLD BAILEY
COURTROOM THREE

ONCE THE JURY MEMBERS ARE ARRANGED IN THEIR SEATS, STEVENS CALLS Harry into the witness box and asks him for his name and address. Harry's throat is dry, and he swallows half a glass of water and tries again.

Stevens smiles. "I have one question for you. Did you kill Mr. Herman?"

"No. I did not."

"Then wait there, please. Others will have questions."

The judge looks around in shock, clearly not expecting this. It has to be some kind of tactic. Why wouldn't he ask any other questions?

Alfred stands and I catch the side of his face as he turns to his junior sitting behind him. He seems furious. He turns back to Harry, giving him no time to compose himself.

"You didn't kill him?"

"No," Harry says, looking straight at the jury.

"Was that an easy enough thing to say?"

"Yes."

"No reason, then, for you not to have said that a year ago when you were arrested and questioned by the police?"

"No."

"Instead you were silent in your interview."

"I went 'no comment' on the advice of my solicitor."

Alfred scratches his head under his wig. "According to the record of interview, you didn't have a solicitor."

"My brother. He came to the station but he couldn't formally represent me. He doesn't do criminal work anymore."

"Your brother told you to give a no-comment interview?"

"Advised me to."

"But then didn't stay long enough to hear out your interview?"

Harry pulls at his collar. "He'd done the same thing earlier when I was arrested for criminal damage. He told me both times that I should get a solicitor, but I knew it would be quicker this way. I hadn't done anything wrong. I didn't need a lawyer."

Alfred leans dangerously forward. "Your daughter, Sophie, went missing just over a year ago."

"She did."

"You, by all accounts, searched very hard for her, didn't you?"

"You would too."

"You weren't satisfied by what the police were doing so you conducted your own investigations, didn't you?"

"Yes."

"According to DS Holly, you went to every house in a radius of half a mile and questioned everyone who answered the door."

"Some didn't answer immediately so I left questionnaires for them, which they filled in."

"But one house in particular evaded you, didn't it?"

"Yes."

"Mr. Herman's house. 210. And you became convinced, didn't you, that he had something to do with her disappearance?"

"No. Not exactly. I wanted to talk to him, that's all. I didn't know why he wouldn't want to talk."

"You wanted it so badly, in fact, that you smashed your way into his house with a hammer less than two weeks before the murder. And you stood over him, according to the crime report he filed that night, with the hammer in his face."

"I didn't have the hammer in his face. He was lying about that."

"But telling the truth about you breaking in with a hammer? Telling the truth about smashing his door in?"

"Yes."

"Tell me. Were you convinced at the time of breaking into his house that he had something to do with the murder of your daughter?"

"My daughter is not dead. She's alive."

"Then her disappearance?"

Harry stops. He swallows. "I had my suspicions, certainly."

"Based on what, Mr. King? The butterfly pendant you told police you found on the pavement?"

"No."

"The butterfly drawing, then?"

"No."

"No. Well, you don't want to admit that, Mr. King, because to do that is to admit you'd seen the one in his bedroom."

Harry says nothing. He is holding his breath, waiting for the assault to pass.

"Well? Had you? Seen the one in his bedroom?"

"No," Harry says. He avoids my eye because we both know it's a lie.

"You didn't fly a drone into his house?"

"No." Another lie.

"He'd complained, you see, Mr. Herman. That a few days before you smashed his door in with a hammer, someone flew a drone in through his bedroom window."

"Okay."

"But that wasn't you?"

"No. It wasn't." He tries to inflect some certainty into his tone but I can see through it. I hope nobody else can.

"But you did buy a drone, didn't you? From Amazon?"

"Yes. I needed a hobby."

"A few days before Mr. Herman complained about one in his bedroom."

Harry swallows hard. "A coincidence."

"Is it?"

"Yes."

"My theory, then, of you buying a drone, flying it into his bedroom, seeing a butterfly mural on the wall"—he stops and reaches for the jury bundle—"the one on page thirty-two. Seeing that and seeing an identical butterfly on a piece of paper found in your daughter's bedroom, convincing you that Mr. Herman had taken your daughter—that theory must be rubbish?"

"Yes. It is."

"You have seen the butterfly picture, though, haven't you? The one from your daughter's bedroom?"

"Yes. My wife found it in her things when she was redecorating the room. But I never saw the mural on Herman's wall—the page thirty-two one."

Alfred turns to his junior, who gives him a small thumb drive. "I'm going to play you some footage. This was recovered from a laptop found in your home."

Before he can press play, Stevens is on his feet objecting.

"My lady. There has been absolutely no disclosure of this material," Stevens says with acid in his voice. "For the Crown to ambush the defense in this way is—"

The judge holds out a hand to stop Stevens. "Let me hear from Mr. Alfred first."

"My lady, a full forensic download of the laptop has been disclosed."

"But we weren't told that any footage was going to be played," Stevens says from his seat, red-faced.

Alfred takes a slow turn. "Well, we didn't know until he was called that he was going to lie. It's simple rebuttal evidence, my lady."

"I don't see a proper basis for an objection, Mr. Stevens. I'm allowing it," Judge Foulkes says carefully.

When Alfred presses play, I see the color drain from Harry's face.

FORTY-FIVE

HARRY

IT'S IN A NEWLY CONVERTED VICTORIAN COTTAGE, ON THE GROUND floor. The upper flat has just been finished and isn't let yet. The landlord, Raj, a small man in his sixties with sparkling eyes, beams all the way through our short meeting.

"Come on," he says, and unlocks the door. He takes me through the flat and points out the gas meter and the cupboard where the boiler lives. I try to hide the tension in my muscles, desperate for him to leave. Finally, he heads for the door, smiling.

As soon as he leaves, I send Katya a message.

> Can you still do this reading?

She responds immediately.

> Yes

> In the morning? First thing?

> Fine for me. Just knock.

The next few hours disappear in toil. I tuck my things away into the spaces built for hiding. Drawers, cupboards, wardrobes. I don't like to see the signs of my old life here in this alien environment. It makes me feel dislocated and seasick when I catch sight of something that is supposed to live on a chair in *our* kitchen or in a closet in *our* bedroom. The bin liner with the materials from the loft is the only thing that I want in plain view. I unroll the map and Blu Tack it onto a wall. Then the flyers. All the notes I made on sheets of A4 I put in a neat pile on the tiled kitchenette table. And on top of that, I put the bundle of cash that Zara found in S—'s room. I need the cash now.

I stare at the map on this foreign wall and at the red line missing from 210 and that sets me off. I rattle every drawer, looking for a marker. I upturn the few bags that haven't been emptied and packed away yet. In the single wardrobe, I pat down the jackets and finally I find it—the red pen—and I take it to the map and scrawl the line in, thick. I was there. I have been there and spoken to him. So now that is every house, spoken to. And of them all, only that one—210—reeks. That's the one. I knew it anyway, by elimination. But now that I have seen him and looked into those eyes, I know.

I know it from the house, the dog, the butterfly, the man, his eyes, and now I know it from his words. *You'll never find her in a hundred years.*

I don't want to wait. I should wait. I should let things settle but I don't want to, not now. I have to make him tell me everything. And then.

And then . . . there's *that*.

IT IS MIDNIGHT. I hate leaving her alone in that house but there are good reasons why I had to leave. There are things I have to do that I can't do from home. I think she'd understand. Or will, when it's all over. One day.

In the main bedroom I put fresh linen on the bed, and then once I have set it up as nicely as I can, I go make up the second room as well and lie down on the bed and close my eyes. The tiredness from the long night and morning in the police station suddenly hits me. If it wasn't for everything I have to do, I'd just slip under the covers and sleep among the scent of laundry detergent, *our* detergent, the smell of home, and all the years that reach back, long before all this misery. If I could, I would sleep. And I would sleep. And I would never wake.

But the things are there like heavy metal tools in my pockets—just there. They're not for being ignored.

I step out into the street. I don't know this part of London at all. Greatorex Street. It has the sound in one's mouth of a street with a dozen ancient red kings behind it. But to look at it, it's a mess of indecision. A new block of flats next to a small 1960s council block. Then all the way in between and along, shop fronts—travel agents, solicitors, even a leather jacket shop. Just this one lone cottage. I think the others were all bombed out in the war. There must have been devastation as far as the eye could see—and this one tiny cottage survived like a lost child.

Although there's a twenty-four-hour Tesco nearby, I choose one that's five miles farther east. I park right at the back. Then with my head down, I drag a trolley from the stack and plow into the electric glow.

I roam the aisles and fill my trolley with everything. Food—breads, fruit, vegetables, cereals, milk, juice, frozen food. I need everything, two of everything, three of everything. I fill up with soap and Fairy liquid and tea towels and cups and plates. And sponges. And clothes. Socks and pants and vests. Every yard there's a fresh leap as I remember— shampoo. Deodorant. Baked beans. Saucepans. Face cream. I don't know which one to get since Zara buys hers and I use whatever she uses. I crouch in the aisle until I see something familiar and red and drop it into the trolley.

I need a knife. My chef's knife is still in the drawer at home so I scour the aisles and find a reasonable set of knives in a block that includes a chef's knife with a seven-inch blade. Then I remember and get a second.

Parcel tape. I find something strong and put two reels in. I need some wellies. I find a pair and put those in the trolley. It's only when I am queuing that I remember something else. Steaks. I run off quickly and find the meat section and pick up a couple of T-bones. And then as I'm turning away, I throw in another two—they look good.

"Two hundred and seventeen pounds and twenty-three pence," she says without looking up.

I count out two hundred and twenty in cash and leave without waiting for the change.

Once I get home I settle on the bed and check my watch. Whenever I look at its black face, a pang runs through me. My wedding watch. A Rolex. Zara bought it for me in duty-free on our honeymoon. It had taken every last penny of her savings and I was mortified when she gave it to me. But ever since then, I wear it when I need some extra luck.

I need a lot of that for what's coming.

I pick up my phone. "Hi, is this the immigration enforcement hotline?" I ask. I am put on hold until someone finally rescues me from Coldplay. "Yes. I'd like to make an anonymous report, please," I say. When the man asks, I give him Katya's address. "She leaves home around nine-thirty in the mornings usually. And I think you should hurry. I've seen a lot of activity at the house. I think something dodgy is going on. Very dodgy."

As soon as the call is over, I call Caspar. "Sorry, bro. I just needed your help with some legal stuff, if you have a minute? It's urgent."

FORTY-SIX

ZARA

IN THE MORNING, I DROP IN AT THE DOCTOR'S SURGERY. THE DOOR OPENS reluctantly, as if the staff have even trained the door in misanthropy. Why all the staff here hate patients I don't know. But they do.

"Just here to collect a repeat prescription," I say to the receptionist. She asks my name without even looking at me. I give it and shift from one foot to the other, waiting. It's supposed to be here, ready. Why do they always do this?

"One minute," she says sourly. "Have to check something." She picks up the phone and whispers into the handset as if I am eavesdropping on my own personal information. Then she nods and replaces the receiver. "Doctor will be down in a minute."

"I don't need the doctor," I say, irritated. "Just give me the prescription, please."

"Take a seat over there," she says, before bending around me to smile at the patient behind me.

"Forget it," I say, and leave. This is why I had wanted to have the prescriptions sent straight to the pharmacy—to save all this.

The air is fresh and mossy but the sky is dull, swollen with rain clouds. I head back toward home, my pace quickening with the threat of rain. At the lights I feel the lightest of touches at my shoulder. I turn.

"Zara. You left without your prescription."

Sadia. The wind sends her hair flicking against her face. She tucks it behind an ear.

"I'm sorry. I couldn't wait."

"It's okay," she says, smiling. "Can we have a chat, though? It'll only take a minute."

I search the traffic hoping for an escape but don't find one. "Sure."

"Coffee?"

A teenager with a violet smile brings us two fat lattes, letting the foam slop over as she settles the oversize cups down.

"The medication is really meant for short-term use only. I know that you're feeling under particular pressure but you should be thinking about alternative ways of managing things. I'm saying this not just as a doctor but as your friend. I can see the effect it's having on you."

I sip my coffee. I still feel guilty about my outburst when we last met.

"Right now, these are the only things keeping me together. I can't sleep without them. And I can't get through a whole day without them," I say, and then before I know it's happening, my eyes are wet with tears. She reaches into her raincoat and brings out tissues.

"I'm worried about you, Zara. I think you're depressed. Clinically, I mean. Have you considered counseling? I can recommend some names for you. You could go together—you and Harry."

I dab my eyes and then scout the table for sugar. There isn't any and it is now the most important thing. I get up, and as I do, the coffees slosh like waves over a dinghy. "Sugar," I say. "I need sugar."

The waitress with the purple lips from earlier hears and brings me a silver bowl with white rocks of sugar. I take it and drop one after the other into my coffee until the bowl is empty. Sadia looks at me, concerned.

"Zara, are you okay?"

"Okay?" I say, and smile, and even as I do it, I know what it looks like. It looks like I am mad.

"Can I call Harry?"

"Harry? No. Harry's gone. There's only me."

She reaches over to touch me on the back of the hand. "Come on. Let me walk you home. We can stop by the pharmacy on the way."

SADIA LEAVES ME at my front door but only once I have reassured her that I am okay. "I can come round after surgery?"

"I'm fine."

"Call me," she says. "Promise me. Day or night." And then leaves wearing the same sad smile that Harry wore when he left.

Even after she's gone, I can feel the electric spikes of human connection. It's as if something in what she has said or done has woken up nerve endings under my skin. I shake off the sensation and take the pills to the kitchen. Two of them I swallow with water. The remainder I divide into two small heaps. One pile I return to the bottle, the other I scoop up and drop into the mortar and pestle and grind into a fine powder. Then I spoon it into a square of foil and press it into a sealed package.

Inexplicably, I still feel Harry. I'm comforted by the thought of him. I pour out a bowlful of cereal and milk, swill it around before tipping the mixture into the waste bin. But I notice a change. My stomach is whining in protest. I pour out another bowl, but this time I sit and crunch through it. I'm not excited exactly, but there is a difference. I feel alive, or if not alive, then as if I am beginning to wake.

In the living room, I sit in the window seat and fire up the laptop. I turn on the VPN and begin typing.

```
Chat forums about grief
```

The search returns six million hits. I find one for coping with the loss of an adult child. I am shocked by the sheer number of people on it. I read down the posts, and the pain people are able to express both breaks my heart and fills me with awe. One member who calls herself Tyson's Mum talks about losing her son. He was eighteen. She doesn't say how he died but writes about the crippling pain and how it overcomes her when her back is turned. How her focus is shattered so the world turns as if behind colored glass.

I scroll to the replies. There's a lot of talk about the myth of time, healing. I'm relieved to hear it. There is no healing. One woman— they are all women—suggests throwing yourself into work. But you can't. Or at least I can't. Work takes things from you that you don't have spare to give. I try to write a comment but I can't participate unless I register. So I register, and then with my VPN off, I log on and post a short note.

```
My child is 18. She's not dead. But she has
been missing for 8 weeks. Those last weeks
have been like drowning. Every day. Not
drowning. Like being held under water.
```

My finger hovers over the send button. But I have to do it. I hold my breath and press return.

For the first few minutes the screen is a blank. My message sits there like an affront. And now I am wondering whether it is an affront. Is my loss not real enough yet? Have I intruded on this world of deep grief with an incomplete tragedy?

I stare at the screen.

Nothing.

I need someone to reply. At least one person.

I go into the kitchen to make some tea. I open the cupboard while the tea is brewing and bring out some cookies. I have no idea when I bought these. They must be months old. But it doesn't matter. My stomach is clawing. I rip the bag open and put a whole one into my mouth and chew. It's not enough. It isn't sweet enough somehow. By the toaster is Sophie's chocolate spread. I spread a thick smear on the next cookie and take a large bite. Much better. The sugar crashes through my body like a tidal wave. It is so strong that it knocks me back. A second later there is a swell of nausea. I add some milk to the brewing tea and gulp until slowly the sick feeling ebbs away.

The light sound of a ping reaches me and I rush into the room to check. There's been a response to my post.

```
I know that feeling. My 16 y/o son, Milo,
went missing a year ago. I feel as if I'm
```

```
holding my breath waiting to find out
something, even that he's dead would be
better than this waiting
```

The person who wrote it has signed off as Luca M. His profile picture is a black-and-white image of a man in a tank top, smiling. He's older than sixteen—forty maybe. I reply immediately.

```
I'm so sorry to hear that. Personally, I'm
not there yet. I feel like she, Sophie, has
to be alive. I can feel her in the world. I'm
sure that somehow the universe would feel
less whole without her in it. To me at least.
```

That had been true once. I search the outer reaches of my senses and pluck at the fabric of time or space or whatever it might be to see if I can feel her still. I don't know if I can anymore. I think if I forced my eyes open toward it, I'd see that she was gone. But I don't feel brave enough for that certainty. And it would be a certainty. I'm a mother. I'd know it about my own flesh and blood. My beating heart out there. I'd sense it if it stopped.

And then Sophie appears again. She's right there—just in my peripheral vision. I want to look at her and speak to her but am afraid if I do it will send her away again. And then I look directly at her and say the words.

Where are you?

I wait for her to answer.

Look, she says. But I can't look just yet. Soon, though. Soon.

FORTY-SEVEN

HARRY

When I arrive, all is quiet. There is nothing happening on the road. Almost no traffic passes, but it is early. I keep my eyes open for anyone who looks formal but apart from a few dog walkers, I see nobody. Finally, at around nine, a small white hatchback pulls up a few doors past her house. A man and a woman sit looking at a clipboard. They have to be the ones.

I hasten to Katya's door and press myself into it so that I can't be seen from the street and I knock.

Katya opens it with a warm smile. She has on a simple cotton dress, but it makes her skin glow somehow. "Come in."

I follow her in and then conspiratorially, I tell her, "Don't mean to worry you, Katya. But I think your bailiffs are here."

"Shit," she says, and begins to mutter to herself in another language and starts flapping her arms in panic.

"Wait," I say. "They can't come in unless you open the door. And if you're not here they can't really do anything. Trust me, you don't want to be turfed out onto the street with all these boxes."

"Then what?"

"Let me do the talking. If it really is the bailiffs for you. We'll know in five minutes. They were just coming up the road."

When the knock comes I hold up a finger to Katya.

"Hello?"

We stand in silence. This feels so dishonest, what I'm about to do. It's making me a stranger to myself.

"Could we have a word please, madam? We're here from immigration."

Katya looks at me in shock. I take her by the hand and whisper to her. "Go to your room." I follow her quietly down a short corridor into a sunny bedroom. There are more boxes in here against a chipped wardrobe. "Give me your house keys."

"They're in the lock."

"Okay. Listen, do not leave this room. Don't make a sound. Switch off your phone." She nods and sits on the bed as I run back into the kitchen. "Coming," I say loudly.

When I open up, I see the same man and woman from the hatchback. They introduce themselves by showing me their ID.

"Could we speak to the resident?"

"That'll be me," I say. "But now isn't convenient, I'm afraid. I'm on my way to work. What's going on?"

They look around at all the boxes. "We're looking for a female occupant that we believe has no right to remain in the UK or a right to rent."

"Oh, you're probably looking for the previous tenant. Yes, she left in something of a hurry, according to the landlord." Their faces drop. "Look, I have to go, but let me take your card. And if I hear from her, I'll give you a bell."

They agree to leave once I've promised to supply them copies of my tenancy agreement.

"You can scan it and email it to us or we can come by next week," the woman says.

I hurry them outside and lock up with the keys Katya gave me as if I'm leaving. At the door they slowly drift away. I get into my car and fiddle in the glove compartment, until they drive off.

Katya is breathless with panic when I burst into the flat. It takes her a few minutes to become calm again. She sits at the small kitchen table taking deep breaths and muttering to herself.

I feel horrible for the panic I have excited in her. But I trudge on, as I have to. "You can't stay here," I say. "They'll be back in a few days."

"Where will I go?" Her eyes are red and frightened now in a way that I haven't seen from her before. I don't recognize this ruthlessness in me. This is as close as I have ever been to finding S——. I can't let her fly through my hands now, no matter how hard her wings beat.

"Let me have a think," I say. I check my watch and see that it's past ten. "Katya, I'm really sorry. I have to get to work. But I'll come back tomorrow," I say. "I promise."

FORTY-EIGHT

ZARA

In the afternoon I try calling Harry. His sudden absence is like a pound of flesh scissored from my side. I need to talk to him, to say the banalities of the day at him. To watch him move thickly through the space here, and to disturb its patterns.

I won't last long without him. I'm so confused and unsettled by it all. I thought I understood the reason—that he was trying to save us. But now it feels like he's just trying to leave. I've become iron around his neck and he can't survive me weighing him down anymore.

Or I'm being paranoid.

I call him but he declines the call. He started back at school today—maybe that's why he didn't take it.

I go into Sophie's room and lie with my feet pointed at the headboard so that I can stare at the dark swirling-pattern wall I have made. After a minute, as before, the wall opens up so that I can see right into the other dimension. Sophie is there waiting for me to come through, wearing a crystal-topped tiara. Her face is fixed with a beautiful but cold smile.

I feel lost.

I think of the word that I have heard in certain devotional songs.

"Mustt." Lost. Not missing or absent or astray, but *entranced*. Lost in memory. How it feels to be lost in devotion—intoxicated by separation. And while I don't feel that, I do feel a shred of solace when I forget myself in her. I close my eyes and try to vanish.

AT FOUR ON the dot, my phone rings. "Harry. I'm sorry. I forgot you were at school," I say.

"Actually, it was just a day with HR, mainly. Start properly on Monday. Is everything okay?" he says, and the familiarity of his voice, its tone and pace, sends electricity through me. I feel it as a rush.

"Just wanted to hear your voice," I say.

And then, ironically, he falls silent. A minute later he coughs. "Look, I have to go. I'm driving."

"Of course," I say quickly. "Maybe come for supper one day this week?"

He considers this, and then when he speaks that same voice becomes suddenly strange. "It's probably not a good idea just yet."

"Okay," I say, and end the call.

IN THE LIVING room, I hide in a corner of the sofa and open my laptop. I go to the bereavement forum that I'm now a member of and look for Luca M to see if he's posted anything. He hasn't. I start a new post.

```
Today is a good day. I walked into the garden
and saw a ladybug sitting on a leaf. And when
I saw it, it was as though Sophie was with
me, looking at it. She loves ladybugs. Or did
when she was younger. But in that small patch
of sunlight, I could feel her arm around my
neck—her small hand grazing my skin—as if I
were carrying her again.
```

It isn't true. I didn't go into the garden. There was no ladybug. There is only that black wall.

When the night begins its descent, I climb the stairs to my bedroom and walk around it slowly. The air in here has shifted with the slightest of changes. Most of his things are still here. His wardrobe is crammed as ever, the jackets and sweaters and shoes bulging to escape. He's taken a few items, but you'd never guess. But with just the absence of those few clothes, and him, the energy has emptied. Not in a freeing way, but in a diminishing way.

I stand on the bed and stare at the chandelier. The light glints from the faux jewels like a promise of innocence. I always hated them—they are things for a child. I jump then, lightly, to see if it is there on top of the wardrobe. I see a wooden box and next to it a bag. I carefully lift the box and bag down. The bag has a catapult in it. There is a laser pointer at the top and some metal balls in the bag. I put it aside.

The box is carpeted with dust. I hesitate only a second before wiping it clear. A swiped palm of glossy wood emerges from the haze. It's there, inside, nestled tight in the dark red velvet. I lift it out and feel its weight in my hand. It's heavy. Just as I imagine a gun should feel.

The words RUGER MARK IV are embossed into the handle and on the other side the word LITE and by the trigger the numbers 22/45. In a column along the bottom are some small brass bullets a couple of centimeters long and no thicker than a pencil. I didn't know Harry in his competitive shooting days. By the time we met he'd lost interest in the sport and had picked up rifle shooting for a while. The law had changed and then all he could legally shoot were those. He had tried but had never got on with them. He preferred pistols. In the amnesty he'd given in all his target weapons. Except this one. I remember he showed it to me once. I'd winced when he opened the box.

"They're just twenty-twos," he said, showing me one of the bullets. "Rimfire. The Americans call them plinkers. Just enough to pierce a target accurately."

"So, you can't kill someone with them?" I'd asked.

"At this range? Two feet? Yes. But practically speaking? No."

I look in the mirror of the wardrobe and hold the pistol to my temple. If I fired at this distance, it would be quick. The blood would be minimal. I think about the mechanics of pain. Would it be real? The brain has no pain-sensing fibers, so one minute I would be breathing and conscious and in agony and in the next, nothing.

And after that a *wissal,* maybe. A reunion.

FORTY-NINE

HARRY

TODAY IS MY FIRST PROPER DAY BACK AT SCHOOL SO I'LL HAVE TO WAIT till the afternoon to see Katya.

School takes me by surprise. The sounds of the children in the playground, the smell of disinfectant, the bustle of the canteen all transport me to a time before she went. If I shove it far enough to one side I can feel a stripe of normality like sun across my face. In the morning Mrs. Cooper stands at the gate to see the children in. She smiles when she sees me. It's a smile of condolence but there's warmth there, as if she is really glad to see me.

At lunchtime, I stay in the classroom to eat a sandwich once the children have been released. I see Robert Delancey, the deputy, hesitate in the doorway before knocking lightly and stepping in. He sidles up to the desk and smiles sadly. It's the first time I've seen him since S— disappeared.

"Good to see you, Harry," he says softly.

"And you," I say. I don't know why I feel especially irritated by him today. I return to my sandwich, hoping he'll go away.

"I never got to say in person how sorry I am about Sophie," he says.

"Okay," I say, bristling.

"We missed you here. I've always thought of the staff at this school as one big family. We really missed you. Both."

"Thanks, Rob," I say, and wait for him to go, but he doesn't.

"If there's anything I can do. I know there probably isn't. She was a lovely girl."

"Okay, thanks. I get it."

He squints, puzzled. "Sorry. Did I say something wrong?"

I put the half-eaten sandwich down and push my chair back. "You sound as if you're telling me she's dead."

"Oh. No, that's not—"

"Okay. Well, it did sound like it. And more than that, your face looks like it."

"I'm sorry," he says, blushing. "I didn't mean—"

"She is alive. I don't want anyone to think she's not alive, Rob," I say, and throw down my cheese and pickle. I watch him retreat into the corridor but am immediately ashamed of how I have spoken to him. But there mustn't be any doubt about it. About how I feel. When it all kicks off, they'll ask people, people like him, what I was saying about S—. Whether I acted like she was still alive or not. They'll want to prove that I believed she was dead. And I can't let there be any misunderstanding about this. She's alive. Everyone who is asked anything by police has to say that I believed, firmly, that S— was alive.

I LEAVE AT the stroke of four and head to Whitechapel Road. Like everywhere in London, it's become smarter over time, as if its destiny was always there, glossy under the old skin. As if it were just a question of sloughing it away. I pass the bank and the café and the anonymous business fronts, and there on the corner is the charity shop I'm looking for. A good old-fashioned one with mismatched pottery in the window alongside dresses and handbags. In the window is a sign that reads

CLOSING DOWN SALE

The clang of a bell follows me in. I'm assailed by the musty scent of dying books. In one corner, a rack of old clothes hangs, neighbors fighting for space.

"Hello," an elderly woman chirps from the counter.

I nod by way of reply.

She assesses me like an expert. "There's half price on the books." An Irish lilt tasting the vowels.

"Just browsing," I say, and go straight to the clothes. I find a long, sun-stained beige raincoat—the kind that a fictional detective would wear. It's a size too big but that's fine. Then I pick up some water-proof overtrousers, a hoodie, and a deep brown trilby.

"Fifteen pounds," she says with a twinkle, as if she is trying it on.

"Got any gloves?"

"Ooh," she says, smiling. "Some came in last week." She rum-mages under the counter and comes up with a shoebox stacked with items that seem to be completely lacking connection to one another. There is a silk tie with the label still on, a pair of cuff links, a garnet brooch, and the gloves that she is now handing me. "I keep the good stuff to the side."

The leather gloves are worn and a little too tight on the knuckles, but they go on.

"Eight pounds," she says, eyeing my Rolex.

"Twenty in total then?" I say, playing along.

She begins to pack the purchases into a translucent white carrier. "Or twenty-five and I'll throw in any book of your choice." Then hurriedly she adds, "From the paperbacks."

I smile and hand her two twenties. "Take twenty-five. Don't worry about the book," I say.

At the flat I try on the clothes. The fit is reasonable but the smell is overpowering. I hang the clothes outside my bedroom window. The gloves and the hat are fine. Inside the hat among the folds of the silk lining is a label: SCOTTS—BY APPOINTMENT TO HER MAJESTY THE QUEEN. I put it on and stare at myself in the mirror. I turn the brim down and then for a second I get a flash of my father. Him and his brothers—my uncles—and their friends. All dressed in suits, standing, cigarettes burning in their hands or mouths, determinedly black-and-white, squinting at the camera. I wonder now what happened to that world. That world of men. And gold cigarette lighters. And mohair suits. And Zodiacs and Zephyrs. And heavy glass ashtrays.

What would men like that do in my place? They wouldn't even have a choice to make because other men, before them, would have gone in. They'd have taken the house apart as the world looked on, muted by inevitability.

But here I am reduced to making these measly choices.

I send Katya a message to tell her I can't come by today. There's too much to do.

My belly is a scrapping wolverine. For Zara, hunger was an easily tamed thing but that's never been me. My hunger still returns as it always has for me.

FIFTY

ZARA

I THREAD THROUGH THE WAITROSE AISLES ON A SOFTENED CLOUD. THE diazepam is coursing now so that the hard edges have all been burned away. But softness sacrifices sharpness. My mind struggles to hold on to any energy. I feel a little drunk.

At the meat counter I find a leg of lamb and heave it into my basket. Then I seek out the other things and get them without really noticing. Milk, bread, cereal, tea, coffee. I pay and then head out onto the high street for the garden center.

It's uphill, and by the time I am there my body is pricking with sweat. A fresh grassy scent welcomes me as I walk in. Sophie and I came here together at the weekends every autumn since she was about eight or nine. Together we'd choose bulbs and then when we got home we'd mix them up until we couldn't tell one from the other and then plant them in the beds. And then when the spring finally came after months of darkness and biting cold, we'd wake to find the garden in a crowd of color. The daffodils clamoring with the tulips. The hyacinths arguing with the lilies. Harry called the garden "multicultural" whenever anyone new came.

I buy some soft neoprene gardening gloves and leave before I can fall into the memories that all these plants are inciting. The scent is so heavy in here that I am glad when I'm finally out. The air outside changes and is suddenly so gray and wet that it washes away any trace of the flowers in seconds.

At home, once the effect of the drugs begins to lift, I stand in the garden and cast an eye over the beds that need clearing. The grapevine is in full fruit, but it won't last more than a week. The tiny berries will be slowly and carefully picked by birds until the stalks stand naked. I clear some of the weeds and gather the bracken into a pile. I had always wondered about these trivialities that occupied the elderly or the dying. Mum used to do this. She was forty-three with only a few months to live, and yet there she was wasting the precious hours she had left to her, left to *me,* picking moss off the brickwork or repairing dried beds. And now I understand it. The minutiae of life *is* life. What else was she supposed to do but to allow it to be lived?

At the back, a wrought iron chair left out in the summer shelters under the shade of a large cherry tree. I stand on it to see the house. But it's too far away.

The pain is returning. At this early stage, I can sit back and watch it roll in, an inch at a time. But soon there will be heat under my skin and my muscles will stiffen. Cell by cell, my body will come alive, screaming its way in like a baby.

I go to Sophie's room and lie on the bed again and stare into the wall. She isn't there yet but will come eventually. I just have to wait it out. I shut my eyes, but then a minute or so in the doorbell sounds. I wade down the stairs and open it.

Sadia.

"Hi, Zara, just checking in," she says, smiling. She is wearing a bright yellow raincoat that makes her look like a preteen child.

I don't know what to do so I ask her in. "I was just about to put the kettle on."

She ducks her way shyly into the kitchen to perch on a barstool. As I fill the kettle, she talks to my back. "Have you thought any more about therapy?"

"Actually, I have. I've found something useful on the internet," I say, remembering.

"Oh, what's it called?" she asks brightly.

I hand her a cup of freshly brewed tea and tell her the name.

"So, not professional therapy?"

"No. But I can take things at my own speed with this. Nobody makes me talk if I don't want to." I sit opposite her with my cup.

She takes a sip and nods slowly to herself. "I'm not a therapist but you know you can always talk to me."

I smile. There was a time when she would have been the person I'd talk to. *Was* that person.

Now the thought of talking to my best friend about anything important has become so alien. She betrayed me. I know that legally she can't give me Sophie's records but that doesn't help.

"Just promise you'll call me if you start to feel low."

I nod as if I'm not already scraping along the deepest seabed.

"No more diazepam," she says, concern once again feathering her brow. And leaves.

I clear away the tea things and draw the blinds against the bifold doors. The lights come on automatically and fill the room with shades of blue. I take the lamb from the fridge and remove the cellophane and then wrap it in a tea towel, to absorb the moisture. The garlic is already sliced into slivers. I stand the meat against the tile running along the wall where it meets the counter. Then, I get Harry's chef's knife. The edge of the steel is sharp and pings as I rub my thumb across it. I hold it tight by the handle and feel its weight. I face the leg of lamb and then with force I run the blade through the cloth and into the flesh. It goes in less than half an inch. I pull it out and this time I put more into the motion. Still it only goes in an inch. I keep at it, stabbing harder and harder each time until finally the blade goes all the way through to bone.

I'm soaking in sweat. I pull the knife clean, steadying the meat with my other hand. A few strings of flesh still cling to the blade with smears of pink blood. I wipe it with a finger. My breath comes upon me in a rush, and then I'm hyperventilating. I fold myself in half to help control the convulsive breaths.

Slowly the world steadies.

I call Harry.

"Is everything okay?" he asks tentatively.

"I just rang to see if you wanted dinner." There is a weighted pause on the line. It lasts so long that I begin to hear the pulse in my ears. "I'm making leg of lamb."

"No," he says finally. "It's too soon. I'm sorry."

FIFTY-ONE

HARRY

IN THE MORNING MY FIRST THOUGHTS ARE FOR ZARA. SHE WAS CLINGING on with the last of her strength but I have let go of her. I've had to, in order to save her. In another version of this world, I'm holding on to her with everything I have. But there is always a thing that is pulling her away from me. A strong, muscular force.

I have to get this done before it's too late.

I dress quietly and then bring the charity clothes I hung outside back in through the window. The smell of fresh rainwater overlays the mustiness.

I have clothes and a knife but haven't given much thought to how I get in. The front is too problematic. There are students passing through the road at all hours of the night in differing states of sobriety. And then there are the houses opposite with twitchy curtains. No. I have to go in through the back. He's repaired the fence, but it won't be any harder to pull away a new plank as opposed to an old one.

And then there's that back door. I search my memory to color in the details: it was glazed. I could smash the window once I've settled the dog. And then see if the door will undo from the inside—keys in the lock or a bolt I can draw back.

Saturday. I can't leave it any later than that because with each passing day and night S— falls deeper and deeper through the fault lines. If I have to recover S—'s body, if that's what it will take to end this hell for Zara, then I'll do it. I know that with enough time and space, I can make him tell me the things he'd rather carry to his grave. *You'll never find 'em in a hundred years.* We'll see.

At night I stare into the ceiling.

It's the only thing that drives me in this. Zara has always been a spiritual person. I don't mean that she meditates and looks at the stars. I mean she believes in life beyond life. I'm grateful for that and at the same time I rail against it. It's because of her belief that she will never kill herself to escape the torment. I'm relieved by it. But I hate the idea of pain she can't ever escape.

I make a mental note to make sure to buy that burner phone.

I pull up outside Katya's and she is waiting at the door with a harried look. She says nothing but looks at me questioningly. Her sleeves are rolled up to her elbows and she has a scarf tied over her hair like a 1950s housewife. She's obviously been working hard.

"I'm sorry. I couldn't find anything," I say, following her into the kitchen. The place is stacked high with bags and filled bin liners and boxes. I look over at her and see she is holding back tears. I feel my stomach kick in disgrace.

"But," I say. "You can stay with me. At the flat. Till you get sorted. There's a second bedroom."

She turns small circles in the kitchen. Every spare inch of floor space is taken. "What about all my stuff?"

I pretend to picture where it might all go. "I've got a lockup. You can store whatever you want there, for as long as you like." I write two addresses down.

Her gaze switches from the boxes to me. She wipes her brow with her bare arm. "How long can I stay?"

"I have a six-month lease on the flat. You can stay as little or as long as you need to."

She hesitates, as if weighing up the dangers. "Are you sure?"

"I'm sure."

She pulls her headscarf off and finally allows herself some relief. "Thank you. When?"

"Can you drive?"

She nods. "Not UK license, though."

"That's okay." I hand her two sets of keys. "That's home. That's the lockup. I have to go to work now but take my car. Move whatever you can to the lockup and I'll see you at the flat later."

SCHOOL IS A blur of admin and scrappy lessons in which my sixth-grade class vibrates with mischief. This happens sometimes without any discernible explanation. The children are alive with this energy that seems to come from nowhere. They become harder and harder to contain as the day winds on until finally someone cries and the storm cloud bursts.

I send them out to their lunch and for their breaks a few minutes early. Anything to use up that electricity they are carrying.

At four I leave and head straight to the shop to buy the cheap burner phone. In the cab home, my usual phone rings.

"Zara?" I say. The line goes quiet and I can hear her breath.

"Can you come? I'll make dinner."

"I'm not sure I—" I begin, but when I hear myself speak I stop. This is all for her. What use am I if I can't comfort her when she needs me?

"Not dinner. But I'll be there in ten minutes," I say, and tell the driver there's a change of destination. I can still be back at the flat for Katya later. But Zara's voice—it felt bruised.

She opens the door and lets me in without a word, just a weak smile on her lips. I wait in the kitchen as she pours me a glass of wine.

"Is everything okay?"

Zara nods and sits at the counter. A whisky glass in her own hand. "I was worried about you."

"*Me*? I'm okay," I say.

"Do you know if the police are charging you?"

I shake my head and I take a sip. We stare at each other, just out of reach.

"How's your leg?"

I look down at my ankle. I'd almost forgotten about it. "What's going on, Zara?"

"Not yet," she says. "I need more." She drains the glass and pours herself another measure of whisky.

"Since when did you start drinking whisky?"

She looks over the rim at me and I see the red around her eyes and the dark smudges beneath. "Since nothing mattered." After another gulp she looks away. "I think you should come home."

In any other world but the one I am in, I would never have dreamed of saying what I say now. "I don't think I should."

"I'm not really asking, Harry. I need you to move back in."

I take in more wine, relieved that at least I'm not driving. "I will. Just not yet."

She walks to the doors onto the garden and looks out. The sun is low and giving the glass shades of gold and copper.

"I'm really worried, Harry," she says with her back turned. Her hands move to her face as though she is dabbing at her eyes. She sniffs softly.

"Zara," I say, and get up to put my arms around her. She turns and then falls into me.

"I don't want to be here anymore."

"I know," I say, and stroke her hair. "I know."

"You don't know, Harry. You don't know what it's doing to me. What it's turning me into."

I *do* know. I can see it. Her skin is being torn off and when it regrows, it's ripped away again. "You can get through this."

"Only if we're together," she says, pulling away. Her eyes are round. "I'm scared of what I might do."

I can't move back in yet. I can't implicate Zara in any way. And I have to do this thing to give her any chance of survival. "I'll come back in a week or two. We need the space." As I say the words, they tear into me.

"And if I do something stupid before then?"

"You won't. I know you." I know that she can't do that. And I am talking over her, telling her not to say things like that, when I realize what she's telling me.

"Harry. I think Sophie's gone. I can feel it now."

FIFTY-TWO

ZARA

As soon as the words are out I regret them. But I have to tell someone and there is only Harry. He drops his hands.

"No," he says. "You can't think that. You have to hang on to hope. Cling to it with both hands, Zara."

"I don't know." There's a look of absolute shock on his face. "I can't stand to live without her."

"I know. But closure can help," he says.

"What closure? There is no closure, Harry!"

He rubs his head as if deciding and then returns a look from somewhere I don't recognize. "Sorry."

"No," I say, moving toward him. I reach out and put my palms on his chest to stop him from avoiding my eye. "What closure?"

"It's Holly. She says there's a chance they're going to arrest Herman soon. But she doesn't want to be bothered endlessly by us about it."

I release him and he returns to where his glass sweats on the countertop.

I'm upset that Holly didn't speak to me about it. I cast my mind back. There were no missed calls that I didn't return. I always call her back. Of course I always call her. "What have they found? Did they find Sophie?" I try to read Harry's expression but there's nothing there.

"I don't know. She wouldn't say."

"Why didn't she call me and tell me?"

He rotates the base of the wineglass slowly on the counter. "She didn't want to get your hopes up. You know what we're like."

"I know what *you're* like, Harry. I'm not like that. Whatever she thinks. I'm not the one who would overreact."

"Overreact? Really? Is that what I do? Our daughter is missing. I am never going to stop doing what I have to."

"Daughter?" I say. "I'm sorry. This was a bad idea. You should go." I can't continue on a loop inside this argument. I don't have enough sanity spare for it. And the whisky has reached me quicker than I expected.

He drops his shoulders and then heads upstairs. When he comes down he leaves almost immediately. And then I am plunged into this sudden loneliness again. It's like a wind that obliterates everything that came before it so that there is no comfort left from Harry's visit. Even the peaty taste of the whisky has gone.

FIFTY-THREE

NOW

OLD BAILEY
COURTROOM THREE

THE PROSECUTOR MAKES SURE THAT ALL THE MONITORS ARE SWITCHED on so that everyone can see what is on the screen. He presses play.

I watch the footage of the drone approaching the open bedroom window. Herman is there, momentarily caught in panic, and then I see the jagged lines of the drone's flight inside the room. The purple butterfly blooms into view before fading out again with an image of a black sky. The drone shudders away before the footage fades out.

I thought my team would have warned me about this.

"That video footage was found on your laptop following a search of your home. That was your drone, that you flew into the house, capturing, as we see, the butterfly mural."

There's no way out of this. "Yes."

"You told us that you hadn't seen the mural and yet there it is in Technicolor, on your laptop. You have lied to this jury."

"I misspoke," I say, feeling the heat creep up my neck. The jury cross their arms as if I am a personal insult to them. "I'd seen the mural but hadn't seen the drawing. I got it the wrong way around."

"There are so many lies, Mr. King, that you can't keep up with them, can you?"

"I didn't kill Mr. Herman. That is the truth. Why would I kill him?"

"Because he'd killed your daughter—or so you believed."

I take a big breath. "I did not believe that. She was—is—alive. The last thing I'd want to do is kill Herman when he might be the only person to know where she was. Ask anyone who knows me. As far as I'm concerned, she is alive."

"If that's true, then would you be kind enough, Mr. King, to tell us what you were doing on the night that he was murdered in his own home?"

"I was in my flat. In Whitechapel."

"Why had you moved out of the family home?"

Zara drops low into her seat as if the question has landed a heavy weight on her shoulders.

"We were having problems. In the marriage."

"What was the cause of these problems?"

I stare at the judge to get her attention. It takes a few seconds for her to notice me. "Do I have to answer that?"

"Unless your counsel objects, yes. And I see that he doesn't."

"Our daughter going missing, as you can guess, didn't exactly make for a happy home."

Alfred puts his fountain pen gently on the lectern. "I don't mean to pry into your personal affairs, Mr. King. But it seems to me that you rented a flat specifically for the purposes of giving yourself an alibi."

"No," I say.

"Let's look at this a bit more, shall we, Mr. King?" He turns behind him and pulls a huge lever-arch file from the row behind. "We'll take this slowly."

FIFTY-FOUR

HARRY

KATYA IS SITTING AT THE KITCHEN TABLE, WHICH HAS BEEN LAID FOR dinner.

"Harry," she says, and then stops. She's changed out of the clothes she was wearing earlier for cutoffs and a T-shirt. Her fingers dance with one another. "This is a bit awkward."

I laugh nervously along with her. "Just a bit." I look around the place and it seems better. More lived-in. There are only one or two boxes of clothes and odds and ends here. "Was the lockup okay?" I ask.

"Yes, good. Dry. Empty." She waits, and then at the sound of an alarm shuffles off to the kitchen. "I cooked something," she says, bringing over a dish sizzling with butter and garlic. "Sorry, I used food from fridge."

"Listen, Katya, you don't have to cook for me. Or do anything. Honestly, it's fine. The room is spare and I can really use the company."

She studies me for a moment, as if checking my meaning. "Tomorrow you can cook," she says brightly, and ladles out the food.

Dinner is stilted. It's my fault, not hers. She tries to make conversation but I'm too busy trying to think about how the hell I'm going to explain it all to her.

"So, your wife and you?" she says over a spoonful of stew.

"We've separated," I say. "Temporarily."

She nods silently and the conversation once again dries to a crisp. We finish and she stacks the dirty dishes. "How much is rent?"

"You mean how much am I paying?"

"No, from me. How much? I was paying eight hundred in the last place."

"Katya. It's fine. No rent. I have to pay it anyway. Don't worry. Save your money. You're going to need it, I'm sure."

"I'd rather pay, please, so there can be no misunderstandings." Again, that anxiety surfacing, and I think how stupid I am for not anticipating it. Of course she is nervous—she has no idea who I am.

"Don't worry. I have too many things on my mind to be misunderstanding anything," I say to try and reassure her.

"Sorry. I didn't mean—" she starts.

"It's okay. We're still getting used to each other," I say, and excuse myself to go to my room.

It feels awful to have done this to her. But I don't have a choice. Seeing Zara earlier confirmed it.

IN THE MORNING, my first thought is Zara. I have to do this before she gets worse. She's so wounded and exhausted by all this that I'm really frightened she'll do something to herself. I didn't think it was possible before now. But when I saw her yesterday she had a look of being hunted. I'm terrified of what it might make her do.

I wonder who she has to help her. Her family is on a different continent but it wouldn't have mattered if they weren't. Zara can't be *reached* by anyone, friends or family. All she wants is to be left alone in her darkness. Sadia still tries. She came to the house at the start of this, so I left them together in the kitchen to catch up. An hour later when I checked, she'd gone. "We just had nothing to talk about," Zara said.

She is bloody with all this pain.

So, it has to be Saturday.

I slip out of the door quietly so as not to wake Katya and head to school. When I come back, I'll have to have a plan for how I tell her. I know it's unconscionable but I have no choice.

FIFTY-FIVE

ZARA

I FEEL MY THOUGHTS GATHERING LIKE CROWS AT THE RIM OF A POOL. I can't let them smother me. I look for Luca M's most recent post and see that he's replied to my last one.

```
Sometimes there are moments, like your
ladybug one, that catch you totally off
guard. I had one this morning. It was stupid
really. All I was doing was brushing my teeth
and then as I looked in the mirror I saw Milo
behind me, sitting on the edge of the bath
brushing his. Late for school as usual. His
tie thrown over his shoulder so that he
didn't get toothpaste on it. And that stupid
non-moment just got me. I just stood there in
tears looking into the mirror at him. I just
wanted to reach in and follow him to wherever
he was.
```

I send him a private message.

> Very moved by that, Luca. So sorry for
> your pain

He replies immediately. Pain is our lot for now. But I think about pain and how it is there to prepare us. To make us strong.

I reply. That's what I'm afraid of. I don't think I can stand another assault.

I see the dots strobing as he types, and then it comes.

Luca M: Sometimes it's just to help you survive. TBH I don't know what I'm talking about!

> Who does?

Luca M: Stelly99 does, I think!

I laugh when I read that. Stelly99 is full of wisdom, delivered in single-line servings.

> Thank God you're not like her!

In my mind's eye, I conjure him in the same tank top, pacing the floor, teacup in hand, composing the next line and then deciding against it.

Luca M: How are you doing generally?

This is an opening. I don't know. Not great.

Luca M: Tell me.

> Usual. Being without her is bad
> enough. Not knowing is worse. My head
> is going into some dark places. I'm
> never sure that I'm going to be able

to find a way out the next time it
happens.

After a minute or so he sends another.

Luca M: Look, I don't mean to intrude but
what's your situation at home? Is there
anyone you can talk to?

I leave a gap. Not really. My husband left.
Then there is a deafening silence. I wait and watch the minutes
tick by. The screen saver kicks in. I refresh the screen, but nothing.

I take the laptop to the bedroom and get into bed, still dressed. I
lay my head on the pillow and stare sideways into the white screen.
The glare begins to hurt my eyes and I close them for just a second.
It's true I haven't been sleeping—not at the right time. I doze in the
afternoons or sleep in in the mornings when I manage to drop off in
the early hours. Now sleep is pulling at me—calling.

A ping wakes me.

Luca M: Can I call you?

I sit upright. Yes, I type, and then send him my number. My
heart begins to kick up a little when a second later the phone rings,
loud.

"Hello—Zara?" His voice is gravelly and older than his picture.

"Hi," I say, and put the phone onto loudspeaker. "Luca?"

"I thought I could check in on you from time to time if you didn't
mind."

I put the phone on the pillow next to me and talk to the ceiling.
"Thanks. That's kind. Tell me something. Anything."

"Like what?"

"I don't know, Luca. Anything at all. I need to sleep and I think
hearing your voice—near me—might help," I say. "Just a few minutes, if you can."

"A few minutes? I have all night," he says. "You try to sleep. I've
been told that my voice is very soporific."

FIFTY-SIX

HARRY

At school, a few of the senior girls, S—'s classmates, give me doe-eyed looks when they pass me in the corridors. But aside from that, nothing has changed. At lunchtime I head to a small corner mini-mart that sells odds and ends. I need tools to get me into the house. A screwdriver for the new fence, and a claw hammer.

I pay and ask for a bag and then I put them in the boot and drive back to school.

The remainder of the day trawls agonizingly on until the final bell goes. In my rush to leave, I find myself backed up in pupil traffic. The older children congregate near the main gate. But as I force my way through I feel a tug on the hem of my jacket. I turn to see Emily— her features those of a character from a manga.

"Mr. King?"

"Emily," I say, and then claw around for something else. "Thank you for coming to her birthday." I say it but have no specific memory of her being there.

"Can I have a word about something—in private?"

I take a step back into the school premises and wait as a throng pushes past onto the pavement. She turns her face up toward me. She is so small.

"It's about Sophie," she says. I feel a spike of nervousness. What does she know? Her fists are small white balls. I move away from the gates so that we are free of the stream of pupils trying to leave.

"Sure. What is it?"

She swivels as if checking for eavesdroppers. "Can we go into the classroom? Or your car?"

The car is out of the question. And there are rules about seeing girls alone in a classroom. "Let me get set up. Come along in about five minutes," I say, and turn back toward the school building.

The classroom is empty and with the lights off, it carries an air of abandonment. Chairs are strewn carelessly far from their desks. The familiar scent that is a mix of dust, cleaning fluid, and sweat fills my nose. I turn on the light and sit at my desk with a lesson planner before me. If anyone were to walk by, I can't just be here waiting for a pupil.

A few minutes later Emily knocks on the door. As she stands waiting to come in, Alexander Musset, a seventh-grade teacher, walks past.

"Ms. Blake," I say over-formally. "Are you lost?"

She picks up the pretense. "Is it okay to have a word, sir?" She hesitates but enters when I beckon.

"Leave the door open," I say casually, and then wave Musset away. He pauses as if about to come in but decides against it when he sees Emily pull up a chair.

"Yes?" I say.

She turns to the door, waiting for him to leave.

"Shall I see if there's another member of staff available, Mr. King?" he asks.

"Yes, please, Alex," I say, and then level my gaze at Emily. "Won't be a minute, Emily."

We sit in electric silence and listen to Musset's steps retreating along the corridor. As soon as he's out of earshot I whisper heavily. "You better be quick."

She sits there mute. There is a well of tears building, I can see them about to burst. But I don't have time for this. "What is it, Emily?"

From the corridor the sound of airy voices comes drifting in— Mrs. Cooper, the head teacher, now with Musset.

"Now or never, Emily. Come on," I say quickly in a low voice.

"I don't know how to say this. You're going to be so angry."

My heart is drumming now in anticipation. Mrs. Cooper's voice is coming closer and closer.

"I'm scared," she says then, her eyes filling.

"Just tell me," I say urgently. They'll be here in seconds.

"I got a text."

"From who?"

"I got it the day after Sophie went missing."

"From who?" I ask impatiently.

The tears are falling freely now down her cheeks. Her voice breaks as she says the single word "Sophie."

Just then Mrs. Cooper comes in. "Emily Blake. So, what couldn't wait till the morning? Nothing serious?"

"Oh. Nothing," Emily says, turning to dry her tears out of view. "It doesn't matter." She bustles past Musset and Mrs. Cooper before they can stop her.

Mrs. Cooper gives me a baffled look. "What was that about, Harry?" she says, stepping in.

"Oh, it really was nothing. She was asking if there was any news about my daughter."

"Yes," she says, smiling softly. "They were friends."

"Are friends," I say firmly. *"Are."*

I SIT IN the car. A text from S——? The day after she went missing? There was no choice but to let Emily go. I couldn't follow her. The school is very rigid about any unchaperoned contact.

Now that I am in the car, it feels as though the plan is rushing up to meet me. All the pieces are falling into place.

In the early days of investigating S——'s disappearance I made a map of the roads with CCTV and traffic cameras in the area. I plot out a longer route. No cameras along here. Nothing. On the way to the flat, I stop at our local Sainsbury's in East Dulwich and park around the front. I get out and check for cameras. There are none at the entrance to the car park, but there's a bank of CCTV cameras by the store itself. Two at the ATMs. As I drive out again, I notice the recycling bins are still there—overflowing, as they always are.

They're going to be important.

FIFTY-SEVEN

ZARA

I WAKE UP IN A COLD SWEAT. I HAVE BEEN TURNING AROUND IN MY HEAD the steps, every one, that I need to take to do it—to stop the pain. Stop the heartbeat. Let the brain switch off. Send us both to rest.

My appetite has returned. My subconscious mind must be telling my body that it needs fuel and strength to do this awful but necessary thing. I take croissants, rip them open, and fill them with cheese and jam. Harry would be horrified. He'd have taken them off me and warmed them in the oven. He'd have brought me coffee to drink with them. And juice. And then inevitably Sophie would come in, circles under eyes—late for school. She'd take a huge bite out of my breakfast and glug down my juice. And I'd protest. Hard.

"Sophie. You can't just steal my breakfast. Get up five minutes earlier and sit down in peace with us and eat. Like a person."

"You mean like a family? No, thanks," she'd say, and I would look at Harry who would be shaking his head.

"It's a phase," he'd whisper.

And now of course I hate that I said any of that. I want to step back into that moment and when she takes the croissant I want to smile at her, hold her, stroke her face, and tell her in every way that I can that I love her. But there's only falling forward in time. We can't go back.

I pick up my phone and dial.

"DS Holly."

"It's Zara. King. Look, I know you're busy and you think I'm just a—a thorn in your side."

"What is it, Zara?"

"You could have called me. You *can* say things to me. I'm not *fragile,*" I say, but as I do, I feel only the weakness in my voice.

"Wait. Can we hold up a second, please, Zara? What is this about?"

"Herman. You're going to arrest him and you didn't even mention it to me."

"Who told you that?"

"Harry. I know it's confidential, but what makes you think that I'm not an appropriate person to share this information with?"

"Look, I don't know why Harry's telling you this but there is no arrest planned. There is no evidence to connect Herman to anything. And as far as we are concerned, we are continuing to treat Herman as a *victim* of crime."

That he has managed to position himself as a victim of crime sends me into a sudden spiral of anger.

"*Victim?*" I say. She begins to answer me, but I cut her off. "I can't do this right now," I say, and end the call.

I collect myself in the silence afterward. Why did Harry lie to me?

Since he left he's transformed so quickly and in ways that I had not expected of him. If he ever comes back, I don't know what he will come back as.

I take out the Ruger case from under the bed where I left it. I examine the gun and see things I hadn't noticed before. The barrel has holes drilled all the way around it. There is what I assume is a sighting attachment to add to the top. I turn the gun around and carefully, with the barrel pointing away, test the buttons and the catches by pressing and turning them. One button on the left-hand side releases the cartridge, which drops out of the handle. It is empty. I put it to one side and carry on inspecting it but can't make sense of it without help.

I get my laptop and switch on the VPN and research how to load the bullets into the clip and find an American video within seconds.

I watch it a few times and learn about the gun. It's a .22 "rimfire." An automatic pistol. One of the catches is a safety catch. The bullets— the "rounds"—slot into the cartridge one by one. By the time I'm done, I know how to strip the weapon. There is a button at the back that you push and the whole barrel just pops off. I press it back into place as the video shows. The weapon is as simple as it could be.

I load a round into the cartridge. My heart picks up as I snap the clip home into the handle. Loaded. In my hands, it quivers with an energy it didn't have a few seconds ago. It wants to be allowed to *be*. To be itself. It's nothing but a lump of metal unless and until it fires.

I press the gun flat against my face to feel the coolness of the barrel against my skin. But all I feel is this lethal hardness, which against the delicacy of my skin feels like a violation. For a second I feel what I often feel looking out of high windows. Not that I might fall, but that I might jump. That I'll have an impulse that I can't control.

I drop the cartridge out and pack it all away. It will be there when I'm ready for it.

I put on my raincoat and leave—the opposite way from 210. I have to get it all behind me. I walk.

In ten minutes, I reach a small park bordered by railings. I last came here at least a decade ago. The roses have died away and in their place the autumn plants have begun to bloom. The trees are beginning to exchange their lustrous greens for gold. A tarmac path wends through the park, dissecting the land, separating grass from bed.

This was our place. Sophie and I spent half a summer here when she was five, nearly six. Every weekday after school, we came here, under a veil of secrecy, for the surprise. Harry's birthday. There was a cake and a present of course, and a handmade card, but this was the centerpiece, if we could only get it right. So, each day after school, under the pretense of a walk to feed the ducks or post a letter or play on the swings, we came here. Against the railing, it would be waiting for us, a red bicycle, locked tight. Sophie would wheel the bike out and straddle. I'd stand behind her and hold the seat as she stirruped her feet into the pedals. And I ran behind her, laughing, trying to keep her upright, trying to keep *up*. And then she would fall, dust her tiny hands across her knees, and chirp, "I'm okay, Mummy. I'm okay." And then she would try again.

I sit down on a bench and close my eyes.

One day, just like that, she got it. She was on two wheels.

The birthday was celebrated in the form of a picnic on the weekend. No friends. Harry didn't want other people there watering down the day. He sat cross-legged over the treats—éclairs, Victoria sponge, sandwiches, and salads. He opened cards and presents and smiled in the sun. And then Sophie made an excuse that she was off to hunt for dandelions, but a minute later she returned on her bike. She came thundering across the grass ringing her bell. Harry stared in shock, eyes wide, mouth open like a dropped hatch.

"My best Daddy birthday ever!" Sophie had said.

And I am here now because I don't have a place I can go to speak to Sophie. There's no memorial because she is not dead. And yet all around, people and her ghost scream at me to tell me to let her go because she is dead.

Because Sophie is dead.

FIFTY-EIGHT

HARRY

KATYA, HER BRONZE HAIR LOOSELY TIED, IS AT THE SMALL KITCHEN TABLE with cards laid out in a pattern. Next to it are what look like printed pages from a cartomancy manual. I wave her a quick hello. She looks up but is too distracted to respond. I go to the bathroom and shower before dressing in my cleanest clothes—a white shirt and some biscuit-colored chinos.

I ring Zara from the bedroom. "What's Emily Blake's number?"

"Harry? Is everything okay?"

"Fine. I just need the number." The line rustles in the pause.

"I don't have it," she says.

"Yes, you do. Come on."

"What?"

"Zara," I say, losing patience.

"What's happened?" she says, breathless. "It's about Sophie, isn't it?"

I can't tell her. Zara's hope has been pulled translucent these last weeks and I can't stretch it any more. "It's nothing. I just have to talk to her. She was upset at school today. Came to find me but we were interrupted."

"Do you think it's a good idea to communicate with her?"

"I'll be careful." I drum my fingers impatiently.

She gives me the number and I immediately send Emily a message: Text me your address.

Once I have it, I dip my head into the living area. "I'm off. Be back in an hour or two," I say to Katya. She begins to speak but I cut her off. "Katya. I do need to talk to you. As soon as I get back?"

She nods. "Okay." And then has her head back in her cards.

I PARK ON Emily's road. The houses are all huge on this stretch. They used to call this the stockbroker's belt back when there were stock-brokers. The retiring sun paints the white woodwork in brushes of watery copper but the warmth has leached out.

I send her a message: I'm outside. Make an excuse. NOW please.

I wait at a small strip of green opposite, edged with railings. Bird-song fills the air and reminds me of a hundred different days all at once. Some when she was small—seven or eight—helping me to row a boat on the lake at Dulwich Park. Some when she was older and made to come with us on hour-long walks across Blackheath. This birdsong has a wild quality. People are wrong about birdsong. They call it music and describe it as beautiful, but it's not. It's not unpleasant but not interesting either. It's—dull. But I know why it's special. It is—a rain cloud of memories. Happy ones. Ones made in the sun to the tune of chirruped song. I could shut my eyes to it and fall back into a blanket of memories.

Emily's door opens and in the distance, I see her slight figure slipping out. She comes onto the green and looks around until she catches my raised hand and runs over.

"I'm sorry," she says, hugging herself with her long sleeves, covered in pilling. Her face is pale with worry.

"Never mind that. Just tell me what you can. You said you got a text?"

"Yes."

"*After* she went missing?" I have seen all the text messages from her phone. I have copies of the full forensic download of the whole call and text history. They don't show messages but they do show *when* messages were sent. And there were none after she went missing.

"Yes. Like the next day."

"I've got her phone records. There were no texts the day after."

She pulls at her arms. "Not from her phone, I don't think. The number was withheld. At the time I didn't think it was even from her."

"Have you got the message?"

"No. I deleted it."

"Why?" I say in anguish. "Why?"

"I'm sorry. I didn't know she was going to go missing." Tears pool in her eyes and spill over her cheeks.

I try to contain this surge of raw emotion that is building up in me. I thought she'd have kept it. "What did it say? Can you tell me that at least?"

She blinks her tears away rapidly. "Yes. I mean, I don't remember all of it. It said she was going away for a bit." She looks up into the sky, recalling. "And that we shouldn't look for her."

"Shouldn't look for her why?"

"I don't know." She is crying again, and in my impatience, I just want to shake her. "She just said that. And we wouldn't find her in a hundred years."

My heart is pumping so hard now that it's making me feel dizzy. That phrase again. Surely it can't be a coincidence. She didn't send that message.

All the way back to the flat, I plan what I'm going to say to Katya. I don't know how to do this because I don't know her, really. When I walk in she is sitting on the sofa as if she has been waiting for me. She is fiddling with a box of cigarettes, which she drops as soon as I come in. Her playing cards are laid in a reading pattern on the coffee table. Face up.

She stands. "Harry. I'm going a little bit mad here. We need to talk. Please."

"Of course," I say, and sit on the arm of the sofa—not too close.

"I know you said no rent, but I need to pay you something." I try to interrupt but she powers through. "No, let me explain. I have to work. And most of my money is from face-to-face. So, I have to have clients in here. But how can I work when I am here for free?"

"You can work here. At least on the phone. For now."

Relief trickles through her features. "I still want to pay."

"I can't let you."

"Why?"

"Because I can't. I'm sorry." Once I say this, everything changes. She waits for me to explain, brown eyes narrowed. "I know I told you that I had this place for six months. But that's not exactly true."

"What do you mean?" She sits up.

"I think we need a drink," I say, and fetch some wine from the kitchen. I return with two tumblers of red. She takes the glass but keeps her eyes on me.

"Well?"

"This is hard to explain."

"Try."

"You might have to leave for a few days."

She stares at the coffee table. The cards seem to shout. "What? When?"

"Not definitely. Maybe."

She grows even more puzzled at this. "But if—then where do I go?"

I have thought about this. "Hotel. I'll pay. But it will just be for a week, maybe, and then you can move back in."

She considers this. Questions appear to flash in front of her face. "Why?"

"I'm sorry, I can't say more yet."

She curls her legs under her and swallows some wine. Her face is struck through with worry. "Okay. If time comes I can move. If I can work, then I can pay for hotel."

"No," I say. "I need your help and it's the least I can do."

I expect her to be angry but instead, worse, she is calm. "I knew this," she says, and points to a card. "Three of diamonds. This is legal trouble. And this. Eight spades is danger. Deceit. And then seven of spades is bad advice. You are getting into some deep trouble."

We sit in silence for a minute or two. Finally, she says what she has to say.

"What help do you need?"

"I'll tell you nearer the time. I'm sorry, Katya. I should have been more open with you."

"Yes, you should have," she says, and goes to her room.

I do the same and set my alarm and lie down and try to forget what I've just done to her. I can't let it get in the way now. I need sleep and to plan. But neither of these things seem as if they'll come to me tonight.

FIFTY-NINE

ZARA

Harry called earlier asking for Emily Blake's number. I hardly ever stop to think about Sophie's friends and how they must be feeling through all of this. I know they have their own grief but I am not the right person to help. I'm drowning in a sea of grief while they're being sprayed by seafoam. Helping them doesn't respect either of our pain.

It's midnight. The time is getting closer but it is not quite here. I call Luca from my bed. The only light in the room now is the glow of my screen.

"Sorry to call so late." I need to line up the pieces.

"Zara. I meant what I said. Anytime you want." There is just the sound of his breath on the line. The softness in his voice makes me think that I have woken him up. But I have to go on. "How are you doing?" he says. I picture him shifting around in his bed and sitting up against a soft headboard.

"Can't sleep. And you?"

"Ha," he says. "Well, I *was* asleep, if I'm honest."

"I'm so sorry."

"It's okay. I tend to wake up at some point in the night anyway."

I lie on my side and put the phone on to speaker. "Can you tell me about your day?" I ask him.

"Only if you try and sleep, as I tell you."

"Deal," I say softly, and shut my eyes.

WHEN I NEXT check my phone it's jumped to six in the morning. The call lasted an hour before he hung up. It's not long enough. Tonight, I'll have to think of something else. I go into Sophie's room. The windows are becoming lucent but the light is low enough in here to feel traces of spirit life. Sophie's been in here. I know it. I unfurl the small butterfly sketch and lie back on the bed with it pressed against my chest.

I am coming for you, my heart, my blood. Mum's coming.

BEFORE LUNCH, I watch the videos again and again for an hour, with the pistol in my lap. I follow the steps over and over until I can feel my way to each moving part without looking down. By the time I finish practicing it's well into the afternoon. My wrists and forearms throb with the exercise.

Later, when it is dark and I cannot be seen, I'll take it into the garden and fire a shot into the grass to make sure it works.

A spike of hunger surprises me and I realize that I haven't eaten since yesterday. I have to eat to make sure I am up to this tomorrow. If I have to force down a meal, I'll force it down. I have the lamb in the fridge, but the thought of it, brutalized, turns my stomach.

Instead I order an Indian takeaway on an app on my phone. By pressing "order again," I know that twice as much food will arrive as I need but I don't care. I just need something in my life to be easy. And then I sit on the sofa and call Harry. I want to know what he said to Emily. And I still want to know why he lied to me about Holly.

He doesn't answer. I wait fifteen minutes and try again without luck.

The knocker goes—they're usually longer than this. I open the door.

"Sadia," I say, irritated. I don't know what I have done to encourage her.

She shows me her small open hand in greeting. "Just checking in."

"Oh," I say, forcing a smile. "No need. I'm fine."

"Can I come in for a second?" she says, stepping up and into the doorway. I hesitate and then lead her to the kitchen and we sit at the bar. "How are you feeling?"

"You mean since the last time I saw you?" I ask. I try to catch the bitterness in my voice but some of it slips through.

She smiles. "I know. But I'd rather check and not need to than not check and wish I had."

I offer her a drink and she accepts a glass of water. "I'm feeling better today. Better than last time."

"And what do you think accounts for that change?"

This tone that she is using with me irritates me and now I can't keep a lid on it. "Can you just talk to me like a person and not a doctor? Like a friend?"

The smile drops from her face. "Sorry. I don't know how to be here for you right now. You're in the kind of pain I've never known and it hurts me to see it. I want to tell you that you'll find a way to get through this. No," she says, catching herself. "What I want to say is that you *will* find Sophie. She is out there, somewhere." And then she goes quiet, into almost a whisper. "But I can't because that is too cruel."

And when she says that everything stops. What if Sophie is there somewhere? Somewhere else, I mean, and what if I'm about to destroy our chance of a life together?

"Stay for dinner. I've got way too much food coming."

She considers it for a moment and then calls her partner to let her know she will be late.

WE EAT THROUGH everything. I open a bottle of wine, which she refuses. For a moment there is only small talk. But then she does something with her expression that ignites a familiarity. And then we are straight back again into the swell of old friendship. Soon it's as if we had never dropped all those stitches. We talk about her and about people we know. We talk about her partner, Tejal. We talk about nothing. And I am grateful to be taken out of these shackles to be able to flee, if even only as far as Sadia and her beautiful, ordinary life.

IT IS LATE by the time she gets up to leave. The kitchen hangs with the scent of cardamom and curry leaves, and chilies and rice. I hug her tightly at the door. "Thank you for coming to see me. For *staying*."

"Don't be silly."

"No. I mean it. You made a difference to me today."

She smiles self-consciously and walks off neatly down the road. And all is well until I realize that her feet will take her in the direction of 210. The house will always be there. In the half-life of that thought, I know for a certainty that there is no light in my world while Herman exists in it.

I go to the bedroom and get the pistol. The weight is reassuring and terrifying. I replay the instructions in my head and load the cartridge. It takes no time at all. The rounds click into place. I switch off the kitchen light and open the bifold doors. I sit on the back step and feel the night's cool breeze on my cheek. The gun lies heavily in my lap. My eyes adjust to the light and soon I can make out the topography of the garden. There is a cherry tree directly ahead of me. To the left is the toolshed. Along the back wall are some climbing plants— jasmine and honeysuckle.

I take the gun and aim it at the foot of the tree. I don't want to damage the trunk at all. I look down the sights and flick off the safety catch. Then I press the trigger. There is a small click indicating the first trigger position. I hold still and then press. The gun makes a sound like a cracked branch, which is followed simultaneously by the soft sound of lead spitting into soil. I'm stunned at how easy it is. The smell of cordite flares and then dissipates.

Soon. Next week, maybe, or the week after, I'll do the only thing that makes sense of my life. There is no clever or complex or sophisticated way of understanding something as simple as this. I can't live without my baby girl. I can't survive without my heart. I'm not just withering here—decaying in a soft, gentle death. I'm exploding in pain.

I call Harry late, when I am in bed, and he answers. I tell him about the aching misery. About everything that is inside, consuming me. And he listens. In silence. Finally, after an hour of me talking, wringing the nerve-burning pain out of my body, he speaks.

"I wrote a long email to you, but couldn't send it. So, it's sitting there."

He pauses then, as if waiting for me to speak. But I can't speak. And he can't speak. And I know finally how it has been destroying him too. His inability to express it wasn't an absence of emotion. It was a surfeit of it.

SIXTY

HARRY

When Zara called, I was so close to telling her, but I couldn't. Instead I wrote her an email that I didn't send. All I could tell her was how much I loved her.

The alarm sounds at five and feels as though it went off as soon as I shut my eyes. I wake and dress as silently as I can in cargo pants and a warm hoodie. The pants have long, deep pockets.

I am at the front door when I have an urge to go back in. At Katya's door, I pause and put my ear to the wood. Of course the room beyond is going to be in silence, but I listen anyway. As I do, I get the overwhelming sense that Katya's dead. That in the night she's done something to herself, or done nothing but that she's stopped living nonetheless. I turn the handle and put my face into the gloom. The thin red curtains make a *Black on Maroon* against the window—a painting I saw once in a gallery. It infuses the room with silence. I stare at her swaddled form and look for the rise and fall of her breath, but at this distance I can't see it. I step closer until I am an arm's length away from her. Her eyes are tightly shut like a child's and her body is curled into a ball. I wait for the breath and finally it comes. I turn to go, satisfied, when I see under her chin, the frog that I gave her. S—'s frog. Robbit.

My eyes are wet when I get into the car, and continue to stream until I am almost there. I don't know what has caused it exactly but I feel it as determination now in my bones. I trace out the exact route I'm going to take. I check for cameras. I check the Sainsbury's car park again. And when I stop and park I make a note of the mileage and the time it's taken me. It's not exact but it'll give me a rough approximation of how long it will all take.

BACK AT THE flat, Katya is at the kitchen table with brightly colored tarot cards laid out. Her phone is on loudspeaker and I see that she is doing a Zoom reading. I step into my bedroom and wait for her to finish. A few minutes later she knocks on the door.

"Sorry."

"Don't be sorry," I say. "I said you could work from here and I meant it."

She hovers in the doorway unaware that her perfume is swaying into the room, warm and heady. "We can do the seven rings of Jamshaid, if you like?" she says, eyes flashing.

"Sure," I say, even though the time seems to have passed for anything to come out of it.

"Okay. Come into my room in fifteen minutes. I have to get into the correct state." She stops. "You're okay to do this? To follow guidance of the reading?"

I shrug. "I think so. I won't know until I know what it's guiding me to do."

WHEN I GO into her room, she is sitting cross-legged on the bed. In her hands is a tarnished pewter cup. I count seven ridges circling it like bangles.

She breathes heavily. "Look, if we are doing this scrying—it is called scrying—then you have to be aware of risks."

"What risks?" I peer into the cup, which contains clear liquid.

She's lost for a moment and then recovers. "I did this once for myself. I did not accept the wisdom. It became very bad for me."

"Bad how?"

"Long story. But I ended here in this country. Alone. It cost me a lot of pain."

"Then maybe let's leave it," I say.

She flicks her eyes up at me. "Think carefully about it. If you are in two minds about this then perhaps better to leave it."

"Actually," I say. "Can you put the cup down for a second?"

She places the cup carefully on the bedside table.

"Remember I said I might need your help?"

She takes me in and it's as though she can see something has shifted. "What exactly do you need from me?"

"It might not make much sense, but you will have to stay awake tonight."

She tenses. "I don't understand."

"I know," I say. "But I can't tell you more than I can tell you."

She shuffles on the bed, agitated, like a trapped mammal. "Why should I help you?"

I run a hand through my hair to release some of the tension I am feeling. "Look. I don't believe in this spirit stuff. When I first saw you, every fiber of my being told me to walk away. Honestly, I still don't believe in any of it. But I do believe in you and in how you see things. And I think you more than anyone else know that sometimes you have to do the thing that makes the least sense. I need your help, Katya, but more than that, I need your faith."

She says nothing for some moments. Finally, just when I think she is about to make a bolt for it, she meets my eye. "What do I have to do?"

I explain it to her in detail, step by step. It's not difficult. But I can't do it without her.

"If I don't agree?" She asks this quietly, as if defeated.

"Then you don't agree. I can't force you and I wouldn't," I say. I let that sit. I know as a guest in my house, she feels obliged to help. But this has to come from her, freely. Her eyes search mine as if digging behind them for something. Finally, she nods.

"I'll wake you when it's time," I say.

"About having to leave—when does that happen?"

This is the hardest part by far. "Not immediately and not even definitely. But if in the next few days there's a night I don't come home, then you have to get out. Straight away. Ideally you need to be packed up now—ready to go."

She lights a cigarette and reaches over to open the window to blow out the smoke. "What are you doing, Harry?"

"The only thing I can."

SIXTY-ONE

NOW

OLD BAILEY
COURTROOM THREE

Last night I hardly slept at all. Sleep is an odd presence in my life. It comes dressed as a stranger, offering nothing and everything. When I fall asleep, even though all it does is extinguish the pain of wakefulness, that is everything. Two of the other inmates on the wing were shouting threats at each other through their cells. Then after midnight others started in an attempt to get them to shut up. By four, the arguing had spread across the whole landing. When they loaded me onto the van for court I hadn't had more than a couple of hours' broken sleep.

I look around the room I've been dropped into. These court cells are little more than strong rooms. There is nothing to see or touch or occupy yourself with.

Four walls. A small window too high to look out of. A heavy steel door. There is a thick rattle of keys and then a voice echoing behind to another voice some distance behind that.

"Legal," the woman says, and opens the door and leads me, un-cuffed, to a small conference room. Inside, my barrister, Nasreen Khan, is waiting with a smile. She's a well-preserved fifty. Beautiful, in a way. And formidable.

"How are you feeling, Zara?"

"Fine," I say, dropping into the seat opposite her. The walls are dirty cream over Victorian brick.

"Have you thought more about giving evidence? Any change of heart?"

"No."

"Even the best witness for us hasn't helped as much as we'd hoped." I think about Luca. He had no idea what he'd let himself in for by just being kind to me. "We've limited the damage but we still have that problem to deal with. That he couldn't be sure whether you were awake for the duration of the call. Or whether you were even on the other end of it."

I take a sharp breath, vexed by this. "But they have to prove their case—that's what you told me. They have to prove I wasn't on the call."

She sighs because she's explained this all before.

She laces her hands together. "You have time to decide. Harry is still giving evidence. But as soon as he's done, it's decision time."

"How do you think he's doing?"

Nasreen narrows her eyes. "For you? Not terrible so far. For him? Car crash." She sees my expression and then adds, "So far. He could recover. There's time," she says, and slides out of the room.

By the time I arrive in the dock, Harry is already there. He touches my arm when he sits down and I can sense how worried he is. His mouth is set in a firm line.

"Are you okay?" I ask him.

"I'm okay," he says to us both.

SIXTY-TWO

ZARA

THE SPLASH OF BRIGHT LIGHT THAT FLOODS THE ROOM WHEN I DRAW THE curtains fills me with memories. Moments like this creep up on me, where the past slams me in the chest when I least expect it.

This light, the particular color of it on the carpet, takes me to my own childhood. Lately all my memories have been of Sophie, so this catches me by surprise. I put my hand into the bright yellow patch and feel the sun like a stare. There are squares of pavement. I am perhaps six years old and I have my hand on the ground and I am trying to rescue a ladybug. It seems to have damaged a wing and is fluttering helplessly. A friend is crouching next to me, dabbing a finger at it too.

And now I remember the message that I sent to Luca M about Sophie loving ladybugs, and suddenly it makes sense, this apparently free-floating memory. They are still memories of Sophie. I'm not disconnecting from her after all. I open my laptop and suddenly what Harry said last night triggers something. He said he'd written me an email but couldn't send it. Couldn't. Not *didn't*. What did he mean?

We know each other's passwords. Not as a deliberate decision, but because he'd forget his or because we'd use the same passwords for

Netflix or Amazon. I log in to his account and scroll down to drafts. There are two emails there—unsent. I open the first. There is a page of text. All it says is I LOVE YOU over and over again, filling the page.

I compose an email too. I KNOW, I say, and leave that, too, unsent but hopefully not unsaid.

Then I open the second and as I read it, my heart drops into my stomach.

> I'm doing something tonight. Just know that I did it for you. For a chance of some peace. And for me. And of course, Sophie.

He's going tonight. I can't let that happen. I delete his emails. Then I call him. He doesn't answer and I can't leave the message I want to. "Call me, please, when you can," I say instead, casually. "Today, please."

I leave for the mosque. If there are last rites, I want to be able to say them. I have considered other words and rituals but Islam is the only mystical world I have any experience with. I'm not religious. I'm not a practicing Muslim but I am dyed in its colors. When I get there, it is empty. The space is cavernous. It didn't seem this big for Sophie's party. Cleared of people and furniture, the wide space makes me shift a little on my axis. The huge open floors send me back somewhere far away.

The imam, Shafi, is a young man. There's no shouting or waving of hands in the Friday prayer from what I remember of the few I have attended here. And now when he meets me in his small office, he looks into my eyes unselfconsciously and smiles.

"Come in," he says, and offers me a seat. "Or we can speak in the prayer hall if you like?"

I sit down and the smell of attar takes me back to Eid days as a child. Dad would return from the mosque smelling of incense. He wasn't religious either but went on Eid, and when he came back he would be smiling from ear to ear as if he'd been received by the queen.

"When someone is about to die, Imam, is there a special thing you can say?"

"If you know you are about to die, it is common to recite *sha-hada*." I nod. I know the declaration of faith.

"If you learn that someone has died, it is recommended to say *inna lillahi wa inna ilayhi raji'un*."

"I don't know this one," I say, and flush from the shame of my ignorance.

"Indeed, we belong to Allah. Indeed, to Him will we return." He recites it then in Arabic, melodically. In the quiet of that moment my eyes begin to spill tears. "And what if we didn't say it. And we didn't know if they were even alive or not?"

"Then we may say it now," he says, and then in the same melody he recites it again, slowly, recursively, until my skin shivers from it.

THE WALK HOME dissipates some of the energy I have gathered around me, but it is only when I am at the door that the fear leaves completely. There isn't room for it anymore. There are things to do. I have to pray.

I have to get ready.

The gun now feels like a comforting thing in my hand. The weight isn't oppressive when you get to know it, when you befriend it. I check that it is loaded. I only need the one round in the clip but I put in two in case. I make sure the safety is on and I leave it on the chest of drawers, the barrel pointing toward the wall. I open the top drawer where Harry keeps his socks. A few are gone but it still bulges with balled pairs. I take two pairs for later. When I walk past the gun I give it a wide berth, as though it is giving off an electric charge. In a way, it is.

I make my preparations and then sit under the hot shower until whatever I can feel has been drummed away to nothing.

As I am getting ready for bed, Harry sends a message.

> Sorry. Just got your message. Will pop round tomorrow to see you.

He's coming tomorrow? What does that mean for tonight—was I wrong about that? If something was happening tonight, surely he wouldn't be coming here tomorrow?

I have to keep to the plan and that thought alone is enough to get my heart racing. I go to the bathroom and take the last two Valium with tap water from a cupped hand. Then I crawl into bed while the buzz is still strong enough to get me to sleep. In the darkness of the room, I set the alarm for midnight and shut my eyes. The drugs pull me quickly into slumber.

And then in what feels like seconds, when the alarm sounds, I am jumping back into my life.

I call Luca for what I think will be the last time. When he answers, I say to him, "Tell me a story, Luca. A really long one. It doesn't have to be about anything. Just keep going. Keep going until you fall asleep."

"Until *I* fall asleep? Not you?"

"Yes," I say. "Till you fall asleep. If I wake, I like to hear you still on the line."

I put the phone on mute and then switch on the bedside lamp. In the soft light, I pad to the chest and pick up the gun. I check the safety.

I go to the bathroom and hang my clothes carefully on the door hook, avoiding the carrier bags that line the floor. A can of WD-40 is in my hand. I spray a little into the barrel.

I'm ready. And then, with the faint sound of Luca on loudspeaker, I leave the room behind.

SIXTY-THREE

HARRY

I STEP INTO THE STREET IN MY NEW OLD CLOTHES.

I woke Katya half an hour ago and made her repeat the instructions to me again when I caught her looking at the pewter cup on her bedside table. "Katya. This is important. You have to do it exactly as I'm saying. Please."

She nodded solemnly, rubbing sleep from her eyes. "Okay. When will you be back?"

"As soon as I can."

From the pavement, I look at the light filtering through the curtains into the darkness out here. The street is deserted but still I pull the brim of my trilby down over my eyes so my face isn't showing. I took a look at myself before I left and I know that if I walked into myself in the street now, I wouldn't recognize me. The stagey beige raincoat and the hat. Anywhere but London, I'd stand out. But here, I'm just another stone in a broken rubble landscape.

I have to do this now. Zara rang me earlier asking me to call her and there was something in her voice that frightened me. Her voice sounded like it was coming from a person made of glass. Before I went to bed I logged in to my email account and saw one email in drafts. Just one—not the two I had left. I opened it and saw it was from Zara. I KNOW, she had written. And I understood then why she sounded so desperate in her voicemail. She guessed I was going to 210 tonight.

I deleted her email and then sent her a text telling her that I'd pop round to see her tomorrow. I hope now that that is enough to persuade her that nothing is happening tonight, if that's what she is thinking. If so, by the time she finds out that I haven't turned up to see her, it will be too late.

I drive to a street near Tower Bridge. I get out and call my smartphone from the unregistered burner phone in my hand. When Katya answers it, I wipe down the handset and drop it into a bush—the call still live. Then I return to the car and drive to Vauxhall. There are no traffic cameras along this route but I keep my eyes peeled as I drive just in case. There are ANPR cameras on some roads but not the ones I have chosen. I keep my foot light on the pedal because there are still speed cameras.

I park and get out. The night air has a taste of rain, which is cool on the tongue. I am about a ten-minute bus ride from Clandon Road—home—but I can't risk getting on a bus with their CCTV. It has to be a run. But first I need to make a stop.

I shove the coat and hat into my rucksack and pull the straps tight. I walk quickly to the twenty-four-hour petrol station and buy some cigarettes and lighter fuel for my ancient Zippo, in cash. I haven't smoked in years, but I automatically rip off the cellophane and whip away the silver paper. The scent of paper and tobacco releases a memory I never knew I'd kept. I fill the Zippo and light a cigarette. The smoke hits my throat hard, making my head spin. How hard it was to stop—how easy to start again.

I double back to the car in a jog. I drop the cigarettes on the seat and lock up. Then I run. I haven't been keeping up my fitness so it takes time to get up a rhythm. But soon I am pounding the pavement steadily. My breath comes in heavy and leaves with a sting. I have on my Rolex for luck. I check it—it's 1:09 A.M. I can be there in fifteen minutes.

I go through what I need to do. I have done this so many times in my head that it feels like muscle memory. At one point as I am waiting to cross the road I have a flutter of panic. Not about the physical act but about the morality of it. What if I am wrong? What if he's just a despicable old man but nothing more? And then I remember the fragments of videotape.

I know what I saw on them. And those words he spat out have followed me around for days now. *You'll never find 'em in a hundred years.* The same as the message he must have sent Emily. I know S— never sent that text. She didn't talk like that. That was him, Herman. He took her. When I think about it like this, the truth is inescapable. He took her. And I can't stand by.

When I am no more than six or seven minutes away I hear or feel a noise behind me. I don't turn but I feel sure that it's the sound of someone following me. When I stop, he or she stops. At the next junction, I pause as if to catch my breath. I turn casually so that I can have eyes on whoever it is. I'm right. It is someone following me, dressed in a windbreaker with the hood up so it's hard to tell their gender. I turn back around, and moments later they stop next to me. Something tells me that they are going to engage me in conversation so I decide to run on. The sound of a bell, and a hurtling cyclist knocks me off my feet. My shoulder burns. The person who was following me kneels to help me up. It's a middle-aged woman. I don't want to be remembered so I thank her quietly without meeting her eye. "I'm okay," I say. "Thanks. Think I'll head home now." I turn back the other way and run until I'm sure she's gone. Then I cut down along a parallel path that brings me back on track.

This alternative route has thrown me. I know the road but it's not in my memory the way the old route is. Halfway down the street, a car pulls onto the pavement and parks. I stop in panic. I don't want to be seen or noted by anyone at all. But if I look back now it will be suspicious. So, I carry on, head turned back as I pass the driver's door, as if I am looking for something—just so that I am not seen.

I zigzag through the roads. I hear the sound of scuffling and knocked bottles. At the end of the road I hear, then see, urban foxes playing. And then a yelp sends my heart racing. I calm myself. But now lights are coming on in some of the houses and curtains twitching to see about the noise. I quickly turn back.

At the top of the road I veer back to join the old route. A few minutes later I arrive at the bottom of the street that runs along the rear of Herman's house, my skin prickling with sweat. I quickly put on the tan raincoat and take out the hat. I roll the waterproof trousers over my jeans and change out of my sneakers and into the wellies. I pull on the leather gloves as I walk silently up the road.

A few houses away from the block of flats, a security light flares on. I curse myself. These proximity lights are always going off on my road. I should have known to stay closer to the road edge.

I walk on. Seeing the flats there, the gateway, really, to Herman's house, brings me back to myself.

It's time.

I have to get through that door again without triggering this floodlight. I'm not passing by here. If the light comes on and someone looks, I'll be there to be seen.

The floodlight is only a problem if the light can be seen. I sidle tight against the wall until I am standing directly underneath the lamp. Thankfully it's not high—maybe eight feet up. I take the hat and reach up and with a jump, hook it over the lamp. The bulb flares but is immediately smothered by the dark felt. I step out from underneath and in the safety of the dampened light, I jump again, to push the hat firmly onto the lamp so that it is snug against the fitting. Now that the light is stifled by the hat, I can approach the wooden gate and fence more slowly. It stands a little over six feet high. I could scramble noisily over it but I'm nervous of the attention that might bring.

And just then a car alarm sounds and I freeze as the sound shatters the night. Shit. I crouch into a ball and wait by the bins for what seems like an eternity. Then the sound of an opening door. The two blips of a reset and finally the air is soft and silent again.

I wait a few minutes and then step back out. I gently lower the lightest of the wheelie bins on its side to the ground, flush against the fence. It will give me just enough height to get over the fence without too much noise. When I stand on it, the bin shudders a little. My head is now clear of the fence, which means I can lever myself over with my hands. I make sure the straps of my backpack are tight, and then as quietly as I can, I vault over.

On the other side, the garden is in darkness. I wait until my eyes adjust and then check the windows to the block of flats. All are black.

No threads of white light peek out from behind curtains or blinds. I know from last time that there are no security lights at the back. I take a breath, get my bearings, and then I move.

I crawl forward, low until I reach Herman's fence. The new fence panel looks rigid and sturdy but there is still an old fence panel at the end that hasn't been replaced. I check for gaps between the panels before taking my claw hammer and prying the slats away. The old boards come off easily and in minutes I have a gap large enough to squeeze through. Once through, I wait for my heartbeat to steady. It's racing from the exertion and from the adrenaline, because I know what's coming next.

The dog.

I reach into my backpack and pull out the steaks I bought. I don't need her to be occupied for long, just long enough to get into the house. I strain an ear for any sound. There is nothing. The house is cloaked in silence. The garden too. The dog must be asleep. I edge slowly forward, crouch right down, meat in one hand, hammer in the other. She's going to wake any moment now. And then I have to be quick. I have to let her scent the meat, put it to her muzzle, and then I'll throw it into the bushes away from the kitchen door. While she is busy with her food, I'll tape up the window with the parcel tape and then knock it through with the hammer, tapping gently. That way the smashing glass won't make a sound and the shards won't scatter as they hit the floor. I'll reach in and open the door and then I'll go in.

Then I will find him.

I am now within feet of the kennel and the back door. My breath is the only sound that I can hear. I wait. The dog will wake soon. I want her to be roused naturally. I don't want to shock her and have her barking to raise the alarm. *Come on, girl,* I say to myself. *Dinner-time.*

I get to my haunches and peer into the kennel. For a terrible moment it occurs to me that she might be inside the house. If she is, that will be a disaster. I can't distract her with meat once I have become an intruder—an attacker—in her master's house. At that point I'm nothing but a target.

The soft edges of the kennel in the night slowly resolve themselves as my eyes adjust and readjust to the darkness. I peer in and think I can make out the sleeping form of a dog. I continue to watch the mound and wait for the telltale rise and fall of a living thing.

I check my watch. It is 1:31 A.M. I want to be in and out and back at the flat before 3:30—I need to beat the light.

I take a step forward. A twig snaps under the heel of my boot. I listen. I take a breath—the meat in my outstretched arm. It's time to wake the dog.

SIXTY-FOUR

ZARA

BLOOD!

I'm home at last.

The hot water rushes over my hands and sends washes of red swirling down the drain. The more water there is, the more blood seems to appear. I roll back my sleeves to see blood in streaks all the way up to my elbows. I peel off my clothes and let them drop. As they hit the floor, I hear the heavy clump of steel striking tile. The gun, I remember with a jolt of panic. The loaded gun is in my pocket. I slide the jeans away to one side and stand on the carrier bags I've left here. My heart is hammering.

I run the shower and sit under the stream, letting the water run over me in hot needles. More blood snakes in rivulets toward the plughole. I never expected so much of it to stick to me. My gut clenches and I am doubled over, throwing up bile onto the shower tray.

Behind shut eyes all I can see is the side of his bloodless, lifeless face. His jaw slack, lips cracked and speckled with something creamy.

He's dead.

Herman is dead.

In the depths of my rational brain I know that there's a lot still to do. Every inch of my body has to be scrubbed. I can't risk the most minute speck. I wash my hair twice. Finally, when my skin has become wrinkled and tender with washing, I crawl out of the shower and wrap myself in a towel and rub myself dry. The clothes I need to change into are hanging off the door. I dress and then from my pockets I take out the socks. I put one pair on and separate the other pair, a hand in each one like a mitten.

I kneel down to fish the gun out of my jeans and then, just as I have been practicing, I put on the safety catch, release the cartridge, and remove the barrel assembly. The socks on my hands make it clumsy but not too hard. Then, still in socked hands, I wipe every part down quickly before spraying it with the WD-40. I remember the wooden carry case with the other bullets in it and retrieve it from the bedroom. I put the gun and the bullets into one bag and the empty gun case into another. I have to get this done soon. Five A.M. is my deadline. The worn jeans, sweatshirt, pants, and bra go into another carrier. These, together with the gun case, are going into a green bin on the street. I check the time on the bathroom clock. It is almost 2:45 A.M. The refuse collection lorries will arrive in just over two hours. The police won't come before that. They won't come today at all unless I'm very, very unlucky.

I make my way down the stairs and see Harry's chef's knife, still in the carrier bag on the mat by the front door where I dropped it. I take it quickly to the sink and run dish soap and hot water over it before wrapping it in its tea towel again.

As soon as I have done that, I remember something else and run up the stairs to get it. I put it into a Jiffy bag, and in the kitchen, I scribble a short note and slide it inside as well. In the drawers I hunt for stamps, and when I find them I put the entire remaining sleeve on the envelope and write the address.

Then I am out the door. I use my key to turn the lock so the door shuts softly. I deposit the clothes and the extra carrier bag with the knife into a green bin a few doors down. I take the other bag with the gun and rounds with me.

I walk as fast as I can to the high street. The entire walk there, my heart is tripping at a dizzying rate. I find the postbox. The street is, thankfully, deserted. I check both ways and empty the gun and ammunition through the slot.

The carrier bag I put into a dog-litter bin nearby.

Ten minutes later I am back home. But I walk straight past my door to the postbox at the top of the road and drop in the Jiffy bag.

When I get back, I pick the ladder up from the foot of my hedge and dump it in the back garden.

My phone! I haven't checked my phone!

I race up to the bedroom to find it where I left it, on my pillow, a few hours ago, on loudspeaker. I pick it up expecting the home screen to light up. It doesn't. And my heart catches in my throat.

Shit. It's out of power. I check the cable and see that the connection to the plug is loose. At some point in the night it must have run out of power and shut itself down. I push the connector into the plug and beg the light to come on. The dark screen stares back at me with just a battery symbol with a line of red. *Come on! Come on. Come on. Come on!*

SIXTY-FIVE

HARRY

HE'S DEAD. I CHECK THE TIME. GOOD. IT'S STILL ONLY 2:25 A.M. I retrace the last five minutes and don't think I have missed anything. On my way out, unlatching the gate, I remember the hat and jump up for it. The light blazes for a few seconds, and by the time it has turned off I am halfway down the road. I slow to a quick walk and roll the raincoat into my backpack as casually as I can. At the bottom of the road, I shield behind a van and take off my waterproof trousers and wellies and bundle them into the bag. The gloves come off last, carefully, thickened as they are, in places, with blood. I drop them into the paper bag that I got when I bought the hammer and put the bag into the top of the backpack. Then with my sneakers on, I run.

My heart hammers all the way to the car. I cannot distinguish between terror and exertion.

I have to be quick. I drive to the nearby Sainsbury's lot and park in the same dark corner as before, where I know there are no cameras. I empty the clothes from the bag into the recycling skip. I pull away what comes easily from the overflowing containers and make room for my stuff. Once I empty in the clothes, I am left with the hammer and the tape. I wipe the hammer down and put it into the boot. The tape I simply drop into a rubbish bin nearby. There is standing water at the foot of the plastics recycling bin. I stamp the backpack into it until it is soaked through and then wipe the knife down with it and toss them both into the large bins.

I head right into a dark corner of the deserted car park and place the paper bag containing the gloves on the tarmac. I pour lighter fuel over it, light it, and once it has taken, I stand and watch. It only takes a few minutes to burn them into a charred mess. The paper bag comes away in embers, floating into the air like tiny lanterns. I kick at them and see the surface of the leather is burned away. I pour on more fuel and relight it. There is no way, I am sure, that blood or DNA will survive that. If the police can even link them to me or to the murder.

I get back into the car and drive to the flat, careful to keep to the speed limit.

When I arrive, it is 3:01 by the clock in my car. I take the hammer out of the boot. There's nothing to worry about with that. There is nobody around, but I keep my head down in case. When I turn the front door key I do it quietly. The sitting room is lit, and just as I instructed Katya, the TV is on BBC One—loud. I sit on the arm of the chair and breathe out a long sigh.

"How was it?" I say, turning to Katya for the first time. There are tears in her eyes and I can't quite puzzle out what's happened. The hammer is still in my hand. Is that frightening her?

"Katya, what's wrong?"

She wipes her eyes but they are still streaming. I look around for clues. Has she phoned the police? Is she injured? What has happened? On the table is the ringed pewter cup. Next to it is my phone. And then I see what's happened. The screen.

My blood runs cold. "Katya. Tell me you did what I asked you to."

"I'm sorry," she says.

I reach down to pick it up. I check it and see that the call from the burner phone ended about an hour ago. So up until an hour ago everything was as arranged. I immediately access my banking app.

"When did you stop?" My voice, shrill.

"Nearly an hour. I'm not sure. I'm sorry." Her face is red with crying. She *is* sorry. I just can't understand why she changed her mind.

"Fuck," I say, and check the call history. The last call she made ended at 2:17.

"Katya. Fucking hell. This is serious. Shit. You have no idea what you've done."

Quickly, I run the bath and I sign in to Twitter and like some tweets from a few people I follow as I wait for the tub to fill. The water swallows my face as I dip beneath the surface. I replay everything that happened. It was all going to plan. I'd thought of everything. I thought I had. But I hadn't counted on Katya doing this. Of course, there was always the chance that she might refuse. But at least if she had refused I could have considered my options. Or reconsidered altogether.

And then I remind myself that if I'd told her what was going on, she wouldn't have done it. But I couldn't tell her. I still can't—it's too risky.

Forty-seven dead minutes before my phone logged back in to my banking app. It might just be good enough. But at this time of night it's a fifteen-minute drive and there would be just enough time to get there and back. I wash carefully and then get dressed. Katya is at the table when I walk into the kitchen, her back to me. Before her sit two cups of coffee. I take one of them.

"I've checked the phone usage. The earlier part of the night is fine. But Katya—I told you how crucial it was—" I begin, but then when I see her eyes brimming, I stop. "What happened?"

"I'm sorry," she says. "It was the cup of Jamshaid. After the first hour when you didn't come back I began to worry. So I decided to scry." She dabs her eyes with the back of her hand.

"What?" I say, holding on to my temper. I can't let this situation fly out of my control. I still need her. My alibi is still salvageable as long as Katya remains onside. I can't afford to alienate her in any way. If she ever goes to the police I am finished.

"I'd seen danger in the cards before. And what am I supposed to think, Harry? You disappeared in the middle of the night and leave me with all these crazy instructions," she says. Her eyes are red but the tears have stopped. "I thought you were dead."

"Okay," I say. "And the cup told you what?"

"Don't you dare, Harry. Don't you dare ridicule me. This is serious. I saw in the cup what was happening. It was not telling me you were in trouble. It was telling me I was too. And I saw death." She stares at me, waiting for me to contradict her. "It told me to run from you. You are using me."

"But you stayed."

"Tell me I'm not in any danger." Her eyes are like flames.

"You're not in any danger." I crouch down in front of her. "I promise."

After a minute she swallows some coffee. "What did you do?"

"I'm sorry for all this. I wish I could tell you more but I have to protect you. And you're right. I have used you. But," I say, "I honestly have tried to keep you from any danger and there's no reason for you to be in any trouble at all." I check my watch. It's 3:55. "I need a final favor. You can say no."

"Of course. I can say no. But I can't say no, can I?"

"I wouldn't ask if there was another way."

"What is it?"

"At five A.M. I need you to call this number from a pay phone at least a mile away and read this to them. Exactly as it is on the paper," I say, sliding over the note.

She reads it and then agrees.

"The police might come and arrest me. I don't think they'll come today, because nobody has this address but Zara. But if I don't make it home tomorrow night or any other night, there is a good chance that they've arrested me. If and when they do, I'll wait at least twenty-four hours before I give them this address. But as soon as I do, they will come and search it. When they do that, you can't be here. Everything you have has to be gone. Use the lockup if you have to."

I hand her an envelope with money in it. "For the hotel. At least a week, okay? Pick a bed-and-breakfast somewhere away from here."

She takes it silently and folds it into her jeans pocket. "I don't want you to be arrested."

"I don't either. And it may not happen. But it might. It's just a contingency plan." I slip off my watch and give that to her too. "If you have to pawn it, pawn it. You'll get a couple of thousand, minimum."

She shakes her head and begins to protest.

"Take it. Just don't lose the pawn slip. I'd like to get it back one day."

I CRAWL INTO bed and my mind inevitably circles round to Zara. All I wanted for her was peace but I think I've given her anything but.

SIXTY-SIX

ZARA

My solicitor is here next to me in the interview room. The last week passed by in a slow haze. I felt like a mosquito being gradually solidified in amber. The last few days I was desperate for something to shift—to happen—to move this all along. I was already paralyzed from Sophie's absence. Another kind of stasis was just too much to stand. When they came to arrest me, it was a genuine relief.

My solicitor has told the police that we are ready, but I don't feel ready. I'd been sitting alone in a cell for nearly six hours when the duty solicitor, Suzy Reive, finally arrived. She only asked me a few questions and then gave me advice I only half understood.

"I advise we do a prepared statement. There's too much evidence to get through and advise you about. You could go straight to saying 'no comment,' but that never plays well in murder cases."

"What's a prepared statement?"

"Well—it's kind of a halfway house. You put your case fair and square on record but you don't answer any questions about the statement or anything else. They'll carry on asking questions but you say 'no comment' to every one."

The interview room is lit but the walls are dark, giving it the air of a recording studio. There are two plainclothes officers here and when they look at me, it is not without sympathy. Their expression seems to tell me that they regret having me here at all. They are both women, and that is a surprise, although it shouldn't be.

The interview starts and I'm cautioned. Those words, "You do not have to say anything but it may harm your defense if . . ." when they are said, set my heart racing so fast that I feel faint. My palms become cold and clammy and a feeling of doom comes over me. I think I might die right here in this room.

"Are you okay?" Suzy asks with genuine concern. I can smell flowers in her hair. At home, with her children, or preparing food, or at the school gates, Suzy would be easy and in control. She'd be the person that people trusted their secrets to. She'd give her advice, seriously, pragmatically. I trust her.

"Yes," I say.

"You sure?" she says, leaning in farther and squeezing my forearm. "Do you want to take a minute?"

"No. Let's get this over with, please."

Suzy holds a sheet of paper in front of her and reads out loud. "On behalf of my client, I would like to thank you for the formal disclosure. On that basis I have prepared a statement for Mrs. King, which she has signed.

"I, Zara King, wish to state that I am not guilty of the murder of Jonathan Herman. I know Mr. Herman lived on the same road as we do. I did not see him on the night of the murder and I was at home, alone, the entire night, leaving only after six the next morning. I have been told by my solicitor that the disclosure puts the murder as having taken place between one A.M. and four A.M. I do not have a clear recollection of what exactly I did minute to minute but I was at home asleep in my own bed. I may have used my phone somewhere around that time and I am happy to provide the police with the PIN for my telephone in order to investigate further."

One of the police officers starts speaking. For a second all I can concentrate on is her hair and face, which are graying in the same way. She has lips like string and eyes like buttons. She takes the prepared statement.

"I'll give you a copy at the end. We do have questions arising out of that if you'd like to help us with those. Do you have any kind of alibi for the night in question? Anyone who can verify where you were?"

Suzy makes a note and then says, "I have advised my client not to answer any further questions but have made her aware that you may ask them anyway."

THE INTERVIEW LASTS about an hour. The gray one, DS Shelly, asks every one of around a hundred questions that are set out on several sheets of paper. When we are done, I'm taken back to my cell. Suzy sits me down.

"They're going to charge you with murder. I'm sorry." The news drops like an anvil. But I have been getting ready for this possibility for the last week. The only surprise is that it took them this long to arrest me. If it wasn't for the dog barking the day after and the neighbors calling social services, it might have been even longer.

"Do I have to stay here till then?"

"The police could bail you to attend the magistrates' court tomorrow. I'll check in a minute."

"Okay," I say, and try to control my breathing.

"I'll get you a barrister but if the police don't bail you, you can't make a bail application until we are at the Crown Court. But I have to stress one thing. The chances of getting bail at the Crown Court are almost zero. It's a reverse burden. The presumption is very much against bail."

I nod, taking in as much as I can, but most of it is water pouring through my fingers. "How long will it be before there's a trial?"

"Honestly? About a year. Could be longer."

A year—said so casually it feels like nothing. But a year away from being able to look for Sophie hits me hard. I know it's a fantasy but I can't let go of it yet.

"And till then where will I be living?"

"In a women's prison. Bronzefield, probably—in Surrey."

Tears begin to fall. It's not the prospect of being in a prison. Of course, I don't want to be in a prison for a year. I don't want to be anywhere. I'm already in a prison. But Sophie.

"Thanks, Suzy," I say, wiping my face dry. I let her go. She has been looking at her watch and must be needed elsewhere. There are people she can actually help.

"I'll go and check whether the police are willing to bail you. You never know."

I wait. Everything and nothing go through my mind. All of it is crucial and yet, to me, none of it matters.

Half an hour later Suzy appears at the cell door. "No luck with bail. Sorry. I'll instruct a barrister to attend court tomorrow. And I'll try and make sure the same one comes along for every hearing after that. Once the evidence is served we can sit down and go through it all. I promise. And I'll start looking for a K.C. straight away. The good ones get booked quickly."

When she is gone I lie back on the bunk and stare at the stains on the ceiling until they blur. There is a peace in knowing that he's dead. It's like the removal of a spear that's been lodged in my side. Every moment that he was alive, *being,* was another moment for him to drive the pain home. And now there is a kind of relief. He died and I felt the lance being pulled clear, though the wound is still there. The wound will always be there, raw and ugly. Nothing can heal the things that he did to her. But I need her back now. I need her.

You'll never find 'em in a hundred years.

Then I'll bleed for a hundred years until I do.

SIXTY-SEVEN

HARRY

"Okay, okay. I get that. But what the prosecution was saying about Zara—are they really going to carry on a trial against her?"

My solicitor, Shah, clenches his beard in his fist. "Sometimes they do that shit to put pressure on the guy. Get him to plead guilty if they drop it against the wife or whatever."

"Did they say that to you, though? That if I plead to it, they'd drop it against her?"

"No. I can ask." He closes his laptop and stands up. "Off the record. And I'll let you know."

"Okay. Thanks, Shah."

He turns at the door. "Sorry about bail."

"It's okay. I was expecting it." I want to keep him here for a little longer. If I can talk about Zara to someone, she feels near again. "I really thought Zara might have been here today in court, though."

"No, they don't list your cases together for bail applications. Next hearing she's going to be there. If they've sorted out joinder by then."

"What's joinder?"

"Don't worry about it. It's a technical kind of thing. It's when they put you on one indictment together. Like on the same charge sheet."

"Why would they do that?" I ask, surprised.

His eyes narrow. "So they can try you both together. At the same time."

"What—in the *same* trial?"

"'Course. Why wouldn't they? It's the same evidence. Except they also got you on the criminal damage for the break-in when you smashed your way in before."

I scratch my head because I haven't understood something here. "When you say they're going to try us together, what exactly do you mean? Are they saying we did it together?"

He steps fully back into the room. "Yes. A joint enterprise. If you're in it together, it's a joint enterprise."

"But how can we both have killed him with one stab wound?"

"Oh. Okay," he says, and sits back down on the bench next to me. "You know, like a bank robbery—like an armed robbery? One does the actual robbing and one does the getaway car? Well, they're both guilty of the robbery. They've got different roles, but both are guilty of armed robbery."

I try to unpack this. "So, they're trying to say we did it together?"

"They haven't said nothing yet. But yeah. Theoretically that is what they could be saying. Can't see any other reason for you to be on together, for one murder."

"Maybe they're saying only one of us did it, but they don't know which?"

He shakes his head. "Nah. Doesn't work like that. They can't have their cake and eat it too. If they do charge her as well, it will definitely be as a joint enterprise. Likely they will say you planned it together."

My stomach lurches and suddenly I think I'm going to be sick. I wait for the nausea to subside. "How can they prove that? We weren't even living in the same place at the time. And there's no phone calls or texts or anything else between us. There is no *planning*."

Shah scratches his beard again. "We'll see when they serve the evidence what they're saying exactly. But even circumstantial is good enough. Look. I'll be in to see you next week at the prison— Belmarsh. We can discuss it more then. I got an important client I need to see now, though. Sorry."

"Shah," I say, getting up. "Ask them, please. If I plead guilty will they drop it against her?"

They can't prosecute Zara. Please God. Don't let them prosecute her.

I have spent five days away. Almost two of those days were taken up with the arrest and the interviews, and the remainder have been on remand. I was taken straight from the magistrates' court to the prison, and apart from this morning's outing to the Central Criminal Court—the Old Bailey—I have been on twenty-three-hour "bang-up." Twenty-three hours a day in my cell—sometimes longer than that when they don't have the manpower.

I'm currently on the induction wing. Induction will take up another five weeks. And after that I have no idea where I'll be shipped out to.

I don't want Zara to have to go through any version of this. It's why I moved out of our home, to create some distance between us. So they wouldn't tie her into this with me. That *was* my plan. It was *my* murder.

I sit back on the bunk and run through the events in my head. The more I consider it the more confused I am that they even arrested Zara. What evidence did they have that she had anything to do with it?

The evidence they've served against me so far is pretty weak. It's more supposition and guesswork than anything else. And that earlier incident, when I'd broken down his door, that's the thing they seem to be harping on about. That's their big play, evidence-wise, but I can deal with all of that. As far as they can prove, that was the start and end of it for me. Nothing else they've shown me even puts me at the scene. I was very careful. I think I can beat this charge as long as I hold my nerve.

But they don't play fair. For example, they told me they'd arrested Zara when they were interviewing me. They let that information slip so that I'd lose my footing. And I did. But since then I've held firm. Haven't given them anything at all. So now they're going to try using her against me. Because they *know* I won't let her be tried for this. They know I'll plead guilty before that happens.

I need to talk to her but that is impossible. What I want to say to her I have to say in private. That I will plead guilty if they drop it against her. But that if they don't agree, I need her to hold tight. We have a good chance here. That they're only prosecuting her to get me to plead. There isn't enough to get me for this and there's even less on her. I *will* get a not guilty verdict. And she *will* get a not guilty verdict. I'm as confident as I can be. As long as we hold firm. We just can't be the first to blink.

And then I think about Zara. A woman who is defined, for me, by her kindness. She doesn't move in the world like these people in here with me. And even though she feels that the world doesn't hold a place for her anymore, I know that she can find her way through all the smoke and come out at the other end. I need her to. I have to be able to believe in some things too. And that is where I have to leave my hope—in her ability, not just to survive but to *emerge*.

SIXTY-EIGHT

ZARA

I'VE BEEN HERE FOR SIX MONTHS NOW. THE DAYS ARE WEEKS IN HERE AND the weeks are months. I sit with my back against the painted breeze-block and try to get my head into the papers that the Crown Prosecution Service have served. The words swim on the page so I close my eyes and lie down. The clatter and clang of doors assaults me from both sides as inmates leave to have their visits.

I hate this place.

Every day brings a streak so dark that I can see it even in my pitch-black world. Outside, before prison, I moved in a predictable world, riding my grief on tramlines, safely, away from danger. Here I don't have the luxury of sadness. Yesterday, during "association," a woman walked past and kicked my feet. I looked up and she snarled at me, "What you looking at, dickhead?" I put my head down and waited for her to leave. But she didn't. Instead she pushed me off my chair and laughed as I scattered onto the floor.

I can't stand the other women. They talk in rhythms and tones I don't recognize. They clamor and shout all the time. The din reverberates through the landing at all hours. When I close my eyes at night, even when the wing is quiet, the noise rages on in my head until morning arrives, heralded by the switching on of electric lights.

I turn the pages. The evidence is slippery, like mercury. I try to focus on it but it won't give me a fingerhold. When I read a witness statement, it feels it's going in one direction, but then always stops short of the final blow. Everything they've compiled has the sense of being *almost* there. When I spoke to Suzy, my solicitor, on the phone, she was confident but realistic. "There isn't any *direct* evidence that we can't account for. But it's the circumstantial evidence that is the problem here. The circumstances add up to make something bigger than the individual strands. I'll talk you through it when I come to see you."

She came in to see me the week after the papers arrived in a big brown package with the words "Rule 39" on it together with my prison number.

"Is it a problem?" I said to her. "The circumstantial evidence."

"It depends," she said seriously. "Some juries don't like circumstantial evidence. And you're a woman. Some juries don't like to convict women—not sympathetic ones like you."

And now I wonder how sympathetic I am and how much of the remnants are still going to be sticking to me by the time of my trial in six months.

My door bangs. A jangle of keys and one of the prison officers that everyone calls Dog comes in.

"Come on, then," she says, and then adds, "Visit."

"What?" I say, getting up, confused. "A legal?" Suzy told me she couldn't book another visit till the barrister was free. She wanted me to meet her properly, not for five minutes before court.

"What am I, your PA?"

I follow her along the landing and down the stairs to the visits hall. The room is full of prisoners and their families sitting in plastic chairs around small knee-high tables. The inmates wear orange tabards and sit separately from their visitors, who are arranged on one of three chairs opposite. I look around for anyone I might recognize but don't see a soul. I don't have family. Not here.

"Zara." I look up and see her.

"Sadia." I sit down in a daze. I hadn't expected her. But I should have. She's dressed neatly in smart trousers and a sweater. Her eyes land momentarily on my tabard before flicking away. I feel the shame rising through my cheeks.

"How did you know I was here?"

"I read about it in the local paper."

I nod, at a loss for what to say.

"Zara, is there anything I can do for you?"

"No. You've already done too much."

She reaches a hand out and clutches mine. "Money or clothes or—I don't know. Anything."

I smile at her kindness.

She coughs lightly. "I can't believe you're in here. And I don't believe you're capable of what they are saying about you. I know how depressed you were. I know the medication you were on. It's not consistent with violent behavior. If you need someone to say that—"

"It's okay. Thank you, I mean. But I can't talk about this. Do you mind—it's driving me—" I want to say insane but it sounds wrong to say that to a doctor.

"Of course. Sorry. There is another reason I came. Harry called me from prison."

My heart hammers. I haven't spoken to him in six months. Prison-to-prison calls aren't allowed. He writes to me every week. He tells me things like not to worry about the house, or that Caspar has picked up the mail. He also tells me he's worried about me and not to bother writing to him in reply. That the mail is all opened unless it's legal stuff. He's telling me to be careful.

"What did he say?"

"Nothing, really. He just wanted me to tell you that you'll be okay. He won't let anything happen to you. That was it."

I nod. There is nothing else to say.

The next few minutes are spent in small talk. "I check on the house from time to time. Once the police finished their search, it was pretty much back to normal."

"Thank you. You don't need to."

"I don't mind. Is there anyone I can contact if, you know, there's a problem?"

"No. Harry's brother has a key. I'm sure he can sort out any issues."

When the buzzer goes, everyone says their goodbyes. Some of the women cry. Others laugh. Sadia stands up. I do too.

She leans in to hug me, and before we can be noticed, she whispers in my ear. "I got the envelope. It's safe."

"Thank you," I say. I try to say something but she stops me.

"I don't need to know," she says.

"Thank you," I say again. "Someone will come for it."

SIXTY-NINE

NOW

OLD BAILEY
COURTROOM THREE

"Let me just ask you again, to give you the opportunity to change your mind if you want to, Mr. King. What were you doing on the night that Mr. Herman was murdered in his own home?"

"I was in my flat. In Whitechapel," I say again.

"Yes," he says, then without missing a beat opens the large file in front of him. "We examined your phone, as you know, and the cell-site analysis shows that your phone was in Whitechapel, but of course that doesn't mean that you were."

"I disagree," I say. "I was using my phone throughout the night. I couldn't sleep. It wasn't unusual for me to be up at random times through the night."

Alfred smiles. "Unless it wasn't you. Someone else could have been using your phone?"

"Like who?" I return quickly.

"You tell us, Mr. King. Two-bedroom flat. Who was it?"

"Using *my* phone? Me." I meet his eye and hold it until he looks away. But he isn't finished.

"You could have, particularly if you'd planned this murder, had someone there, babysitting your phone. Using it. Creating a false alibi. For instance, there was rather a long call from a pay-as-you-go sim. Who was that?"

"A mate."

"Are we going to be hearing from him?"

"Her. And no. Her husband doesn't know that she was on the phone to me."

"But just so we know there was a real person on the other end of that call with you, are you prepared to give us her name?"

"No."

"Perhaps you were out murdering Mr. Herman and someone—a *mate*," he says, emphasizing the word, "was using your phone. Making it appear that you were at home."

"I was on my banking app for some of the time. Did I give this imaginary person my banking PIN too?"

"If they were staying with you. And you trusted them enough to shore up an alibi, then why not?"

The jury waits for the answer. I have one but it's not a great one. "If I trusted them enough, then why wouldn't I call them to be the alibi—in person?"

"Maybe, Mr. King, her husband didn't know she was there."

I smile at the cheap trick. "No. I was in the flat alone. Using my phone. There was no other tenant. Check the tenancy."

He ignores me and turns a page. "There is a period of forty-seven minutes that is unaccounted for, where your phone wasn't being used. What were you doing?"

"I fell asleep."

"Convenient."

"It doesn't feel convenient from here. If I hadn't fallen asleep, I might not be on trial."

"Those forty-seven minutes also happen to coincide with the time that your wife can't account for her movements."

I glance over at Zara and she is looking straight down at the floor. I feel the jury follow my gaze.

"You'd have to ask her about that. I wasn't with her," I lie. They are so practiced in my head, these untruths, that to say anything else would feel more like a lie. I have steeped myself so deeply in them.

"But I'm asking *you*, Mr. King. You're the one in the witness box.

Both of you were unaccounted for at a time consistent with Mr. Herman's estimated time of death."

I remember the report and am relieved that I read all the case papers over and over.

"The pathologist gave a window of between one and four A.M. That's a pretty big window. Zara can't say where she was for twenty-odd minutes, according to her call records. But she's allowed to sleep, isn't she? And within those twenty-some minutes, you can see from my phone usage and my cell-site information that I was at my flat. So, you're right, Mr. Alfred. Zara and I were unaccounted for a short period between one and four. But not at exactly the same times."

"Mr. King, I'm going to run with your theory and accept for the moment that you were at your flat in East London for the time your phone was in use. The forty-seven minutes between 2:17 and 3:04 that your phone was not being used, give you, don't they, enough time to make it to Mr. Herman's house, break in, and murder him and then get back to your flat?"

I give out a hollow laugh. "I don't think they do. The drive is at least twenty minutes each way."

"The officer in the case has told us that at that time in the morning, one could do that drive in twelve minutes. In fact, *he* did it in twelve minutes when he tested the route. Under the speed limit."

I put a finger between my collar and neck. It is sticking to my skin. But I'm fine. I've rehearsed these answers. "He did it on one particular morning. But even Google Maps says at that time in the morning it can take up to twenty-four minutes," I say. I have asked the solicitors to check this. I know it's correct.

"Twelve minutes," he says, ignoring me completely. "Assuming the same time to return, that gives you twenty-three minutes to break in and put a knife into Mr. Herman's neck."

I wait for the question.

"Well?" he says. "Doesn't it?"

"No. I'm pretty sure committing a murder doesn't work like that. You can't break into a person's house and kill them and leave, all within twenty minutes. It's ludicrous. It takes them," I say, pointing at the dock officers, "twenty minutes to bring me up into court from the cells downstairs."

A few of the jury chuckle at this but I don't mean to be amusing. A drive there and back and murder in between, all in forty-seven minutes, is a stretch too far. I don't think even Alfred believes it.

"Then, Mr. King, you're making my argument for me. Someone else must have been using your phone."

"No."

"Do you love your wife?"

"Yes," I say.

"Despite the separation?"

"Of course."

"You were living apart. But did you miss her?"

"Yes, I did."

"Then can you tell us why if you were awake in the middle of the night, and she was awake in the middle of the night, you didn't just call your wife instead of someone else's?"

"I didn't know she was awake in the middle of the night."

"Was the reason that you didn't want to leave evidence of a plan? Between the two of you?"

"There was no plan."

"Are you telling us that you didn't act together?"

"Yes. We didn't act together."

"You knew nothing about a murder?"

"No." Then to head him off, I add, "Until I was arrested."

He opens and closes his blue notebook and folds his arms. He is basking in the moment. Something is coming. "Then it must have been your wife, acting alone."

"No," I say, looking straight into the dock. Zara lifts her head to meet my eyes and smiles sadly.

Alfred looks around the room and allows his gaze to land softly on the jury box. "How do you know?"

"Excuse me?" I say reflexively.

"It wasn't you. You didn't speak to her that night. You were at your flat, miles away in Whitechapel. How do you know it wasn't her?"

"Because——"

"Because what?"

"I just know."

"Do you? She was desperate about Sophie, wasn't she?"

"Of course she was," I say angrily.

"She was grieving—her disappearance, at least, if not her death. Her loss."

"Yes. As any mother would."

"And if she came face-to-face with the person she believed was responsible for her disappearance, she would have stopped at nothing to find Sophie. Isn't that true?"

In the dock, Zara looks smaller than ever. Her shoulders are so thin. Her body looks brittle. Before I can answer, Zara has cast her eyes up. And she is nodding at me. Willing me, giving me permission to agree with him. "Yes," I say, and then am surprised by the tiny sound of a drop of water hitting the polished wood of the witness box. I scratch at my eyes and realize I am crying, and suddenly the weight of everything I have been holding back breaks through from somewhere at the back of my head. It rises, I can feel it catching me, and I try to hold it at bay. The speed and severity of it are shocking.

And then I am bent over, crying ugly, heaving sobs and I can't stop it. The courtroom is a blur. I cover my eyes and face in shame. I feel a ghost part of me step out from my racked body to watch me. The jury looks on unblinking. Waiting.

"Perhaps, my lady, a break?" Stevens says, shuffling to his feet. I continue to sob as the judge and jury file out.

When the room is cleared I take a moment before I look up. The lawyers are still in the courtroom, but Zara has been taken back down into the court cells. Stevens calls across to me, unconcerned. "You okay, Harry?"

I wipe my face and wave him away.

"Good. We're back in five minutes. Get yourself together. Drink some water."

I do as he says and then run through the events again in my head, as I must. Everything is accounted for as well as it can be. The clothes disposed of. The gloves burned. I might be on a garage forecourt CCTV if they have picked my car up on an automatic number-plate recognition camera somewhere. I have a receipt for a packet of cigarettes and lighter fluid to explain that. I have prepared that story— *I forgot. That was the night I'd driven to get some fags. I've given up smoking so it didn't stick in my memory until now when you presented me with the footage. That's why my car is on that camera.* It gives me an out. But there's been no hint of any CCTV evidence and they'd have disclosed it to us if there was. It's there for me to use if the time comes. And then there's the package. There's still that. When that comes, it will throw all the pieces in the air.

I just need us both to hold our nerve. I can't talk to Zara but I trust her. I don't mean trust—not in that way. Trust isn't even a question here. I mean I can rely on her. She's fractured but she's one hundred percent reliable. All her cracks have been glued and gilded like kintsugi. She can do this.

I think back to that night in Herman's house. What I saw. What I heard.

We have to get out of here for that reason if no other.

SEVENTY

ZARA

WHEN WE RECONVENE, HARRY LOOKS AS HE DID BEFORE. HIS FACE IS A little redder around the cheeks but he's composed again. An offended air encircles him again, like vultures looking for a chance. I have been expecting the moment but I am so nervous now that I can't look at him when he's speaking. Instead I stare at the floor and count.

Alfred is cross-examining him again. He seems to always ask questions that result in terrible answers.

"Were you aware that your wife had been prescribed medication?"

"What kind?" he asks.

"Tranquilizers. Sedatives."

"I don't know if I knew. She was having trouble sleeping, I know that."

"Did you steal any of her medication?"

"No," he says, puzzled. He doesn't know what's coming but I do.

"Do you have access to any diazepam yourself?"

"No."

"It's not being prescribed for your sleep issues?"

"No." His face creases in concern at the direction of these questions.

"Then you presumably can't account for the large amounts of the drug found in a leg of lamb at the premises?"

"No," he says, confused.

"For Sheba, I assume."

"Sheba? I'm not sure I—"

"Mr. Herman's dog. She would have been knocked out by the high level of benzodiazepines in her blood had she eaten it."

He looks over at me for a second before returning to Alfred. "What? You think my wife tried to poison the dog?"

"Well, did she?"

"Of course not!" he exclaims.

"Again, Mr. King, since you weren't with her, how can you possibly say?"

Harry points at me before he answers. "Because I know my wife. She's not capable of doing something like that. We're not murderers. We're teachers."

"*Were* teachers. If she did intend to poison the dog, would you agree that you don't know your wife at all?"

Harry meets him in the eye. "I know Zara. And everything you're saying about her is wrong. She did not murder Mr. Herman. She did not have it in for his dog. For one thing—" he says, and then cuts himself off.

"What?"

"Nothing."

"Not nothing, Mr. King. You're in a courtroom giving evidence in a murder case. This isn't a lounge. For one thing—what?"

"How do you think she'd manage to get Herman into a chair and tied up?"

Alfred smiles, amused. "Oh, you know the answer to that, Mr. King, don't you?"

"No. I don't."

"That's why it needed the two of you. Acting in concert. Acting together. Planning together. Executing the plan *together*."

"No. I wasn't there. There was no plan."

He continues without a pause. "At around five the morning after the murder, the police took a call from a woman alerting them to the presence of a firearm that had been posted into a letter box. What can you tell us about that?"

My heart begins to thump at this question. I knew there was something about this in the "unused" material. This was supposed to mean the prosecution weren't using it. I hold my breath, waiting for it to be over. My chest pounds so hard that I wonder whether they can hear it.

Harry is calm.

"Nothing. Why? Was a gun used in the murder?" Harry asks.

"Used? As in fired? No. But was this the method by which Mr. Herman was persuaded into the chair—a gun in his face?"

"No."

"Again, Mr. King. How do you know if you weren't there?"

"Well, I assume you meant that I was the one holding the gun." Alfred takes in the room. "You assumed it? Do you own a gun?"

"No."

"Ever owned a gun?"

"No," he says much too quickly.

"The PNC checks show that you used to have a firearms license."

Harry colors. "Many years ago. In my twenties. I was a target shooter."

"Then you did own a gun. These aren't questions capable of multiple answers. You did own a gun, yes?"

"Yes."

"What was your gun of choice?"

Harry rubs his chin and looks at the judge. "Is this relevant?"

The judge leans back. "If it isn't, Mr. Stevens will, I am sure, object," she says coolly.

Stevens, hearing his name, shifts in his seat. This feels as if it's spooling out of control. "My lady, what is the relevance exactly, if the gun wasn't used?"

The judge smiles benignly. "He is suggesting that the gun was used by Mr. King to secure the deceased's compliance. Indeed, it is difficult to see how, if Mr. King wasn't involved, Mrs. King could otherwise have secured it. If anything, Mr. Stevens, this helps your client."

"But he's suggesting that it was my client holding the gun."

Alfred, who sat down during the exchange, gets to his feet. "I'm not suggesting it was Mr. King holding the gun, my lady."

"Well, as long as that is clear," Stevens says, and hurriedly sits down again. There is more shuffling on the front bench and I see that my barrister, Nasreen, has been slipped an envelope by the solicitor, Suzy. It's done with such skill that nobody else notices. She opens it and then looks back to me. I don't know what she has seen so I don't know how to react.

"Mr. King, I'm not, to be clear, suggesting that you were holding the gun, necessarily. But I am suggesting it was your gun."

"I don't have a gun."

"But you did, didn't you? When you were a target shooter. You had your own pistol."

"As I say, many years back. More than twenty years."

"What did you use? Twenty-twos?"

"Mainly."

"The police found this gun, when they got a call from a woman alerting them to its presence." Alfred rustles among his sheets of paper and produces a photograph of Harry's gun laid out next to a ruler. He hands it to Harry whose face is set like ice. "Is this your gun?"

"I don't know. It's a similar model."

"There is a serial number on this weapon, you see, and to save the mystery I can tell you that's your weapon, registered to you."

"If you say so." Harry holds his gaze. "I turned it in decades ago to the police in the amnesty. If that's been used, that's on you lot. Not me. Someone let it back on the streets." I watch Harry's face for a flicker but there isn't one. He's nearly convinced himself this is true.

Alfred consults his laptop. "You did turn in a number of weapons. Three in all. But the fourth, this one, wasn't handed in."

"Maybe I'd sold it before they banned them."

"Maybe you sold it? Do you have difficulty remembering guns that you've sold?"

Harry flushes red. "No. But I did occasionally sell old guns to other target shooters if I was upgrading."

"Or maybe you kept this one at home. And maybe you took it with you to point at a terrified Mr. Herman before you killed him?"

"No."

"So you could tape him to a chair and then drive a knife into his neck."

"No!"

Stevens stands up again. "He specifically said he wasn't suggesting that Mr. King was holding the gun."

Alfred smiles and holds his hands up in mock surrender. "If not you, Mrs. King."

"No."

"The evidence is overwhelming. There's still time, Mr. King. Still time to do the decent thing and accept your guilt. If your wife wasn't involved, you can tell us. This judge, I am sure, will take it into account. Even now."

The judge doesn't flinch and watches Harry open his mouth to answer. Then Nasreen, my barrister, gets up. "My lady. I see the time is rapidly approaching four. There is a matter that has just arisen that I need to take my client's instructions on. May we rise now and resume tomorrow?"

The judge looks at her watch.

"Mr. Alfred. Is it a convenient moment for you?"

"It is, my lady."

"Very well. Tomorrow at ten. Members of the jury," she says, and gets up. The other courtroom actors follow suit, standing until she is out the door.

I look over to Nasreen but she is speaking in hushed tones to Suzy. Harry is escorted back to the dock and as he gets nearer, I see how tired he looks. He walks as though he has been beaten with sticks. Every joint seems to be giving him trouble. I smile at him and he returns it with a half one of his own.

A hand slapping the glass gives me a shock until I see it's Nasreen, her hair escaping from the wig in strands. "I'll come and see you now. Don't let them put you onto the van." She turns to the guard. "Jailer. Can you hold her down there till I've seen her, please? It's important."

The guard doesn't answer Nasreen. Instead she looks at Harry and says, "He took a bit of a beating. Bet he's glad of a breather."

I nod. What they don't say is that it wasn't him who was being beaten. It was me.

SEVENTY-ONE

HARRY

I DON'T KNOW WHY I'M HERE IN THE CONFERENCE ROOMS AND NOT IN the cells. I ask the guard whether my legal is coming to visit me. "Nah, mate. You're in the middle of giving your story still. He can't talk to you till you're finished in the box. Nobody from your lot can."

"Then why am I here?"

"The cells are full. When the first van goes back to the prison, we can move you."

I sit down on the hard wooden surface of the short bench and breathe hard. The air is damp and carries the scent of mulch or mold. I stretch my arms across the table and then lay my head softly on it.

I run the cross-examination through in my head to work out how much damage Alfred did. The gun is a problem. Of course it had a serial number. I knew that. But it wasn't used. No shots were fired. I didn't think it would be an issue. And I knew that if the police had found it in the house when they searched, it would have been five years in prison for Zara, just for having it. So, getting rid of it was definitely the right call. And now that they have found it, it's just nothing. A stray piece of evidence that doesn't really link to the murder, even if it does connect to me.

But what else did they have? The timeline doesn't work for the prosecution—not really. Twenty minutes just isn't long enough for the jury to be sure that I did it. And I've seen all the evidence there is on Zara. Her phone was on a call until almost 2:35 and then died. It powered on again just around 2:55. That's just twenty minutes to explain, where I have forty-seven lost minutes to explain. If they can't prove she wasn't on that call, she has to be home and dry. All they have is that Luca guy's statement, which says he wasn't sure whether she was on the line the whole time. It's not enough for a conviction.

I think back to that night. The blood flowing all the way to the floor in streams. His eyes rolled back in his skull. I still can't believe what I saw that night. There was no part of me that was prepared for it and yet now, when I look back on it, it's the only thing that makes sense.

I hear Zara's voice along the corridor, frail, as her door opens and I can hear Nasreen bustle in to see her. Despite craning for every sound, I hear only stray words from Zara, buried under Nasreen's heavy, soothing tones. "I wanted to play it in front of you," I hear Nasreen say. "—watch it together."

Zara mumbles in reply and then there is a hush.

Suddenly my door opens and it's the guard. "There's a cell ready for you now."

"Can't I stay here?" I say.

"No. We need these free for legals."

I'm led, cuffed, back to the cell and wait on another bench. When I lie back and the blood rushes to my head I am overtaken by a feeling of sadness so I sit back up again. Whatever happened, he deserved to die. And I don't think there was a way of avoiding it. Not after what he said.

THIS LAST YEAR in prison has been lonely. It's been lonelier than a bereavement. When you're in your grief, you are in a room that other people have been in or will be in sooner or later. But in prison you're alone. Nobody you know on the outside will ever understand it. But if I had to do it all again I would. The only thing I would change is

Zara. I would have made sure, somehow, that she didn't have to suffer the way she has.

I miss her. I miss S— too, but Zara is alive and here and within reach, and yet when I stretch my hands my fingers grasp only her ghost. She can't talk to me, and if she can, she won't. I don't know what she's thinking. I have no way of knowing how she survived prison this last year. I write to her every week. Nothing risky, just letters, written as letters used to be written. I write slowly and form the words after thinking about the right ones. On paper there is no delete button, and in the pen there is an emotion that won't be controlled or contained. Every scratched letter leaves a trace of me in the slips and quivers of its lines.

When I get back to the prison later, I empty the bag of the papers I took to court and start work on them again. This is the critical period. I have been working on this case every day since my arrest. Before the papers were served, I was making notes so that my memory wouldn't slip. When they arrived, I went through every page again and again until I could tell you what page which witness's statement was on, which were the important exhibits, what the weak points were for me.

And now that we are in the middle of my evidence, I can't relax. It's the final stretch, and as much as I want to switch my little TV on and watch something mindless to drown out the banging and shouting on the wing, I can't. This has to go exactly to plan. I have to get out.

I haven't let myself be distracted with the idea of losing the case. If I am in here for life, then what? There is no way my head can process that notion. I can't imagine another full year, let alone a full life of an untrodden future. It doesn't mean anything to me, and more than that, I can't let it mean anything to me. There is no what-if.

I have to get out of here. It's already been too long.

I eat something hot and flavorless for dinner and then one of the prison officers comes in with a package.

"That for me, guv?" I say. Even after all this time of saying it, the word "guv" sticks in my throat. It feels fraudulent.

He tosses it over to me. "You missed post when you were in court. I said I'd bring it to you."

The packaging has been opened already. Everything is opened and searched except for legal papers. When I see what is in it, a swell of emotion rises up from my chest and all I want is for him to leave me. I hold back the tears and swallow. "Thanks," I say, and put it under my pillow.

He must see the effect because he smiles and leaves quietly. No ribbing about getting cuddly toys in prison or how the inmates will react when they see it. Just a quiet exit so I can cling on to a strand or two of my dignity.

When I am sure he is far enough away, I pull the frog out from under my pillow and bring it close.

The scent of S— is still there, deep within its soft middle.

I close my eyes tight but it's no use. My body curls around the frog, racked with a pain I can't hold back. My face is streaming tears, and a low guttural bellow escapes as I try to stop it from overtaking me. I can't let it. But now it's tipped so far forward that I can't do anything but let go and fall into this cloying darkness.

SEVENTY-TWO

ZARA

I AM BACK IN THE CELL CONFERENCE ROOM WAITING FOR NASREEN. YES-terday after court she couldn't play the video she wanted to show me on her laptop. It loaded and then froze. We couldn't even see the first frame. I know what is on it. She doesn't.

Last night while lying on my bunk, I turned over and over how I was going to explain the footage to her. Now as I wait, the words I'd rehearsed yesterday sound hollow when I replay them.

The opening door shakes me out of my thoughts. Nasreen bustles in, carrying her wig rolled inside her robes, papers balanced precari-ously on top. Her face is flushed and refreshed. She smiles. There is always a smile for me, even when the circumstances don't predict one. Suzy follows her in, her expression grave.

"So, we both tried to play this, me on my laptop and Suzy on hers."

"I even tried my kid's laptop," Suzy adds.

"But?"

"But," Nasreen continues, "no dice. Yet. The solicitors have a techie guy who's pretty sure he can get it playing."

I nod but don't know what else I can add. I am relieved but at the same time, I know it's a false dawn. It will have to be played.

"I don't like surprises," Nasreen says, laying her robes on the table and sitting across from me. "Not only do I not know what is on there, I don't even know why I have it or who sent it."

When she came to see me yesterday, she told me it had been delivered to the court with a typed note saying only "Video Evidence in the case of R v King and King."

"We don't even know it's meant for us. It could have been meant for the prosecution team."

"Then should we even be trying to view it?" I ask, searching their faces.

"Well, if it's relevant—they'd have to serve it on us anyway. If it's not, then we're no worse off. At least this way, if it's bad, we have a bit of advance notice to do what we need to do."

"To do what?" I say, trying to contain the drumming in my chest. "You mean get rid of it?"

"What? No. I mean prepare for it. We can't just destroy evidence. That's unethical."

"No, I didn't mean—" I say, and then feel the words drying on the line stretched between us. Nasreen flicks her eyes to Suzy who nods almost imperceptibly.

"So, when Harry's finished, we have to make a decision."

"I know. And I've already decided."

"We know your feelings about this, but we always said we'd review things once Harry had finished giving evidence. Everyone goes into the witness box the same way, Zara, but they don't all come out of it the same."

"What do you mean?"

"Well . . ." She stops and looks across at Suzy again. "I'm sure he didn't intend to, but Harry has not done you any favors so far."

"I don't understand." I know this but I can't give them an excuse to pressure me now at the last.

"I mean everything he has said, not directly, but obliquely, points to you. All this mention of a gun. The prosecution isn't saying it's Harry holding a gun to get Herman to comply. What they're saying is that it's you. *You* need the gun. Harry can just go in with a hammer. As he has in the past. But how would *you* get him into a chair? By pointing a gun at him."

"But that isn't what he said."

"Not yet. But the closing speech is coming. And the gun was found a few hundred meters from your house. A house that Harry was not living in. Yes, he could have dumped it there before going home, but why would he? He was on the clock. He had to move quickly."

A curtain of heat drops over my head. I stare at them both. "Anything else?"

"His timeline. It really doesn't allow for him to have gone in and killed Herman. It might just be possible, but ultimately nobody will believe he went out and committed a murder and made it all the way back. With no hiccups. But you're so close. They're not going to have the same trouble with you. And your Luca Marco—his statement raises the uncertainty stakes for you."

Suzy coughs and opens her notebook. "And there's the leg of lamb, laced with your Valium."

"Not *my* Valium."

"Well. Yes," Suzy says. "Not your Valium necessarily. But Valium. And you have a prescription for Valium. There was some in the house. It's too much of a coincidence."

"So, what do you suggest?" I say, trying to digest all of this information.

"We think you have to reconsider not giving evidence. Once you are in the box and the jury hears your voice, hears what you say— you'll be sympathetic. You'd be a good witness, Zara."

"But I'd be exposed to Alfred. I can't do it the way Harry is doing it. I'm not good at that."

"Look, you don't have to decide right now. Wait till he's finished. When he's all done then I'll ask for more time to talk to you. But Suzy and I agree here. If you don't give evidence, you'll be going against clear advice. You'd have to sign an endorsement to that effect."

They squeeze out of the narrow room. I stare at my hands until I hear the heavy door shut after them, keys jangling in the lock. This was supposed to have been decided. My head had been clear. I had mapped out the way through this trial and this wasn't how it was to finish. I can't give evidence.

All I can hope for now is that Harry repairs some of the damage he caused me. But I don't know how that's possible if he doesn't even know what he's done.

An image of Herman floods my mind. I remember the expression on his face. And now the footage rolls across the back of my eyes.

I still can't believe any of it happened.

SEVENTY-THREE

HARRY

In court, the jury files solemnly into their seats. I am standing in the witness box, which still seems to carry the imprint of every question that took me apart yesterday.

Alfred gets up, mumbles at the judge, and launches straight in as if he'd never stopped. The questions come like nine-foot waves. They are relentless and heavy and the weight of them is hard to withstand. Every time I return for air, another wave heads in my direction.

At one point I look at the clock on the wall behind the judge and see that I have been here under cross-examination for over an hour this morning.

"Are we boring you, Mr. King?" he says then.

I shake my head. "Sorry. No."

He returns to his questions. "And the footprints. Can you account for those?"

"Which ones?" I say. There are dozens of them. Some in the bedroom, some in the kitchen, and some at the front door.

"The ones that are covered in blood, Mr. King. Two sets. One smaller. One larger. One Mrs. King's. One set, yours."

I feel myself stiffen. "Not mine. Not hers. The police searched my flat and the house and didn't find any shoes that matched the tread pattern. As you know."

"When most people are asked whether they stole some apples, in my experience, if they're innocent they don't say 'I don't even like apples.'"

Stevens stands up to object but Alfred bats him down to his seat. "You disposed of the shoes, didn't you?"

"No."

"Do you agree that the existence of two sets of bloody footprints— which are different sizes—suggests that two people, whoever they might be, were involved in this murder?"

"Yes. Potentially. Not definitely." I see him winding up for another assault so I add, "But it does suggest that."

"Were those two people you and Mrs. King?"

"No."

"She was holding your gun?"

"No."

"Pointing it at a man who you believed had killed or taken your daughter?"

"No."

"Did you drive a knife into his throat?"

"No. And there was no murder weapon found in my flat."

"But there was a knife found in your house. A chef's knife. Your chef's knife. One consistent with the injuries."

"There's probably a knife like that in your house, Mr. Alfred. In most houses."

"And did you dispose of the gun and call it in to the police? Or did Mrs. King? Not wanting it to be found in a search of your house?"

"No."

"A final question from me. Do you know anyone else that wanted Mr. Herman dead, more than you did?" The question hangs in the air for a second but before I can answer it, he adds: "Other than your wife?"

"I didn't want him dead. I just wanted him to answer some questions."

Alfred sits down without any ceremony and I am left to vibrate in the witness box as the entire court scrutinizes my face for things that might have been unsaid.

I hear the sound of a file of papers being opened and closed and I see Stevens cursing under his breath before getting to his feet.

"Mr. King, have a look at the pictures of the footprints. Can you tell me the time they were made?"

"The pictures?"

"No. The prints. The prints."

I smile. "No. I can't."

"So, can you say from looking at them whether they were made when the two people were together?"

I see from the look on the jury's faces that this isn't the best point he has made. "No, I can't. But they are in blood. So they would have had to have been made when the blood was still wet enough."

Stevens ignores my answer. "Well, now. You've been cross-examined up hill and down dale about a firearm. Do you own a revolver?"

"No."

"Have you ever owned a revolver?"

"No."

Stevens looks taken aback by the answer. "Not even in your target-shooting days? This revolver," he says, holding up the photograph.

"Oh. That's not a revolver. It's an automatic pistol. Yes. That is mine."

"When was the last time you saw it?"

"Years ago. I thought I'd given them all in during the amnesty."

"But you accept you might have missed out this one?"

"Yes. When we moved house we meant to install a new gun safe but then the legislation changed and I made the decision to hand them in."

"And what happened to this gun?"

"The Ruger? I don't know. I could have sold it at the gun club. Or we had a break-in last year. It might have been taken then."

"You didn't report it?"

"No. I didn't know it had gone missing. I hadn't thought about this gun for twenty years or more."

"Do you still shoot? Targets?"

"No. Not with firearms. Not for two decades."

"Not with guns? What else does one shoot with?"

"Some use crossbows. There are some good ones on the market now."

"Do you have a crossbow?" he says, startled.

"No. Not me. I occasionally target shoot catapults—slingshots. That's as far as I go these days."

"Okay. So, getting back to the gun. You didn't dump it in a mailbox and then call the police?"

"No. It was a woman who called, according to the police."

"Thank you," he says, and sits down.

"Can we play the call?" I say to him. When he doesn't respond, I look at the judge.

"Is there a reason why we can't?" the judge asks plainly.

"Well," says Stevens, standing. "I assumed that Mrs. King's counsel took the decision not to lead it into evidence so I haven't pressed it. It doesn't affect me. It's more my learned friend's problem. It was a woman who called."

The jury all lean around to look at Nasreen. I know what she's thinking. If she doesn't play the recording, then the jury will suspect it's her client, Zara, on that call. But if she does play it—then what? That's what is speeding through her mind.

SEVENTY-FOUR

ZARA

"WILL YOUR LADYSHIP BEAR WITH ME A MOMENT?"

Nasreen walks over to me and presses her face into the gap in the glass. "Fucking Harry. If we don't play it, it's going to look bad. So, unless you instruct me not to, we might have to play it. There are no voice experts, so if you didn't give evidence it still wouldn't be fatal. They wouldn't hear your voice to be able to compare it."

That question makes me realize something for certain. Nasreen isn't sure if I am innocent.

I nod. "Okay. Play it."

"Okay. I don't think we have much choice." She takes a long look at me before she returns to her seat. The anxiety breaks into her voice. "May I ask that it's played?"

Alfred stands and leans casually into his lectern. "Mrs. King had the opportunity to ask questions and chose through her counsel not to." The memory of Stevens tendering the witness in that way he did returns. Nasreen couldn't have asked any questions. It would have destroyed the element of surprise.

"Well, I'm not going to stand in the way of it if Mrs. Khan would like it played," the judge says. "And if we don't, this jury is going to wonder why. You'd like it played, Mrs. Khan?"

"Yes, please," she says, her throat dry.

The courtroom falls into hush as the 999 call is played. The first voice heard is the breezy voice of the operator. And then there's a pause before there is the sound of a woman talking, in a soft accented voice, over the line.

"Yes. I just want to report a gun that I have drop into a letter box on ah, Copeland Street, in SE22."

"Can I just take some details, please?"

"No. Just go and get it, please, before any young people finds it." And then the call goes dead.

Everyone in the courtroom turns to look at me, even Nasreen. I notice her smiling with relief. She knows I don't speak with a Spanish accent. And Harry knows. But nobody else here does. Yet.

We are soon back in the cells, Nasreen having asked for some time before making a decision about whether to call me to give evidence. Before they took me down, Harry reached out a hand. "Don't blink," he said. "Not now."

"So. We are here now, Zara. It feels like an odyssey for me. God knows how it must feel for you."

The tears are collecting behind my eyes. I want to tell her that the last year has been easier than the ten weeks before it. That you can't put a person in prison who is already imprisoned. I think of Harry up there, struggling each second to escape this charge. The desperate fight to leave prison shines on his skin. I know why he has to leave. But I don't know why I do.

"I think you have to give evidence."

"Nasreen. We spoke about this. I don't want to."

"I know. But . . . just hear me out. Suzy will tell you the same thing when she comes down. That call from the woman plainly isn't you. But we can't put that into evidence unless you speak—for two reasons. First, you have to say it's not you—that's the evidence that it isn't you. Second, they have to hear your voice to know it's not you."

I nod along to this. "Can't you just play a recording of my voice?"

"We could. But think about how it looks. You're jumping through hoops to avoid having to give evidence."

I hear Harry's voice in my head. *Don't blink.* "No," I say. "I've made my mind up."

Nasreen sighs heavily and leans back. "Okay. But I need you to endorse my brief." She takes a pen and starts to write out something in her blue A4 notebook.

The door then bursts open and Suzy walks in, her cheeks flushed. "Nas. We've got a problem." Before we can ask what's wrong, she has her laptop open on the table. "Lionel, our tech guy, managed to get the thumb drive to play the file."

"And?" Nasreen says, getting up to look at the screen.

"It's probably easier if I just play it."

IN THE SILENCE after it's finished playing, the room begins to hum. We have watched this two-minute clip a dozen times now. Suzy and Nasreen switch between looking at each other and the ceiling. Finally, Nasreen speaks. "What the hell?"

"I know," Suzy says.

Nasreen picks up a pen. "So, the first question is what do we do about it?"

"I don't think we have a choice. We have to disclose it," Suzy says.

"Do we? Let's think this through. Do we have a duty to disclose evidence that harms our client? I don't think we do," Nasreen says, answering her own question. "We're not the Crown. We don't have that obligation."

"No. But it could help Zara."

"How?" I ask quietly.

"Well. It's obvious that there's only one person, apart from the deceased, who's there on the video. One person committed this murder. Not two."

"I'm sorry," I say. "I know I sound slow. But why couldn't there be two people there?"

"There could be—but it's highly unlikely given the context. We see only one person—just out of shot. The same person switches the camera on and off. And you heard what the deceased said. *In context*, it sounds like the other person has gone."

She lets this sink in.

"There is one way it doesn't help," Suzy says.

Nasreen nods and answers before I ask. "He used the word 'parent.' If the jury sees that video, they will be sure that the person who killed him was Sophie's parent. That one of you two is definitely the murderer. And one of you two will get life."

The air crackles as if filled with static.

"Zara," Nasreen says seriously. "Where did this clip come from?"

"I don't know," I say. I have lost control over the finer muscles in my face so I don't know if I am betraying my anxiety.

She chews her pen and then leans toward me. "It must have been Harry. He must have taken it. And left it with someone." She doesn't know how close she is to the truth. I hold my breath and will her to look away from me.

Suzy nods. "And that someone had a crisis of conscience."

There is a knock on the door and the jailer is there with an apologetic look. "They want you back up in court."

Nasreen turns to me. "Okay. Look, Zara. We're going to need more time to decide about what we do with this video. Let's go up. I'll ask the judge for more time and come down again."

I wait to be taken up. Harry's team is up there oblivious to what has happened down here—that one of us is guilty of murder. Oblivious to the hell that is going to break loose when they find out. When it's out, there's no going back.

You can't ever go back.

I think of all the times I tried to go back. All those concerts I went to after Sophie was born. All the girls' nights, just to try to recover some of that feeling. But I realize now that it was impossible because what I had when I was younger was something I couldn't re-create afterward. It wasn't better skin or more energy. It was the lack of responsibility for anyone else—for a child. I had freedom. It was the freedom that allowed the excitement to bloom. But I didn't know it then. It was only after years of trying to re-create it unsuccessfully that I saw it. You can never go back.

"If we play the video, will Harry get the chance to say his piece about it?" I ask.

"You mean get into the witness box again? No."

"But he won't have had a chance to say anything. It's new evidence."

"In a way it's new. But in another way, it's not. He's had the chance to say whether he killed Herman. On that basis, he's already answered the video. Look, we better go up. I'll get more time and then we can talk."

I pull her back by the arm. "No. I don't need more time. I want to give evidence after all. And the video—"

I know how this ends now. Harry has to go.

Nasreen stares at me in shock. "I need time to think about it and to advise you properly about the implications of this video."

I grab her arm. "No. I've decided. This is what I want you to do," I say. "Please," I say as I am led away. "I have to."

SEVENTY-FIVE

HARRY

THIS IS NOT WHAT IS SUPPOSED TO HAPPEN. WE AGREED. THE ONLY THING I needed from Zara was to not give evidence, but there she is, standing in the witness box, taking the affirmation.

"I'm going to start with the easy ones, but they'll get harder. What's your name?"

She is so small in that wooden box. The entire courtroom is looking at her and she seems to stoop under the weight of their gaze. She answers in a small voice and is then reminded by Nasreen to *"Keep your voice up nice and loud. So that juror right at the end can hear you."*

Nasreen takes her through the day and the evening before in meticulous detail. What time she got up. What she ate for breakfast. Whether she left the house. When she had lunch. Who she spoke to that day.

"I haven't yet asked you about your husband, Harry," she starts, and then slowly, skillfully, draws out the silk and satin of our relationship. And then the nails on which it snagged at first and then later tore.

An hour slips by almost unnoticed, every question oil on water.

"That 999 call. We all heard it in this courtroom. Was that you?"

"No."

"Putting on an accent, perhaps?"

I half smile as she answers. "No."

And then more questions. Every detail is unfurled from her. The call she made to her friend Luca from the support group. "He talked until the phone went dead. I thought I'd plugged it back in but the connection wasn't right. It didn't finally charge up enough to come on for twenty minutes. Faulty cable, I think."

"But did you leave your home? At that time in the morning?"

"No. Of course not."

"Armed with a gun and a knife and rolls of tape?"

"No."

The jury hangs on every word. The questions are so choreographed that what passes between the two of them is like a dance. I hold my breath through it all but I know that the damage is going to be done when the prosecutor, Alfred, starts his questions. This is safe ground with Nasreen, but my heart is in my throat. I can't fathom why she has decided to give evidence. The plan was going perfectly.

Last night I got the call from Katya. *It's delivered,* she said. I assume the prosecutor will apply to reopen the case once he's seen the video. But will it be too late or too soon? There's some low-level security on it. I know it won't stand firm. Overnight, the CPS would crack it open. This morning it would be ready to play. I stare over at Alfred but there's no hint of any excitement. Has he even seen it? But then I see that the officer is not there behind him. If he comes back with the video now, we are in trouble. Zara has to be finished before he sees the video. Her being in the box when they see it ruins everything.

If Zara hadn't chosen to go into the witness box, the prosecution could play it but couldn't force her to give evidence or force me back into the box to answer questions. And with that video showing what it does, it would mean only one thing. One of us did it—not both of us. And without being able to ask either of us questions about it, Alfred would have been stuck with it. I've thought hard about this. Caspar has helped me understand the legalities of it. The jury can't convict us *both* if just one of us did it. And they can't convict even one of us if they don't know which one of us it was.

That was the plan, the whole plan, and now it's gone up in flames just like that.

— — —

NASREEN IS WINDING down and finally closes her blue book. "Did you murder Mr. Herman?"

"I did not."

"Wait there, please. Others may have questions."

Mr. Stevens stands up. "No questions."

Alfred gets up slowly and something in his slow movements telegraphs to me that he hasn't got the video. And by the time the first questions are out of his mouth, I know he doesn't have it. Thank God.

I only hope she's finished before he sees it.

"Your daughter means the world to you, yes?"

"Of course," she says, defiant. There is still a chance that if she holds it all together, we both walk away from this.

"You would do anything for her—do anything it took to find her?"

"Again," she says, "of course. But if you mean would I commit murder? Then no."

"Not even if it meant the safety of your daughter?"

"Do I wish I could murder someone for Sophie and have her back in my arms? Every day. There isn't a second that goes by that I don't make that bargain in my head."

"So, you agree you would kill?"

"No, it's not what I said. I *wish* I could. But look at me." She holds her arms out, and bent at the elbow they look like broken wings. I'm so impressed by her.

Alfred continues his slow and menacing drill down into the fissures. "Did you take the gun?"

"I didn't even know there was a gun until Harry gave evidence about it. As I told my barrister, we had a break-in last year. It must have been taken then."

"Because a gun, even one that was never fired, would have been useful to force Mr. Herman to comply, wouldn't it? In theory, I mean."

"Maybe."

"Especially if you don't have brute force to rely on. Because the gun that you say was taken in a burglary last year then showed up in a postbox on the very day of this murder. Quite the coincidence, wouldn't you say?"

"It's only a coincidence if Mr. Herman's murderer was also the person who took the gun." Zara's answers are confident and well thought through. She has prepared for this, despite what we had agreed about her not giving evidence. "And you know that's not my voice on the call."

"And I suppose you don't have a friend who might make a call for you?"

"*A* call? Yes. *That* call? No." This is more than I have heard her speak in a year and the sound of her voice sends electricity through me. I look at her and as she answers the questions she flicks her eyes at me, signaling something to me. If I had to guess, she's telling me that she's in control of this.

He asks her question after question. He presses every weak point as if they are bruises on her skin.

"Your friend Luca Marco. He wasn't so sure you were even awake when he called you on the night of this murder. Wasn't this just a clumsy attempt at an alibi?"

"No. He was talking me to sleep. He did that sometimes, as you can see from the call records. It wasn't unusual."

"He did it twice. No doubt, you thought it wise to make it appear to be a pattern of behavior?"

"I met him on a grief forum," she says, indignant. "Not everything is suspicious. Sometimes a thing is what it looks like and nothing more."

At lunchtime the judge asked Alfred how long he expected to be. "I'll be finished today," he said.

Shortly before three I am taken through to the rooms just along the corridor for a legal visit. Stevens is already there.

"I thought she wasn't giving evidence. Your wife," he says rapidly. His nervous energy ricochets around the room.

"So did I," I say. "But I think she's doing okay."

He sits and starts biting the skin around his nails. "I think she's cutting your throat."

I'm taken aback. "Why do you think that? She hasn't blamed me at all."

"She can't say it's you. That would incriminate her. What she's saying is that it's so clearly not *her* that it has to be *you*."

I consider this. "I don't think so. She's obviously been spooked by something Nasreen has said."

"Maybe. I know she likes her clients to give evidence if they can. Especially in murders."

"That's it, then. What happens after Zara's been questioned?"

"A few legal issues to iron out. Then it's closing speeches."

"What kind of legal issues?" I say because I don't know what else to say. I'm not sure why he has interrupted his lunch to see me.

"The prosecution has served a video, apparently." I feel a lump the size of a large stone land in my stomach. The video. I'd hoped that he wouldn't get it in time.

"What is it?" I say.

"I haven't viewed it but the junior is looking at it. I think it's too late for new evidence, especially since you've finished giving evidence. It's prejudicial."

"Can we exclude it?"

"*We* don't have to. It's on Nasreen, really. It's her client in the box. It's affecting her more than you. You can't be cross-examined on it, whatever is there, and I can always tell the jury to disregard it since you have never had the chance to deal with it in evidence."

"But you don't know what's on it."

"Not yet. But—"

"What if I *want to* answer questions about it?" I say, cutting him off.

"Usually I advise strongly against defendants getting back into the box. It can be fatal. Every question he forgot to ask you first time round will come out. And everything that your wife just said will be put to you as well." He gathers himself but gives me a hard look. "I better go and see what this new evidence is all about."

I sit staring at the painted wall once he's gone. Zara might be okay. If she's smart she'll tell him what we know already. That it doesn't show who is on the video. That's all she needs to remember.

Almost home free, Zara. Why did you get into the witness box?

SEVENTY-SIX

ZARA

THERE IS AN UNDERCURRENT OF TENSION. I HEAR THE BARRISTERS MUT-
tering to each other and catch the words "footage" and "video."
When the judge comes into court, Stevens is on his feet first.

"This is really disgraceful on the part of the Crown. Not even at
the eleventh minute of the eleventh hour but at the twelfth hour, we
are served with footage of the murder. It's really too much, my lady.
My client is going to be prejudiced beyond words. He'll be looking
at evidence from the dock without any opportunity to challenge or
answer it."

"If you were to make an application to recall your client to deal
with it once Mrs. King has finished in evidence, I would listen sym-
pathetically to it," she says evenly.

"I know you would. But the appearance of justice here is as important as anything. Does it appear *just* if the Crown is allowed to
ambush the defense with material at this late stage? There's been no
explanation for the delay. We don't know the provenance of this
footage. Where did it even come from? Who, for example, can say
that it shows *this* murder? I know that sounds trite, but there is an
evidential process here. Someone has to produce and exhibit this.

And that's before we get into the quality of the video. The sound for some of it has been deleted or redacted or edited or something. It's an incomplete piece of evidence and there's no continuity at all for it. In effect, it's a tampered piece of evidence."

Alfred gets to his feet. "The fact is we don't know where it came from. It landed sometime today on the officer's desk. It had nothing on the package to indicate the sender. It was marked only VIDEO EVIDENCE IN THE CASE OF R V KING AND KING. That was it. But it is obvious that it shows the murder in question. Mr. Stevens can't seriously be arguing that it doesn't. And as for evidential procedure, I can put it to Mrs. King. It goes into evidence that way, perfectly permissibly."

The judge agrees with Alfred, and twenty minutes later the jury is looking at a large video screen. There is an intake of breath as soon as the image flickers into view. The camera is pointed at an ordinary kitchen chair in a bedroom, the wrought iron bedstead just visible at the edge of the screen. Behind the chair is a huge purple-and-black mural of a butterfly. In the chair, to the left of the screen, struggling, is Mr. Herman. Through the speakers, his breath comes jagged and panicked.

"Let me go, please," he says, almost screaming the words. Then the sound is cut.

When it comes on again, it's Herman speaking.

"And you'll let me go?"

The footage goes blank once again. It soon is clear that the other person's voice has been cut from the conversation. The effect of the one-sided conversation that is left is nauseating—like being seasick.

"How many times do you want me to say it? It wasn't me. I didn't do anything to 'em."

Just then the tip of a knife comes into view and is held to his eye. The hand holding it is out of shot.

"Your Sophie. I didn't do anything to 'em. It was—" he says, and then the footage begins to hiss again to remove the other person speaking. When it returns, it feels as though the footage itself has been cut. There is a definite but intangible snap in the timeline.

"Yes. I did. I had 'em here. Yes, that's true. I had your daughter."

"Yes. That's what I'm saying."

"About three days."

"Kept 'em gagged. In the—in the—" he says, and then the tears begin to leak from his face, leaving snail trails across the sallow skin. "In the cellar."

There's a collective intake of breath when he says "cellar." The video cuts out again.

"I didn't kill 'em. I had a girl meself. Gone now. You're a parent. You couldn't kill someone's child. I couldn't either. I didn't kill 'em. Yes, I kept 'em. Yes. I kept 'em. I did."

On the screen the knife drops slowly from where his eye is and points downward into the dip between his chest and neck.

"She wanted to stay with me. If you'd a seen 'em, you'd a seen," he says, his voice becoming shrill with fear.

"Where's your other half? Why aren't they here? Get 'em here. Please. Talk some sense into you."

"Please, please," he says, tears continuing to flow. "Get 'em on the phone, then. Let me explain it to 'em. I didn't kill her."

Whoever is holding the knife now turns it. A second later it comes plunging down. And then the screen goes blank and a CPS logo screen saver bounces around the screen.

"There is more, my lady, but it's not appropriate for general viewing. By agreement, we can summarize it by saying that immediately before the footage ends, there is a second or so where the knife enters Mr. Herman. It enters in a way that is consistent with the injuries described by the pathologist and the resultant severing of the carotid artery and jugular vein. One cannot make out the identity of the murderer. The hand doesn't even come into view."

A thick silence hangs in the air. The jury looks at me and this time I stare back through blurred eyes. Some of the jurors turn away as if made ashamed by their own acts of watching. Now they know what Herman did. And if I were them, that's what I'd be struggling with. Not just what he did but also what he didn't do. What was done to him and whether it was forgivable, knowing what he implied he did to Sophie.

Alfred stands, as if he can't let the mood permeate and cloud everyone's common sense. He knows he has to shatter whatever sympathy might have been building for me and Harry.

"What we didn't see on the footage was the stabbing of Mr. Herman. It's there but it would be too harrowing to watch. We know that he would have fallen unconscious within a few seconds and died within a few minutes." He turns to me. "Mrs. King. Had you been standing behind him, hearing what he said, that would have made you indescribably upset, wouldn't it?"

"Yes."

"That he'd kept her. That he'd kept her for three days, in his cellar."

"Yes," I say through tears.

"Angry?"

I nod, but he wants an answer. "Yes."

"Your husband too? From what you know of him?"

"Yes."

"We know from the footage that Mr. Herman described the person with him as Sophie's *parent*. I had your *daughter,* he said." He looks around the court slowly before resting his gaze calmly on me.

"You and your husband are Sophie's parents, right?"

"Yes."

"So. Which one of you was it that drove the knife into his neck? You or him?"

My heart begins to race. My face is hot with tears but my hands grow cold, clammy. The world around me condenses under the pressure of the question. The unwritten futures wait, baying at the rump of that question. Whatever I say can't be unsaid. Whatever I do now chooses fates.

I wait.

"Well, let me help, if I can. Your husband was prepared to use violence toward Mr. Herman when he broke in just a few weeks before. He was prepared to smash his way in, on nothing more than a hunch. To buy a drone and fly it in through his window. He knocked on every house within a small radius of your home. Spoke to every occupant. He owned a gun. He had access to your Valium.

"And according to DS Holly, whose statement you've read, he'd broken in some weeks beforehand and taken remnants from the deceased's garden bin. And we've seen the police body cam from when he was arrested. We've all seen how Mr. King was. How angry. How insistent.

"So, tell us. Was it you or him, Mrs. King? It's the moment of truth."

I look over at Harry in the dock as I wipe away tears. His face has gone white. He is sitting at the edge of his seat. And then he is standing. The guards in the dock pull him gently back down, but he is back up a second later.

The sound of him slapping his hands against the glass of the dock vibrates across the room. Everyone turns to Harry.

Then come the words.

"It was me."

SEVENTY-SEVEN

HARRY

I KNOW WHAT SHE IS GOING TO SAY BEFORE SHE SAYS IT. I STAND UP AND slap on the glass so that all the attention is on me. I want to stop her—will do anything to stop her. If I have to fight the guards off and cause a scene, I will do it just so that I can stop her. But it's too late. She's said it. And now here is Alfred asking her to repeat what she has said.

"It was me. I did it. I crushed up the pills. I took Harry's gun from the wardrobe and I forced Herman into the chair with it. It was me. I stabbed him through the neck." She says it. Defiant now.

The jury fizz in their seats. There are murmurs between them. A few scratch urgent notes into their pads. One who has missed some detail is having it repeated to him in a whisper by his neighbor.

Then they turn to look at me, their minds slowly crystallizing. Open-mouthed, some of them, grim lipped, others. They blame me. Alfred looks wrong-footed by this and the glow of satisfaction I'd have expected is not there.

"Tell me about your reasons for killing him."

Zara looks at him, aghast. "You heard what he said. You *heard* what he did to Sophie."

"But according to him, at least, he didn't kill her."

Zara's knuckles are white as she grips the file on the top of the witness box. "There is more than one kind of killing." Her voice shatters as she speaks.

Alfred sits.

Nasreen stands. In all of that commotion she's been forgotten.

"My lady. I have no questions. May I have a fifteen-minute break so that I can speak to my client?"

"Certainly, Ms. Khan. If you'd like her to be rearraigned once you have spoken to her, send a message through my clerk."

Nasreen races to the back of the court as soon as the judge has risen and looks straight past my pleading eyes. "Jailer. Can you take her straight to the conference rooms, please? I'll be straight down."

I see Stevens behind her, signaling to me. "You don't need me, do you, Harry?"

"Yes. Yes," I say. "I do."

"Okay," he says, as the door behind me opens. Zara is ahead of me. I call out after her. "Zara! What did you do?"

She turns and smiles sadly. "What I had to."

BY THE TIME Stevens arrives, I am all but climbing the walls.

"That was unexpected," he says, throwing his wig off. "But it's obviously good for us. She's going to have to plead guilty after that. I'll see what the Crown says about dropping the case against you. They have to, really. The video suggests that it can only be one of you that did it. And if they have her—"

Suddenly I am overwhelmed by anger. "You have to do something. You can't just let her plead guilty. She didn't do it."

"Now, be careful, Harry. Don't tell me anything I don't want to hear. At the moment, you get off. That's good for you. It can't get better than that."

"You don't get it," I say, crying out in frustration. "If she gets convicted, there is no good left for me."

"Well, it's too late for that now. She's admitted it from the box. There's no choice."

"What if she retracts it?"

"She can't. She's finished giving evidence. She can't be recalled. Apart from anything else, she has spoken to her counsel. It's not permissible to recall her once she's talked about her evidence to her lawyer. And it wouldn't make a jot of difference. The jury wouldn't believe she was innocent, not after she's confessed."

I think back to the conversation Stevens and I had earlier. My throat is tightening. I feel as though all the muscles that are holding me up are disintegrating. "You said I could be recalled to give evidence. After I'd spoken to you, even."

"When did I say that?"

"When the video evidence was served. You said that I could give evidence even though, using your words, you'd strongly advise against it."

"But that's different," he says, staring at me. "That was new evidence that was being relied on that you hadn't yet had a chance to deal with in your evidence. She has had a chance to deal with it. There's no recalling her."

"At all?"

"At all."

I lean my head against the wall, feeling the bricks against my skin. "Then do it."

"I don't know if you're being dim, Harry. But I can't call her."

"No. Recall *me*."

"What? Are you crazy? Why would I call you? What could you possibly say that would help you more than Zara already helped you?"

"I don't know. But I do know that I want you to recall me."

"No," he says firmly.

"At our very first meeting you told me that you had to follow my instructions and not the other way around."

"And?"

"And I instruct you to recall me."

"And if I don't?"

"Then I'll have to sack you and call myself," I say.

He scrabbles around for his wig and puts it back on his head as soon as his fingers find it. "You might have seen that on TV. But let me tell you. This isn't TV. This," he says, stabbing the plastic table-top with a finger, "is real. Do you have any idea what life in prison is like? It's not the fucking holiday-camp remand crap you're in now. It's a cat A prison. It's a visit once a month. It's serving eighteen to twenty years, at the very least.

"And the parole board isn't a joke either. You might think you'll get paroled first time, but you won't get parole on even the fifth time. You'll be in with all the scum. With people who murder children and shoot people and stab prisoners for drugs. And people doing life sentences don't care about getting done for your murder. They're already doing life. You won't survive."

He leaves. A second later I see him turn back and approach the door again. "You can't get anything out of this, Harry. Let it be. That's my advice. Take the win. Help your wife from the outside. She's going to get less time than you would. She's got a ton of mitigation. But at the end of the day, I do what you tell me to do."

I nod. "That is good advice, Mr. Stevens. Thank you."

SEVENTY-EIGHT

ZARA

I READ A BOOK ONCE WHERE THE HERO LOST EVERYTHING. HE'D STARTED out with nothing. His health was bad and he'd had the worst start to life imaginable. It was a story that begged for joy, begged for light, and promised both. A story that starts so low has nowhere to go but up. Except each time he climbed to some place of safety, I turned the page only to find some new horror flinging him back to the depths. And every time, he would wake, soaked in blood and his own mess. His bones would be shattered. His resolve and confidence withered away to nothing, and still he'd carry on. Heal. Mend. Slowly edge out, terrified, back into the burning light. Cajoled each time by loved ones into believing the world to be safe. And out he'd step, only to be met once again by calamity. Each successive one worse than the previous. I'd always been impressed by his courage. He had a faith that his life should not have allowed him.

But now, looking back, I no longer see him as brave. I see him as a coward who was too afraid to let go. Life was telling him that it was time, but he was too frightened.

Nasreen has tears in her eyes when she comes in.

"*Why, Zara?*"

"You know why."

Harry needs to be free. His plan isn't secure enough. It had sounded good when he'd left those emails in the drafts folders for me to read the morning after. Each of us denying responsibility. Each of us creating just enough doubt to make a jury uneasy about convicting two grieving parents. He would give evidence and take the brunt of the questioning. I would remain silent and not give evidence. What could the jury do with that but decide we were in it together? But then, once they were convinced that we were in it together, there was the video. He'd send it to the prosecution. A video that made it clear that only one of us could have done it. An edited video that would ensure that neither of us could be identified. It would be timed to arrive just after Harry had finished giving evidence. And by then it would be too late to force either of us to answer questions about it. It would have to just speak for itself.

Except the theory was better than the reality.

Alfred knew it. It was why he had played the footage even though it proved only one of us was involved in the murder. Looking at that video, even though you couldn't see him, you *felt* that Harry was there. Herman wasn't just scared. He was terrified. In a way that made it obvious it wasn't me there with him. When I saw that footage in court, I was certain the jury would find Harry guilty.

I couldn't let that happen.

I watch Nasreen go. Her red eyes are the last thing I see of her as she leaves the room.

When I am back in court, Harry is brought through and sits next to me. He reaches out his hand but I can't take it. Not yet.

"Zara," he says. "I know you think you're helping, but you're not."

I look at my feet because to look up at him is to risk weakness at a time when I need strength. "I'm sorry," I say into the floor.

"Listen to me," he whispers. "Do not plead guilty."

I turn my body but avoid his eyes. "It's too late, Harry. I confessed. They all heard me."

He shakes his head. "Look. I spoke to Stevens. He says that the case is carrying on against me regardless of you changing your plea to guilty. They won't drop the case against me. The best thing you can do for us both is to see it through to the end. If it's just me on the charge, they could convict me still. But if you're still in it, they're more likely to acquit me. I'm sorry."

"How can they convict you if I plead guilty?" I ask, shocked.

"Juries. Can't predict them. Stevens says it's safest this way." His face is folded in concern. His eyes beg. "I'm sorry, Zara. Please. I need to be out. You know that."

I look into his eyes. They are like shattered glass. The light refracts from them in a hundred different directions. I nod. "Okay," I say, and write a note to pass to Nasreen.

When the judge comes in, Nasreen stands, alone.

"Do you want the indictment put again?"

She reads my note to herself. "No, thank you, my lady."

Judge Foulkes looks at Nasreen in surprise but says nothing more to her. "Jury, please."

Once the jury is in place, Stevens jumps up. "Your ladyship said that she would look favorably upon any application I had to call my client to deal with the video."

She stares at him quizzically. "Are you asking for leave to recall your client?"

"Yes, my lady."

She turns to the prosecutor, Alfred, who shrugs. "Very well, Mr. Stevens. I can't tell you how to run your case."

It takes me a second to catch up and when I do, Harry is heading back into the witness box. I don't know what he's doing. It's suicidal for him to go in there and be questioned about the tape. No matter how clever he is, that video hurts him.

Stevens starts talking before Harry's even settled in.

"You've seen the video. You've heard what your wife has said about it. She accepts that it was her. No doubt you're relieved about that?"

"Not really," Harry says. "She's not guilty."

"Thank you. Wait there." Stevens sits down and as if on a seesaw, Alfred rises.

"Then it must be you."

Harry looks across at me. The silence once again drops over the room like a weighted blanket. "Then it must be me." All eyes are on Harry.

"Well, was it? You?"

"Yes. I killed Herman"—adding, after a slight pause—"alone."

Alfred leans dangerously forward. "Is this a game to you both?" His shoulders hunch as he turns to stare at me.

"No."

"Your wife says it was her and you say it was you. Yet, we know only one of you did it."

"She's lying. To protect me."

"And you're *not* lying to protect her?"

"No."

"What did you do with the murder weapon?"

"I threw it away. And threw away the clothes I was wearing, including the boots."

"And the other bloody footprints?"

"No idea. They weren't there when I was. Whoever they belong to came in after I left. They would have found Herman already dead."

"I see," Alfred says in disbelief. "Well then, maybe you can help us with this. If this was you, you must have recorded the footage?"

"Yes."

"So then where is the camera you recorded it on?"

Harry's cheeks flush and I can see a tremor beginning to colonize his hands. "Disposed of it."

"Where?"

"A large commercial bin. It's long gone."

"Of course it is. Tell me. Where is the unedited footage?"

"Excuse me?" Harry says, flicking away something from his forehead.

"Well, the footage has plainly been edited—to edit out your voice. Or your wife's. So, if this was you, you no doubt can furnish us with the original footage and we can hear you on it."

Harry looks at the floor. "Destroyed it."

"Well—it's digital footage. You'd have had to edit it on a computer. You can delete files as much as you like but they don't stay deleted, Mr. King. Deleting just leaves an instruction that the file is available to be overwritten."

"I don't know anything about that," Harry says.

"You don't need to. I do. Tell us where the computer is that you edited this on, and our team will do a forensic download and recover the data."

My heart starts up a new beat, thrumming like butterfly wings. Harry looks as though the earth is sinking beneath his feet.

"I can't give you that information."

Alfred looks at him long and hard. "Even to save your wife? Where is it?"

Harry presses his lips together hard as if afraid of the words escaping without his consent. "I can't tell you."

"If you can't tell us where it is, perhaps to protect whoever is holding it, maybe you can get the footage for us?"

"I can't do that either."

"Can't or won't?"

"Does it matter?"

Alfred looks at the ceiling. "If you're guilty of this murder, as you say, then why not enter a guilty plea?"

Harry looks down at his hands. "No. The jury should decide." The jury's eyes bore into him like drills.

Alfred throws up his hands and sits, and even from here, from just his back, I can tell he is furious. The side of his face that I can see is blood red, the skin as tight as a cooked apple.

SEVENTY-NINE

HARRY

ONCE I'M FINISHED IN THE BOX, THINGS MOVE VERY QUICKLY. STEVENS wakes up for the first time in the trial and tells the judge he has an application to make and the jury is sent away. He hasn't told me what it is, so I press my head forward against the glass to hear.

"A submission of no case to answer, my lady. In accordance with that case, the well-known one—the name's gone from my head. The plums and duff one."

The judge remains inscrutable. "Crown and Galbraith."

"Yes."

"First or second limb?"

"Sorry, my lady?"

The judge stares through him. "Are you saying that there is *no* evidence against your client or that there is *some* evidence but of poor quality?"

"The second one. The problem the prosecution has in this case is that there is clear evidence that only one person was guilty of the offense of murder. The video makes that as clear as it can be. It's circumstantial of course, but a strong inference can be drawn from the evidence."

"Your client says that it was him—that *he* was the one person."

"Yes. As does Mrs. King. And that is where the problem lies. The jury cannot convict them both as a matter of law."

"But Mr. Stevens, they could decide that your client is guilty and not Mrs. King. Or vice versa. Or that they were in a joint enterprise, the presence of the one encouraging the other. Why shouldn't I leave it to them?"

"They'd have to be sure, my lady. How can they be sure of guilt when two people have admitted to a crime only one of them could have committed? Where they had the same motive, the same opportunity, and both have unexplained portions of time to account for. They are both in the same window. They could each have committed the murder. But what no jury can say, on the evidence that they have heard, is which of them it was. And as for the joint enterprise, the Crown would have to be able to say who played what role. As it is, they can't say which of them was the stabber, let alone prove the other was present and giving their encouragement."

The judge furrows her brow and stares at the red notebook she's been writing in. "Let us say that you are correct in that analysis, it would be deeply unsatisfactory, wouldn't it, for the two of them to walk free, when we know as a matter of fact that one of them committed this murder?"

Stevens wraps his arms around himself as he speaks, sweeping up his gown as he does. "That's the famous principle we operate under, my lady. Better to let nine guilty men walk free than have one innocent hang."

As the sense of what he's saying filters down, I see the logic of what he is saying. I look across to Zara to see how much she's picked up. She looks at me, her face full of questions. I reach a tentative hand over and grasp her fingers tightly.

"I'm deeply troubled by this. Mr. Alfred, what do you say?"

Alfred rises slowly as if he's still processing what to say. "I'm troubled too, my lady. One of them murdered Mr. Herman in cold blood. Both of them have admitted the murder. They could be convicted on the basis of their admissions. The jury might, for example, find that the other evidence in the case supported a conviction of one rather than the other defendant. My submission is that the matter ought to be left to the jury to decide."

Nasreen then gets up. "Your ladyship has to direct the jury in this case. What would you say to them in summing up? That only one of them is guilty, but that they, the jury must decide which one it is? It would, in our respectful submission, be an impossible task."

The judge looks again at the ceiling for answers. "But suppose Mr. Alfred is right. The other evidence might point to one defendant over the other. That, surely, is within the jury's province?"

"It might be in other circumstances. But here, even the Crown don't say which they prefer for the candidate. And there's a reason for that.

"If the prosecution say that their case is that Mr. King is guilty, not Mrs. King, it would be an abuse of process to try Mrs. King at all. In fact, there is an argument to say that it's an abuse of process to try two people when there is clear evidence that one of them must be innocent. It's tempting for my lady to make a decision on the basis that one of the two of them is guilty, but it is just as true and more important to proceed from the footing that one of the two is surely *innocent*."

The judge finishes hearing the arguments and adjourns to consider her decision. Stevens comes downstairs into the conference rooms in the cells to see me.

"I think there's a good chance. I can't see a jury being able to decide this. Foulkes has to kick the case out. She has to. I have to hand it to you, though, Harry. I thought it was a mistake. But now I think it was ingenious. You couldn't have planned it better."

"I didn't plan it. But, Stan, I do feel I owe you an explanation."

"No. You don't. I don't need to hear it. I *can't* hear explanations."

We sit in silence after that for a few minutes until he becomes twitchy and gets up. "I'll see you upstairs when the case is called on again."

In the cells there is a wicket gate that is normally left shut but it's so warm down here that they have left it open. Through the hatch I can see the cell opposite but not the occupant. To the left of it is a whiteboard with one word scrawled on it in blue felt-tip—*Female*.

I call out, "Zara."

A second later her small face appears in the aperture, and suddenly all there is separating us is tears. I push my fingers through the bars.

"I love you," I say to her.

She smiles sadly and nods. "I know," she says.

If I could carry the weight of the love I feel right now with me, wherever I went, then it would be enough. I'd never need anything more. She continues to look at me, and I remember what I had forgotten. That she's not Zara anymore. She is a thing transformed by the love wrenched out of her. Her face isn't hers anymore. *She* isn't hers anymore.

"Not long now," I say as softly as I can, but my voice echoes in the corridor. A prisoner down the corridor starts shouting out for food, and Zara retreats out of view.

As the minutes pile up, I begin to dissect the arguments again and at first, I am reassured by the logic of it. There are two of us in here. Only one is guilty. But when I consider it again, I know that if the jury makes the decision, I'm sunk. I'm a man. I'm not especially likable. I've smashed into Herman's house before. I've flown a drone into his bedroom. It's my camera the footage was recorded on. It's my gun that was found the next morning by police. In retrospect, it was a mistake to think that the prosecution wouldn't understand the significance of the gun. It hadn't been fired so I didn't think that the police would make a connection. I thought it would make them wonder about gangs or drugs. Now I think that if I'd had time, I would have disposed of it myself—far away. To be discovered much later. But I didn't know when they'd be coming for me. I did know, from Caspar, that if they'd found the gun in the house, Zara would have been given a five-year-minimum sentence just for having it there. I had to make sure it was gone. But I didn't want it in a bin for a kid to find. It had to be safely away. I thought that Katya's voice, when she made the call, would be enough to filter the suspicion away from Zara to nothing.

I hear a door clang in the distance and now all I can think of is a future behind doors like this one.

But life. I can't do life. I have to be out of here. And Zara. She can't do much more prison than she's already done—her flesh is barely attached to her soul.

EIGHTY

ZARA

WHEN I SAW HIS FACE FRAMED IN THE METAL DOOR OF THE CELLS, IT HAD the feeling of an omen. He felt so close. But sitting once again in the dock, Harry just a few feet from me, it is as if he's been spirited away again to another world.

I can cope with the justice of whatever decisions are made or reached or stumbled accidentally upon in this courtroom. It's all just. It is all unjust. There are no poetic movements here that weave threads of right and wrong. It's all just tapestry. After Sophie died, that is the one thing that I know for certain. Nothing is fair or just.

The judge is delivering her judgment on the applications to dismiss the case. I can't hear everything, I can't even hear most of what she's saying, so I am left to try to decode the decision from the body language of the barristers' backs, bent as they take down the words on keyboard, or paper.

When she is finished, I look at Harry, breath shallow. His face, always washed through with exhaustion, is now streaked with confusion.

"Did you get any of that?"

"No," I say. All I can hear is my own heart pounding.

Then the judge calls for the jury, and I'm filled with a sickening sensation as they slowly take their places. I hold my breath. I don't know what is next, but whatever it is will change lives.

The jury gathers, silent. Intrigued.

"Members of the jury," Judge Foulkes says finally. "As you will have no doubt gathered, this case is causing all of us, lawyers and judge alike, some difficulties that have required careful consideration from me. Counsel for each defendant has made an application to me to dismiss this case and, for reasons that I am bound by, it's my determination, made with a good deal of reluctance, that the case has to be stopped."

Harry collapses onto the floor.

The guard gathers him up quickly. My breath comes evenly for now. I can't quite believe this, although a part of me prepared for no other outcome.

"I can see by some of your reactions that this is both an unexpected and, for some, an unwelcome decision. But there are strong legal reasons why I have to stop the case here. It will not have escaped your attention that both defendants have admitted committing a murder that we know from other evidence in the case can *only* have been committed by one person. By one of these defendants.

"We have an important principle at play in the system that I was reminded of earlier, but of which I can assure you, I needed no reminding. That principle is that it is better to let nine guilty people go free than convict one innocent person of a crime that he or she did not commit. We now know that one of these two defendants is innocent. The law cannot in good conscience allow the prosecution of two people for a crime for which only one of them is responsible. For that and for other reasons that I will not trouble you with, you will, on my direction when asked by my clerk, find each of these defendants not guilty of murder."

Time stops. My pulse throbs in my eyes. I see the world as if through frosted glass. The world is slow, like syrup.

AFTER THE FORMALITIES of the verdict, Alfred reminds the judge that Harry still has to be sentenced for the criminal damage to Herman's property.

"How long has he spent in custody awaiting trial?" Foulkes asks.

"Three hundred and forty-one days, my lady," Alfred says.

"Very well. He's served the equivalent of almost a two-year sentence."

Stevens gets to his feet and begins to speak, but the judge cuts him off. "I don't need to hear from you. Eighteen months custody. Deemed served. Any other applications?"

"May they be discharged?" Nasreen says, bobbing up.

"Yes. But let me say this." The judge looks at us hard. "It is not, as you have heard, Mr. and Mrs. King, without very considerable reluctance that I am dismissing this case. It is, of course, a tragedy that you have lost your daughter. It is a further tragedy that the circumstances strongly suggest that she is no longer alive. I am also very much aware of the fact that Mr. Herman appeared to have made some admissions to some serious conduct toward your daughter. And it is a tragedy that, as far as one of you is concerned, you have spent a year of your life in custody needlessly, although I stress that that is not a criticism of the Crown.

"But the fact remains that one of you murdered Mr. Herman. That is something you must live with. If other evidence comes to the fore that makes it clear which of you that was, be in no doubt, you will be prosecuted once again for his murder. The rule against double jeopardy no longer survives. The CPS will, I am sure, have no hesitation in prosecuting you."

IT TAKES ALMOST an hour to process me out of the cells, but even so, when I am finally free and standing on the sunlit pavement outside the court, I am still in a daze. Nasreen has gone. She came downstairs into the cells earlier to congratulate me. I thanked her as much as I could, but in the moment, it fell flat. No amount of thanks can reach the heights of what she did for me.

"If it makes any difference to you," she said quietly as she left, "Herman deserved everything he got."

I walk opposite a low granite wall and sit facing the front step of the Bailey. I sit absorbing the sun into my skin. I haven't felt it in so long. A large plastic sack with my belongings sags next to me on the pavement. I'd have left all of it behind if I could. I don't want to see that bag or anything that's in it ever again.

A few minutes later, I turn to see Harry struggling out with his bag. As soon as he sees me, he drops it and runs over the road to me. His arms are around me, squeezing hard. The scent of him knocks me back a dozen years. I don't know how I've survived this last year without him, now that I see him and feel him here by my side.

We don't speak during the short taxi journey. Instead, we hold hands and let the blood rushing in them swap messages. Only when we are home and at the front door do I remember that Harry had left. Left me.

Inside, the house smells stale as a church. I run through the rooms and throw open the windows. Harry opens up all the taps and switches the boiler on. I feel like a stranger here, but the sensation doesn't last. By the time I fill the kettle, the house is welcoming me back. The shadows are still there, but those that begin to peek out are like visiting friends.

"I'll order a takeaway for dinner."

I'm not hungry but I nod along. I finish making some mint tea and take the cups into the garden to catch the last of the falling light. The shrubs have grown and there are weeds peering out from beneath the flowerpots. Caspar has been doing a decent job maintaining it, but he's no gardener.

Harry joins me. "Can I stay?" he says after a sip.

I hold his hand. "I'd be upset if you didn't."

And then to fill in the silence, I ask him, "What about all the stuff from the flat? What happened to it?" As soon as I say it, though, a flood rises over me. There's so much time to recover. So much to catch up. We haven't spoken in a year.

"I gave it all away."

"All of it?" I'm surprised.

"I kept one thing," he says, and rushes back into the house. When he returns, I see him and the tears gather and slowly flow.

He hands me the frog, Robbit, and I hold him to my nose. The scent it carries is still of Sophie. In it I imagine I can smell her hair, and that more than anything takes the wind out of me.

"We need to talk about all this," Harry says after a while.

"Not now," I say. "Later." We sit until the sun has dipped under the horizon and thrown flames across the sky. And when finally we leave, we do it to leave the gathering cold behind.

EIGHTY-ONE

HARRY

THAT NIGHT

I TAKE A STEP FORWARD. A TWIG SNAPS UNDER THE HEEL OF MY BOOT. I listen. I stand still and hold the meat in my outstretched arm. It's time to wake the dog.

I inch forward, heart racing. I keep low to the ground in case anyone should be looking into the garden. I am right upon the kennel and the dog hasn't woken. I have meat in my hand but the scent hasn't roused her. I peer in. There is no dog, but a large cooked leg of lamb lies half-eaten on the floor.

Then I notice the door. The glass has been shattered and lies on the kitchen floor in jagged shards next to a large stone. The door has been pulled to but the catch hasn't caught. It's open. Shit. I can't deal with the dog if she's inside the house. I push into the kitchen, carefully stepping around as much of the glass as I can to avoid making a noise. The stale smell of dog food and unwashed dishes fills my nose. I stop. There is a faint rumble of voices, coming from deep in the house. I shouldn't stay here. It's too dangerous, and what I had expected to be a controllable environment is now anything but.

There's someone in the house. Who's broken in? The dog is God knows where. The yellowing fridge is an arm's length away, and I need to get rid of this meat in my hand. I open the freezer compartment and toss it in.

More noise from upstairs. The voices are familiar in tone. One is Herman's. The other is S——. I consider the possibility in disbelief as I lope quietly out of the kitchen and into the hallway. The stairs are to my right. I stop at the base and listen. I hear the padding and snuffling of what can only be the dog. She must be locked in one of the rooms downstairs.

Then I hear that second voice again. It sounds like S——. But it can't be.

Now it's as clear as a bell. I know that voice. Not S——. *Zara*. Before I realize it, I am racing up the stairs. She's in trouble. I don't know why she's here but she's in danger. I charge straight into the bedroom. Herman is in a chair, eyes wide with fear.

Zara is standing in front of him and as I enter, she points a gun at me. My old Ruger.

"Zara! What the hell is going on?"

In the second that the gun is off him, Herman leaps up. Zara turns it back on him. "You sit down."

"Arms on the chair," I say, stepping in front of him. Now I am moving as if everything has been practiced a hundred times. I reach into my backpack and pull out the tape and wind it round each of his arms a dozen times until I'm sure he can't escape. Then I do the same with his legs, wrapping the tape around his ankles and the chair legs.

"Zara," I say, turning my attention to her. "What are you doing here?"

"I know why you're here but I can't let you do it."

"Go home, Zara. It's not too late."

She shakes her head slowly. "I can't. I can't leave him now. Not after what he's told me." The gun in her hand quivers as she levels it to Herman's head.

"I didn't say anything," he says then. "She's a liar."

I pull Zara away gently. "Come with me. He's not going anywhere." Her face is wet with tears, red with anger. She comes away reluctantly, moving as if in a dream. When we are on the landing, I lay my hands on her shoulders. "That thing isn't going to do a good job of killing him," I say, nodding at the gun.

"I had to do something," she says, her eyes red with anger.

"Go home, Zara," I say.

"No. I can't let you. My life is done now, Harry. You go."

"What did he tell you?"

"That he took Sophie." The words hit me hard and for a moment I can't formulate my next thought.

"Where is she now?" I say, coming back around.

She shakes her head, and her face crumples into tears.

"Go home, Zara," I say, reaching into my bag. "I have a camera. I'll make him confess on video. But I need you away from here or it won't work." I keep my voice low so that he doesn't hear us on the landing.

She dabs away at her face. "No. You're going to kill him."

He makes a noise like a yelp from inside the bedroom. "No. I promise. I just need the confession."

"I'm staying," she says, and begins to follow me in.

"No. You can't. He won't believe my threats if he thinks you're here. He has to know it's just me and him. Alone." I turn her toward the steps and lead her down the first few of them. "You have to leave, quickly. The police might come any second. And you can't have that gun in the house. Wipe it down and get rid of it."

"Where?"

"Somewhere safe. Put it into a Royal Mail letter box. This morning, before first collection. I'll report it so it gets picked up by the police. And separate the bullets."

She nods and then heads toward the front door.

"Go out the back," I say. "Be careful of the dog."

"I made him put her into one of the rooms."

Zara opens her mouth to speak again when Herman's voice splits us apart like cleaved wood. "Help!"

"Go," I say, "before he wakes all the neighbors. Now!"

Back in the room, Herman is fighting against his bindings but they are holding fast. "Help," he shouts again when he sees me. I race over to him, pull out my chef's knife, and hold it immediately in front of his face. "Any more of that and this meets your throat." His voice dies down into a whimper.

I take the camera from my backpack and set it on top of a chest of drawers and position it so that I am out of shot when I stand behind him. It's the drone's camera so I know it will record good footage.

"You can start by telling me what you told my wife," I say.

"Let me go, please," he screams.

"First you tell me what you told my wife."

"And you'll let me go?" he says.

"I will. But if I even think you've left anything out, I'll end you here and now. So, think carefully."

He gathers himself for a few moments. When it comes, his voice is splintered. "She came one day, sent by the other fella to take my order."

"Order?" I say. But I know what's coming.

"E. Ever since the injury, the MDMA is the only thing that takes the edge off."

My pulse is racing. I have to be quick. "Then what happened?"

"Nothing at first. She took my order and she left."

I find the details sticky and hard to process. "But you don't open the door to anyone. How did she get in?"

"The main fella sent a message to say she was coming, so I was expecting her."

"Then what?"

"Then the next week she brought the gear and we got talking."

A shiver runs through my body, knowing that she was here with this man. I push the point of the knife into the skin of his neck. The urge to ram it home is so strong that I feel my hand ache with it. He squeals when the blade cuts through. "Then?"

"No. You're going to kill me. When I tell you, you're going to kill me."

I put my mouth to his ear. His head reeks of dying flesh and urine. "If you tell me what happened, I'll tell the police. But you'll live."

He breathes, but in shudders. He thinks about it until I press it in harder. "Okay. Okay," he says. "Give me a second. So, then she came. And I noticed she was wearing this necklace. Which, you know, I said I liked. And she said she drew butterflies as well. I asked 'em if she'd, you know, like do a mural in my bedroom for a hundred pounds."

"What?" I say in disbelief. "You mean *she* painted that?" I'd convinced myself that she'd copied his mural, not painted it herself.

He nods. I'm standing behind him so I can only see his face as it appears framed in the camera. Too small to see his expression.

"She came a few days on the run to paint it. Then one night after she finished, she asked to stay the night."

"You're lying," I say, and feel the blade pulsing in my hand.

"She did. She did. I swear. Just the one night. Had been having a hard time at home, she said."

My blood runs cold to think of her wanting to stay here at all. I think about the padlock on her door. How we had to push her and hold the door closed. "Then what happened?"

"Then," he says, looking down, "I got attached to 'em. She wanted to leave but I didn't want 'em to go."

"So you *killed* her?" I say, the anger sending flashes into my eyes.

"No. I didn't kill 'em. I didn't."

"You're lying, Herman. I know you killed her. Because if you didn't, where is she?"

He doesn't answer but something like a sob leaves his chest.

"Admit what you've done."

He stops as if weighing up his options. "Okay, okay," he says finally.

A fistful of bile rises immediately into my throat. "Did you kill her?"

"How many times do you want me to say it? It wasn't me. I didn't do anything to 'em."

I bring the point of the knife level to his eye. My hand shakes with temptation.

"Your girl, it's Sophie, right? I didn't do anything to 'em. It was—"

"It was what? An accident? What—what was it? You had her here, in this house!"

"Yes. I did. I had 'em here. Yes, that's true. I had your daughter." His breathing is so erratic now that I wonder whether he is going to pass out.

And now I am overcome by panic. The information is too hard to digest. There is so much of it and it is so dark I can't find my way through it.

"You had her here right under our noses? That's what you're saying?" I hiss into his ear.

"Yes," he cries. "That's what I'm saying." He is shaking with fear.

The sight of his tears fills me with fury. "How long? How long was she here?" The need to scream every word at him is so strong that I am almost out of my body. But I can't scream. The neighbors would hear.

"About three days."

My tears are coming now and I choke them back because I need to be here, completely. "Three days?" I can't believe how near she'd been. "Where? Not here. You couldn't have kept her in this room. She'd have shouted out of the window. Someone would have heard her."

"No. Kept 'em gagged. In the—in the—" he says, and then the tears begin to drip onto his yellow skin. "In the cellar."

And the realization hits me. "Wait. You killed her here, in the cellar?"

"I didn't kill 'em. I had a girl meself. Gone now. You're a parent. You couldn't kill someone's child. I couldn't either. I *didn't* kill 'em. Yes, I kept 'em. Yes. I kept 'em. I did."

I take the knife and point it downward into his neck. I can't hear more of this. But I must.

"*Kept?*" I say in a rage that is taking over me now. I feel like I've been possessed by a second spirit. I'm losing my grip on myself.

"She wanted to stay with me. If you'd a seen 'em, you'd a *seen*," he says, croaking.

I turn the knife so that it's vertical. I grip the handle with both hands, ready to plunge it in.

"Where's your other half? Why aren't they here? Get 'em here. Please. Talk some sense into you. Please, please," he says, bawling.

"She's not here," I say.

"Get 'em on the phone, then. Let me explain it to 'em. I didn't kill her."

"I'm not doing that," I say, and press the knife down. My face is wet and it is everything I can do not to wipe the tears away so that I can see.

"Wait. No. No. It was—"

"What?" I say. "What?"

"It was Andy. Andy took her."

The name sends a bolt through me. "Andy who?"

"The fella who was supplying the gear," he says through sobs.

"What's he got to do with it?"

Herman's jaw begins to shake and he lets out a howl.

"On the third night I heard a noise and went to check on 'em. And give 'em some food. But she were gone."

The information cascades so fast that I can't keep hold of it. "What do you mean she was gone?"

"She'd escaped. She slipped the ropes. They weren't on tight enough. My fingers, see. Arthritis. She'd forced the door open. Rotten frames. Sheba had been in the kitchen and I thought she'da barked if something were up. But the kitchen door were ajar and the dog were outside. Then I saw the kennel had been moved. And I seen her using it to scramble over the back fence."

I think of how she banged and kicked the door when we'd locked her in. She'd almost split the wood. I think of the pen marks down her leg. She'd have hated being locked in.

"You're lying. If she'd escaped, she'd have come home. She'd have called the police." I grab a fistful of his yellow hair and yank it back to expose his throat. I lay the blade against it.

"I swear. She escaped. I saw her go over."

"So where did she go?"

He squawks from the pressure of his stretched neck. "That Andy fella's got 'em."

"What do you mean?"

"I called him straightaway. I didn't know what else to do. He was angry. So angry. Kept saying how could I be so stupid to try and kidnap her. That the police were going to be all over him now. *What we going to do?* I asked him.

"We *aren't going to do anything*. I'm *going to fix it,* he said. Told me he knew where she lived and that in the car he could get to her before she got home."

"You're telling me that Andy's got her?"

"Yes. I swear."

My heart stops.

EIGHTY-TWO

ZARA

THAT NIGHT

I'M STILL IN HERMAN'S HOUSE. HARRY'S VOICE CARRIES EASILY OVER TO where I am standing outside the open bedroom door. I can't leave. I walked toward the back of the house until Harry returned to the bedroom and then I crept quietly up the stairs.

I have to hear this for myself.

Herman's voice when it reaches my ears is pinched and wet. Every word he utters sends a wave of disgust through me. But I know Harry. It won't be disgust he's feeling as much as anger and hatred. Any second he's going to drive that knife in. Every time Herman speaks will be the last, I think. But then I hear him say the words. That he kept her in a cellar. Like it was nothing. Like she was nothing—disposable. My beautiful girl.

I step into the open doorway and see Harry's back and in front of him, Herman's head twisting in the chair. The knife is on the floor by his feet and Harry is bent at the waist, sobbing. Herman is wailing, crying to be let free.

I pad silently to where Harry is standing and put an arm around him. If he is surprised that I'm back he doesn't show it. He continues to sob. I crouch quickly and pick up the knife and hold it loosely in my hand. Herman arches his neck again, aware of me. He's smelled me or seen me in the video camera.

"You're back. Miss. Please talk some sense into 'em. Let me go. I ain't done anything to her."

"You killed her," I say softly.

"No, miss. I didn't. Ask him. I didn't."

"Inna lillahi," I say. And then slowly and deliberately, I slide the knife deep into his neck. With two hands on the hilt. When Harry sees the blood, his mouth opens before he falls heavily to the floor, out cold.

WHEN HARRY COMES to, he is frantic. He sees the lifeless body. "Zara. What did you do?"

"You better go," I say. He looks at me, frozen for a moment as if suspended in air. It's a few seconds before he lands. He blinks rapidly and starts to move quickly and fiercely. He leads me out of the bedroom into the corridor. He stops and holds my face.

"Zara. Listen to me carefully. After we leave here we can't speak. If you need to pass on a message or I need to, then write an email on my Gmail account. You know the password to get in. But don't send the message. Leave it in the drafts folder as before. I'll do the same."

"Okay."

"Take the gun. Do what I told you. Lose everything you're wearing. Everything."

"I know," I say. "I've already thought it through."

"And you need an alibi? Did you think of that?"

"Yes," I say thinking of the call that was still connected to Luca. "You?" He nods.

"Tell the police nothing. Don't worry. Don't panic. I'll take care of it all. Come on now. We have to move."

I go quickly down the stairs and head round to the back. My head is pounding.

He calls after me in a heavy whisper. "Which way did you get in?"

"I used the ladder to get over the fence where it's lower and then pulled it over."

We are now in the garden. The air smells wet and slippery. "Go back the way you came. No noise. I'll leave in five minutes. We don't want to leave at the same time," he whispers.

As I turn he pulls me in close. "Zara. Don't say anything to the police. Promise me. I will get us out of this but I need you with me all the way."

"Okay," I say, and swallow back the tears I feel rising and tighten the straps on my backpack.

"Wait," he says. "When you get rid of the gun, you need to post this memory card from the camera," I say, slipping it out of the body. "We cannot afford to have it found. If I'm stopped on the way I can't have it on me. If in doubt, get rid of it."

"Post it to who? Caspar?"

"No. He'll try and play it—can't let him see it. Someone you can trust not to open it."

"Okay," I say, and then Sadia comes to mind. "I know someone."

"Remember. The gun and the card—both must be out of the house before the police come."

"Okay," I say. I look into his face. I may never see him again, I realize. His eyes are trembling. He tries a smile for me but can't complete it.

"Go now."

I face the mossy expanse of the night. I scramble through the weeds and grass until I reach the fence. It's only when I'm on the other side of it that my heart starts thumping with the realization of what I have done. I climb it quickly and as silently as I can and drop to the ground before reaching to lift the aluminum ladder over. Then I go home by the shortest route. When I reach our front gate, I lay the ladder gently along the base of the hedge. It plinks as it touches the ground.

I crouch down and put my face in my hands. I'm shaking. I need a minute to gather all of my senses close. There is so much to do and so much to keep in my head. I have to be strong for what's coming but images of Sophie, my little girl, keep flooding my head. What he did to her? I see her pain and overlaying it, the terror—black and hopeless. And then just like that something in my head makes a sound like a cracking branch. I can't carry it all with me. There is too much and it is too heavy. I can't breathe air and have all of this welded to me at the same time. There's only life enough in me for one thing—that or this.

EIGHTY-THREE

HARRY

NOW

IT'S TAKEN A WHILE TO ADJUST TO LIFE OUTSIDE A PRISON CELL. TWO DAYS out for every day inside, they say. Occasionally I shout out in the middle of the night, Zara tells me, but it's happening less and less frequently.

I shout, but she cries. I wake to the sound of her quiet sobs. Sometimes she's awake and sometimes I wipe her tear-soaked face only to see that she is still sleeping.

Sadness is still thick in places. It comes on without notice. But there are moments of happiness too. A dash of light across Zara's face in the morning. Coffee. The scent of jasmine after the rain has fallen. But there are long corridors of darkness.

I saw Katya three weeks after I'd been released. She sent me a text and we met in a café in Clapham. She smiled when I walked in and waved. I almost didn't recognize her. She looked well. Happy even.

"You look like terrible," she said, putting a hand lightly to my face.

"Thanks," I said, laughing. "How kind."

"In my country we are only polite to strangers. Not to friends," she said, and then sat down.

A silence settled between us. "Thank you," I said at last.

She waved her hand to dismiss me.

"No. Really. It saved our lives."

There were two coffees on the table. She picked up one and took a sip. "I have a job." My eyes widen. "You mean an official one?"

"Yes. Nothing special. But they sponsor me so finally I have papers."

"No more tarot?"

She laughed and I saw the amber light in her eyes. "Cards or cups or runes. Is just a medium to hear the conversation. I can't turn off the sounds."

Later when we were standing on the pavement she embraced me quickly. "I'm sorry," she said.

"You're sorry? For what?" I was genuinely puzzled.

"I think I might have give you false hope."

I thought about this. "Hope is hope. It's never false or true, it just is what it is."

Her smile held for longer than I'd ever seen it. "You sound like me," she said. Then as I turned to go she held me back. "Wait." She fished into her bag and held out my watch. I waited a second before I took it. The weight of what I had done to her poured over me.

"I have to tell you something," I said. She cocked her head and waited, amused almost. "I don't know how to say this."

She tucked away a stray hair and waited, serene.

"I lied to you. Worse. I manipulated you into helping me."

She nodded like the ebbing of shallow waves. "You mean the immigration people?"

"I'm so sorry. I was desperate. It's no excuse," I said, before drying up.

"I knew at the time. You came to my place. They came. I worked it out."

"You didn't say anything."

"By then I was . . . without choice. I had to move. Your place was good. You did not charge me rent. I felt safe."

"It was a shitty thing to do."

"It was," she said. "But I forgive you."

— — —

NOW AS THE darkness collects, I watch the people leaving this building. As they go, I feel myself return.

I was inside it until a little under half an hour ago, in the corner, with my back to the rest of the room, facing out into the street. It was a quiet night. Wednesday. When I left, there were seven people remaining. Now, well after "Last orders," every last customer has decamped. Only two are left—the girl with the pink hair, Lola, and him, Andy. I take the catapult out of my pocket. It's a professional hunting slingshot with spirit level and laser sighting. I check the laser sighting.

I concentrate on the pub. I know the procedure well by now. This is my third visit at this time of night. Lola will mop the floor and wipe the tables. Once the glasses are all dried she'll put on her short leather jacket and pull down the shutters on the windows and lock them. Then she'll drop the keys off to him. A few minutes later, Andy will switch off the remaining lights and lock the door. Except he won't.

Not this time.

I hear the shutters being rolled down, and before Lola's turned the key, I pull on some gloves and am across the road, obscured by a van. She runs back in to drop off the key to him, and a second later she is out again and fast-walking through the night. From the street, the pub is illuminated from just the light that spills from the door.

A second later, I walk in, pull the door shutter down and the door closed behind me.

"We're closed," Andy says, looking up from behind a small table. He looks the same as before. A little puffier around the eyes, but that's it.

"I know," I say, and pull out the slingshot and fire a ball bearing as I walk toward him. It hits him square in the chest and sends him collapsing onto the floor. That will have snapped a rib. At full stretch, it would have gone straight through. I load another as I stand over him. I pull the band taut and aim it at his head.

"Up you get, Andy."

He groans and fights his way upright, clutching his chest. "Aren't you supposed to be in prison, you fucking psycho?"

"Yep," I say. "I am. Let's go to your office."

The office is a small room, no bigger than a large broom cupboard. There is CCTV recording equipment, a desk, and a chair in there but almost nothing else.

"Sit," I say. He does as he is told and then I indicate the CCTV. "You know how to reformat that disk?"

"What the hell is going on? I'm calling the police," he says, and gropes for his phone. I let another shot loose. It strikes him on the thigh and sends him into a scream.

"I've got about a hundred rounds. CCTV. I want you to format that disk. Now."

He rubs his leg trying to soothe what I know will be agonizing pain. These slingshots can bring down wild boar.

"Erase the whole month?" he says, and limps a step forward to access the options on the screen. I watch carefully as he sets the process in motion. In seconds, the machine is deleting all the stored footage.

"And leave the CCTV off."

"What do you want?" he says, turning in his swivel chair toward me.

I keep the catapult aimed at his head, at half stretch. At this distance, with this bearing, it's a lethal shot. I throw him a cable tie. "Put it in your mouth and then tie your arm to the chair."

He does what I tell him, and as soon as he is done I step behind him and tie his other arm down.

"The fuck you want?" He struggles but the ties are strong.

"What did you do with her?"

"Who?"

"Really? My daughter, of course."

"I don't know what you're talking about," he says, but I spin him round to face me.

"Save your breath," I say. "Herman told me. I know you took her." He begins to protest but I silence him with a stretch of my slingshot. "Where is she?"

"I have no idea," he says, and then immediately winces in the expectation of a shot.

"You told the old man," I say. "You told him that you were going to get her before she got home."

He nods furiously. "I did. But I never found her. I thought I was too late. Thought she must have got home by the time I drove there."

"Bullshit!" I say. "What did you do with her?" The end of the catapult is millimeters from his eye.

"I didn't take her," he says, and squeezes his eyes shut, ready for the assault.

From my pocket I pull out a large, thick, clear plastic bag and a roll of tape with my gloved hand.

"What you doing with that?"

I don't answer. Instead I pass the bag over his struggling head and tape the bag shut around his neck. His breathing quickens immediately. "You psycho. They'll life you off for this, you fucking loon."

I lower my face so that it's level with his. "You need to conserve the oxygen. If you save it, you've got maybe three or four minutes."

He stares at me through the bag and opens his mouth to say something but then thinks better of it.

"Some people call this an exit bag. I quite like that," I say. "Not an easy exit, though."

He thrashes around in his chair, gasping for breath.

"Wait," he says, his voice muffled. "I know who she must've gone to." His words steam the inside of the bag.

"You."

"No," he says, frantic now. "D. It was D."

"You're D," I say. "An-dee. D."

"No! No. I'm not. But I know who is." Something in his eyes convinces me. He knows something.

I cut his right wrist tie and watch as he rips the bag desperately off his face. It is wet with condensation. He hyperventilates, and I leave him for a second to recover his breath before readying the catapult.

"They came in a couple of times. I didn't think anything about it. She was younger than him, but so what? I prefer them younger myself."

I pull the catapult back and fire a steel ball into his knee. He screams out in pain.

"No," he says quickly, rubbing his knee. "I mean that it wouldn't have stood out to me."

"What wouldn't?"

"That she was with an older man. That they were *hiding*."

"What do you mean?" I say, but even as the words are in the air the thought is solidifying.

"I mean," he says, catching his breath still, "hiding the relationship. You told me she was underage when you came into the pub with her. That's when I knew she was seeing someone she shouldn't."

"What are you talking about?"

"She was here. Your daughter. She came sometimes. Sat in a corner by herself and would leave after an hour. She drank *Coke*."

"And?"

"One of these days he came in. He was at the bar and she came over and tapped him on the shoulder. And then a second later they go in opposite directions. He's off joining some others. She's gone back to her corner. I knew something was up."

I conjure up the pictures of my daughter and this man meeting illicitly. Him panicking. "Who is it?" I say.

He says nothing.

"I'm not sure you deserve to live, Andy. I'm really struggling here." I take another plastic bag from my pocket. "Who is he?"

"I don't know his name, but she called him D. That's as much as she would tell me."

I put the bag over his head and stretch out some more tape.

"Wait! I can show you what he looks like. I have him on tape. It's what I used to blackmail them into doing the work. I've got a recording of it."

EIGHTY-FOUR

ZARA

NOW

HE DIDN'T TELL ME WHERE HE WAS GOING. BUT I KNOW.

I also know that he's not going to find Sophie there. She's not there, with Andy. It wasn't him. I can't tell you how I know it but I do. It's more than just the certainty of feeling. It's the certainty of *knowledge*. Sophie's talking to me.

She talks to me every day now. When the case was finished, I came home and lay on her bed. I did it every day at dusk. And then one evening when the sky was burned toffee, I saw her. I looked into the black of her wallpaper and beyond it, into the darkness, and I saw Sophie. She looked like a princess of some snowy land. At first, I thought it was Narnia. I thought that all the times I had read the books to her had re-created the land and her in it. I thought that all those stories had left my mouth and exerted a magic that was stored somewhere, waiting for her to claim it. But I was wrong. *Am* wrong. She isn't in Narnia. I don't know where exactly she is. But I'll know it when I see it.

The night is bright tonight. I have a sensation of something elemental coming toward us. It can't be stopped. It moves with heavy, steady, unwavering steps. It tramps its way to us like a giant machine.

But I am not afraid of it. Nothing holds any terror for me now. I am fearless. But the price, if you want to know, of fearlessness, is the loss of everything you love.

EIGHTY-FIVE

HARRY

NOW

I KNOCK GENTLY AND WAIT.

It is after midnight and he will need time to wake and open the door. I knock again, louder this time. A car hisses by behind me on the wet tarmac.

I knock for a third time, and I can see the hallway light come on through the ornamental glass panels. I wait.

The chain is hooked in and the door opens a few inches. He peers through, confusion scrawled across his face. His shoulders are bare, giving him a childlike look. He stands there focusing, assessing who it is that has hammered on his door after midnight. Then finally he recognizes me and smiles uncertainly through the gap.

"Just a second," he says, and shuts the door. I see his shadow retreating into the house. Two minutes, maybe three pass. I am about to bang the door again when his shadow returns, slowly. It unclasps the chain and pulls the door open. "What are you doing here?"

"Can I come in?"

He checks his watch. "It's late, Harry."

"It won't take a minute," I say, and he lets me in. Of course he does. We're *family*.

He is dressed in striped pajamas as though he is in a sitcom. "Everything okay?"

"I'm so stupid," I say. "I trusted you."

"Harry?" he asks, crossing his arms tight. "What's happened?"

"You were seeing her."

"Who? Seeing who? What's this about?"

I push him back into the living room and onto the sofa. He sits stunned.

"You're D."

"What?"

"Sophie." Her name, out loud, catches in my throat. "She called you D. She didn't want to give you away."

He tries to stand but I push him back down. "I don't know what you mean." There's a hint of outrage in his voice, but it hasn't quite crystallized, as if he hasn't fully committed to it.

"You do. I know. I know you were seeing my daughter—your pupil! I trusted you. *She* trusted you."

"Harry," he says, splaying his hands. "I don't know what rumors you've heard but they're not true. I swear." He is speaking in this loud and stagey way that immediately tells me everything.

I sit down next to him. "I've seen the CCTV, Rob. From the Pig. Where you met her that time. I saw the look on your face. How scared you looked that some of the other staff you were with would see her."

He blanches. A second later he is on his feet. I lunge forward and tackle him to the floor. He kicks out, but he isn't a match for me on a good day, and this isn't a good day. I punch him hard in the face three times before dragging him back onto the sofa.

"I need to know what you did with her. Look at my face, Rob," I say, and take out the catapult. I load it with a ball bearing. Slowly. And then I stretch it. "Look closely, Rob. You only get one go. Where is she? Where is my girl?"

He puts his head into his hands and a moment later he is sobbing. He says "sorry" repeatedly, but the sound of his words is muffled by the sobs. I drop the catapult and slap him hard across the face. "Where is she?"

"Here," he says finally. "She's here."

Hearing it said so blandly like that knocks the wind from me. I am wheezing. "Why?"

He looks up, confused.

"*Why* did you do it?" I ask him.

"I couldn't help it."

I feel a sudden slug of pain to my gut and I double over. My own body is assaulting me. I am kneeling now as if at his feet. I can't fight the weight of it all. His head is still in his hands.

"It wasn't like that. I swear, Harry."

I raise myself from my knees just enough to punch him once, hard in the face. He whimpers and begs me not to hit him again.

"What happened?" I scream now, tears falling down my face and hands. "What did you do?"

He puts his palm under his nose to catch the blood that is flowing. "It would have all been okay, Harry. I swear it. When she'd escaped from that house on your road, she called me from a phone box. I went to get her. *I* was the one she called. And when I got there, she was terrified and cold and hungry. She was in an awful state. I brought her back here."

"Here? Why didn't you bring her home? To *us*?"

His face is still behind his hands. "I wanted to. But she didn't want to go home. She refused. And then later—"

"You're lying."

"I'm not! She told me what you did to her."

The blood rises in my face and threatens to overcome me. "What are you talking about?"

"She told me. You locked her in her room. With a padlock. Like she was a prisoner!"

"You don't know what you're talking about." I grab his pajama top in one fist.

He flinches and shuts his eyes, tensing for another blow. "She just wanted to spend one night here just to get her head right after all that had happened. Then one night turned to two and then three. The number of times I begged her to call you, but she wouldn't." He drops his hands and looks at me. His face is smeared with blood and tears.

"You. *You* could have called. You knew how desperate we were for any news, anything."

He nods rapidly. "Yes, yes. You're right. I should have. But by then the whole city was looking for her. I couldn't tell you she was here. How could I tell you that?"

"You could have lied—made something up. That she'd just escaped from 210." My words feel raw in my throat.

"The police wouldn't have believed that. She'd left there three days before. They'd have done forensics on her, Harry. She'd showered by then. And we'd—" He stops.

I bellow from somewhere so far and so deep that for a second, I am lost to myself. When I open my eyes, he is watching me in the way you would a cornered animal. He starts talking again. Slowly. Feeling his way.

"She wanted to come clean about us. She was nearly eighteen. She said we could be together openly but I told her we had to wait. Just until it was calmer out there and people weren't looking as hard. She was saying we could go to Scotland. Get married. But I tried to explain to her that we couldn't. I'd lose my job and then where would we be?"

His face is like a plum now, bruised, and all I see is its softness where the blood has gathered under the skin. I could break it so easily. He sees the look in my eye.

"I was trying to *protect* her. She couldn't just go home after she'd been missing all that time."

"What did you do to her?" I ask him, getting up. He stares at his feet. I aim a hard kick at his legs. "What did you do to her?" I shout, absent to everything but him. "Where is she?"

"In the basement."

I stare at him.

"The freezer," he says. "I should have called the police. But I couldn't."

"Couldn't?" I say, hunting frantically for the basement door.

"I couldn't. I was scared. I'm so sorry."

Before I know it, I have him by the throat and I am pressing my thumbs on his Adam's apple. He flails around, trying to break the choke. "You were supposed to be caring for her. You were her teacher!"

— — —

I LEAVE DELANCEY collapsed in a heap on the floor and find the cellar door and pull. Inside the smell of damp brick rises to meet me. I scrabble around for a light until I find a switch on the wall. The room, a narrow brick gulley, emerges into the light. There is a chest freezer in the corner. My girl is here in this rotting room. Has been here for more than a year.

The bricks hum. The low ceiling and its flickering light hum. My steps falter. There is such electricity in here. And I know it. It's the sound of misery. It's my despair running wild in this terrible, awful, low place that has held her for so long. She is here.

I approach the freezer. I lay my hands on the warm, smooth surface. I should call the police now. They need to be here and to deal with all of this carefully and to record and to log it. But I don't want her logged. I don't want them to come and pull everything apart as I watch. They'll be here soon enough, swarming, prodding. I need to be here with her alone for a second. Just me and her.

I pull the lid of the freezer open. It hasn't been closed properly, the weight of it almost nothing in my hands as I lift. My breath is forcing its way out of my lungs. I raise the lid all the way up. The air becomes still. I stare into the sarcophagus. There is a sheet over whatever is inside. I pull it away.

She is here. My beautiful Sophie, pressed into a layer of soft blankets, the material dusted with glitter. Her once-pink lips seem to be about to speak.

And then the door to the basement opens. At the top of the concrete steps is Delancey framed in the warm light of the hallway. In his hand is a huge hunting knife with a serrated blade. There is something crazed in his eyes.

EIGHTY-SIX

ZARA

NOW

I AM DRESSING IN CLOTHES THAT I HAVEN'T DRESSED IN FOR TWO AND A half years. I stare into the mirror and I see a person who I hadn't expected ever to see again.

I waited all night for him but Harry isn't back. I tried calling him but he didn't answer. Not that long ago, I would have worried, panicked. But nothing is capable of exciting that in me anymore. He will be back soon enough. I know. Things are changing today. When I open the garden door, something new is there on the wind. I can feel her ghost again.

I pour the cereal as I wait for the coffee to brew. I am just about to sit when the doorbell rings. My heart flips.

The shadow in the glass is one I recognize. "Holly," I say. But when I see the line of her mouth the tears begin to stream. I am in ecstasy and in abject misery, both at the same time. "You found her. You found her, didn't you?"

"Yes," she says, and I crumple into her arms. And then I am being passed gently to someone, another officer, and walked back along my own corridor. I already know. I have known what she is about to tell me for a long time now. Even so. The pain is like a tearing open of healing skin.

The officer sits me down and fetches a glass of water for me. She smiles and sets it down brightly. The air is wrong. It all feels off to me. I search Holly's face and though there are tears in her eyes, unbelievably, she is smiling.

I stare at her in disbelief, but she is smiling still. And then it hits me and I scream.

"Sophie's alive?"

"Yes!" she says. "It was Harry. He found her."

I stand up and look between them. My eyes are streaming. "Sophie. She's alive? You can't—this can't be a joke. Please." I am crying now, pleading with them both.

"Sophie's alive. She's okay, Zara. I promise you. She's alive," Holly says, wiping her own tears away.

IN THE CAR she tells me what she knows. She is jittery, and when she speaks the information comes in snatches. Harry found her, she tells me, at Delancey's house. At first, I'm confused by what she's saying.

And then a wave of nausea overtakes me. "Rob's house?"

She nods as she steers quickly through the traffic. "She's been there the whole time. She'd escaped from 210 and Delancey picked her up."

"Rob? Why Rob? Why didn't he call us? I don't understand."

She shakes her head. "They were hiding her. From what we have pieced together, she wasn't locked up or imprisoned."

"Then what?"

"Are you sure you want to do this now?"

"Yes!" I say. "I need to know."

She sighs deeply before answering. "She believed they were in a relationship."

"A relationship?"

"Zara. Look, it's important you understand this," she says, turning in to a car park. I see the letters S A R C on a signpost. "This isn't her fault at all."

I try to absorb this but can't. "And nobody knew? He must have had people visiting him at his house! It's been more than a year!"

"They did. And she'd hide in the basement, she said. In an old chest freezer. That's where Harry found her."

At first it's just a thought, but then it becomes so overwhelming that I can't contain it. The world collapses and is immediately remade as I'm trying to understand what I'm hearing. And then I do. There's no other way to understand what Holly is saying.

"Where is Delancey? I'm going to kill him," I say.

"He already did the job himself, Zara. He cut his own throat. Harry tried to save him. Couldn't."

On the way to the building I break into a half run. I have to see my baby. I have to be able to hold her. But I don't know where I am going. Holly catches up and then tries to keep up with me. It's not long before we are in the building.

Inside the walls are salmon pink, the doors blond. Harry is already there. He runs to me and wraps his arms around me tight. I am overcome. He holds me, and all I can feel is the release of our long-held pain twisting around each other in warm ropes.

Everything moves quickly now. It has to. I need to see my girl.

Harry takes me by the hand and leads me swiftly along a corridor to a nondescript door that could open out into any room. When I step inside, I register the sea of pastel. And then. My heart explodes.

Sophie.

I am cemented to the spot. I stare at my beautiful baby. Her face is pale, like putty. Her eyes are bruised circles, but she is so beautiful that it catches at my throat. I don't know if I am seeing her. And I turn to Harry to check my bearings. And he is smiling his still-damaged smile. And then Sophie is too. Smiling through tears. And my mouth is open. My eyes blur so rapidly that I wipe them furiously again and again because if this moment were to vanish now I would vanish too. But her eyes stay open. Butterfly wings opening and closing. I run to her.

"My life," I say. "My life."

EIGHTY-SEVEN

HARRY

NOW

SOPHIE DOESN'T SPEAK VERY MUCH. BUT THAT'S OKAY. FOR WEEKS ZARA shadowed her, as though any second she might wake up and find that it had all been a dream. She melted into her so completely that they each were in danger of becoming warped by the constantly exerted pressure. For the first few days Zara slept on the floor by Sophie's bed. When she cried out in the middle of the night, Zara would leap up and soothe her until she fell quiet again.

The therapists tell us that everything we see is to be expected, but they can't tell us what to expect. At first, all Sophie would say was that she loved him. She couldn't understand where he had gone and why he wasn't there with her. But slowly—so slowly—she has begun to see him remade, as he really was. Months of being told, being counseled, being shown, being *reminded,* that Delancey had groomed her, has finally triggered an awakening. He'd made her believe that he loved her and that she was there by choice.

We pressed her psychologist repeatedly about how Sophie was doing. "I can't tell you very much in terms of detail; her therapy is confidential. But she's better than she was. She has at last found a way to *locate* her rage."

Sophie sees two professionals regularly. Zara and I have our own therapy—both individually and as a couple. We even have counseling together, as a family. It helps and it doesn't. Before all of this when my head was mainly light spaces interspersed with the odd stripe of shade, I couldn't have conceived of the need for therapy. Even when we were in the grip of our grief, when we'd first lost Sophie, I couldn't see how a stranger probing relentlessly into my head would ever help. But no matter how dark it was in those grief-swamped days, my mind was still a recognizable place.

Now it feels like an occasional torture chamber.

I have rage too. I have tried to talk to Zara about it but she doesn't have the room for it. My therapist encouraged me, finally, to talk about it to him in our sessions.

"A year, Jim," I said to him. "She was there for a *year*! She couldn't have called or messaged us once, let us know she was safe? I don't understand. I genuinely don't understand what she was thinking for all of that time."

He made a note and then put down his book. "I'm not her treating psychologist, Harry. But I expect that she has very complex situational traumas. She's a candidate for abandonment disorder. These cases are incredibly difficult, clinically. She was abducted by one person and ran straight into the arms of another abuser. But to her, you have to understand, that person took on the mantle of savior. I am certain that while she was there with him, she would have experienced complicated emotions around guilt and gratitude." He paused to see whether I was still following before continuing. "Her frames of reference had all been destroyed, Harry, by what was, on any view, an extremely painful period of forced captivity and assault. The world outside Robert Delancey's house would have represented to her a deeply frightening place. And she loved him. Love is a very powerful drug in the blood of a teenager."

He looked at me, waiting for me to say something. "You mean she was brainwashed." It wasn't a question. That's what he meant. But I know that I would have escaped if it had been me. Or tried to. Or called home just once.

"I mean," he said kindly, "that she trusted him because she had no other choice. Look, Sophie was at such a formative stage of her life when she formed an attachment with this man. She believed she loved him. To avoid being found out, she'd even been prepared to sell drugs to keep her relationship with him secret."

She'd never spoken to me about this herself, but I remembered the CCTV the pub landlord had showed me. He'd kept it to blackmail them.

He continued. "She'd invested so much personal and emotional capital into this man."

I took it in and tried to digest it as far as I could, but I wasn't built for this kind of explanation. "I can't understand why she'd do that for him. I don't get it. Why wouldn't she just leave?"

He nodded as if anticipating the question. "He made Sophie feel vulnerable in a planned and concerted way so that he could *control* her. That's how abusers exercise control. He'd have made her believe it wasn't safe to leave him. Remember, she'd just escaped a far more obvious danger in the form of that man Herman. And now here he was, this man she loved, who had rescued her, made her feel protected."

"Until she wanted to leave," I said.

"Yes. And then he would have convinced her all over again that it was just too dangerous to leave."

"Too dangerous to call home?"

"Actually, yes. Because it would have meant that her whole existence for the past year would have unraveled."

I WORRIED ABOUT how Zara would cope with what she'd done to Herman. He was innocent of murder, we know that now. But we also know that between them, Herman and Delancey, they killed the last of her childhood. That Sophie would never return to us. She is into adulthood now, feeling her way, cautiously, but inching ever forward into it. On one of those days yet to come, maybe not this year or the next year, but one day, Sophie would leave us again and we'd have to grieve again.

Zara is sitting in the garden sipping coffee. There is the soft, rain-washed scent of flowers in the air. She smiles as I approach.

"She still asleep?"

"Yes," I say, and take my coffee to sit with her awhile. Whatever else has happened, there is a definite sense of that depthless darkness having lifted from her. She has the glow of having been saved from a calamity.

We sit and sip. A robin flutters and lands at our feet. Zara tosses a crumb from a half-eaten pastry. The bird chirps and whisks the morsel away. The light is low in the sky. Zara's eyes meet it with light of their own and she couldn't be more beautiful.

And then I am overtaken by an idea, and I put my cup on the grass and take hers and lay it softly next to mine. I stand and take her by the hand. She throws me a questioning look but doesn't resist.

I lead her wordlessly into the house and up the stairs. One day we *will* have to grieve.

We look at each other, breaths held. I push open the door quietly. Inside, Sophie is lying there, her dark hair splayed across the pillow like fronds in a coral reef.

One day, we will have to grieve. I will cry for Zara or she for me or us both for Sophie. Or Sophie for us. One day we will wail the loss of us. We will feel desperately the need to hold close a warm body but won't be able to.

But that day isn't now. For now, we are here. So let us, I think, hold one another's breathing bodies now, while we can.

I nod to Zara and she walks around to the far side of the bed and at the same time we both climb in next to our daughter. Who is here. And who we love. And who we love and love and love.

ACKNOWLEDGMENTS

To Mama, whose daily prayers remind me of her love and her strength. Thank you for life. And for love. You shaped me in my childhood, through your care and kindness and love, so that now in my adulthood I can always see the man I should aim to be.

To Dad who wanted me to read—always—to make up for the reading that wouldn't come to him. Thank you for all those stories you left for us. And for that smile. And for being proud whether I deserved it or not. We are coming to you, slowly but surely. We are all but a blink away and the thought of your face is enough to make me braver about it.

To Sadia, my wife. My life. My love. And now the best lawyer in the world (having been third last year!). Thank you for all your belief. I love you. I can't imagine a life without the brightness and the warmth of your sunlight. Thank you for finding me.

To my brothers, Kash, Omer, and Khurrum, and my baby sis, Aiysha. I miss you all. Each of you helps me find myself in this mad world. I'm always grateful that I can reach out to hold your hands whenever I need to.

To the peerless Camilla, my agent. Thank you for always making my books better and for all the championing you do for me. A more constant and protecting friend cannot be found in this game. Thank you for taking me on all those years ago! Everyone I meet tells me how great you are. And I have to tell them that I already know.

To the entire constellation at Darley Anderson who combine their energies on my behalf. Thank you to Sheila and to Jade, Mary and Kristina, Georgia and Salma. You are all of course brilliant and fierce but you are also so lovely, which is a rare combination.

To Jenny Chen, my insightful and talented editor. Thank you for pulling the very best book out of me and also for doing it with such poise and grace. Thank you for welcoming me so warmly to the Random House and Ballantine families. To all the brilliant minds there including the countless sales and publicity and marketing stars who work behind the night skies and who have done so much to bring this book into being, I am in your debt.

Thank you to Scott Biel, who designed such an evocative and striking cover, and to Loren Noveck and Sheryl Rapée Adams, my production editor and copy editor.

I remain ever grateful to Alex Tribick, who knows why there would be no books without him, for all the interesting and varied work he allows me to help with. It's such a privilege to work with you. (Sadia once more adds her thanks and in a message for Sue says she is still sorry, and I'm still not sure why.)

Next, the Chillies. The Red Hot Chilli Writers are my writing support group. Or at least they started off that way but now they are all thrilled to have me as their friend! In alphabetical order, then: Amit (AA) Dhand, who once made a £90,000 samosa. Nadeem (Alex) Khan, who is starting a new adventure abroad. Vaseem Khan, who has never called it right even once in his life but whom we love anyway. Ayisha Malik, who might be awake before noon these days but who still can't drive. And finally, Abir Mukherjee, whose books I often sign at book festivals because I can and because they're just so good.

They are all talented, brilliant writers and in their own ways have blazed trails, wide and bright, for others to follow. Read their books if you can! Guys, you all make me a more betterer writer.

Thank you to all the readers and the reviewers and the bloggers.

The ones who tweet and the ones who silently read and breathe life into dusty pages. I fully and readily acknowledge what a huge privilege it is to be able to write at all and be published. But it is the readers who bring the books into existence as stories. Thank you one and all. Special mentions for all the Goldsboro Books beautiful people. And also shout-outs to Fiona (I will come soon, I promise!) and Tracy and a thousand others, all of whom I wish I could namecheck here. Oh, thanks to Tejal too for your help!

Finally, to Zoha and Shifa. I am so proud of you both. You are startling and funny and cheeky and remind me how to experience joy in tiny things. Long may you laugh. Long may you continue to make us laugh. If you could occasionally just pipe down, though, and give us all a second's peace, that would be very welcome. (Also, I'm well aware that having spent all our time teaching you both to walk and talk, we now spend a lot of it telling you to please sit down and be quiet!)

ABOUT THE AUTHOR

IMRAN MAHMOOD is a practicing criminal barrister in England and Wales with over thirty years' experience fighting cases. His debut novel, *You Don't Know Me,* was chosen by Simon Mayo as a BBC Radio 2 Book Club Choice for 2017, long-listed for the Theakston Crime Novel of the Year and the CWA Gold Dagger Award, short-listed for the Glass Bell Award, and made into a hugely successful BBC One adaptation in association with Netflix. It reached number three in the world on Netflix charts and received a BAFTA nomination for best actor. Mahmood was born and raised in Liverpool but now lives in London with his wife and two daughters.

X: @imranmahmood777